D1264458

Dusty Britches

Center Point
Large Print

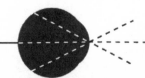

**This Large Print Book carries the
Seal of Approval of N.A.V.H.**

Dusty Britches

Marcia Lynn McClure

Center Point Large Print
Thorndike, Maine

The text of this Large Print edition is unabridged.
In other aspects, this book may vary
from the original edition.
Printed in the United States of America
on permanent paper.
Set in 16-point Times New Roman type.

ISBN: 978-1-62899-694-4

Library of Congress Cataloging-in-Publication Data

McClure, Marcia Lynn.
    Dusty britches / Marcia Lynn McClure. — Center Point Large Print
edition.
       pages cm
    Summary: "When Ryder Maddox left the Hunter ranch, Dusty's heart
was broken. When her fiancé proved unfaithful, she hardened her heart
towards men. Now Ryder has returned to work on her father's ranch
determined to soften her heart and make their dreams come true"
    —Provided by publisher.
    ISBN 978-1-62899-694-4 (library binding : alk. paper)
    1. Frontier and pioneer life—West (U.S.)—Fiction.
    2. Large type books.
    3. Domestic fiction.
    I. Title.
PS3613.C36D87 2015
813'.6—dc23
                                                    2015020462

Chapter One

Dusty Hunter looked up into nature's painted splendor of a heavenly blue sky. Raising one hand to shade her eyes from the intensity of the late spring sun, she paused for a moment in her efforts to rid the vegetable garden of weeds. As she marveled at the soothing beauty of immense velvet clouds wandering slowly across the canvas of sapphire, their tranquil grace gave her cause to smile. Somehow the task at hand didn't seem quite so tedious anymore.

Inhaling deeply of the dry western air, she wondered at how long the day seemed to be. She had been weeding the garden since the first rays of morning sunlight broke over the mountains. In addition to all the troublesome weeds meeting her at dawn, some rotten little varmint had nibbled the leaves of her cabbage plants during the night. She wasn't sure she could save them now.

"Rotten ol' skunks," Dusty mumbled. Resting her hands on her hips, she glared down to the seemingly endless task before her. Tossing a handful of ragweed into a nearby wooden bucket, she removed her well-worn leather gloves and carefully inspected the blisters in her palms. They weren't as sore today as they had been yesterday, but sore enough all the same. Pulling the gloves back on and sighing heavily, she dropped to her knees and returned to the monotony of maintaining the garden.

Dusty's father, Hank Hunter, had been away on a cattle drive. For weeks he'd been gone; it was a long way from Texas to the Hunter ranch. Hank had lost nearly all of his calves during the early spring calving season. Mother Nature had been brutal. Even though several calves had been saved by bringing them right into the house at night, most were lost when their mothers suffocated from snow and ice obstructing their nostrils. Others died simply from cold and exposure. New cattle had to be purchased in Texas, and Hank had gone to drive them home.

Dusty found herself glancing up from her labors —toward the south. She knew at any moment her father, whatever cowboys he'd hired to drive the cattle home, and at least a hundred head of cattle would be arriving in a cloud of Colorado dust.

"They'll never get that fence done in time," Dusty mumbled. Her daddy's top ranch hand, Feller Lance, and the rest of the ranch hands were working from sunup to sundown on the fence and windbreaks needed for the new cattle.

Dusty wiped the perspiration from her brow. She began yanking weeds out of the ground once more. She wished she hadn't sent Becca to gather the eggs. Having Becca's company and help would have been nice. Yet she immediately cast aside the useful piece of the idea, for Becca would simply sit and ramble on endlessly—on and on and on. Dusty had no patience for, and definitely no interest in, hearing about the shallow affairs of Becca's young heart.

Dusty Hunter had no heart. Long ago it had been stomped on and ground into the dust under the boot heel of a man. Dusty had no interest in repeating such an experience. Therefore, she couldn't see why any woman would trust any man or find anything attractive or redeeming about one. Her younger sister's naive, lighthearted ways only served to irritate Dusty most of the time. Therefore, after thinking about it again, Dusty was, as usual, content in her lone misery.

Becca would've complained anyway. The temperature must be in the high eighties, and Becca would only tell Dusty they shouldn't be out working in the heat. She would claim "heatstroke" and end up back in the house, sitting in the rocker with a nice glass of water for company.

Not Dusty. Hard work was good for the body and soul. And the mind! It kept one occupied and unable to linger on . . . on the frivolous things most young women spent far too much time thinking about. Besides, Dusty knew her limits. She'd only fainted from the heat once before, and that was last year. Becca was just—just . . . Dusty sighed and smiled at the thought of her sister.

Becca was simply a very normal, very sweet, very pretty young girl—the little blue-eyed blonde of the family. The jewel—with the personality befitting a jewel too! No wonder all the ranch hands liked her. She was kind to them, witty, and didn't mind someone finding humor in her misfortunes.

Dusty reflected on the day only a week before when Becca had gone out to slop the hogs. There she'd been, treading awkwardly through the muck in the pen. Never mind that she could've gone around the outside of the pen and slung the slop into the trough that way. No! Becca had put on a pair of her daddy's old boots, hitched up her skirts and petticoats, and tucked their hems firmly in her waistband. She treaded out then—a bucket in each hand—to feed the hogs. Naturally, anyone with any sense could see what was going to happen. Dusty had been watching from the back porch. She saw the ranch hands pause in their usual chores to watch what promised to be no less than a hysterical exhibition by Becca Hunter.

Sure enough, Becca had no sooner entered the pen than the hungry hogs began snorting around her feet.

"Now, all you hogs . . . you leave me be!" Becca ordered in her strongest voice. Becca's strongest voice more resembled that of an indentured servant trying to timidly whisper an order to her mistress.

But the hogs, in their impatience to eat, began bumping against her legs, and before she could act—before anyone could act—Becca lost her footing. The two buckets she was carrying leapt into the air, emptying their contents the length of Becca—from the newest hair of her head to the tip of her tiniest toe. She found herself promptly, and not very gently, sitting in the mud and muck of the hog pen.

The way every ranch hand anywhere near flung himself into the pen to assist Becca caused Dusty to think for a moment that perhaps her sister's dramatic "accident" had actually been intentional. The thought was only fleeting, for Dusty knew Becca hated nothing more than getting dirty. And slop and hog manure surely were in the "dirty" group. Still, as Dusty giggled at her sister's predicament, she noted Becca managed to laugh at herself as several of the men helped her escape her snorting captors.

What a sight Becca had been! Dusty smiled broadly, feeling a little less dismal, as she continued to pull weeds.

Her knees were sore from kneeling on the moist ground and her fingers stiff from ripping up unwanted roots. Yet she smiled when she looked up to see Becca approaching at almost a dead run a few minutes later.

"Dusty! Guthrie's seen Daddy!" Becca called, stopping a few steps from the tomato plants Dusty

11

was tending. Becca placed a dainty hand to her panting bosom. "They'll be comin' in any minute!"

Dusty's heart felt almost happy for a moment— as though something had just filled her body with a warm, sweet liquid. It had been weeks since their father left! Dusty had missed him terribly. She pulled off her gloves, tossing them into the bucket of weeds as she stood.

Brushing off the seat of her skirt and smiling warmly at her sister, she said, "Well . . . let's go then! I love to watch them bringin' the cattle in."

Becca smiled. Taking her sister's hand, they both hurried off toward the corral. Sure enough, just as they approached the south fence of the corral, they saw a cloud of dust in the distance. Dusty smiled and sighed with delight when she heard the soft bawling of the cattle—the whistles and shouts of her father and the men on the drive.

"I love this," Becca sighed, smiling lovingly at her sister.

"Me too," Dusty agreed, returning her loving smile.

Rebecca Hunter had always secretly envied her sister. She loved Dusty like she loved no one else on earth. Still, it had been difficult—being Dusty Hunter's little sister. Dusty was intelligent, strong, witty, and beautiful! Even now, after Dusty had hardened her heart toward people and life for years, her dark eyes, shaded by long, thick lashes, sparkled with strength. She was an inch or two shorter than Becca with a smile that lit up any room—when she chose to smile anyway, which wasn't very often—nearly never now. Her skin was unblemished, her figure flawlessly curved, her hair the most absolute shade of chestnut brown ever given a woman. Becca wrinkled her nose a little—completely disappointed in that moment at the way Dusty had taken to pulling her lovely hair back into a tight, spinsterly knot on the crown of her head. To Becca, Dusty was ideal—except for the blackened heart she now carried about in her bosom.

"Quit starin' at me, Becca!" Dusty demanded.

Still, even Becca's disapproving eyes could not dampen Dusty's spirits. Since she was a little girl, Dusty had loved to hear the approach of a cattle drive. Even in the fall when her father and the cowboys started bringing the cattle in to winter close by, she loved the sound of it—hundreds of hooves approaching, the snap of the whip some cowboys used to turn them, the soft bawling of younger heifers and steers, the whistles and shouts of her father and the cowboys who rode for him.

Her mind wandered back for a moment to the year she was fourteen. She'd stood just where she was now—perched upon the south fence of the corral watching the cowboys bringing in the cattle for fall. There had been one particular cowboy she'd favored. Actually, she'd been in love with him! Becca was always in love with one ranch hand or cowboy, it seemed. But it hadn't been so with Dusty. She had her varying crushes as a young girl, but her feelings for this one particular cowboy went far beyond a little girl's crush. He had seemed so mature to her—so handsome and strong—though he was only twenty at the time. Dusty remembered the way he rode, the snap of his bullwhip as he drove cattle. There had been several cowboys that had carried a whip since, but none had been as skilled as that young cowboy years ago. He could crack it so perfectly she could hear him coming long before the sounds of the cattle were audible. In that very moment, Dusty fancied she nearly heard the crack of his whip—remembered how excited she would be in knowing he was bringing in the cattle and would be home in time for supper at the ranch house with the family. Shaking her head, she scolded herself for dwelling on such sap as being melancholy over a cowboy from years back. She returned her attention to the approaching cattle.

"Oh, surely Daddy's bought more than a hundred head, Dust!" Becca remarked. "Look how many!"

"Maybe he decided to be safe. Last time he lost so many on the drive," Dusty said, realizing the snap of a whip echoing in the distance must have been what sparked the never-forgotten memory.

"Listen there, Dusty. Daddy's hired a cowboy with a whip," Becca noted, also having heard the echo of the crack. "It always puts me in mind of . . ."

"Yes, I remember." Dusty fought to keep her thoughts from floating back through time again.

Her father came into view, riding in front and to the right of the herd. She and Becca waved excitedly, and Dusty felt warmed as he waved back.

"He'll water 'em at the creek and come on up," Feller Lance chuckled as he appeared from behind them and joined them at the fence. "Your daddy's come home to ya, my girls!"

Ruff, Guthrie, and Titch arrived, hopped up onto the fence, and began whistling and waving their arms in greeting. Dusty smiled at the three hands. They'd stayed on the ranch for near to three years now. All of them were local boys who wanted to cowboy but had no desire to roam the country far and wide.

Ruff was a handsome enough fellow with green eyes and sandy-colored hair. He was short and squatty but strong as a bull. Guthrie and Titch were brothers, sons of a farmer in a neighboring county. Both were tall with black hair and eyes as gray as rain. All three hands were hard workers and good men. Dusty thought how lucky her daddy had been to keep them on.

Looking on as the cattle were allowed to head toward the creek, Dusty waited impatiently as her daddy spurred his horse into a gallop and rode to them.

"Whoa, boy," he mumbled, reining in his horse and leaping off like he were no more than a boy. "Sugar plums!" he called, chuckling as he swaggered toward his daughters, weathered cowboy legs bowed and strong arms outstretched.

"Daddy!" Becca exclaimed, rushing forward.

Dusty was as excited as her sister, but as tears of joy and relief welled in her eyes, she swallowed them, not wanting to cry in front of everyone. She reached him soon enough and found herself melting in his fatherly embrace.

"Did ya take care of my girls while I was gone, Feller?" Hank Hunter asked, winking at the weathered cowboy.

"They look right as rain to me, Hank," Feller chuckled.

Hank kissed Becca square on the forehead. After doing the same to Dusty, he took her face in his hands. "And did ya soften ol' Dusty up a mite . . . I hope?"

"A mite," Feller chuckled again.

Dusty smiled happily up at her father.

"Well, my girls," Hank began. He tucked a daughter under each arm, squeezing them tightly, and began walking toward the house. With each step he took, dust and dirt from the drive lifted into the air like smoke curling out of a chimney. His normally black hair was more a plain old dirt color and matched his dust-covered skin. "I got us some good stock. Yep. Some good stock! Cattle *and* cowboys. Got me a fair price, a new pair of britches, and a back that's aching like it ain't laid down for a year!"

"You needed the britches more than anythin', Daddy," Dusty assured him, smiling.

"Don't I know it! And I might have to have you and little sis patch them new boys' britches up a bit too! They're all as hard on 'em as me," he chuckled.

Dusty could hear the shouts of relief, the splashing noises made by the cowboys as they quickly refreshed themselves in the creek. She smiled, relishing the sounds and knowledge of tradition. The cowboys would no doubt be stripped down to nothing in a moment or two— washing the layers of trail dust from their bodies before they came to the house for the big meal her daddy always insisted on after a drive.

"Get that fire pit goin', Feller!" Hank hollered over his shoulder. "I brung home a starvin' mob."

Becca and Dusty watched, giggling happily as their charmingly bowlegged daddy released them. Whooping and hollering, he stripped his shirt off over his head and climbed awkwardly into the big watering trough under the windmill.

"Boots and all, Daddy? For Pete's sake, you'll

slop for a week!" Dusty called after him through her laughter.

Hank spit water from his mouth like a cherub fountain as he sat on the bottom of the trough, enjoying its cool refreshment. It was good to see her daddy happy. Losing her mother several years back nearly killed him. It was months and months and months following her mother's death before he even smiled, let alone spoke to anyone—unless it was absolutely necessary. It was good to see him happy.

"Bring some wood from the shed, Titch," Feller ordered. "And, Ruff, you get that beef out we done yesterday . . . 'fore them boys start into eatin' that herd they just brung in."

"Come here, my girls!" Hank called. Dusty and Becca rushed to where he sat in the trough. "Did you miss me?" he asked with a knowing grin on his face.

"That's the silliest question you ever did ask, Daddy," Becca said. Both girls leaned on the trough's edge.

"Well, I'll tell you what," Hank began, lowering his voice and reaching out and taking a hand of each daughter in his own. "I missed you girls somethin' awful. If it weren't that you were ladies now . . . needin' comfort, privacy, and a soft bed . . . I'da brung ya right along, 'cause missin' you is too hard on me these days."

Dusty smiled lovingly at her daddy. Then, as

the all-too-familiar expression of mischief crossed his face, she sensed his intentions and tried to pull her hand from his grasp.

"Daddy!" she warned. "Don't you dare!"

But it was too late. In an instant, she found herself sitting next to him in the trough, having been pulled in headfirst. She heard Becca's delighted shriek a second later, followed by a splash to match the one she'd just created. Looking over, she erupted into giggles at the sight of her sister sitting on the other side of her father, completely drenched.

"Now you girls stop your foolin' around!" Feller shouted. "I'm gonna need some help sloppin' this mob." He stood chuckling, amused at the sight before him.

"Daddy!" Becca exclaimed in a horrified whisper. "Look at me! And all the new cowboys are walkin' this way!" She pointed in the direction of the creek. Dusty saw four or five men, themselves dripping wet, some fully clothed, others missing shirts, walking toward them.

"For Pete's sake, Daddy!" Dusty exclaimed. "I'm wearin' a white blouse! It'll be plum see-through from bein' wet." She made her way awkwardly out of the trough, pleased by her father's laughter, and ran to the house, not waiting for Becca to catch up.

Dusty entered the house not a second before her sister.

"Daddy's the devil of a stinker," Becca giggled, heading toward her room.

"Wait, wait, wait!" Dusty exclaimed. "You'll soak the floor." Becca paused, and both girls unfastened their skirts, dropping piles of petticoats with them where they stood. "He's a fool. That's why we love him," she giggled as she unbuttoned her shirtwaist, tossing it on the heap of clothing at their feet.

Her smile faded, however, when Becca asked quietly, "You ever gonna love anybody else, Dusty?"

Dusty looked at her sister, frowning with irritation. "I love you—you and Daddy, and that's all I need." Becca looked away, obviously wishing she had never asked. Trying to ease her sister's discomfort, for she knew Becca meant well, Dusty added, "And Feller. I love Feller too. How could anyone not love ol' Feller?"

"He is a loveable ol' mutt, ain't he?" Becca whispered, smiling.

"Yeah." Dusty offered a forgiving smile. "And he makes a dang good roasted beef."

"Come on!" Becca squealed, grabbing Dusty's hand. "I gotta get cleaned up. There's a whole new crop of cowboys out there we gotta look over."

Changing into dry clothing, Dusty listened to the low hum of masculine voices—the good-natured chuckling and conversation floating from the roasting pit through her bedroom window as the new hands talked with Feller and the others. Times were she would've been as excited about the new hands as Becca. Several years ago, before . . . and she would've bathed in that excitement exactly as Becca did now. However, experience had taught Dusty Hunter there was more to life—so many things to be taken far more seriously than flirting and love, sparking under the hay wagon, and dancing at the town socials. There was work to be done. Hard work! The garden, the house, the meals, the mending— that's what life was all about. That and tending to her father and his needs since her mother had died.

Still, deep down inside, somewhere in the pit of her stomach, somewhere in the aching of her heart, burned a tiny resentment as she heard Becca leave the house and greet each new cowboy in turn—her silky, soft voice no doubt mesmerizing them all instantly. To all those tough men that had been riding a dusty cattle trail for so many weeks without the sight of a woman, Becca was an angel of heaven personified. Her daddy would pay them all just after breakfast tomorrow morning, and most would leave, not wanting to tarry. One or two others would perhaps be hired on for a while. Becca would probably have her heartstrings plucked before the winter was over. But not Dusty! She'd stopped falling in love with ranch hands and cowboys when she was fourteen years old—the first time her heart was broken—

21

shattered by an intriguing, handsome, capable young cowboy. But it was the second man who hammered the final nail in her coffin of romance and love. And since then, she'd had no use for matters of the heart.

Dusty dressed, and as she smoothed back a stray hair, she watched the goings-on at the roasting pit from her window. Feller was busy talking to several new hands as he tended the meat on the skewer. Dusty's heart panged a twinge when she saw the bullwhip strapped to the saddle of one of the horses tied to the corral fence. *Why today?* she wondered. Why was her memory tarrying on the young cowboy from five years ago?

Becca had the complete attention of three or four men as she smiled and sweetly tossed her head in conversation. Her daddy, dried off some and sitting on the old tree stump with Guthrie, Ruff, and Titch, was no doubt telling them details of the drive. As she quickly straightened her skirt, Dusty noted that several of the drive hands were quite tall, a couple with dark hair, a few with blond. One had hair as black as night like Guthrie and Titch. As the scent of the beef beginning to cook reached her, she turned and left the room, intent on helping Feller with the meal.

Oh, how she hated the porch door—the way it always slammed shut! Why had she let go of it so easily—let it slam? Instantly, every set of eyes at the pit turned to look at her—watch her approach. There was nothing to do but walk quickly toward them and wave a greeting.

"That there's my daughter Angelina," she heard her father announce. She felt her face turn crimson. She was . . . uncomfortable with her first name. She hadn't gone by Angelina since she was about ten years old. *Dusty,* she corrected him silently in her mind. *Dusty!*

As she reached them, all the cowboys nodded in turn. She found herself unable to meet any of them eye-to-eye. Her father's announcing her by her given name was humiliating. It seemed so . . . too . . . familiar. Only her father and sister called her Angelina—and only on occasion. She focused on Feller, who grinned with understanding.

"What do you need me to do, Feller?" she asked.

"I need ya to help Miss Becca keep all these young pups occupied while I fix some supper," he chuckled, knowing full well it was the last thing on earth she wanted to do.

"Well . . . now," a deep, masculine voice said from behind her, "if it ain't Miss Dusty Britches."

Dusty felt the warmth and color fade from her face. Her very blood seemed to drain from the rest of her body and puddle in her feet. She was dizzy and nauseated all at once. She looked again to Feller, who raised his eyebrows and grinned a knowing grin.

"I think your daddy picked himself out a

23

cowboy that's crossed your path before, Dusty," Feller said quietly.

There was no need for him to have spoken this information aloud. She already knew. Only one person on the whole of the earth had ever called her "Dusty Britches." That was the cowboy who had given her the nickname in the first place. Feeling she might die of shock, of . . . of something, Dusty slowly turned to see standing before her a man whose eyes were those of a boy she'd once known—a boy who grew into a man. A man who . . .

Ryder Maddox's broad smile was even more captivating than Dusty remembered. "You remember me, don't ya, Dusty . . . uh . . . Miss Hunter?" he asked in a voice heartbreakingly familiar, yet deeper than she remembered.

"Of—of course," Dusty stammered. She stood in awe of his height and staggeringly handsome face and form.

He'd grown! At least three or four inches by the look of him. His shoulders were broader than when he'd been twenty and worked for her father those many years ago. His upper torso, arms, and legs were thick and firm with the muscular development of a fully matured man. Had it not been for his eyes—those oddly tinted, brown-sugar-colored eyes, accented by dark eyelashes—she would not have known him. His face was much broader, his jaw chiseled and squared, his hair darker than she remembered—almost a cedar-bark brown. He had grown to be a very, very, very attractive man!

"Um . . . Ryder Maddox," Dusty added, realizing she'd been standing in awed silence for several moments.

"Yep," he confirmed. His smile broadened. He chuckled as he studied her from head to toe. "You done some growin' since I last saw you, Miss Britches."

Dusty blushed from the top of her scalp to the soles of her feet. The sensation quite unnerved her, for it had been years, literally, since she'd experienced it. *Miss Britches.* She'd almost forgotten he'd called her that. How divine it was to hear him say it again! And then Dusty Hunter, the woman—no longer the fourteen-year-old girl prone to matters of the heart—pulled her thoughts, feelings, and self up short. Stone cold. No feeling. Only irritation.

"Yes. It happens to us all," she stated flatly, forcing a friendly smile. "I'd say you're a mite taller yourself."

Ryder's brow puckered. He said, "I guess so."

He seemed to study her intently for a moment, especially her eyes. It made her uncomfortable. He'd always made her uncomfortable. Now that wasn't exactly true, she admitted somewhere deep, deep down inside her soul.

"We met up with old Ryder in Tucumcari," her

25

father interjected. "He'd just finished a drive and was hangin' 'round the yards. I talked him into comin' on home with me."

Dusty looked to her father as he slapped the man on the back. Hank's smile was wide, and his eyes had a pleasant, delighted twinkle. Dusty remembered how fond her mother had been of Ryder Maddox. Elly Hunter always said that if she'd had a son, Ryder Maddox would've been the spitting image of him! If her mother had favored the man, it stood to reason her father had too.

"Well, welcome back to the ranch, Mr. Maddox," Dusty said. "If you'll excuse me . . . I must get to helpin' Feller." Turning away from her father and Ryder, she walked to where Feller was spooning his special sauce over the skewered beef.

She felt the unfamiliar, yet all too familiar, sting of tears rising in her eyes. He was perfect! More perfect than she even remembered. And she wasn't. There she stood before him, having just been wrung out of trough water, hair wet, simple brown skirt and calico shirtwaist. Even more infuriating and upsetting was that she cared!

"Smoke gettin' to ya, Dusty?" Feller inquired innocently, noticing the moisture in her eyes. After all, Dusty Hunter didn't cry anymore—ever.

"A bit, Feller," she lied. "I'm all right. Here . . . let me do that," she said, smiling and taking the large spoon and pail full of sauce from him. Feller stepped back as Dusty continued to baste the meat.

"What do ya think of that, Dusty?" he asked quietly.

"Think of what?" she asked, though she knew full well what.

"'Bout your daddy pickin' up Ryder Maddox along the way home. Small world, ain't it?"

Dusty knew Feller was all too aware of her past concerning Ryder Maddox, but she played the innocent anyway. "Yep. Small world."

Feller Lance decided not to push his young friend about the matter. His eyes narrowed as he watched her nervously basting the beef. She was a complete emotional mess. He knew her all too well. The handsome cowboy who'd arrived with her daddy had looped her rope entirely. And Feller loved it! It was about time Dusty climbed out of the deep, dark hole she'd sunk in two years before when Cash Richardson did her heart in. And Feller knew if there were a man on earth to dig her out, it was Ryder Maddox.

Feller's and Dusty's heads both popped around when they heard Becca exclaim suddenly, "Oh my heck! Ryder Maddox!"

Dusty fought the painful twinge of regret and jealousy pricking her heart as she watched her little sister throw her arms around the handsome cowboy's neck in a warm and welcoming hug. It should've been her place—her arms around him, her body receiving his returned embrace. After all, she thought—watching Ryder hugging Becca in return, wrapping his arms around her waist and lifting her off the ground—it had been her place before. Becca giggled as her feet swayed back and forth like the clapper of a bell.

When they finally ended their rather long embrace, Becca sighed, "Ryder Maddox! Where on earth did Daddy dig you up?"

"Tucumcari, New Mexico, sweet thing," the man chuckled in his warm, deep voice.

"You got so big," Becca said.

"And old," Ryder added.

"And *handsome,*" Becca added. Dusty flinched at her sister's innocent flirtatious honesty— though somewhere in her mind she knew where her sister had learned it and tried to forget. She wanted to crawl into the roasting pit with the intended supper when Becca added, "Did ya see Dusty? She's grown up too since last time we saw you."

"Oh, yeah," Ryder agreed. "Both you girls have . . . changed," he admitted, drawing out the last word for emphasis. "Makes me feel like an old man."

"Think on how it makes me feel," Hank chuckled.

Old. The word echoed through Dusty's mind hauntingly. She did feel old—like she'd lived for more than nineteen short years on this green earth. And Ryder? He would be, what, twenty-five by now? A true man, in years—a man who'd most likely lived a lot of life—a man who'd undoubtedly had women in that life. Dusty shook her head, turned, and handed the sauce pail back to Feller.

"We'll be needin' more forks," she mumbled. She left quickly and tried to keep from running too headlong toward the shelter of the house.

Once inside, she said, "Stop! Stop, stop, stop, stop, stop!" She had to quit thinking of him—had to block the memories of her youth and Ryder Maddox. She had to remind her heart what a man could do to your life—what he'd done to her life! And with new resolve, she went to the silver drawer to get more forks.

But as she rummaged through the drawer housing all manner of eating utensils, she could not keep her thoughts from him. Everything—every moment of those days so long ago—seemed to be rushing back into her mind. There were too many things to remember all at once: visions of Ryder snapping his whip as he herded cattle—images of his walking toward her, smiling the delicious, mischievous smile he owned. Sounds echoed through her mind: the low intonation of his chuckle, his voice. She fancied she could actually hear him singing in the barn as he tended the milk cows during the dark morning hours. She could almost, not quite but almost, smell the scent of soap and saddle leather clinging to him.

It was incredible! For just an instant, for just a breath of time, she closed her eyes and was fourteen years old again—fourteen years old and untainted by the disappointments of life—fourteen years old and completely in love with her daddy's favorite cowhand.

Forcing her eyes open, Dusty remembered the rest. She felt her eyebrows pucker into a frown as familiar pain pricked her heart—reminding her how it had ended and of what had gone on years afterward. Grabbing a fistful of forks, she slammed the drawer shut, spun around, and stormed out of the house. As she stomped her way toward the roasting pit, her mind filled with angry, hateful thoughts—any thoughts that would harden her heart and stop her confounded memories from being so sentimental and sappy. Because she was being hateful and determinedly unhappy, she didn't hear the wild drumming of unrestrained hooves. She was so set on mounting her defenses against anyone's offer of kindness, she didn't hear her daddy shouting, "Dusty! Watch out!"

It wasn't until she looked up to see Ryder Maddox in a dead run toward her—her daddy and several other cowboys at his heels—that she stopped dead in her tracks. Only then did she hear the approach of a runaway team and a woman screaming.

Chapter Two

Dusty looked to her left to the team pulling a wagon, heading straight for her and entirely out of control! In those few seconds, Dusty noted Miss Raynetta McCarthy bouncing about on the wagon's seat like a cricket in a frying pan. Holding on for dear life now and again, the woman was screeching for help at the top of her lungs.

Suddenly, Dusty's breath was violently driven from her. For a moment, every inch of her body throbbed with pain as she was thrown backward to land hard on the ground. The horrible panic and pain of not being able to inhale a breath kept her silent.

Ryder Maddox raised himself from on top of her and mumbled, "Who saved your bacon when I wasn't around anymore?" Dusty watched in painful, breathless silence as he stood. He turned to watch Dusty's father and several hands struggling to control the team some distance away. Turning back to her, he smiled, offered a hand to assist her to her feet, and said, "I see Miss Raynetta is still a wild hare."

Without thinking, Dusty placed her hand in Ryder's, and he pulled her to her feet. In the next instant, her wits had returned, and she abruptly yanked her hand from his. The cowboy responded with a puzzled frown.

Finally able to draw a breath, Dusty said, "Thank you, Mr. Maddox. I should pay more attention to where I'm goin'."

Her chest hurt from lacking breath. Though her body still ached as well, it was her pride that was most damaged. How humiliating—to be so distracted she hadn't heard the danger! Further humiliating still was Ryder Maddox having been the one to save her. How completely mortifying he'd saved her by coming at a dead run, grabbing her body, and lifting her out of the way as they sailed through the air together—landing in a heap in the dirt! At least she hadn't dropped the handful of forks. She glanced down, amazed to see she still held them tightly in her fist.

"You're welcome, I guess . . . Miss Hunter," he told her awkwardly. The puzzled frown on his face deepened.

Dusty didn't like the way he studied her with obvious disapproval. She could almost hear his thoughts. *What have you become?* she felt him thinking. She thought back at him, *The end result of what you began!*

With a scowl, she turned from him and headed toward the wagon where her father and several hands were dealing with the team and a hysterical Miss Raynetta McCarthy.

"Oh, good gravy, Hank!" Miss Raynetta

32

exclaimed breathlessly. She dramatically pressed her hand to her bosom as Hank Hunter helped her down from the wagon. "I thought I was goin'! I just thought I was plum a-goin' up to gossip with the geese there for a moment!"

"Now settle down there, Miss Raynetta," Hank chuckled. He nodded at Feller in a gesture he should tend the team.

Miss Raynetta shook her head, fanning her face with one tiny hand. "Truly, Hank!" she assured him emphatically. "I seen it all!" She opened her hands and stretched her palms toward the sky. "My whole life a-flashin' before my eyes like lightnin' in the heavens!" Dusty watched as her daddy looked to Ruff and smiled knowingly and completely amused. "There I was," Miss Raynetta continued in an awed whisper, "there I was when I was eight, a-stealin' molasses from my mama's cupboard." She looked to Hank and shook her head. "Truth be told, Hank . . . everythin' I ever done wrong . . . just a-flashin' in front of me like judgment day!"

"Well, if stealin' molasses was the worst thing you ever done, Miss Raynetta," Hank began, taking her arm and leading her toward the roasting pit. Dusty followed, all too aware of Ryder Maddox walking behind her in ponderous silence.

"Oh! But it weren't the worst of it!" Miss Raynetta exclaimed, intent on proving her villainy. "I dare not tell ya the rest, Hank! You'll send me down to the devil yourself!"

Dusty's father chuckled, and even for her angry, dark mood, Dusty couldn't help the smile spreading across her face as she watched the eccentric woman.

Miss Raynetta was the county character. Everybody thought so. She was thirty-five years old and had never married. She always wore the brightest colored dresses anyone had ever seen. Purple and red were her favorite colors to wear, and that alone gave birth to many a raised eyebrow. Dusty couldn't understand why Miss Raynetta had never married. Oh, it was true she was someone who you had to learn to under-stand, but she was adorable all the same. She was tiny, not quite five feet, with dark brown hair and big brown eyes. She unknowingly boasted the complexion of an angel—soft, smooth skin that was never marred by the tiniest freckle or blemish. Her smile and laughter were a pure remedy for anything causing anyone else to frown. All she had to do was enter a room, and the air of eccentricity, wit, and curiosity that was her aura immediately set even the grouchiest of souls to grinning. Sometimes, over the past five years, Dusty had wondered if perhaps Miss Raynetta McCarthy had been a victim of heartbreak—abandoned in the wake of a heartless man as she herself was.

"You all right?" Ryder asked from behind her, diverting Dusty's attention from Miss Raynetta's confessions of sin.

"I'm fine," she stated, not looking back to him. "My pride seems to be the only bruise that'll linger."

"That and the dirt mark on the back a your . . . skirt," he mumbled.

Dusty stopped cold in her tracks, whirling around to glare at him. He stood grinning mischievously, and Dusty fought the instinct to be moved to emotion by the familiar expression.

"It might be best if you were to go before me then, Mr. Maddox," she spat at him.

His grin broadened, and he nodded to her. As he strode past her, he lowered his voice and said, "All righty then. But it ain't like I haven't dusted off the seat of your britches before."

Dusty's mouth gaped open in astonishment at his remark. He was unbelievable—his comment completely improper! "You haven't changed a bit!" she scolded.

He paused and looked back at her. His expression changed. His eyes narrowed, a frown puckering his handsome brow. He somewhat glared at her and said, "You have." He turned from her. Catching up to Hank and Raynetta, he offered his arm to the tiny female eccentric.

"Well! Bless my soul!" Dusty heard Raynetta exclaim. "I'd know you anywhere! Mr. Ryder

Maddox. Hank Hunter, where'd ya dig this boy up from?"

Dusty was hateful in spirit and didn't want to chance being cheered up by her father, Miss Raynetta McCarthy, or Ryder Maddox, for that matter. So she turned and began walking in the opposite direction.

"You wanna help me with this team, Dusty?" Feller asked as she passed him. She didn't want to help, but she knew Feller was trying to distract her. She nodded, dropped the forks into her apron pocket, and silently matched his stride as he led the team back to the barn.

"Ain't like you to nearly be run over by a team of horses, Dusty," Feller noted when they'd reached the barn. He began checking the harnesses, the lines, and the horses themselves— searching for anything amiss that might have caused the team to bolt. "Well, it ain't like you . . . anymore," he added when she remained silent.

Dusty had no desire to hear one of Feller's sneaky sermons on the evils of how she'd changed. Therefore, she offered, "Miss Raynetta gets in more fixes than anyone I've ever known."

Feller chuckled. "Yep. She's somethin' else. But it's her love for livin' that gets her through . . . makes her somebody that people like to be around."

"You know everythin', Feller," Dusty ventured as she watched him. She stroked the velvety nose of one of the horses and then the other. Feller *did* know everything. Dusty believed that to be a fact. He knew everything that was important anyway. She looked to him, wondering why such a good-looking cowboy as Feller Lance had never settled down. Feller was tall, slim, with dark hair and light-colored eyes. She'd seen many a girl in town pine away after him. "Why didn't Miss Raynetta ever get married?"

He was silent for a long time. Then he said, "I . . . uh . . . I'm not certain."

Dusty frowned. He was lying to her. She could sense it. He knew why.

"You do too know. Why don't ya want to tell me?" she asked. "Is it as lewd a story as all that?" Her curiosity was truly stirred.

"Ain't lewd at all. Just . . . just a little too close to home," the weathered cowboy mumbled.

"Tell it to me, Feller," Dusty begged. "I wanna know."

It seemed odd to Dusty in that moment that Feller should know so much about life. The way he talked and the knowledge he owned made him seem so much older than his mere thirty years. As a child she had once asked Feller why he'd never married—why he'd never had a family. He always just told her he hadn't found anyone that could love him. It had forever saddened Dusty. She had loved him once—followed him around like a lovesick kitten, in fact. But then

37

she'd fallen in love with Ryder Maddox and left Feller for young Becca to fawn over for years and years. Sometimes Dusty fancied that, even now, Becca's eyes twinkled when she listened to Feller telling stories around the fire at night.

"Miss Raynetta fell for a cowboy . . . long while back. 'Fore you were born. But she was young, and he was older . . . and he hitched up with somebody else 'fore she was old enough really to have a chance to catch him."

Dusty turned and looked to where Miss Raynetta sat next to Becca, both of them surrounded by adoring hands. Miss Raynetta was magic! She had a way of drawing people to her like bees to honey. And yet . . .

"She seems happy enough," Dusty mumbled. If Miss Raynetta could be happy without a man in her life, then . . .

"Fact was . . . the man didn't even know how she felt. He went off and married his darlin' not even knowin' that he'd broke some other little girl's heart." Dusty watched Feller as he now inspected the wagon for something that might have caused the team to run. "Took her so long to quit hurtin', and she sure didn't want any other man that come along . . . well, by the time she was over it, she'd missed the best years of her life—them carefree, flirtin', courtin', sparkin'-on-the-porch-swing years."

Dusty was irritated. Somehow Feller always

managed to work in a sermon and preach to her. "And she seems fine for havin' the wisdom to avoid it all," she grumbled.

"Seemin' and bein' are tricks of the trade, Dusty," he told her frankly. "Never had her own children or a husband to keep her warm and safe . . . to laugh with and work alongside of."

"And how is it that you know so much about her?" Dusty asked a bit too sharply.

"Me an ol' Willy McCarthy used to be good friends. Willy's Miss Raynetta's little brother and the same age as me. We started cowboyin' together for Miss Raynetta's daddy. We had a lot of time to talk. Willy told me." Then he looked up at her and reminded, "You asked me about it, Dusty. Remember that."

"Yes, I asked you," Dusty whined, "but you always turn it into a sermon. I'm fine where I am, Feller. I'm fine and happy. I tried the 'lovin' a man' part of life once . . . and once was enough for me."

"You tried it *twice,* Dusty," he corrected her. "Then ya tucked tail and ran."

Dusty couldn't be angry with him. He was right on both counts! She knew it. So she tightened her jaw and stroked a horse's nose.

"How are you feelin' just now, darlin'?" he asked unexpectedly. "Ol' Ryder Maddox rides in after five years a-lookin' as big and strong as anythin'. And I ain't much of a judge when it comes to good-lookin' or ain't . . . but I suspect he's the handsomest boy any female ever laid eyes on. And . . . I'm a wonderin' how you're feelin' about now."

Dusty stared at the horse in front of her, never seeing it. "I feel like I've been thrown to the ground and trampled until I can't breathe . . . or get up . . . or go on. I hate him. I hate him more than I did five years ago." She walked away with loathed moisture in her eyes, a pounding in her head, and hatred in her heart the like even she'd never imagined.

Feller sighed heavily and shook his head. That little girl concerned him more than she'd ever know. And that Raynetta McCarthy—he'd told Dusty more than he planned, and he hadn't told her all of it.

"Sure ya hate him, girl," he said to himself. "If ya hated him . . . ya wouldn't be so miserable."

ॐ

Miss Raynetta had been saved, Feller had finished up the cooking, and now everyone sat enjoying the cool of the evening and a good meal.

"That Becca," Ryder chuckled as he sat with Feller eating his meal. "She ain't changed a lick . . . 'cept in growin' up a mite."

"And that Dusty has, you mean to be sayin'," Feller stated with the awareness given an experienced man.

Ryder nodded and smiled at his friend's insight. "Yep." He paused a moment before going on. "Ol' Hank . . . he told me how he lost Mrs. Hunter. She was the finest woman I ever knew."

"Amen," Feller whispered in emphatic, reverent agreement.

"But . . . I reckon there's somethin' he ain't told me about Dusty." Ryder let the comment hang in the air, knowing Feller Lance would tell him what he wanted to know if he felt it were the right thing to do. And he wouldn't if he didn't.

Feller chewed and swallowed a bit of beef. He inhaled deeply and began. "Well . . . I'll tell ya honest, boy . . . I don't usually take it as my place to tell anybody nothin' where Dusty is concerned, but I think since you mighta had somethin' to do with it . . . you oughta know."

Ryder looked down at his plate—guilt-ridden. "She was fourteen years old, Feller. You know that."

"I know it, boy. I ain't blamin' you. I just said when it comes to the heart of Miss Angelina Hunter . . . you were the first one there. That's all."

Ryder nodded, and Feller knew he'd made his point. "Well, boy . . . you remember the Richardsons in town? Man who owned the bank?"

"Yeah. Yeah, I do."

"You remember their son, Cash?" Feller asked.

"Yep. Little wormy, pampered kid . . . didn't

know how to get his hands dirty," Ryder answered. "That'd be the one. Well . . . he took a likin' to Dusty a year or so after you left. When she was . . . oh, 'bout fifteen, he started really payin' her court. Not official, mind you. But he rode out here a lot, danced with her a bunch at all the socials in town, sent her little love notes, and all that." Feller noticed the disapproving frown on Ryder's face, the way he wrinkled his nose in distaste, so he added, "Now mind you, Ryder . . . that boy filled out. And fast! He's a big ol' boy now. Not a hair under you and perty handsome for a town boy. Weren't a girl for two counties wasn't plum gone on that boy. Oh, and let me tell ya . . . he was a charmer. Charmed every female in the county clear down to her toes. And he took to our little Dusty like kittens to cream."

Feller watched as Ryder looked up to where Dusty sat alone eating her meal. He knew the cowboy owned an ocean of guilt where Miss Angelina Hunter was concerned. "Anyway," he continued, "for two years that boy charmed, courted, and coaxed that girl. Treated her good . . . I can't deny that. And she fell for him—as much as a girl can fall when someone else is always a-lurkin' in the back of her mind."

"Yeah, yeah, yeah," Ryder grumbled. "You done made your point, Feller."

Feller chuckled and slapped the man on the

back. "Anyway . . . 'bout six months after Dusty turned seventeen, ol' Cash proposed marriage."

"Really?" Ryder seemed surprised. "And she said . . ." he coaxed.

"She said . . . she'd think about it, as I recall. Seemed she wanted to talk it over with her daddy, bein' that her mama had just passed about a year or so before and all. So our little Dusty—and she's a good gal—she wouldn't even consider it 'less she was really lovin' that man in some way . . . I assure ya of that. Anyhow . . . she decides some young cowhand she had her heart set on has grown up and got hisself married somewhere . . ."

"Ah, now come on, Feller! Cut me some rope here," Ryder chuckled.

Feller smiled. "All right, boy. All right. So Dusty . . . she decides to marry Cash. He gives her a ring . . . big ol' rock of a diamond and gold band. He gives her a ring, and they set a date. Then one day, Dusty goes into town to surprise him with a birthday cake she made for his twentieth. Walks up to the Richardson house . . . knocks . . . no answer. She hears somethin' comin' from their barn . . . walks over, opens the barn door . . . and sees Mr. Cash Richardson hisself a-smoochin' and rompin' in the hay with one of them loose girls from the saloon."

"Ouch," Ryder sighed, rubbing at the whiskers on his chin. He shook his head and frowned.

"Oh, the smelly dog begged and groveled, sent

her gifts, cried . . . did everythin'. But you know Dusty. She's got a good head on her shoulders, and she wouldn't have nothin' to do with him. Bad thing is," Feller added, lowering his voice, "she wouldn't have nothin' to do with nobody. Not for the longest time. She still ain't got no use for men other than her daddy and, I'm proud to say, me. Don't trust 'em."

"Betray a woman's trust, and ya murder her soul," Ryder mumbled, looking up to where Dusty sat, having been joined by her father.

"Yep." Feller looked up to Dusty too. His own heart ached for the suffering endured by a young woman he loved like a little sister. "She cried and cried and cried off and on for weeks. And she ain't shed a tear—that I seen, anyway—since. She's hard, Ryder. Hard as stone. Works herself like a mule, won't let nobody close . . . 'cept Alice. You remember Alice Maxwell?"

"Oh, yeah. They were friends when I was here," Ryder recalled aloud.

"Yep. But Alice got married and has two babies and her husband to care for now. So she don't get over much."

"Banker's son. Dirty yeller dog," Ryder mumbled, shaking his head as he watched Dusty talking with her father and now Becca.

"Yep. Wanted to shoot him myself. I think ol' Hank had a hard time not beatin' the waddin' out of him," Feller told the man.

"Why don't *you* heal her heart, Feller?" Ryder asked, an unreadable expression on his face. "Ya said yourself she still takes to ya."

Feller couldn't really tell whether the man were in jest or not. "Tarnation, boy! Even if I had the inclination—which I don't—you think she'd fall for another cowboy?" Then pure determination drove him to his next statement. "I figure . . . that's what the Lord, fate, or her daddy brung you back for."

Ryder chuckled, shook his head, and took a swig of water out of his beat-up old tin cup. "That girl don't need the likes a me. I been around and back since I was last here, Feller. One thing a broken-hearted woman don't need . . . it's a man with a yoke 'round his neck hitched up to a wagon and a-haulin' bricks." Feller watched as Ryder Maddox inhaled a deep and grievous breath, exhaling long and hard. "But . . . I will say that this here's the best meat I ever tasted!" He smiled and stood up. "Since I left here five years ago, that is. I'm thinkin' I need a bite more." He walked away to where Becca was now serving up seconds.

Feller watched him go. "Yep. Fate or heaven." Then he looked to where Becca was feeding the men. He didn't even realize a smile had spread across his face as he watched her fumbling around trying to serve—wasn't even conscious of the wink he gave her when she looked over at him

45

and sighed in frustration. He simply stood up and went to her rescue.

ꕹ

All evening Dusty had been quiet. She hadn't felt like talking. Her conversation with Feller had squelched any desire she might have had to socialize. *He is such a nag sometimes,* she thought to herself. But she loved him all the same. She had a powerful twinge of regret at the thought of him ever leaving the ranch.

"Oh, Dusty!" Miss Raynetta exclaimed as she plopped herself down on the bench next to Dusty. One thing about Miss Raynetta—she didn't sit down; she plopped. Dusty forced a smile, not really feeling like a chat with Miss Raynetta— mostly because Miss Raynetta always had a way of making her feel better, and Dusty wanted to wallow in her misery. It was how she stayed guarded.

"Oh, Dusty! I am so sorry that I nearly ran right over you with the team! I can't even think on it. I just start to feelin' like I'm gonna upchuck right here and now!"

Dusty smiled. The woman was an angel. Her sincere dramatics were also far too amusing not to smile at. "I know it wasn't your fault, Miss Raynetta. I shouldn'ta been daydreamin'."

Raynetta McCarthy smiled. "Well . . . if'n I was nineteen and Ryder Maddox came a-ridin' up again one warm May afternoon with my daddy . . .

46

I'da been daydreamin' too!" She winked, and Dusty shook her head, delightedly irritated. "Actually, even now if Ryder Maddox came a-ridin' up . . . I'd be a-daydreamin'!"

"Now, Miss Raynetta . . . you know I don't—" Dusty began.

"I know, I know," the woman sighed. Then tactfully, Raynetta changed the subject. "I thought I was gonna meet the Maker, Dusty. Right here on your daddy's ranch. My heart's a-beatin' like a hammer on a nail just thinkin' about it!"

"But Daddy saved you," Dusty reminded her in an effort to calm her down once more.

Instead, Miss Raynetta's excitement and smile disappeared in one breath as she said, "Yes. He did."

Dusty frowned. The woman seemed oddly void of her usual zest. "What's the matter, Miss Raynetta?" Dusty was genuinely concerned. It was unlike the woman to look so defeated.

But Raynetta just shook her head. "I'm just weary, sweet thing. Just weary. I been in town most all the day, and then comin' home the team got away from me. Your daddy's always tellin' me that I should stop in and get one of the boys here to take me in to town. But I don't need that, Dusty. Now do I?"

Dusty smiled. Here was a true kindred spirit— a woman who understood what a man could do to a woman's life!

"No, you don't!" Dusty agreed wholeheartedly.

Raynetta smiled understandingly at the girl, yet Dusty did not favor the look of pity accompanying her smile.

"You best be gettin' on, Miss Raynetta," Hank said as he sauntered toward them. "That team may be a bit skittish yet, and I think somebody oughta go with ya . . . make sure you get there safe."

"All right, Hank. I'd appreciate it," Miss Raynetta agreed.

Dusty frowned and looked to Miss Raynetta, puzzled. Hadn't she just said she didn't need a man's help?

"Ryder says he'd be more'n happy to see ya home," Hank offered.

"Oh. Okay."

Miss Raynetta seemed disappointed. Dusty wondered how she could possibly be disappointed that it was Ryder who was going to go with her. After all, she'd implied she found him attractive.

"Ryder," her father shouted. "Take ol' Red with ya outta the corral. I figure he ain't been ridden much since I've been gone."

"Yes, sir," Ryder called, rising from his place near the fire and heading toward the corral.

Dusty watched him go—watched him walk—noticed the way his shoulders moved in rhythm with the rest of his body. Ryder Maddox didn't walk, she remembered then. He swaggered. And as her mind began to linger—began to drift back to the days when life was happy, full of adventure and flirting and dreams—she stood.

"I'm done in, Daddy," she managed to say. "I have to turn in if I'm gonna be up to feed this bunch breakfast in the mornin'."

"All right, darlin'," Hank said, hugging his daughter. He kissed her adoringly on one cheek.

"Good night, Miss Raynetta," Dusty offered. In the next moment, she fled.

Hank watched his daughter walk away—the ache in his heart for her own pain almost unendurable.

"You done good by your girl in bringin' that boy back, Hank," Raynetta told him. "She needs to close that book and start over."

"I know," Hank admitted. "I just worry that . . . that the book is too good . . . too interesting . . . too perfect for her to let go of."

"Closin' a book don't mean ya burn it, Hank. It just means ya can start readin' it again . . . that's all."

Hank smiled down at Raynetta. "You're a wise woman, Miss Raynetta McCarthy. A wise woman indeed."

Raynetta smiled up at him. "You'd be surprised at how unwise I truly am, Hank," she told him.

Hank shook his head. "I doubt that. But it is unwise for ya to keep yourself out this late. You make sure Ryder gets ya home safe, and don't stay away so long this time. You're welcome here any minute of the day."

"Thank you, Hank," Raynetta mumbled.

Hank Hunter watched the wagon leave, Ryder at the lines and Raynetta at his side in her racy purple dress. She was a beauty, that Raynetta McCarthy—as cute as she'd always been. She didn't look all that much different from when he'd been a young cowhand himself on her daddy's farm. Hank stood watching them go, wondering why a little gal as pretty as Raynetta had never married.

He looked back toward the house. He watched as the light in Dusty's room got brighter, indicating she'd lit her lamp and turned it up. His heart ached for her. And yet, at the same time, he was angry with her. Why had she let life beat her down so? It never truly seemed to be part of her nature. That yellow Cash Richardson! He'd like to wring that boy's neck! It hadn't been the same with Ryder. Dusty was fourteen, and the ranch was in trouble. But Cash!

Hank turned back to the pit. Feller was still cleaning up, Becca alongside him as ever. The other hands all looked done in.

"You boys get bunked in for the night. It's been a long, long day, and tomorrow ain't gonna be any shorter," he announced. "Leave it for tomorrow, Feller," he said. "It ain't gonna run away while we sleep."

Becca walked to him, smiling as ever, and threw her arms around his waist. "I'm so glad you're back, Daddy," she said as she leaned up, kissing him soundly on the cheek.

"Me too, darlin'," he chuckled. "Now you get to bed. It's late. Dusty'll need some help with breakfast in the mornin'."

"Yes, Daddy," she said, releasing him and heading toward the house.

Hank looked up into the night sky. A million stars winked back at him, and he inhaled deeply of the clear night air.

"What more could a man ask for, Feller?" he sighed as Feller walked over, folded his arms across his chest, and looked up into the same dazzling sky. "Two purty daughters, hard work, land, air, and the sky. What more could a man want?"

"Love of a good woman, maybe?" Feller mumbled.

Hank looked to Feller, puzzled. "Already had that myself, boy. I figure it's way past your turn though."

Feller chuckled. "Yep. I guess I ain't the lovable kind." Feller looked to Hank and added, "But you . . . ain't nothin' would please Elly more than to be up there in heaven and a-lookin' down to see you havin' someone to love again, Hank."

Hank smiled at the memory of his little wife.

He'd loved her more than life itself. It had nearly killed him to lose her. He often wondered if he would've just shriveled up and died alongside Elly—if it hadn't been for his girls.

"You're a fine one to talk, Feller. Got all the advice in the world for everybody but yourself, don't ya?"

"Yep," Feller admitted.

Hank watched the stars twinkling. He liked knowing Elly was safe with the angels. And the thought struck him again—Raynetta McCarthy was a sweet-looking little gal.

Dusty sat on the bed brushing out her hair when Becca knocked on the door. "Can I come in, Dust?" she asked, entering without waiting for a response.

"Becca, what're ya knockin' for?" Dusty asked, trying to sound irritated. "You're gonna come in whether or not I'm buck naked!"

Instantly, Becca was sitting on the bed next to Dusty—eyes as wide as supper dishes and as curious as any old maid gossip. "How do you feel, Dust?" she asked.

"What are ya talkin' about, Becca? I swear you send me into fits." Dusty knew darn well what Becca was talking about. But the fact was—she didn't want to talk about it.

"I nearly fainted dead away when he turned around and I saw who it was! How can you be so calm? He's . . . he's fantastic! More fantastic than he was when he was here before! How can ya sit there so calm and—"

"Because I am calm," Dusty lied. "That was so long ago, Becca. I can hardly remember what all went on."

Becca's smile and excitement were squelched—completely. She slowly stood, hurt and disappointment evident on her pretty face. "Why do you lie?" she asked. "Why do you shut me out? You're my sister—my only sister and the only person I can talk to! And you slam the door on me at every turn."

"Becca, I'm sorry," Dusty began. She had been cold, unfeeling, rude. She regretted it—as she always did when she did it.

"No," Becca whispered. "Nevermind. I'm tired of tryin', Dusty. I'm tired of never havin' anybody to talk to."

"You talk all the time, Becca. You got every man on the ranch eatin' outta your hand. What do ya need me for?" Dusty was building up the wall again—the strong, impenetrable wall, the wall keeping her from feeling.

"What *do* I need you for?" Becca asked, completely dejected. "After all, you ain't Mama. You don't have to listen to my concerns, my fears . . . my heartache. Now do you?" She turned and began to leave.

"What could you possibly know about heartache?" Dusty asked. Emotion caused her voice to falter, betraying her feelings.

Becca turned looking back at her, the all-too-familiar tears already streaming over her cheeks. "A lot more than ya think, Dusty. Don't think you own the only broken heart in the world." She left, slamming the door behind her.

Dusty released a heavy sigh and fought back her own tears. Then, shaking her head with discouragement, she blew out the flame in her lamp and crawled into bed. The night was unusually warm, and she felt uncomfortable even with the weightlessness of the cotton nightgown she wore. She closed her eyes, intent on sleep. It had been a long day, and breakfast came early.

But as she lay in bed, all she could see in her mind's eye was that danged Ryder Maddox. The way he smiled, the way he walked, the smooth, deep intonation of his voice—the way he put on his hat, the way he rolled up his shirtsleeves. The boy had become a man, but the man had retained so many things belonging to the boy. *He's beautiful,* she thought, angrily turning to her side and hugging her pillow.

She tried to force her mind onto other roads of contemplation. Miss Raynetta's purple dress had been quite lovely. What a sight she had been—screeching at the top of her lungs atop her runaway wagon! Dusty smiled at the thought and scolded herself for finding any amusement in the woman's misfortune. And then the memory of Ryder Maddox "saving" Dusty's own "bacon," as he had put it, snuck in. In that brief moment when he'd grabbed her and thrown her out of harm's way, her heart had leapt with delight at his touch! And then he'd remarked about the dirt mark on the back of her skirts. *How dare he!* she thought. He most definitely must've been looking at her seat in order to notice such a thing.

She remembered the first time she'd ever seen Ryder Maddox. At first she fought the memory overtaking her mind and senses. But then, as she always inevitably did, she let it wash over her like a warm summer rain. Closing her eyes and trying to control her tears and quickened breath, she remembered it all.

She had been ten years old that spring. Ten. Becca was eight. They had been playing down by the creek, and Angelina Hunter, in her infinite ability to stumble into a mess, had fallen in the water and soaked her dress. Well, naturally, she simply took it off and hung it over a tree branch while they continued their play. It had been such a fun day. Angelina and Becca had hauled their small tea table out to the creek. Their daddy had made the little table and matching chairs for them for Christmas several years before so they could have their imaginary tea parties together. That day the table was set under the big willow growing on the bank of the creek, and Angelina and Becca had spent all afternoon "entertaining" imaginary guests. Oh, the fun they'd had pretending butter-cups were corn freshly cut off the cob, that willow leaves were greens! And they'd made the most marvelous mud pies that day; they'd flopped out of the tiny pie tins holding their shape perfectly. Furthermore, the girls had been set upon by imaginary renegade Indians. Of course, their imaginary cowboy beaus had saved their lives! All too soon, the sun was telling Angelina it was late afternoon, nearly time for the hands to be coming in for supper.

"I don't want to drag the table all the way back to the house, Angelina," Becca whined.

"But we can't leave it out, Becca! It might rain tonight, and then it would be ruined," Angelina explained.

"I'll take the chairs if you drag the table," Becca offered finally.

"Becca! You're such a baby!" Angelina took hold of the table, pulling it along behind her as she walked toward the house. In her irritation with having to go in for the evening and having no help dragging the tea table home, Angelina had completely forgotten she'd left her dress and petticoats behind. The mirth was blatantly evident on her daddy's face as she and Becca approached looking like something the cat dragged in.

"Well! You girls been havin' tea today?" Hank Hunter asked.

"Oh, Daddy!" Becca exclaimed. "We've been havin' all kinds a stories!"

"And now Becca made me drag the table home all on my own!" Angelina complained.

At that moment, one of the table legs bumped into an old tree root sticking out of the ground. Irritated, Angelina turned around and pulled hard on the table. It bumped up over the tree root and gave a bit but caught immediately on another exposed root. The sudden jerk of the table stopping cold after she'd pulled so hard caused Angelina to lose her grip and sit down flat in the dirt.

Of course, her father, Feller Lance, and several other hands burst into laughter as Angelina stood up and dusted the seat of her bloomers, only then realizing she'd forgotten to put her dress back on. Now she stood for all the world to see in just her underthings.

"Humph!" Angelina breathed as she haughtily stood up and tugged on the table again. But again the table leg cleared the tree root only to hook itself on another, and Angelina was again rear-end down in the dirt.

"Well, now, little Miss Dusty Britches," some-one said. And Angelina looked up into the face of the handsomest boy she'd ever laid eyes on. "Looks to me like you could use a hand," he

57

said, grinning mischievously at her. He offered his hand to her.

Tentatively, Angelina placed her hand in his. He pulled her to her feet and dusted off the seat of her bloomers. Reaching down and picking up the table, he carried it toward the house.

Angelina ran to catch up with him. "You're new," she stated.

"Yes, I am. Come in just this afternoon, and your daddy hired me on. My name's Ryder Maddox," he said. He set the small table down on the back porch and offered her his hand again.

"Angelina Hunter," Angelina said, taking his hand and shaking it firmly.

"Really?" the young cowboy chuckled, bending over and kissing the back of Angelina's hand quickly with a wink. "I thought your name was Dusty Britches."

Ryder had taken to calling her Dusty Britches from the very first moment they met. It caught on like a house afire, and it wasn't more than a few days until even her mama was calling her Dusty. And now, resenting the fact that insipid tears had soaked her pillowcase, Dusty turned over and stared out the window. She watched the breeze billow the light curtains into her room. What a day that had been. Such fun she and Becca had— and her life had changed forever! She hadn't known it at the time, but that had been the most pivotal day of her life. Ryder was a gold-strike of a boy! Tall, handsome as heaven, smart, a hard worker, witty, kind, polite—there had been nothing like him to be seen before or since.

Dusty remembered how all the girls from town would find excuses to follow her home from school every day that next fall. The older girls in town were complete ninnies—fawning all over Ryder at every social he attended—but he'd always been Dusty's boy. He'd do anything she asked, within reason, and some things without. Like the time she begged him to help her know what it was like to fly—Ryder had helped Dusty with the rigging in the hayloft. What a fit her mama had when she came home from town to find Dusty swinging this way and that—in and out of the hayloft—swinging from a harness and some ropes Dusty and Ryder had rigged. And who was it that always wiped her tears, when he'd find her out by the creek crying about something someone had said to tease her or some other thing that had made her sad? And when she was thirteen and at the harvest social in town, who was it that had asked her for a dance when no one else would? Ryder Maddox, of course—like some handsome prince in an old fairy tale book.

She remembered how heartbroken she was at finding Ryder and Jenny Morris flirting on the porch swing of the Morris's house at Jenny's sister's wedding. But even then, when Dusty had fled the scene in tears, Ryder left Jenny on the porch swing to seek out Dusty and reassure her that someday, when she'd grown up, he'd catch her out by the old creek and spark with her a bit. He, in his masculine naivety, hadn't realized she'd believed him—hadn't realized she'd dreamed it would really happen. Then came the droughts, and the ranch began failing.

Sighing heavily, Dusty closed her eyes and let the low hum of the cowboys' voices in the bunkhouse drift in, comforting her somewhat. Oh, how she hoped Becca would never fall for a cowboy—really fall for one. Becca flirted mercilessly with them all—enjoyed far too much attention from every ranch hand in the county. But she'd never fallen in love, and Dusty hoped when she did—for it was destined to happen—Dusty hoped Becca wouldn't be hurt like she had been.

Poor, sweet Becca. Guilt washed over Dusty and caused her to weep all the more. She'd treated her sister so miserably all day long! Dusty covered her face with her hands to silence her crying. She only cried in bed now. For so long she'd cried when anyone even looked at her. Now her tears were few and very far between, but Becca hadn't deserved the treatment Dusty had handed down to her a short time before.

"What is wrong with me?" she cried out in a whisper. "I'm mean, cold . . . selfish!" A vision of Becca's face, hurt and rejected in expression, printed itself in her mind. "Please, God," Dusty prayed in a whisper. "I don't want to be like this. Help me! Heal me!" And then she added, "Why did you lead him back here?"

That night even the low hum of the cowboys and ranch hands settling into the bunkhouse couldn't comfort her—for, above all the rest, one very familiar, very beloved voice was all she could hear. She finally fell asleep with an ache in her heart that seemed more unendurable than ever before.

Chapter Three

It was still dark when Dusty awoke. It was a bit earlier than she'd planned to start the day, even for her. Still, something had awakened her, and she knew herself well enough to admit she'd never get back to sleep. Even if she did, she'd feel worse getting up in half an hour after dozing again. She pushed the covers aside and stretched for long moments. Breathing deeply of the morning air, she relished the smell of dust, the creek, the trees, and pasture grasses. Her eyes widened, however, when she realized just what had awakened her.

"Are you pretendin' tonight, little darlin'," came the first line of the familiar tune. Frantically, Dusty kicked the rest of her covers off, leaping out of bed and racing to the window. She looked

out into the darkness of early morning. There was a lantern on in the barn. She could see its glow through the open door.

> *Pretendin' I'm your Prince Charmin',*
> *Though I'm nothin' but a cowboy . . .*
> *a-ridin' for the brand?*
> *Are you pretendin' I'm a gentleman . . .*
> *a-askin' for your hand?*
> *Well, I'll kiss you tonight, little darlin'.*
> *And I'll hold you real tight in my arms.*
> *And if you're thinkin' that my kisses . . .*
> *aren't really who I am,*
> *I'm not pretendin', little girl,*
> *A dream unendin', little girl,*
> *No more pretendin', little girl . . .*
> *I'm your man.*

Oh, how she'd adored the song as a child! How she'd awakened every morning long before the sun just to lie awake in her bed or sit by her open window and listen to Ryder's deep, masculine voice as he sang during morning chores. His voice owned a richness it lacked all those years back— its intonation all the more dreamy! As she saw him come out of the barn, she stepped back so he could not see her watching him from the window. He set down two buckets of milk and closed the barn doors behind him, whistling the tune instead of singing it this time and heading for the back porch. There he'd set the milk buckets down outside the back door and cover them with the old dishcloth Becca had left out the night before.

For a moment, it was as if nothing had changed. Yet making busy to dispel any further sentimental reminiscing, Dusty dressed and went to the kitchen to start breakfast. By the time Becca came rushing into the kitchen, Dusty had all but finished the flapjacks and bacon.

"I'm so sorry, Dust. I-I really thought I was gettin' up early enough," the girl apologized sincerely.

"It's fine, Becca," Dusty assured her with a kind smile—an apologetic smile. "I was up earlier than usual and thought I'd just get it done."

"I'm—I'm sorry for last night, Dust. I was so cruel to you," Becca told her.

"It was me, Becca, not you. How well you must know that by now." Dusty hugged her sister tightly. It had been so long, far too long, since she'd hugged her little sister. "I did want to ask ya about something you said though," Dusty ventured. "About me not bein' the only one who—"

"Good mornin', my sugar lumps!" Hank greeted as he entered the kitchen, stretching his suspenders up over his shoulders.

"Oh, Daddy!" Becca whined delightedly. "Sugar lumps?"

"Yes, Daddy! Please! I certainly hope we're not

lumpy yet," Dusty teased. She returned her father's morning kiss as he paused in passing her.

"Them hands up yet?" he asked as he sat down at the table.

"Well, I saw Ryder millin' around out there while I was gettin' dressed," Becca offered.

"Yep! That boy's still got a mighty fine voice in his gullet, don't he?" Hank yawned and stretched again. "But Feller oughta have them other boys up by now."

"It was a long day, Daddy. I'm sure they're wrung out," Dusty defended. The silence was deafening, so she turned to see both her daddy and Becca staring at her with raised eyebrows. "What?" she asked.

"Well, if you'll pardon my sayin' it, Dust," Becca ventured, "you're nearly harder on 'em about gettin' up early than Daddy is."

Dusty's initial reaction was to get angry with her sister. Of course she was hard on them all! She was the one who had to prepare their meals most of the time, and it was a lot of work. Why shouldn't she expect them to be prompt? But her musings of the night before gave her reason to pause. She was mean, and she was trying to change that now. "I am, aren't I," she stated rather than asked. Her daddy, obviously not wanting to say anything unkind, simply rubbed at his whiskery chin and looked away.

"Mornin', all," Ryder said as he entered the

kitchen through the open back door. For a moment, his eyes met Dusty's, and he grinned. She smiled slightly at him but looked away quickly. How was she going to live through this? How could she endure having him so close—so wonderful—so untouchable?

Feller was right at his heels and said, "Mornin'."

"Mornin', boys! And ain't it a beauty?" Hank greeted.

"It is that, sir," Ryder agreed, taking a seat at the table.

"What's on the list today, boss?" Feller asked, taking a seat next to Ryder.

"Mornin'," Ruff mumbled as he entered, followed by several others.

Hank nodded at each man as he entered, answering Feller's question at the same time. "Figure after everyone who's leavin' has rode out, we'll get to brandin'. Might as well get it out of the way."

Dusty dropped the spoon she was using, and it clattered to the floor. Her breath had stopped, and there was a terrible constricting pain in her chest. She hadn't thought of it before now. What if Ryder were drifting? What if he hadn't planned to stay on? What if he'd only joined the drive out of loyalty to her father and now planned to leave with the others who were moving on?

"You all right?" Becca asked, her expression that of true concern.

"What's the racket, Dusty?" her father exclaimed. " 'Bout to give a man a heart attack."

"Sorry, Daddy," Dusty mumbled.

"Anyhow," Hank continued, "we need to get them cattle branded today and look 'em all over good so we can get on with the regular work tomorrow."

"Yes, sir," Feller agreed.

The talk turned to low, mumbling, man kind of things. Dusty and Becca sat down together to eat their breakfast at the small drop leaf in one corner of the kitchen.

"You're as white as snow, Dusty," Becca whispered. "What's the matter? You feelin' all right?"

"I'm fine," Dusty told her, trying not to speak in her usual short, irritated manner.

"Well, all I know is you and I are gonna find ourselves doin' more chores 'round here, since Ryder's the only one of the drive cowboys who's stayin' on. The rest are leavin'. That leaves only Daddy, Feller, Guthrie, Titch, Ruff, and Ryder to run the cattle and everythin' else!"

"Who told ya that? That Ryder was the only one stayin' on?" Trying to cover her obvious interest, Dusty added, "At least four stayed on after the last drive, and Daddy didn't bring all that many cattle home last time."

"Ryder told me last night. Said the others didn't want to stay . . . that he was the only one

66

stayin' on," Becca said as she concentrated on eating her eggs.

A wave of anxious relief washed over Dusty, and although it was merely first thing in the morning, she felt tired—drained already as if she'd worked all day.

"I saw this dress in Miss Raynetta's dress shop window, Dusty!" Becca began, lowering her voice excitedly. "It's all yellows and greens! Do you think I might talk Daddy into letting me have it for the Fourth of July picnic in town?"

Dusty smiled. Becca's eyes were lit up like train lanterns. "I'm sure ya can, Becca," Dusty answered. "He never says no to you, now does he?"

"He never says no to you either, Dusty," Becca reminded with a smile.

"That's 'cause we're good girls. We never ask for more than we should."

Breakfast went along, the men having their own conversation at the big table, Dusty and Becca listening most of the time. At last, Dusty finished off her biscuit and stood. Placing her plate in the sink, she watched as her daddy and each hand, in turn, put his plate in the sink, snatched his hat off the rack by the door, and left with a, "Thank you, Miss Dusty."

Ryder was the last one to leave the table. As he approached the sink where Dusty still stood, she felt as if a blazing, fiery torch were moving toward her. With each stride he made toward her, she began to feel hot and uncomfortable. He deposited his plate in the sink, and as he took his hat from the rack, he said, "Your mama never did better, Dust—Miss Dusty. Thank you."

"You're welcome," she managed to reply, trying to sound unaffected by his presence and compliment.

"Miss Becca," he nodded to Becca before leaving.

Becca rose from her seat and joined Dusty at the sink. "You're gonna have to love him, ya know," she whispered.

"Rebecca!" Dusty scolded. "What is wrong with you?"

"Nothin'. I've just decided I'm not gonna let you ruin your life or anybody else's anymore. It was fate that brought him back here . . . fate or a greater power. And I ain't gonna let you ruin it!" Becca told her.

"Becca . . . stop it now. I don't want yo—" Dusty began.

"Nope. You ain't gonna bully me about this one, Dusty. Now let's get these dishes done up. I got other things I wanna get done today."

"Do 'em yourself," Dusty spat. "I did the cookin'! Remember?" And throwing her apron into a nearby chair, Dusty stormed off—all determination to be kinder and more understanding to her sister completely obliterated.

She had meant to go down to the pond and pout. It was, after all, her favorite pouting place. But no sooner had she left the back porch than she heard her daddy call to her.

"Dusty. Dusty! Run in the barn and get that smaller brand for these heifers."

Sighing heavily and with irritation—for her self-centered pouting session had been interrupted—she stomped to the barn and retrieved the brand.

"He's got two thousand hands out there just a-standin' around waitin' to be paid! You'd think one of 'em could come in here and find the small iron!"

Angrily, she walked back to where her father stood paying the cowboys who were leaving and thanking them for their help. Feller already had the fire going, and Guthrie and Ruff had several head waiting nearby ready for branding. Dusty glanced over to where Ryder stood near Feller. She knew Ryder would do most of the wrestling. He always had. She remembered he could take a cow down faster than any hand they'd had before or since. Dusty used to love to sit on the fence and watch him help in the branding. It was always so impressive when she was a young girl to watch his strength and dexterity—the way he'd throw a heifer or steer to the ground like the easiest thing in the world. So without being conscious of what she was doing, she leaned back against the fence and watched as Ruff sent a heifer toward the fire. In a split second, Ryder grabbed the heifer's head, twisted her neck, and forced her to the ground. Feller was just as fast with putting the iron to her. Dusty wrinkled her nose at the familiar yet dreadful stench of burning hair and hide.

The cowboys making ready to leave joined Ruff, Guthrie, and Titch in hollering and whistling with admiration. Ryder simply released the cow, stood up, and rubbed his hands back and forth in anticipation of the challenge. "Bring 'em on! We'll have this done 'fore lunch!" he said.

Dusty, totally unaware of the broad smile that was now part of her expression, continued to watch the men brand. Before long, the cowboys who were drifting were gone, and her father was branding the smaller heifers and steers while Ruff and Titch took turns wrestling. Guthrie was bringing the big ones in, and Ryder took down two or three to the other men's one.

Dusty stood watching for a long time before Becca finally joined her. "I've finished the dishes," Becca stated rather resentfully.

"Thank you, Becca," Dusty said. "I'm sorry, Becca. I—I shouldn't be so cross. It's just that—"

"I know, I know. Let's not talk about it anymore." Becca stepped up onto the lowest fence rung to watch the men work. "Ryder's still the fastest I ever saw," she commented.

Dusty remained silent. They watched as Guthrie led an enormous cow in on a rope.

"She's huge!" Becca exclaimed. "She's gotta be near half a ton!"

"She's still got her horns too. I bet she's ornery," Dusty added.

"Think he can get her down?"

"Naw. She's too big. Daddy'll just butcher her early." Dusty watched as Guthrie nodded toward Ryder and Feller.

"Find any elephants to bring in for us, Guthrie?" Feller chuckled.

"What you boys think I am?" Ryder asked, sizing up the cow and rolling up his shirtsleeves.

"Stinkin' immortal!" Ruff shouted with a chuckle.

Everyone stopped to watch and see whether Ryder could take the monstrosity of a beef down for branding.

"I'll wager you, boy!" Hank shouted. "You get her down, and I'll give ya the whole day off week from Friday!"

"You're on!" Ryder laughed, pointing at Dusty's daddy. "She's gonna break my dang legs though!"

"Then I'll give ya two days off!" Hank chuckled.

"That's a big beef," Dusty mumbled. "He shouldn't try her." She looked at Becca, who nodded, her eyes widening in agreement. "Daddy!" Dusty shouted. "Shame on you!"

"Ah, don't ya worry, punkin!" Hank shouted.

"Ain't yet seen a cow that Ryder can't lay down!"

But Dusty felt more than frightened. This cow had enormous horns! She watched, helpless, as Ryder nodded his head at Guthrie to let his rope go. Ryder stepped up behind the mammoth animal, put his arms under her horns, and started twisting. He twisted her fast enough she couldn't run from him or get away, but she didn't go down immediately. She was big and strong and heavy, and her neck was nearly as thick as the rest of her. But after a few long seconds, she started to lean toward the cowboy, and maneuvering his body carefully, Ryder managed to get his legs out of the way, falling back to the ground and pinning her head as she hit the dirt with an earthshaking surrender. Feller wasted no time in branding her, even though all the other men stood around clapping and shouting with admiration.

"He did it!" Becca squealed, clapping wildly.

Dusty stood completely upset and frightened. "He's gotta let her up now," she mumbled. Instinctively, as Dusty watched the cow's eyes wide with fear and seeming indignation, she stepped behind the fence. She knew what a big, angry cow could do. Sure enough, as Ryder let her go and she got to her feet, she immediately turned on him.

"Oh, she's mad now!" Hank chuckled.

Ryder eluded the angry bovine as she charged him several times. Hank, Feller, and the others stood laughing as they remained aware the cow might turn on any one of them next.

Ryder hollered, "Look out!" and made straight for the fence behind which Dusty and Becca stood. In one clean, very impressive leap, Ryder cleared the fence. Turning he grabbed the girls' waistbands, yanking them safely away from danger a second before the angry cow ran headlong into the fence—her long, sharp horns plunging through the rails like two spears.

With a triumphant grin, Ryder shouted to Hank, "Week from Friday?"

Hank chuckled and conceded, "Week from Friday!" All the ranch hands roared with amusement as the giant critter turned and took out after Feller. Dusty watched as all the hands and her father, save Guthrie, who was still mounted on a horse, ran this way and that, leaping fences to avoid impalement.

Becca squealed with delight. Dusty wanted to enjoy the merriment, but the danger of it all was still far too apparent.

"I knew she couldn't best you, Ryder," Becca giggled.

"No, ma'am," he answered with a smile.

"You all are actin' like a bunch of children," Dusty grumbled as she turned to walk away. Her attempt at departure was short-lived. The tug at her waist indicated, without question, that Ryder still held her by the skirt. Slapping awkwardly at his hand, she turned to find him grinning mischievously down at her.

"Let go!" she demanded.

"Can't," he teased. "That cow scared the tar outta me, and I can't unclench my fist."

"Let me go," she snapped.

With a disapproving and disgusted frown, he growled, "Ease up, Miss Hunter."

"Grow up, Mr. Maddox," she spat at him, yanking her skirt waist from his grasp and storming back toward the house.

"She ain't nothin' like I remember her," Ryder mumbled.

"Yes, she is," Becca assured him. "She's just— just lost. That's all. She's lost herself." Becca paused and then said, "You can find her."

Ryder smiled affectionately, cupping Becca's cheek with his hand. "You can't help nobody home if you ain't there yourself, sweet thing," he said solemnly. He turned and jumped the fence again. Guthrie had brought in another heifer; there was work to do.

As she reached the back porch, Dusty turned to look back. Already she was regretting her lack of lightheartedness, but when she turned to see Ryder looking down adoringly at Becca, his hand affectionately on her cheek, all regret hardened into stone. Oh, how well she remembered the

74

effect Ryder had on girls and women! Every female in the county used to take to swooning when he walked by. They used to rain pies and cakes on him, trying, no doubt, to impress him with their culinary prowess—to remind him that a good cook made a good wife.

She wouldn't care that he was back. Truly! All an interest in Ryder Maddox gave a person was grief. She'd learned that. She didn't need to learn it again. And thus, as was the case anytime Dusty found herself in a fit of weakness—almost becoming a caring, loving, normal woman again —she dug up the hurt and resentment that had kept her sane since Cash Richardson entered and exited her life. She could be nicer to her sister, kinder to her father, but she would not soften up where Ryder Maddox was concerned.

As the sun rose higher in the sky, Dusty kept herself busy with hard work. She quickly finished her outside chores and then moved into the house. She worked furiously even though the house didn't need such fiery attention. The lunch hour arrived far too soon. She didn't realize how occupied she'd kept herself until she heard the men filing in for their meal. Since Becca took care of the noon meal, Dusty had kept right on working. She soon heard the deep voices of men raised in conversation—her father calling her to join them.

Upon entering the kitchen, her gaze fell to

Ryder—though she had sworn to herself to ignore him. He smiled and nodded. She nodded in return without cracking even a polite grin. She became angry, for at the mere sight of him, her heart fluttered, and her stomach seemed to flip, stirring up a sensation of elation she hadn't felt for years. *Stop it!* she thought. But then Ryder picked up his fork, spinning it around in his fingers twice, as had always been his manner before plunging into his meal. The familiarity of the habit further fed the response of warm melancholy in Dusty, and she winced.

"These here boys got the whole herd branded 'fore lunch, girls!" Hank boasted. "Whatcha say to that?"

Dusty stood silent. Becca jumped in to fill the obvious void. "Was there ever any doubt about it?"

"Nope! Don't suppose there was," her father chuckled. "I forgot to ask ya, Dusty," he began, "did ol' Leroy come by while I was away to pick up that beef I offered him?"

"Um . . ." Dusty stammered. Ryder again captured her gaze, winking and causing her to lose her train of thought. "Um . . . yes. Yes, he did. He said to thank you kindly, and he left off a couple of hams in exchange." She looked away quickly. Becca stared at her with a knowing smile. Dusty frowned at her sister and went about fixing herself a plate of food.

"Now, I told that old boy he didn't need to do anythin' in return," Hank grumbled.

"You know how ol' Leroy is, Daddy," Dusty reminded him, sitting down at the small drop leaf nearby. "He won't take anythin' without a swap."

"Ol' Leroy's a fine feller," Ruff commented.

"Yep," Feller agreed. "Ol' Leroy gave me my first horse."

"Really?" Becca asked.

"Yep. I was eight years old and worked for him all summer one year a-helpin' to butcher hogs. He gave me a little bay mare and paid me a right good wage on top of it too." Feller paused to chew and swallow a bite of food.

"I can see that," Ryder mumbled.

"Yeah," Feller agreed. "He's a good ol' boy."

"Well, that he is . . . but I meant I can see you at eight a-ridin' the range, causin' trouble and givin' your mama fits."

Everyone chuckled. Hank reached over and tousled Feller's hair affectionately.

"Now, go on," Feller grumbled, completely embarrassed.

"I 'member that bay," Hank sighed. "You rode that poor ol' girl into the ground near to every day." Everyone ate and waited for the boss to continue telling tales on the top hand—who was so often serious and solemn. "What was her name?"

77

"Daisy," Feller mumbled.

"Yep, Daisy. You and ol' Daisy really used to tear up the town!" Dusty watched her father chuckle, the wrinkles at the corners of his eyes born of so many years of merry living—so familiar—so endearing.

"Come on now, boss," Ryder coaxed. "Give us a tale on ol' Feller here!"

"Ain't no tales to tell, boys," Feller said, smiling and shaking his head.

"You 'member the time you was playin' Paul Revere and got the tale mixed up with that Lady Godiva story?" Dusty's father offered.

Feller immediately began shaking his head as Ryder asked, "Ain't that the woman rode through town buck naked 'cause . . ."

"Ol' Feller . . . he comes a-ridin' through town one Saturday night." Hank paused to swallow a bite of food. No doubt he feared choking were he to start into chuckling as he told the story.

"Oh, for Pete's sake," Feller grumbled. "No need to bring that up."

"What, Daddy? Tell us!" Becca demanded. She was entirely intrigued and delighted.

"Hold on! I heard this one!" Ruff interjected. "You mean to be tellin' me that it was Feller done that?"

Hank chuckled and nodded. "There we all were, all us cowhands. Let's see, I was . . . oh, 'bout nineteen, I suppose. Been cowboyin' for a rancher in the county. Anyhow, there we all was, a-sittin' out on the porch in front of the old general store . . . and here come Daisy! She's a-trottin' down the middle a town like nobody's business . . . and sittin' there as tall in the saddle as an eight-year-old boy can . . . was Feller Lance, buck neked as the day he was born and a-hollerin', 'The redcoats is comin'! The redcoats is comin'!' "

Becca and the men burst into laughter, and even Dusty couldn't restrain a smile. She glanced at Ryder, who was looking at Feller as he laughed. Ryder always drew people out—always got her father to talking and telling stories somehow. He made people feel important. He made them feel happy. Except for her, she reminded herself. She was beginning to feel too warm and cheered within. He wouldn't pull it on her! No, indeed!

"Feller! Really?" Becca squealed.

"I was eight, Miss Becca. Had myself thinkin' that I'd stir up the town by hollerin' like ol' Paul," Feller explained.

"Yep! You stirred up the town all right!" Hank laughed. He sighed heavily as his chuckling subsided. "Them were some fun days, weren't they, Feller?"

Feller nodded, and gradually the conversation turned to matters of running the ranch. Dusty helped Becca clean up as the men finished. For the remainder of the meal, she'd kept her gaze away from Ryder—though her thoughts lingered on him constantly. Every time she heard his voice, her skin tingled, and her mind whispered, *It must be a dream! He can't really be here!*

Her undoing came as she stood at the sink, working the pump to fill the washtub with water. Ryder rose from the table and brought his plate to her. His arm brushed hers, causing goose bumps to break out over her arms and legs like yeast brewing in warm milk.

"Thank you, ladies! It was a fine meal," he sighed, putting a hand to his stomach in satisfaction.

"You're welcome, Ryder!" Becca said, smiling.

When Dusty did not respond or acknowledge him in any way, he reached out. Taking her chin firmly in one hand and turning her face to his, he asked, "Did you dump all your manners in the slop bucket too?" Surprised, Dusty could only stare at him indignantly. "I said thank you," he repeated.

"You're welcome," she growled through clenched teeth.

He smiled sarcastically and whispered, "Now, that's the way your mama taught you." Releasing her face and taking his hat from the hook near the door, he left.

Dusty looked over to her father for support. Surely he wouldn't let any man, any ranch hand or cowboy, even Ryder Maddox, treat her so rudely! Her father only raised his eyebrows and shrugged his shoulders, signaling his agreement with Ryder's actions.

"Daddy?" Dusty whined.

"Boy's right, darlin'," her father mumbled. Rising from his place at the table, he walked to her and kissed her warmly on the forehead. "Ain't many excuses for bad manners," and he left too.

Shaking her head in disbelief, Dusty watched her father walk across the yard toward the barn. Was the whole world going to turn against her in favor of Ryder? *Ryder Maddox has always been too big for his britches!* she thought angrily. Plunging the plate he'd handed her into the water, she tried to think angry thoughts about him. Some men were too good-looking for their own good— thought they could boss others around just because they had charisma!

"Remember how Ryder used to stay and help Mama and us do the dishes after supper some-times, Dusty?" Becca asked quietly.

"Ryder was always tryin' to be Mama's favorite," Dusty grumbled.

"Ryder didn't have to try," Becca reminded her. "He helped Mama 'cause he felt she deserved it after cookin' for that big bunch of men." Dusty scrubbed furiously at the plate, trying to ignore Becca as she continued to list the virtues of Ryder Maddox. "Remember how he used to help us with our arithmetic? Even after the other hands were asleep, him and Feller would be up helpin'

Daddy finish up chores or helpin' us with our school-work."

"Some friend he is to Feller, anyhow!" Dusty interrupted. "Gettin' Daddy to tell that old tale on Feller!"

"Feller needs to have the attention, Dusty. It helps everyone else respect him more and understand him better if they know he's human!" The scolding strength in Becca's voice was so unfamiliar that Dusty turned to look at her. "The hands always liked Ryder 'cause he made them feel important! He respected and admired Mama and treated Daddy like he was the greatest rancher in the world!" Becca threw the dish-towel onto the table. "And he's scarin' you! You still love him, Dusty, and—"

"You don't know me, Becca! Don't tell me what I feel and what I don't!" Dusty argued angrily.

"You do! You do love him!" It was obvious Becca would not be bullied this time. "I seen it in your eyes ever since he got back yesterday. But he won't love you back, Dusty—not when you're so hateful and selfish!"

Dusty couldn't say anything to her sister that wouldn't be angry and cruel. So, whirling around, she fled from the house. Her eyes fell upon none other than Ryder watering his horse at the windmill trough before riding out to check stock. It was too perfect! He was bent over, leaning on the edge of the trough looking down into the water as his horse drank. Motivated by anger and humiliation, Dusty walked up behind him. Lifting her skirts and placing her foot squarely into the seat of his pants, with one good shove, she sent Ryder tumbling over into the trough with a splash.

"I am not a child anymore, Ryder!" she shouted at him. "What gives you the right to stand in there and correct me like I was a—"

"What's wrong with you?" he shouted as he stood up, brushing the water from his face. "I got work to do! I don't have time to be foolin' around with your tantrums!"

Ryder's face was tight with irritation. He reached out, taking hold of Dusty's arm. Tucking his hand into the waist of her skirt, he pulled her into the trough with him.

"Ain't nothin' gonna get done on this ranch with them two goin' at it all the time," Hank mumbled under his breath to Feller. The smile on his face told the top hand that the boss favored his daughter getting a talking-to from somebody other than her father for once.

"Ryder won't put up with her poutin' the way the rest of us do," Feller told him. "Wisest investment you ever made was payin' that boy to cowboy for you again." Mounting up, they rode away to leave Dusty to fend for herself in her battle with Ryder.

• • •

Dusty stood up, coughing and sputtering. Wiping at the water in her eyes, she met Ryder's angry glare with one of her own. "You!" was all she could exclaim.

"Now, listen here, sugar," Ryder began, pointing an index finger in her face. "I know I've been gone a long time and that you want my attention—"

"What?" Dusty shouted, completely in awe at his conceited remark.

"But your daddy's payin' me good money to work for him, and you know that when I take a man's money, I work hard! There's plenty of time for your horsin' around when the day's through. You wanna play with me, Dusty? Then you wait 'til my workday is done—just like it used to be." Dusty could only stand panting with fury and indignation. "I'm glad we agree," he muttered, nodding triumphantly.

Dusty's vexation was at an explosive level. She raised her hand to slap him for teasing her, but he caught her hand and grabbed the other. Holding them at her back, he pulled her body to his. Instantly, Dusty felt the anger draining from her to be replaced by a thrill she hadn't experienced since . . .

"Don't you raise your hand to me, girl," he exclaimed. She saw a hint of mischief flash in his eyes as he attempted to frown—but an amused grin spread across his face. "I can take you on anytime." He gently pushed her backward. Losing her balance, she sunk into the water once more. "Now, you sit there and cool off. Your temper's even worse than I remember." Stepping out of the trough, he took his horse by the bit and sloshed off toward the bunkhouse.

"Never turn your back on a woman, boy," he chuckled as he left Dusty sitting in the trough.

Looking around to see if anyone witnessed her impetuous and now humiliating act of vengeance toward Ryder, Dusty rose from the trough, lifted her heavy skirts, and climbed out. She continued wringing the water out of her skirts and petticoats and tried to ignore Becca casually walking toward her on her way to the chicken house.

"And to think," Becca muttered as she passed her sister, "he ain't even been here one whole day!"

Dusty was furious. She was also delighted. No! She was furious! Reaching down and unlacing her boots, she tossed them aside and stripped off her stockings as well. She was so determined to remain angry she didn't care who saw her strip off her stockings. Reaching up and pulling the pin from her hair, she gave it reprieve from the tightly wound knot. Running her fingers through her hair, she relished the feel of the morning breeze as she fairly ran away from the house and toward the waterfall feeding the creek some distance off.

She hadn't been to the pond and falls for ages.

It was about time she took a moment for herself. Angrily, she plodded along, trying to think of every unlikable character flaw possessed by Ryder Maddox. To think she'd cried tender tears over him the night before! She growled to herself as she let her skirt and petticoats drop to the ground near the falls. After all, she reminded herself, she was already soaked and wet. What did it matter if she went wading now?

Sitting down next to the cool pool of water fed by the waterfall, she let her feet slip beneath the water's surface. "Ahhh," she sighed, closing her eyes. She opened them immediately when the first vision to pass before them was that of Ryder and his mischievous grin. She hated that grin—that triumphant, "I-got-the-better-of-you" grin. He'd grinned it forever. For as long as she could remember, that teasing, adorable, infuriating grin had always existed. And yet, as she thought of their proximity in the trough, as she contemplated how exhilarating it had been to have him holding her against him as he bound her hands at her back, she began to give in.

There was no fighting it. There was no fighting the reality that the man was fantastic—even more magnificent than he'd been five years ago! She would have to accept and learn to live with it—learn to live with him! Undoubtedly, he would winter at the ranch. He'd already told her father so; she'd heard him that morning during branding. And if she were going to survive—if she were going to be able to soften herself toward her father and sister as she'd promised herself—then she was going to have to come to terms with the fact that the perfect, wonderful man who had been so out of reach to her before was going to be near to her every day, a painful reminder of what she still could never have.

She let herself fall backward into the cool grasses lining the banks of the pond. She breathed deeply of their green fragrance and the warmth of the day. Though her mind fought surrender for several moments, she finally allowed memory to flood her mind. From the moment she'd turned to see Ryder standing behind her the day before, they'd called to her. There were so many memories—too many to count, too many to recall. And they were, all of them, good—almost.

"Mama, I can't do this! I tell you, I can't!" Dusty whined. Putting her head down on the table, she dramatically banged her fist on the top of it. "Mrs. Fitzpatrick is a demon of torture, Mama! This arithmetic is far too hard. I can't do it. I can't!"

Dusty heard her mother's impatient sigh. Still, she spoke rather calmly, considering how long Dusty had spent whining about her schoolwork instead of doing it. "She wouldn't give you that assignment if she didn't think you were capable of figurin' it out, Dusty!" Elly Hunter untied her apron and folded it, laying it on the counter. "Now, I've done all I can to encourage you. I'm worn out. I'm goin' in the other room to do some readin' of my own, and when I come back in thirty minutes . . . I want that assignment finished and you ready to turn in. You hear me?"

"But I can't!" Dusty sobbed. "It's too hard and—"

"Angelina Hunter! I've had it!" Her mother left the room, shaking her head.

It wasn't more than a few moments before Dusty heard the door to the kitchen open. Assuming it was her father coming in for the night, she sniffled, wiped her tears, and straightened in her chair. There would be heck to pay if her father found out how she'd been whining at her mother.

"I can hear you whinin' all the way out to the corral," Ryder whispered. Dusty turned to see Ryder walk quietly into the room.

"I thought you boys were all in bed," Dusty sniffled.

"With you yowlin' like a hung cat?" he chuckled quietly. "What's ol' Mrs. Fitzpatrick torturin' you with tonight, Britches?" he asked.

Ryder always came to her rescue. Always.

Dusty smiled. He had helped her through all of Mrs. Fitzpatrick's awful arithmetic assignments.

It was fairly often he'd come sneaking into the kitchen well past his own bedtime to help Dusty and Becca with their schoolwork—patient as ever in spite of being completely wrung out from a hard day's work. Dusty's heart twinged as she thought of her mother. No doubt her mother had been wise to it the entire time. Looking back, it was too coincidental that her mother would disappear each time there was a dramatic schoolwork complaint, only to suddenly reappear the moment Ryder walked out the door.

If you wanna play with me, Ryder had said, looking down at her in the trough that afternoon. Ryder's voice echoed through her mind. He had played with her when she was younger. They'd played marbles and kick the stick. He'd been the one to teach her to waltz, for pity's sake. She and Becca had even talked him into being their patient on occasion when they wanted to play nurses and hospital. Sometimes Feller could be talked into it too—on a hot afternoon when the work was done early. Both men would always end up lying under a tree by the creek, wrapped up like mummies in bandages the girls had made out of scraps of any kind of fabric they could find. Eventually, Becca and Dusty would get tired of their drifting in and out of sleep and leave them to nap—pink calico bandages around their heads and all.

In fact, when Ryder first arrived, he'd been

more like a novelty cousin or something to Dusty. But things changed as she grew older—as he grew older and more comparable to a knight in shining armor than a friend.

He is beautiful, she thought with a sigh, her body finally relaxing. *A beautiful dream that I'm living again. But dreams end. They always do.*

Sleep was peaceful by the pond, and she accepted it gratefully.

It was that sense of someone watching her that woke her. Even before she opened her eyes, she knew who it was—for the air around her was charged with his presence.

"You sure have a lot of time on your hands for braggin' about what a hard worker you are," she grumbled as she opened her eyes to see Ryder was indeed hunkered down beside her, chewing on a blade of grass—a mischievous grin plastered across his face.

"Yeah, well," he mumbled, "I got a bit of a talkin'-to from your daddy 'bout pullin' his young woman of a daughter—who ain't a little girl anymore—into the horse trough . . . even though it was that young woman's foot planted on my behind that found me there in the first place." He raised his eyebrows accusingly and then continued, "So . . . I figure . . . if I wanna warm bed to sleep in this winter and food in my belly . . . well, I guess I gotta say I'm sorry."

"Well, don't say it if it's gonna choke ya to

death," she grumbled, pulling herself to a sitting position.

"It ain't," he chuckled. "I'm sorry. Sorry that I was a pill in the kitchen . . . not that I pulled you in the trough with me. That you deserved."

"Well," Dusty said, brushing her hair back from her face. She suddenly realized what a complete mess she must look. "If that's your apology, I'd hate to hear what you'd have to say if ya didn't feel guilty at all."

"I just wouldn'ta said nothin'." He grinned and groaned dramatically as he sat down beside her.

"Things are different than when you were here before," she blurted out.

"Yep," he agreed. He did not elaborate.

"No, really," she assured him. "I-I want you to be able to stay here and work for Daddy. Daddy's a good, fair man and . . . but I can't . . . you have to . . . I've changed. I'm not a child anymore, and . . ."

"Yeah, I noticed that," he mumbled with insinuation. He winked at her when she looked to him, astonished.

"That's what I mean! I'm . . . you can't treat me like I was ten."

"Not even when ya act it?" he asked, his grin disappearing. She was hurt into silence, and he continued, "You've changed. And I don't mean the way you fill out a dress now or that you grew up. I mean—and yes, I've heard the tale about what happened a couple of years ago—but I mean, your heart has changed. You used to be this wild, excited, happy little girl. Most times people like that grow up to be wild, excited, happy adults. But you're wallerin' in self-pity and hate . . . and that makes for a mighty unhappy woman."

"You've been here one day, Ryder! One!" she argued, raising her voice. "How can you suppose to know—"

"Because you were already mostly grown when I left. And I knew ya then, better than anybody. Don't deny it," he growled. "Heck! I was in trouble over you most of the time I was here . . . not to mention the way I . . ." He silenced himself and clenched his jaw tightly for a moment. "I come out here to apologize to ya . . . but, dang it all, if I don't want to take you over my knee and paddle your behind by now!"

It was her only hope of survival to hate him. Otherwise she'd be lost—lost in the heartache of loving someone she couldn't have. Yet something about him sitting there next to her, arguing with her—it wasn't so unlike it had been before when he would sit, listening to all her trivial troubles of youth and giving encouragement. Fact was most of what she complained to him about she over-dramatized on purpose just to have his attention. She figured he'd known that all along. But this was different. This was real and grown-up.

She stood, intent on leaving, but he brazenly took hold of her ankle to stall her. She looked down at him indignantly.

"I'm sorry, Dusty," he told her. "I'm sorry that I hurt you."

There was hidden meaning in his words. "Which time?" she asked. Reaching down, she wrenched her ankle free of his grasp and stormed away.

She stopped just before she entered the clearing to put on her skirt and wipe her tears. She'd said too much—revealed too much to him. Now where would she find her strength?

Ryder sighed heavily, took the blade of grass he'd been chewing out of his mouth, and tossed it into the pond. The thought struck him—was it Cash Richardson's betrayal that had turned the girl he used to know into this resentful woman? Or—and he had to admit it to himself—should the blame be placed more squarely on his own shoulders as Feller had implied? She was there—that girl whose heart he'd unintentionally broken. He could find her in this woman's eyes at times —see the smile wanting to curl the corners of her pretty mouth. Could she ever gift him the forgiveness he'd come back seeking? Would he ever be able to shed the guilt he'd carried around for so long? The guilt that was even worse than the other yoke of guilt he bore?

Dusty was quiet at dinner. She avoided looking at Ryder, or anyone else for that matter. She helped Becca clean up and went directly to bed. A good night's sleep would help. Ryder understood her now. There would be no horsing around like there had been in the old days. She was a grown-up now, as was he. Yet from her own observations, she knew women gave into adulthood a lot more quickly than men did—especially cowboys and ranch hands.

Chapter Four

Dusty awoke the next morning somewhat puzzled —puzzled in finding herself somehow feeling more friendly toward others, more tolerant of her sister's lighthearted manner. Somehow Becca's silly antics didn't irritate her as much; somehow she found a measure of joy in watching the cowboys and ranch hands talking and chuckling as they worked.

Ryder, however, seemed to play the part of a scolded puppy—a helpless puppy that had piddled on the rug and been sent out to sleep in the barn. For nearly two days he behaved this way—two days during which Dusty began to feel guilty somehow, as if she'd been the one to scold the puppy. She didn't like him this way.

What was she thinking? She didn't like him at all! But it was unsettling to have him sulking, as it were.

However, in true Ryder Maddox form, he could only be beaten for so long. One day just after lunch, as Dusty was returning from an errand to the barn, she saw Ryder sitting in a chair—propped up against the outer wall of the bunkhouse and whittling away. She knew he was waiting for old Leroy to ride in with some supplies her father had requested. Upon seeing him smile and nod a greeting to her, she felt relieved and somewhat forgiven for having been the puppy-scolder.

"I named me a dog Dusty once," Ryder mumbled, pausing in his whittling to look up at her.

"Really?" Dusty asked, rolling her eyes. Yet she was secretly elated that he would speak to her after seeming to ignore her since their argument at the pond.

"Yep. I always regretted havin' to leave her behind when I was movin' on . . . 'cause she was a good little mutt."

"What? Is that supposed to make me think better of you somehow?" Dusty asked. "Am I supposed to be flattered that ya named a dog Dusty?"

"Nope. I was just thinkin' out loud really. She was a good little mutt though." He returned his attention to his whittling as he continued, "She used to follow me around like the sun rose and set by me. She took a likin' to me first off . . . even 'fore she was weaned."

Were his words conveying a message to her? Was he saying the puppy had been similar to the way she had been as a girl?

"Really?" Dusty asked, the sarcasm thick in her voice. "Puppy love? Is that it?"

Ryder chuckled and looked up at her, smiling. "Now that there was almost funny, Miss Dusty." Pointing his pocketknife at her, he grinned slyly and mumbled, "Maybe you'll get weaned enough off'n that sour taste of men in your mouth one day yet."

"Don't hold your breath, Mr. Maddox," she said. Ryder was still leaning back against the side of the bunkhouse on only the two back legs of the chair. Dusty reached down, taking hold of one chair leg, and yanked hard. Ryder tumbled backward, bumping his head on the bunkhouse wall.

He wasn't provoked, however. He simply chuckled and righted his chair. Sitting in it once more, he briefly rubbed the back of his head in amusement and returned his attention to whittling.

"Be careful, Miss Dusty. You may be the boss's daughter, but I don't take too much of a beatin' from nobody 'fore sooner or later I take 'em down hard," he said.

She ignored his insinuation and the thrill

traveling through her. Turning, she walked away. She had taken no more than three steps when she heard three quick, consecutive whistles. Pausing, she looked back at him. Realizing the three quick whistles were akin to those any man might use to summon his dog's attention, Dusty was instantly irritated by the amused grin on Ryder's face.

"Ol' Dusty used to come a-runnin' when I done that too," he chuckled, tipping his hat at her.

Why did she tolerate his smart-aleck remarks, his endless teasing and taunting? Why didn't she slap his face whenever something pestering came out of his mouth—his mouth—his perfect mouth? How tantalizing his smile was—that sly, all-knowing, teasing grin. Well, she thought, pulling herself up short, she never slapped him because . . . because no doubt he'd thwart her attempt and send her sitting in the trough again.

Still, she felt better—better than she had in days. When she heard the rumble of a wagon and team and turned to see Alice approaching, she felt her heart lighten even further. She felt . . . happy.

"Are you givin' your mama grief today, Makenna?" Dusty asked as the tiny angel personified in human form fairly leapt from the buckboard and into her arms.

"Hi, Dusty," the little girl cheerily greeted.

Dusty adored Alice's daughter. Makenna was all of two and a half but boasted the vocabulary of a child much older. She was a living angel with soft, blonde hair and the brightest of blue eyes, pinchable chubby cheeks, and a smile that lit up any situation.

"I comed to see you!" Makenna exclaimed.

"You did?" Dusty asked, smiling with delight and raising her eyebrows in feigned surprise.

"Um-hum. I did! And I bringed my mommy and my baby brudder!" she chirped, putting her hands to Dusty's cheeks as Dusty held her on one hip. "Where's Becca?"

"Becca's over helpin' Miss Raynetta with some sewin' this afternoon. But I'm so glad you came for a visit!" Dusty told her.

"Baby Jakie, him's my brudder, and him's got runny drawers, and him's cryin' a lot! So I bringed mommy to visit you!" Makenna added.

Dusty couldn't help but giggle. "Runny drawers? Oh, no! I bet your mama surely does need some visitin' time, huh?"

"Um-hum!" Makenna said, smiling and pinching Dusty's cheeks.

"Is he teethin', Alice?" Dusty asked, turning to look at Makenna's mother. Immediately Makenna put her hands back to Dusty's face, forcing Dusty to look at her.

Alice Jones had once been Alice Maxwell, Dusty's dear, dear childhood friend. She'd married a nice man some four years ago. Dusty missed their usually profuse visits. Seems they'd dwindled to one a month, or even less, after Alice married.

"I think so, Dusty. He's just fussier than any old half-dead dog, and I'm about to lose my mind!" Alice answered, sighing heavily as she climbed down from the wagon with baby Jake. Almost as if he understood what she was saying, the baby boy began whimpering and sucking on his two middle fingers.

"Well," Dusty began, starting for the house, "you just sit here on the porch with me, and let me take a turn at him."

"You has to play with me first, Dusty," Makenna reminded her.

"I do want to play with you, Kenna. But what's say we see if we can get this little-bit to settle down awhile, huh?" Dusty pleaded in her sweetest voice.

"Is you ever gonna get married, Dusty?" Makenna asked suddenly.

"Well, I . . ." Dusty stammered.

"You run on and let me and Dusty visit, Kenna," the child's mother told her firmly.

"But I don't got nobody to play with, Mama," the little girl whined.

"Why don't you come on over to the henhouse with me, sugar? We'll see if we can dig up an egg or two from under one of them old hens, huh?"

Dusty whirled around, astonished by the sound of his voice. Yet her ears had not deceived her.

Ryder stood just behind her. As both Dusty and Alice stood looking at him, mouths gaping open, Makenna instantly stretched her arms out in a gesture for Ryder to take her.

"Ryder Maddox, ma'am," he said as he gathered Makenna into his strong arms. "Surely you didn't forget me."

"For Pete's sake! Ryder Maddox!" Alice exclaimed as she shook Ryder's hand. She quirked one eyebrow and looked at Dusty. "I'm Alice Jones. Alice Maxwell Jones."

"The longer I stay on here . . . the older I feel! Don't tell me these young-uns are both yours," Ryder chuckled. "You can't be old enough to have a family this far along. I remember when you was in short skirts."

"Ryder rode in with Daddy from the drive, Alice," Dusty explained, shifting uncomfortably as Ryder smiled down at her and Alice. He kept looking back and forth between them. She knew he was sizing them up and remembering when they'd been two silly schoolgirls in love with one of her father's favorite ranch hands.

"I'm good with little angels like this here one," he said, tweaking Makenna's cheek.

Dusty watched, mesmerized as Makenna took Ryder's roughly shaven face between her hands and forced him to look at her. Makenna was usually averse to strangers and very stingy with her attention and affections.

"You're pretty!" Makenna giggled as she looked at him.

Ryder chuckled. "Well, thank you, sugar. But ain't nothin' in the world as pretty as you!"

Makenna smiled. "I'm goin' to the henhouse with Ryder Magics, Mommy. You can have Dusty now."

"Well, thank you, Makenna. Um . . ." she paused, looking to Dusty for reassurance.

But it was Ryder who answered. "You know me, Miss Alice . . . um . . . Mrs. Jones. Trustworthy as time."

Makenna took his face in her hands again and forced him to look at her. "Look at me!" the child demanded of him.

Ryder chuckled. Even though Dusty knew there was no need to further reassure Alice where Ryder was concerned, she said, "She'll be fine with him, Alice."

"I don't doubt it," Alice giggled, watching Makenna with Ryder.

"I'll look after her, ma'am. You stay and visit with Miss Dusty. Maybe you all can settle that boy down a bit." Ryder turned and started toward the henhouse, Makenna's hands still on his face, a smile still revealing the dimples in her own chubby little cheeks.

When he was well out of earshot, Alice exclaimed, "Good gravy, Dusty. Ryder Maddox! Of all people! I hadn't heard he was back. Are ya just ready to drop dead right on the spot? I'll be! If he ain't still the handsomest thing ever to walk the earth!"

Dusty felt a hot blush rising to her cheeks. It was plain Alice had forgotten, or at least was in awe of, how unusually attractive Ryder was.

"I bet you 'bout died when he came ridin' up again," Alice said knowingly. When they were young girls, it had been Alice in whom Dusty had confided her feelings for the young cowboy.

"Actually . . . I nearly did," Dusty admitted. "It was a . . . surprise, to say the least of it."

Alice smiled and shook her head, "Mmmm mmmmm mmmm! Look at the way he fills out his blue jeans. Ain't nothin' like a good pair of blue jeans on a man like that!"

"Alice Jones!" Dusty exclaimed. "I can't believe you!"

"Oh, Dusty . . . relax! Many's the time you and I sat on the porch in front of ol' lady Watson's general store and watched the cowboys walkin' into the saloon," Alice giggled. "And many's the time we sat right where we're sittin' now and watched Ryder at his chores for the same reason!"

"Yes . . . but . . . but . . ." Dusty stammered.

"But nothin', Dusty! You know I love my Alex more'n I can even tell . . . but it don't mean I still don't notice a good-lookin' man. Ain't nothin' like one! And don't pretend to me *that* man hasn't turned your head . . . again!"

"I'da had to be blind," Dusty admitted with quiet resentment.

"Even then I think you could smell one that looks as good as he does!"

As Alice burst into girlish giggles, Dusty began to laugh. It felt good to laugh so unguarded. Dusty was again reminded of how much fun she and Alice had growing up—how much they had shared—how much she missed seeing her friend now that Alice was married with a husband and family to care for.

"Sakes alive!" Alice began. "You remember that time we were up in the tree by the pond a-waitin' for Ryder to come along? And lo and behold, here he comes a-strippin' himself down to go swimmin'!"

"And we closed our eyes like a couple of silly Sallys," Dusty grinned.

"And when we looked up again, it was to see his britches and his drawers a-lyin' on the ground at the foot of the very tree we was hidin' in!" Alice laughed. "I 'bout got too big a lesson in male anatomy that day."

Dusty began to giggle wildly. She hadn't giggled as much in years. Furthermore, once she started, she found she couldn't stop! It was as if a sort of hysteria were overtaking her. Try as she might to talk plainly through her giggles, she couldn't. "Remember . . . how we had to stay up there in that tree for near to an hour . . . because . . . because . . ."

"Because we couldn'ta gotten down without Ryder seein' us! And we couldn't watch him for fear of bein' corrupted!" Alice roared. "Land's sakes, he had a build for such a young man!"

"Alice!" Dusty exclaimed through her laughter. And they giggled for long, delightful moments. "I've missed you," Dusty told her friend. Sighing heavily, she led her to sit on the porch swing.

"You've missed a lot, Dusty," Alice sighed.

"Don't you start with me, Alice. I—" Dusty began to argue.

"But . . . at least there's hope for you. And he sure wears his britches mighty fine!"

"You come to Aunt Dusty, little-bit," Dusty said to Jakie. She held her hands out, and the baby gladly clung to her. "So . . . he sure seems to be chewin' his fingers. I think he's just cuttin' teeth, don't you?"

"Don't you try changin' the subject on me, girl," Alice warned with a smile. "That man's got you thinkin'. I can see it plain as day. I ain't seen your eyes light up like that in a long, long time. Not since we was fourteen, in fact. That smelly old lump of cat manure Cash Richardson you tried to love never had you a-twinklin' like I see ya now."

"My eyes did not light up," Dusty defended herself.

"Oh, come on! Don't he just stir up them ol' butterflies in your tummy with that handsome smile, Dusty?"

"Alice!" Dusty was starting to feel a great melancholia rise in her again. She wanted to laugh, not think about what she could never have.

"He'd give ya some mighty handsome sons, that's for sure!"

"Alice Jones, you stop! Now, one more word about Ryder Maddox and I'll leave you here to love on this fussy boy all alone," Dusty warned, feeling her face go warm and red again.

"Well, all right," Alice sighed, teasingly. "But ya better trap him into bein' your lover 'fore Kenna grows up, 'cause she's plum smitten herself."

"That's enough, Alice." Smiling, Dusty added, "She did take to him, didn't she?"

"Who wouldn't?"

"Alice!"

"Oh, all right, you old stick-in-the-mud," Alice relented in defeat.

"Where's Alex anyway?" Dusty asked.

"Oh, he had to take some cattle over to the Springs. I miss him so much when he's gone! That might be one reason Jakie is so crabby."

Dusty and Alice sat for a long while talking about things and people. When little Jakie would start fussing for one woman, the other would take a turn at rocking him or walking him around the porch until he settled for a while.

Sometime later, however, the attention of both women was drawn to the tall, fascinating man striding slowly toward them, holding the hand of a little blonde angel. Makenna skipped along briskly to keep up with Ryder's stride.

"Ryder Magics showed me the new puppies in the barn! He says they gots the sweetest smellin' brefs, and they do! I was sniffin' theys brefs, and one of 'em licked me right on the nose! Ryder Magics says that's how they kiss you! And I gots free bird feathers that we found in the hayloft, and one of them's blue, and Ryder Magics says that maybe a blue jay lost it up there! And there was a nest in that old tree by the corral! And it gots free white baby little tiny eggs wif blue speckles! And Ryder Magics says we can look, but don't touch!" Makenna babbled as she approached, still not letting go of Ryder's hand.

"My goodness!" Alice exclaimed, clapping her hands together with excitement. "You have been busy! What else did Mr. Maddox tell you?" she asked, smiling at Ryder.

"Oh, lots and lots! We singed. Ryder Magics knows lots of songs . . . and we danced and . . ."

As Makenna babbled on, Alice raised her eyebrows in approving astonishment at Ryder. He simply shrugged his shoulders as if it were all in a day's work.

"Well, I think Ryder oughta be able to settle down Jakie since he's such a perfect type of fellow," Alice teased, handing the baby to Ryder. "Don't you think so, Dusty?"

"Oh, definitely," Dusty agreed, staring at Ryder and quirking one daring eyebrow.

"Fine," he mumbled, willingly taking the baby. "You ladies take a stroll. I got things well in hand here."

Dusty saw Alice wink at Ryder in thanks as they set out toward the fields. The walk was nice, and Dusty was glad her daddy had left Ryder home to wait for the supplies. It gave Alice a much-needed break, and it was good for her own soul. They talked for quite a while, and Dusty realized that Alice was worried about Alex working too hard. He didn't want to spend the money to hire a hand, so he was working himself into a state of great fatigue. Dusty assured her she would let her father know so he could drop in and try to talk Alex into getting some help.

All at once, they realized they'd been gone far too long. Alice and Dusty were both concerned the fussy little baby boy might have sent Ryder into yanking his hair out by the handfuls.

Yet when Dusty walked into the parlor, her mouth dropped open in astonishment. She could not believe what she saw before her! There was Ryder, rocking back and forth, back and forth in the old, squeaky rocking chair—and there was baby Jake sound asleep on his chest. One of Ryder's powerful hands patted the baby softly, if not somewhat awkwardly, on the back; the other cradled him comfortably, providing a perfect rest for his tired little body.

"Poor little fella. He was just plum tuckered out," Ryder spoke quietly, and Dusty imagined the low booming of his voice was a further comfort to the sleeping baby—ear nestled firmly on Ryder's chest. "Look at his little face. That there's a tired pup."

Certainly, the baby did sleep soundly—his peaceful little face porcelain white and pressed flat against Ryder's body, his little mouth open, a steady stream of slobber already leaving a wet mark on Ryder's shirt.

"Why, Mr. Maddox," Alice exclaimed, "I'm just . . . just . . . so grateful! I thought I would fly into screamin' fits if he didn't settle down soon."

Dusty still stared disbelieving at Ryder as he stood and carefully laid the baby down on a quilt lying on the floor—for there, next to the now-sleeping baby, lay a sleeping Makenna.

"You put me to shame as a mother, Mr. Maddox!" Alice exclaimed in a whisper.

"Nah. They was just tired," he answered. "But I gotta get out to meet ol' Leroy. I hear him comin' just now." He looked at Dusty and nodded. "Miss Dusty. Mrs. Jones."

"Well," Alice began as Ryder retrieved his hat

from the hat rack by the door and started to leave, "it's mighty glad I am that you've come back to the ranch, Mr. Maddox."

"Same here, ma'am," Ryder said, smiling.

"You'll make someone a good daddy someday," Alice added.

"Well, let's hope so," he chuckled, winking at Dusty.

Immediately, she felt her face go crimson and hot. Nodding at Alice, he left, closing the screen door quietly so as not to disturb the sleeping children.

"For cryin' in the bucket, Dusty!" Alice exclaimed once Ryder was out of earshot and the two women had returned to the swing on the front porch. "Are ya really gonna turn him out on his fanny every time he speaks to ya?"

"I didn't turn him out on his fanny," Dusty argued.

"And it's such a nice fanny at that," Alice teased.

"Alice! Stop that!" Dusty ordered.

She was beginning to hurt inside. She didn't want to talk about Ryder anymore. She didn't want to think about how gentle and kind and adept he had been with Alice's children. She didn't even want to think about Alice's two beautiful children. She wanted to think about heartbreak and hurt. She wanted to think about Cash and how he'd humiliated her—how Ryder

Maddox had hurt her long before that. She wanted to remember that she would never let it happen again. Never!

"Oh, sweet Angelina," Alice sighed, hugging her friend suddenly. "Where did those two little girls go who used to sit in trees and spy on skinny-dippin' cowboys?"

For the first time in a long time, Dusty fully accepted the comforting embrace from her friend—even returned it. It was true. She had to admit it to herself—what her mother had told her so long ago was true. *A hug can heal a hurting heart,* she'd always said.

"They've turned into two women with responsibilities," Dusty sighed.

"Naw," Alice sighed. "One of 'em just needs to open her heart again."

Dusty remained silent and simply smiled at her friend as they sat enjoying the shade on the porch together.

ॐ

Evening lingered. As Dusty washed dishes, she gazed out the kitchen window to where Feller, Ryder, and Ruff stood around the fire pit with the others. Everyone had finished their dinner and was gathered outside around the pit as usual. It had been such a long time since Dusty had joined everyone for the traditional evening talk. Lingering around the fire pit had been near habit at the ranch for as long as she could remember.

She longed to go out—to sit with Becca, her father, and the others and listen to stories and talk about life and the world. Still, to do so would be a risk. To do so would leave her too open to feeling.

Ryder and Feller stood listening to something Ruff was saying. Ryder stood with his arms folded across his chest, his feet planted firmly apart, nodding his head as he listened. Suddenly, he threw his head back, breaking into laughter. The rhythmic bounce of Feller's shoulders told Dusty that whatever Ruff had said had ended in humor. Dusty didn't even notice the heavy sigh escaping her lungs as she watched Ryder slap Ruff on the shoulder before sauntering over to take a seat on one of the giant logs around the fire. It was a small fire—small ones in the early spring and summer, bigger ones in the fall. Looking down at the plate she was washing, she was unaware of the smile breaking across her face as another memory rinsed over her.

Her daddy had brought home a new kitten for Becca and Dusty one sunny summer afternoon. Dusty was ten—she'd never forget it. It was the same summer her daddy had hired Ryder on, and he'd only been with them a couple of months. Dusty and her sister had been absolutely beside themselves with delight over the kitten. It was all black, except for a few white markings on its backside. Dusty shook her head at the memory of how she and Becca had unintentionally tortured the kitten all day, cradling it in their arms like a mother would a newborn baby and never putting it down.

"Put that poor creature down, girls!" Elly Hunter called from the front porch. Dusty could still see her mama standing on the porch, drying her hands on her apron, the skirt of her blue calico dress dancing in the soft breeze.

"Oh, but, Mama," Dusty whined, "he's our baby!"

Their mother laughed, her smile as beautiful as an angel's—her laughter like the music of heaven.

"He's gonna run off and not come back if you don't give him his space," she told them. She smiled. "Now put him down, and find somethin' else to do!"

Becca relented and released the small kitten, who, in its desperation to escape, nearly flew as it bounded off toward the creek. After shaking her head, knowing full well that as soon as she went back inside the girls would be off to find the kitten again, Dusty's mother blew them a kiss, turned, and disappeared into the house.

"Come on, Becca!" Dusty whispered. "Let's go find him!"

Becca giggled and nodded, and both girls lit out for the creek. "What if he trees himself?" Becca asked. "We'll never be able to climb up high enough to get him."

"Ryder will get him for us," Dusty assured her. After only a few weeks, Dusty had confidence in the fact that Ryder Maddox would do whatever she asked him.

Carefully, the girls combed the bushes and trees growing along the creek bank, but there was no sign of the cat. After a while, Becca lost interest in hunting for the elusive feline.

Sighing heavily, she whined, "I'm tired of lookin' for that ol' cat. He's hid too good. We'll never find him."

Dusty sighed herself but with irritation. "You can't give up that easy, Becca. He's here somewhere!"

Becca stood looking around, having given up in spite of her sister's encouragement. Suddenly, however, she exclaimed, "I think I see him! Over by the barn!"

Dusty turned and looked to where her sister was pointing. "He couldn'ta gotten by us that easy, Becca," she told her sister. "We would've seen him, and I don't see nothin' over there."

"I'm tellin' you I do!" Becca argued. "You can waste your time over here! But I'm gonna look by the barn."

"Fine," Dusty sighed, with an air of great superiority. "But if I find him, I'm playin' with him first."

"Fine," Becca mumbled, angrily storming off.

Several moments passed, and Dusty, all the

more determined to find the missing cat, was looking so diligently in the bushes she didn't hear Ryder approaching until he was standing right behind her.

"Whatcha lookin' for?" he asked.

Dusty gasped and, putting her hand to her chest to calm her startled heart, turned to face him. "You scared the waddin' outta me, Ryder!" she scolded.

Ryder's face immediately broke into an amused grin, as it more often than not did whenever Dusty found herself face-to-face with him.

"Sorry," he apologized with a chuckle. "What're you rootin' around for?"

"That kitty Daddy brung home," Dusty answered. "I sure hope he hasn't treed himself."

"I'll fetch him down for you if he has," Ryder mumbled, looking up into the branches of the tree beneath which they stood.

Dusty smiled with secret delight. She knew he would—even without him having to say it.

"What're ya doin' over here anyhow?" Dusty asked the handsome cowboy.

"Your daddy sent me to the house for lunch," he answered, looking back to her. "Saw you nosin' around in the bushes and thought I'd see if ya wanted to come in for lunch with me."

Dusty smiled at him. His eyes were so warm!

She wanted to wrap herself up in their inviting color.

"You gotta girl in town yet, Ryder?" she asked bluntly.

He burst into laughter. It took him a moment before he drew in a deep breath and, shaking his head, sighed. "And if I do?"

Dusty suddenly felt very irritated that he didn't assure her he did not have his fancy set on a girl in town. "Who is she?" she asked.

"Who?" he asked teasingly.

Dusty rolled her eyes with impatience. "The girl in town you've set your fancy on?"

"Why do you wanna know?" he asked her. "You gonna blab it all over?"

"No," Dusty truthfully told him. "I was just wonderin'." Then, without even knowing why, she blurted out, "You ever kiss her yet?"

Again Ryder chuckled and shook his head. "Now I don't see how that's any a your business, Miss Britches."

"What's it like?" Dusty asked him—though she really didn't want to know. Or did she?

"What's what like?" he grumbled, feigning innocence.

"Kissin'."

Ryder grimaced and wrinkled up his nose. "Why're you askin' me this kind a thing, girl? You're only ten years old. Ain't nothin' you should be worryin' about yet."

"I'm nearly eleven," she corrected him. It had hurt her when he'd reminded her of her youthfulness.

At that moment there was a rustling in one of the bushes nearby. Too close to tears from hurt feelings to want to continue talking to Ryder, Dusty turned to the bush. "There he is . . . that sorry little cuss!" she mumbled.

"What did you say?" Ryder asked, the pitch of his voice going higher—an indication he was surprised by her vocabulary.

"He's in there, Ryder!" she whispered excitedly. "I can see his rear end . . . all black and white! Yep! It's him all right."

"You sure that's your cat, Dusty?" Ryder asked. He seemed hesitant to join her in peering into the shadowy innards of the bush. "Your mama says the skunks've been in her garden somethin' fierce this year and—"

Yet before he'd finished his warning, Dusty had picked up a stick, using it to try to prod the scared kitten out of the bush. She hardly had time to blink before a quick mist of liquid squirted out of the bushes—accompanied by a familiar, nauseating odor. Instantly her skirt and boots were saturated as an angry skunk backed out of the bush. A moment later it waddled away toward the garden. Dusty screamed as if someone had just lopped off her arm and immediately began running in place, frantic and sobbing.

"Now ya gone and done it, girl!" Ryder scolded as he took hold of her arm and began dragging her toward the creek.

"I'm gonna die! I'm gonna die!" Dusty screamed in panic.

"You ain't gonna die," Ryder mumbled as he took hold of the collar of her dress and effortlessly ripped the garment in two.

Dusty stopped bawling as she saw her favorite play dress drop to the ground at her ankles. "You tore my dress!" she hollered at him.

Ryder simply directed her to step out of the ruined garment, sitting her down hard then on the ground. Pulling a pocketknife from his boot, he cut the laces of her shoes, pulled them off, and tossed them aside. He wiped his watering eyes on his shoulder before taking hold of her arm and pushing her into the creek. It was at that moment, as Dusty looked up to the young cowboy—his eyes watering and looking down at his own skunk-scented hands as if he'd never seen them before—that she inhaled her first good breath through her nose instead of her mouth. Immediately, her own eyes began to water. She began to cough and gag as she burst into dramatic sobbing again.

"I smell like a skunk!" she cried.

"Well, sugar," Ryder told her, a smile spreading across his face, "that's what happens when you poke a stick at the hind end of one!" He chuckled and doused his hands in the creek, shaking his head. He knew washing them in the creek would do little to rid them of the smell of skunk. In cutting the laces of Dusty's boots and removing them, Ryder was now tainted with the odor too. "Now slip off them stockin's and your petticoat. I figure your mama will be out shortly."

Dusty's face puckered. Tears ran down her cheeks as she sobbed quietly and did as she was told. Standing in the creek dressed only in her underthings, she began to shiver—still gagging as she breathed in the stench covering her.

"Now come on, sugar," Ryder said as he simply walked into the creek to stand towering before her. "It'll wear off . . . eventually." Again Dusty's crying increased, and he chuckled, "Oh, ho! Now come on." He unbuttoned his shirt, pausing a moment to sniff at his own hands before removing it, placing it about her shoulders and swooping her up into the cradle of his arms. "Ooo, whee!" he teased. "You smell like somethin' the dog rolled in!"

Not at all encouraged by his teasing manner, Dusty smacked him hard on the chest as he carried her toward the house. He only chuckled.

"For Pete's sake!" Elly Hunter exclaimed. She dried her hands on her apron as she stepped out of the house and onto the front porch. "What've you gotten yourself into now, Angelina?"

"Miss Britches's been keepin' company with them varmints that've been gettin' to your cabbages, Mrs. Hunter!" Ryder explained brokenly through his coughing.

Dusty's mother started down the porch steps. She stopped dead in her tracks, however, bringing her apron up to her face to try and lessen the stench.

"A skunk?" she squealed. "Dusty, I swear . . . I never know what to expect next!"

"Oh, it ain't nothin' a little scrubbin' and a week or so won't wear off, Mrs. Hunter," Ryder assured her.

"Well, for cryin' in the bucket, Ryder," Dusty's mother sighed. "What'll I do? I can't scrub her up in the kitchen. It'll send the whole house to stinkin'!" Dusty watched as her mother leaned forward and sniffed Ryder. "Good grief, boy! You smell nearly as bad as my poor baby!"

Ryder just nodded, asking, "Well, where do ya want the little onion?"

Elly shook her head. Dusty could tell by the look on her face her mother's irritation was already gone. Fact was, she was struggling not to laugh. "Well . . . I'll get Feller to haul the washtub out to the barn. I guess that's better than stinkin' up the house!"

"Yes, ma'am," Ryder nodded. He turned and carried Dusty toward the barn.

Dusty still wept, tears rolling down her cheeks.

Yet the quiet chuckling overtaking Ryder comforted her. It was obvious he wasn't angry— only amused. They reached the barn soon enough, and he set her down just inside.

"I guess all we got is each other for a few days, Dusty," he told her.

Dusty nodded, oddly consoled. Suddenly, Becca appeared, running toward them, the elusive black-and-white kitten clutched tightly in her arms.

"He was in the barn, Dusty!" she called. "He was just where I told you he . . ." Becca stopped short about ten feet away. She grimaced and pinched her nose closed. "Dusty! You stink!" she exclaimed, and Dusty burst into bawling.

Dusty smiled. She giggled quietly to herself as she placed another plate into the dishwater. How funny it all seemed now. How ridiculous she must've looked to her mother all wrapped up in Ryder's shirt and reeking of skunk.

There was a tap on the window in front of her. Drawn from her reminiscing, she looked up to see none other than her fellow skunk-mate of long ago looking at her through the window.

Flicking water at the window with her fingers, she called, "You scared the waddin' outta me!"

He smiled, shrugged, and told her, "Your daddy wants ya out here. And where's Feller gone to?"

"Do I look like his mama?" she asked, trying to

rid her face of the smile still there plain upon it.

"No, ma'am . . . you do not!" he chuckled, tipping his hat to her. He winked before turning and sauntering toward the barn.

Dusty dried her hands on her apron and put them to her cheeks to cool the blush. She hated the way he made her feel! It would be her undoing if she didn't get a handle on it. His wink and smile had delighted her so she'd felt the same as she had on that first skunk-stinking night all those years ago—when her only companion had been her champion.

Her mother had tucked Dusty in the barn for the night as comfortably as possible—on a nice bed of straw with an old blanket she didn't mind getting ruined with the odor of skunk. Moments later, Ryder had sauntered in. The whining of the other ranch hands in the bunkhouse over the detestable odor about him had forced Ryder to the barn too. Dusty remembered how he'd looked that night—so handsome and strong—and tired to boot.

"Make sure she stays warm, Ryder," Elly Hunter told the young man. "And thank ya for offering to stay out here so the smell won't drive everyone else out."

"You're welcome, ma'am," Ryder mumbled as Dusty began to weep quietly.

"I love you, peach," her mama whispered.

She bent and kissed Dusty lovingly on the forehead. "It's a fine, brave, and kind thing you're doin' by sleepin' out here for a few nights so things don't smell inside."

Dusty only nodded.

"Mornin' will come soon enough, punkin. And when it does . . . the smell will already be fadin', okay?" As Dusty nodded, her mother whispered, "Thank you, Ryder."

"The boys don't want me in my bunk anyhow, Mrs. Hunter. Might as well enjoy the summer night," Ryder sighed.

"You're a fine boy, Ryder Maddox. A fine boy," Elly said. She kissed him affectionately on the cheek before she left the barn.

Dusty wiped at her tears, embarrassed they'd started again. Ryder groaned as he put a blanket down on the straw several feet from where Dusty was tucked in for the night.

"I feel like I been spit at and hit," he moaned as he lay down. "What a day, huh, sugar?"

"A rotten day," Dusty mumbled.

"Ah, come on now," he said, stripping off his shirt, sitting down on the blanket, and removing his boots. "You and Becca were havin' a fine time 'til ol' Mr. Stinky-Rear showed up, now weren't ya?"

Dusty couldn't help but smile. His voice was so soothing. She nodded at him as she watched him stretch out on his back, cross his feet, and rest his head on his hands. He winked at her and looked out the barn door to the stars in the night sky. He released a heavy sigh—tired after a long day.

"You see the Big Dipper out yonder?" he asked.

"Yeah," Dusty answered. Her daddy had taught her long ago about the constellations. She found them fascinating in their starry beauty.

"Well," he continued after sighing again, "I always thought it looked more like a beat-up ol' pan or somethin' . . . 'stead of a drinkin' ladle."

"Me too," she agreed, somehow warmed that he would think similarly to her.

"Yeah . . . I woulda named it 'the ol' beat-up pan Mama used to smack skunks with' instead."

Dusty smiled at him warmly as he continued to stare at the stars. It was comforting, and somehow exciting, to have his attention so completely to herself.

"You never did tell me, Ryder," she ventured then.

"Tell ya what?" he asked, yawning.

"Whether or not you've been sparkin' that girl in town you're sweet on." At ten years old, nearly eleven, Dusty herself didn't understand why her curiosity was so inclined toward that particular subject regarding Ryder. All she knew was that it was.

Ryder chuckled and turned on his side to face Dusty. "Well, sugar . . . that's my own business," he told her. She looked away from him for a moment and then back when he continued, "But since we're such good, stinky friends together . . . I'll tell ya just this once." He winked at her again, and she smiled. "Just this once, mind you, nosy-Rosy!"

Dusty nodded, wondering if she really wanted him to tell her. It bothered her to think of his attentions being focused on someone else. Especially at that moment when they were so focused on her.

"Her name is Miss . . ." he teased, quickly whispering, "Nobody!"

"Ah, quit teasin' me," she whined at him, scowling.

"I ain't teasin'," he chuckled. "Why . . . I figure . . . no one'll ever be as pretty as you're gonna be when you grow up. So why waste the time?"

Disappointment and delight mingled in her. Yet Dusty was dazzled by his compliment, while still bothered that the secret was still his own. Playfully she drew up a handful of straw and threw it at him.

"You're a skunk yourself, Ryder Maddox!" she giggled.

"Least I know better'n to poke a stick at somethin's rear end!" he chuckled, brushing the straw from his hair.

He yawned again, and Dusty knew she was

selfish to be keeping a cowboy from his sleep. Ranch hands worked hard. If they lost sleep, well, it wasn't right. Still, she had his undivided attention! How could she give it up?

"Now," he yawned, "I'm tired, wrung out, and I gotta get some shut-eye, Miss Skunk-Britches," he told her. "Still . . . there's always time for a good bet."

Dusty raised her eyebrows expectantly.

"I'll bet I can keep my eyes open longer'n you."

"Deal," Dusty said.

She snuggled down onto her bed of straw and began returning Ryder's amused stare. His eyes were so warm and soothing even in the moonlight. She knew it wouldn't be long before she lost the battle and drifted into pleasant slumber—knowing she would always be safe with Ryder so near to her. His smile was the last thing she saw before her eyes finally closed for good that night in the barn. Even the prominent odor of skunk did nothing to tarnish her pretty dreams.

Dusty breathed a heavy sigh and finished drying the last plate. She put it in its place in the cupboard before going to find her father. She wondered what he wanted of her. As she left the house, something caught her attention, and she glanced at the barn. Looking up to the sky, she wondered where the Big Dipper might be that night. She would go to the barn when everyone was settled in for the night. She'd go to the barn where she and Ryder had once slept; she'd gaze up into the stars and find their Big Dipper. Not because of the sentimental reminiscing she'd been doing while washing the dishes—simply because she hadn't looked for it in so long.

Hank Hunter was sitting on one of the large logs near the fire pit as Dusty approached. Becca sat next to him with Ruff, Guthrie, and Titch. Ryder and Feller were walking over from the barn.

"What did ya need, Daddy?" she asked him. She wanted to find out what he needed so she could return to the house and avoid everyone— avoid Ryder.

"I want ya to come on out here with the family and talk awhile. It'll do ya good to get out of the house," he told her.

"Alice and I took a good long walk today while she was over and . . ." Dusty began to argue. She glanced to where Feller and Ryder both now sat on one of the logs.

"Sit down, Dusty," her father said. He was firm—not cruel, but very firm.

Sighing heavily, Dusty sat down next to Becca, grinding her teeth with irritation. It wasn't long, however, until the light conversation concerning ranch life and townsfolk lulled her into a state of relaxation. Ruff told a funny tale he'd heard in town concerning old Leroy's latest antics.

"I always thought ol' Leroy oughta hook up with Miss Raynetta McCarthy," Guthrie offered.

"Heck, no," Hank argued. "He's near to seventy year old! She's a kitten compared to him."

"Yeah, but they're both so . . . so . . . you know," Guthrie stammered.

"Eccentric," Dusty finished.

"Yeah, that's it. 'Centric," Guthrie chuckled, nodding at Dusty in thanks.

"I think Miss Raynetta is an angel," Becca sighed. "I wish I had the guts to wear purple like she does."

"She's the sweetest lady I've ever known," Ruff agreed, yawning.

"Send us to sleep on a tale, boss," Titch suggested.

"Yeah," Ryder agreed. "Somethin' along the lines of Lady Godiva a-meetin' up with Paul Revere." Everyone chuckled, even Dusty and Feller.

"Oh my, boys," Hank sighed, "don't know if I've got it in me tonight."

"How 'bout the time Grampa Hunter had the kickin' fight with the mule, Daddy?" Becca suggested.

"That's a good one, Daddy," Dusty heard herself say.

She nervously glanced around to see if anyone were looking at her—thinking how ridiculous she sounded in entering the conversation. Still, all heads were nodding in agreement—all eyes already on Hank as he began the tale.

"Well, ya see, my daddy had this here old mule name a Ross."

Dusty watched her father begin to tell the tale. She loved to listen to her father tell stories. She'd missed so much by avoiding the evening fire outside.

"Ol' Ross up and kicked Daddy in the rear-end one day while they was out plowin' together. Well, Daddy, he don't take nothin' from a mule . . . so he hauls off and kicks ol' Ross in the leg. Ol' Ross kicks him back, and Daddy kicks him, 'til all of a sudden my mama looks out the window and hollers, 'Henry! You get out there and stop your daddy from kickin' that mule!' Well, when my mama said, *'Go,'* I went! So I trot on out there, and Daddy's still exchangin' kicks with that mule . . ."

Dusty didn't hear the rest of the story. She didn't need to. Just being there with her family—bathing in the warm security of friendship with the hands—was enough. Enough to send her to bed with another new resolve to be a better, friendlier person—to let her guard down—let it down in front of everyone except Ryder Maddox, that was.

Chapter Five

Eight days had passed—eight days since Hank Hunter and Ryder Maddox had returned from the drive. Dusty had expended most of her energy each day trying to avoid Ryder. Certainly it seemed they'd made a kind of unspoken peace the day Alice visited. Still, he unsettled her, and she kept her distance as much as possible. Other than at mealtimes, she endeavored to avoid him entirely. It was less painful, less vexing that way—for whenever she was near him, or near enough to see him, her heart would begin to ache. Heartache was a threat—a threat of feeling something—and Dusty didn't want to feel.

On that eighth day, it was decided everyone would take a trip to town. Hank, good to his word, had given Ryder the day off for besting the big cow while branding. He'd thrown in half a day for everyone else to boot. Becca, with hardly any effort whatsoever, had also talked her daddy into buying the yellow dress in Miss Raynetta's shop for her. There were supplies for the house Dusty needed, and several of the men had business to do in town. So sitting high on the wagon seat between her father and sister, Dusty listened to the low, easy conversation of the ranch hands as they rode alongside. Even Feller, who rarely found any use for town or the people there, was accompanying them.

"Wipe that sour-pickle look off your face, girl," Hank told Dusty. "I'm gettin' tired of that frown ya wear. It ain't you, Dusty."

"Don't start chewin' me, Daddy," Dusty whined.

"I'll start into chewin' anytime I want to! And I want to now."

Dusty sighed. She knew what was coming. She'd heard it so many times before—how she needed to get over the wrong, the heartache heaped on her by Cash—how a person couldn't let others ruin their life. Yet this time—this time Hank hit her with something new—something unexpected.

"How do ya think it would make your mama feel to know you're carryin' on like this?"

Dusty looked to him quickly, all too aware of Becca climbing from the wagon seat beside her to the wagon bed behind. Becca habitually slunk away whenever the subject was raised by their father.

"That's not fair, Daddy," Dusty told him.

"Yes, it is!" Hank argued. "Your mama wouldn't have allowed you to do this! You wouldn't have done this to her, but ya do it to me . . . feelin' sorry for yerself and throwin' self-pity to all the world."

"I'm not that bad, Daddy," Dusty argued, feeling mostly angry but hurt too—hurt by her daddy's disappointment in her.

"Yes, ya are. You are that bad . . . and it's selfish,

Dusty. Plain selfish." Hank looked to his daughter for a moment. "I mean . . . what's this?" he asked, gesturing to her hair. "Ya look like some ol' tight-lipped spinster. Heck! Everybody calls Raynetta McCarthy a spinster, and she don't look so severe as you."

"Severe?" Dusty asked, unable to believe she had heard him correctly. Before she could move to avoid it, her father had reached over and pulled out the pin holding her hair in a tight bun at the back of her head. "Daddy!" she scolded as her hair fell in thick, brown cascades over her shoulders and back. "We're goin' to town!" she complained, reaching for the pin a moment before her father flicked it into the air.

"Then braid it up soft and nice like ya used to. I'm sick of it, Dusty! I know you're better than what you've become, and I ain't gonna tolerate it no more." Dusty could see her father's jaw clenching and unclenching angrily. He was mad. She knew arguing with him just then was pointless. "And I want ya to have Miss Raynetta hook ya up in a new dress too."

"Daddy—" she began to argue.

"I mean it. We're goin' to the picnic on the Fourth as a family, and I won't have ya detractin' from your sister and ruinin' her fun this time with your starched-up, arrogant attitude."

Slowly and very self-consciously—for she noticed the conversation between the ranch

hands riding behind the wagon had stopped—
Dusty began to work her hair into a loose French
braid. When she'd finished, she twisted a strand of
hair at the end and tucked it, securing the braid.
She tired to ignore the heated blush on her cheeks
—tried not to hate her daddy in that moment for
making such a fuss in front of the hands.

Sometime later, when her daddy pulled the
team to a halt in front of Miss Raynetta's dress
shop, Dusty hopped down from the wagon and
began marching up the steps to the shop.

"Get your attitude straightened out before I get
back," Hank told her.

She glared back at him—anger and humiliation
raging within her. He simply raised his eyebrows
in a silent scolding, and she bit her lip to silence
her frustration. She watched as Feller took
Becca by the waist and lifted her out of the
wagon. All the other hands looked away in
discomfort when Dusty looked at them—all of
them but Ryder. Ryder simply stared at her with
no apparent expression.

"Come on, Becca," Dusty urged with irritation.

Becca paused, uncertain about joining her.

"Oh, come on."

"I'm sorry Daddy got onto you, Dusty," Becca
offered in a whisper as she followed Dusty into
the dress shop.

"Don't worry about it," Dusty mumbled.

A bell rang, triggered by the door when the girls

entered Miss Raynetta's shop. In the next moment, Miss Raynetta McCarthy fairly floated in from the back room.

"Well, lookie here!" she greeted, obviously delighted to see the girls. "Angels! I tell ya, you two are simply angels!" She took each girl by the shoulders in turn, kissing them on both cheeks. "And what brings ya into the shop today, ladies? Perhaps a certain yellow dress I've had set aside?" With a wink, she nodded knowingly at Becca.

Even for her dark mood and prideful attitude, Dusty could not help but smile at the woman. She wore orange today—the brightest pumpkin orange Dusty had ever seen anyone wear, a bright orange dress with no collar. She had a simple black ribbon tied around her throat and long, dangling, beaded earrings. This was, with the exception of her mother, the most delightful woman Dusty had ever known.

"Daddy says I can have the dress, Miss Raynetta!" Becca told her with delight.

Miss Raynetta smiled. Her eyes widened, and she shrugged her shoulders excitedly. "I knew he would! And wait until he sees you in it!" Turning to Dusty, she said, "I haven't put a new dress on you in quite a while, Dusty. What do ya say we find ya one today? Oh, and I love your hair like that. It's so very becomin'." Miss Raynetta reached out and pulled a strand of hair from the braid, letting it hang in a soft curl from

Dusty's temple. "You really should wear your hair down, sugar plum. You're far too young to be stretchin' it back all tight in an old knot."

"So I've been told," Dusty informed her.

"And I think," Miss Raynetta began, taking Dusty's arms and holding them out to her sides, "I think I've got a red dress in the back that'll do just fine on you!"

"Oh, no, no, no," Dusty argued. "You're the only one I know who can wear red and get away with it, Miss Raynetta."

Miss Raynetta giggled and lowered her voice. "Me and the devil, ya mean?"

"Oh, no," Dusty protested. "I didn't mean—"

Miss Raynetta giggled again. "I've got a rather brown-sugar shade of calico made up. What do ya think of that?"

Dusty wanted to think it was wonderful. She wanted to think about looking pretty, wearing her hair down. She wanted to think about being dressed in something the color of Ryder's eyes. But try as she might, she built a wall against it in her mind. She'd been trying for over a week to be kinder to Becca—to her father and the hands too—even to Ryder. For all she'd avoided him, she'd been more civil to him when she did have to be in his powerful presence. Still, to change the way she wore her hair would certainly draw too much attention already! A new dress at the picnic? Could she endure that?

"Come on, Dusty," Becca pleaded. "Just . . . just be yourself for once."

It was an awkward attempt at telling Dusty to change. Dusty chose not to flash anger at her sister. She meant well, after all.

"It'll surely become ya, pumpkin," Miss Raynetta assured her. "Don't be afraid to try somethin' new." The woman paused and put a ponderous finger to her lips. "Tell ya what. You wear that new brown calico to the picnic, and I'll wear my loudest purple just to take the attention offa you."

Dusty smiled at the woman's sincere offer, knowing perfectly well that it wouldn't bother Miss Raynetta McCarthy one bit to wear purple up to meet St. Peter at the pearly gates.

"It'll be a sacrifice on my part," Miss Raynetta sighed dramatically. "But . . . I can do it for you."

The Hunter girls spent near to an hour in Miss Raynetta's shop while Dusty and Becca were completely doted on by the dress shop owner. It was as if, Dusty noted, the woman were expending every bit of energy on her and Becca that she never could on daughters of her own—daughters she never had.

"I'll hem that up for ya right this minute, Dusty," Miss Raynetta called after her as Dusty crossed the street toward the general store. "You drop in and pick it up 'fore ya leave, you hear?"

Becca was staying behind to help Miss

Raynetta, and Dusty walked along the board walkway, wondering how in the world she would ever find the courage to wear a new dress to the picnic.

"Now ain't you somethin' to look at," a man seated on a bench outside the carpenter's shop chuckled.

Dusty ignored him and kept walking. It was obvious he was a drifter of some sort, for she'd never seen him in town before. She hadn't even noticed the rest of the unfamiliar men sitting nearby until the man had spoken. She'd been too lost in her own thoughts. Yet when one of the men reached out and took hold of the hem of her skirt, she wished she hadn't been so distracted. She tugged at the fabric, giving the man a disapproving, prideful glance. Still, he continued to hold onto it, in fact, lifting it up somewhat until her stockings showed nearly to her knee.

"You'll not treat me with any disrespect, mister," she told him—although, as several of the men stood and formed a circle around her, her confidence began to wane.

"Oh, I don't mean no disrespect, miss . . . just that ya look like ya taste sweeter'n honey," the man chuckled. His breath reeked of liquor. It was obvious that all of them were drunk.

"Stand down, sir," came a very familiar voice from behind. Dusty closed her eyes for a moment, irritated that it should be Cash Richardson who had come to rescue her reputation.

"Go on, boy!" the first man growled at Cash. Dusty turned to see Cash standing in the street nearby. "This don't concern you."

"If you're bothering the lady, then it concerns me," Cash said.

Cash was handsome. His dark hair and even darker eyes were unusually striking. He was very tall, broad-shouldered, square-jawed, and firmly built. Yet something about the fair color of his skin and the perfect cleanliness of his immaculate suit struck a sudden cord of distaste in Dusty's stomach. It wasn't hurt, heartbreak, jealously, longing, or anything the like she felt as she looked at him. More it was distaste. An odd wonderment entered her mind as she tried to think of what it was she'd ever found in him to like.

"He said," one of the men began, stepping off the walkway and standing nose-to-nose with Cash, "it don't concern you, boy!"

"I've no desire to make this unpleasant," Cash told the man—though Dusty noted he took a step backward. "Just leave the lady alone." Cash looked to Dusty and said, "Run along, Dusty. These fellows will leave you be now."

Dusty frowned, unconvinced, as she tried to step past the three men standing before her. It was not at all surprising to her that they blocked her way, grinning with triumph when she tried to move past them a second time. When she tried to turn and go the other way, two other men

137

blocked her way—the first man that had spoken to her taking hold of her arm.

"You'll go when we say," he said.

Dusty looked to Cash, who swallowed hard.

"Men . . . let's remember . . . you've been drinking, and this is a lady here . . . not a saloon girl," Cash said.

Dusty raised her eyebrows at him. The irony of his words, considering his past behavior, was so hypocritical it was almost humorous.

The men, save the one standing nose-to-nose with Cash, ignored him as the drunken leader pulled Dusty closer and spoke directly into her face. "Is that so? I ain't never tasted myself the kiss of a lady!"

"Well, you ain't about to start now neither!"

Dusty glanced up when she heard Ryder's voice. He was striding angrily toward them. He paused when he reached Cash and the other man. He studied Cash for a moment—looking at him as if he were looking at the lowest form of life on the earth. Without further pause, Ryder took hold of the other man's shirt and let loose with a merciless, tightly fisted punch to the man's face! Dusty gasped as she watched him forcefully throw the man, with a now-bleeding nose, to the ground. Leaping up onto the walkway, he turned another degenerate around by the shoulders and let go a fist to his face as well, sending him falling off the walkway and sprawling to the ground.

Taking Dusty's hand, he pulled her from the drunken man's grasp and pushed her behind himself. Distracted in doing so, Ryder was momentarily off guard. Dusty screamed as the man punched Ryder in the mouth. Ryder stayed on his feet and simply began delivering his own punches in sober superiority. Two men jumped Ryder from behind. He took several hard blows to his midsection before breaking free. Reaching up, he grabbed one man by the hair of the head, slamming the villain's face down onto his knee and tossing him aside as if he were no more than an old rag doll.

"Three to one still ain't a fair fight!" Feller shouted as he cast a disapproving look to Cash before jumping up onto the walkway and throwing fists himself.

Dusty couldn't move. She simply stood in astonished, paralyzed shock at what was going on in front of her—and because of her! She watched as Ryder and Feller eventually knocked the three remaining men to the ground, leaving them bleeding and unable to stand. Ryder and Feller stood near panting with the exertion of their efforts. As Ryder wiped the blood from his lip and battered knuckles, he turned and glared at Dusty.

Dusty shook her head in dismay and tried to speak. "I . . . I . . . just . . ." she stammered. She couldn't think of what to say to him.

Feller reached out and took Dusty's hand, helping her to step over the bodies of the men sprawling every which direction as he assisted her down from the walkway. Ryder stepped off the walkway. Dusty felt sick to her stomach as she saw the anger blatant on his face when he stepped up to Cash.

"How long were ya gonna stand there and watch, huh, boy?" Ryder nearly shouted.

"I had everything under control," Cash assured him calmly. "This . . . this mess could've all been easily avoided," he said, gesturing to Ryder's bleeding lip and the drunken men on the ground.

A crowd had gathered, and Dusty saw her father, Becca, and the other hands walking toward them. Her father's attention was on Ryder, not on Dusty. Dusty looked at Ryder still glaring at Cash.

"He shouldn'ta even had the chance to talk to her, let alone touch her, you coward!" Ryder shouted.

"A gentleman uses the strength of his mind in such situations," Cash told him. "Fists are left to those who can't think out a situation with civility."

"Oh, no," Dusty mumbled.

If there was one thing Dusty remembered about Ryder Maddox, it was his distaste for a man who wouldn't protect a woman's honor at any length. Somehow knowing what would happen next, she watched as Ryder rubbed the whiskers at his chin. Without another word, he looked Cash

Richardson in the eye, slamming his fist into the "gentleman's" face. Cash's feet flew out from under him. He sailed through the air for a moment, his arms and legs outstretched, before landing with a solid thud square in the dirt.

Ryder immediately walked over to him, placed one of his own dusty boots square on the man's chest, and growled, "Go take a bath, boy." Then he sniffed the air with exaggeration. "You stink."

"Come on, there, son," Hank said, having reached the scene of all the excitement. He took hold of Ryder's arm and pulled him away from Cash. Dusty watched as Cash got to his feet much faster than probably anyone standing around had expected.

Cash glared at Dusty for a moment. Then he said, "And you complained about the company I keep?"

Hank grabbed Ryder around the waist as he growled, "You dirty . . ." and tried to get back to Cash, who stepped backward while wiping the blood from his lip.

"Hold on there, boy," Hank told Ryder as he struggled to confine the young man. "Feller! Help me out here!"

In the next moment, Feller and Hank had Ryder settled down. Dusty couldn't hear what they were whispering in their low, mumbling tones. Still, it seemed to keep Ryder from flying at Cash with his already bloodied fists.

Cash straightened his collar as he walked past the group. His pride was damaged, but his superior attitude intact, and he said to Miss Raynetta, "I do wonder about the company you and the Hunter girls are keeping these days, Miss Raynetta." Then, proving himself a true coward, he turned and landed a fist in Ryder's midsection.

"I've about had my fill of you, boy!" Dusty heard her father shout. In the next moment it was her father Feller and the others were pulling off Cash Richardson—Cash Richardson, who'd now been sent reeling again by Hank Hunter.

"Daddy!" Becca screeched.

"Hank!" Miss Raynetta shouted. "Hank Hunter! You quit a-wallerin' in the dirt like a schoolboy!"

Dusty watched her father's chest rise and fall angrily as he turned and walked away, pushing his way through the crowd and toward Miss Raynetta's shop.

"You're a disappointment, Cash," Miss Raynetta told him, helping him to stand. "You've disappointed more people than you ever had a right to know." She shook her head, clicking her tongue with disapproval a moment before she followed Hank through the crowd. "Ryder! Feller! Get on into the shop, and we'll clean ya up," she called over her shoulder.

"That boy deserved a good whoppin'!" Ruff exclaimed as he and the other hands gathered around Ryder.

"Somebody shoulda knocked him on his . . ." Titch glanced at Becca a moment and then finished, "hind end a long time ago!"

"Sure enough," Feller agreed, dabbing at a cut over his eyebrow.

"Come on," Becca said, pushing at Feller's back. "You all heard Miss Raynetta."

As Ryder turned to follow them, Dusty felt herself reach out and take hold of his arm. He stopped, turned, and looked at her expectantly. She wanted to thank him. She wanted to throw her arms around his neck and kiss him squarely on the mouth! She wanted to kiss him so badly the thought of it made her mouth water. She wanted to tell him how wonderful it was to have him rescue her—to have him champion her virtue and her pride—to have him so close she could touch him!

Yet fear overcame her—fear of rejection, of loss. And when she opened her mouth, all that she could manage was a stammering, "I . . . I . . ."

He sighed with disappointment and frowned down at her. "Don't thank me, Dusty. I wouldn't want you to hurt yourself." Yanking his arm from her grasp, he followed the others through the crowd.

Everyone was staring at her—not at Cash, who was storming toward his parents' home in town —not at the drunken, bleeding men that were now struggling to their feet. They all stared at her. Dusty had caused this all—unwittingly, of course.

Still, she had caused it; she knew they were all wondering how.

Without a word to anyone, Dusty pushed her way through the crowd of onlookers and walked toward the dress shop. Stepping inside, she was greeted by Miss Raynetta handing her a wet cloth.

"Now, put some pressure on Feller's head there, sweetheart," the woman instructed without waiting for a response.

Humbly Dusty walked to Feller and pressed the cloth to his head. "I can do that, Dusty," Feller grumbled in his shy, mumbly way.

Dusty pushed his hand away. "Let me do somethin' for you for once, Feller," she whispered, forcing a smile—though she felt like sobbing.

The whole incident was too much to take in. Being nearly accosted by strange, vile men—the fact the mere sight of Cash made her certain she'd been insane to have ever been attracted to him—having Ryder come so powerfully to her rescue—Feller helping him—even her father involving himself! And what had she done but stand there mute and seemingly ungrateful? She looked over to where Miss Raynetta was forcing Ryder to sit in a chair.

"You chewed your knuckles up good enough, didn't ya, boy?" Miss Raynetta said, though talking more to herself than to Ryder. She showed Becca how to tend Ryder's knuckles. Then the woman in orange turned to Hank. "And you!" she exclaimed. "Have ya got rocks in your noggin?" She shook her head and pointed a dainty, scolding index finger at him. "You could've been hurt!"

Dusty quickly looked back to Feller as she felt tears fill her eyes. She opened them wide, refusing to blink and trying to will away the extra moisture there as she dabbed at Feller's forehead. Still, the tears were too many, and as they trickled down her face, she whispered, "I'm sorry. I'm so sorry." She couldn't even imagine how it must feel to have the power of a man's fist meet full force with any part of one's body. Ryder and Feller had endured great pain and injury because of her. The knowledge, though somehow comforting and flattering, was not easy to bear.

Feller put a roughened and familiar hand to her cheek, brushing away her tears with his thumb. "It's all right, Dusty. It ain't none of it your fault."

"Well, if I ain't as dumb as a post!" Miss Raynetta exclaimed suddenly. "Here I am a-makin' over these men like they was babies, and I didn't even stop to ask if you're all right, Dusty, honey!"

"I'm fine," Dusty lied. She forced a smile as the woman took her by the shoulders and studied her face.

"Thou shalt not lie to Raynetta McCarthy," Miss Raynetta cooed, gathering Dusty as best she could into her short little arms. "Them men was just a bunch of drunken filth, Dusty! Just drunken filth! You don't pay no mind to the things they may have said to you. And these here boys . . . don't let 'em fool ya! Cowboys take to brawlin' like fish take to water. Even ones that should be old enough to know better," she added, glancing over her shoulder at Dusty's father.

When Miss Raynetta released her, Dusty watched a moment as Becca dabbed at the blood at the corner of Ryder's mouth. A hot rush of jealousy suddenly washed over her—and greatly disturbed her. She thought, *I should be taking care of him.* Shaking her head, she tried to dispel the feeling. Her gaze met Ryder's for a moment. His expression was no longer that of anger. His temper had settled, and his knuckles bothered him more, no doubt.

"Let's haul this bunch home, boys," Hank sighed suddenly. "Come into town once or twice a month . . . can't even get supplies without all heck a-breakin' loose around ya," he mumbled as he made for the door.

"You boys keep somethin' cool on them cheeks and fists," Miss Raynetta instructed. "And Hank . . . you make sure that girl knows whose fault this all wasn't! You hear me?"

"I hear ya, girl! I hear ya," Hank chuckled.

"Did ya put your dress in the wagon, Becca?" Miss Raynetta asked as Ryder stood and began to follow Feller out of the shop. "I'll have to send Dusty's along later, I guess."

"I did, ma'am. Thank you so much," Becca answered.

Ryder started to leave the shop but paused behind Dusty, motioning for her to precede him.

"Oh. No. You go ahead. I . . ." Dusty stammered uncomfortably.

"After you," he ordered. "I don't want to be accused of not bein' a gentleman."

"Now stop that, Ryder Maddox!" Miss Raynetta scolded, smacking Ryder hard enough on the back of the head that he mouthed, *Ow!* "What do you want the girl to do?" she continued. "Drown herself in the pond over guilt?"

Ryder smiled at Miss Raynetta. "Thank you, Miss McCarthy," he said. Reaching out and taking hold of Dusty's elbow, he forced her out the door ahead of him. Dusty looked back over her shoulder to see Miss Raynetta wink encouragingly.

You thank him, Miss Raynetta mouthed authoritatively. *He deserves it.* With another wink, she waved to the others as they mounted their horses or climbed into the wagon.

"You all right, honey?" Dusty's father asked as Dusty settled down next to him on the seat. When she didn't answer right away, he took her chin in one roughened hand and forced her to look at him. "I mean, really? You all right?"

Dusty nodded and fought the urge to shrug off her sister's comforting arm around her shoulders.

The wagon ride home seemed long and tiring.

Periodically the hands would burst into laughter, and Dusty caught bits of their conversation.

"He'll have a shiner for weeks!" Guthrie chuckled.

"I hope so," Ryder said. " 'Cause I sure as heck'll look like somethin' the dog upchucked for at least that long."

"Ah, come on now!" Feller added. "You see the way them town women was a-swoonin' every which way when you come a-walkin' into the dress shop after the go-'round? They'll be a-swoonin' still come the Fourth."

"That Miss Raynetta," Dusty's father mumbled unexpectedly, "she's a pistol, ain't she?"

"Well," Becca began, "I don't know if I'd call her a pistol exactly, Daddy . . . but she's a dear, dear soul. I wonder why she never married."

Hank shrugged his shoulders, and Dusty didn't hear any of the conversation her sister and father shared on the way home from town. All she could think about was suppressing the morbid delight rising in her each time she thought of Ryder hitting Cash—laying him out on the ground.

The rest of the late afternoon and suppertime were pretty solemn around the ranch. Dusty felt very uncomfortable when Ryder, sitting down for his evening meal, unconsciously let a groan slip from his throat. The grimace on his handsome face reminded her, yet again, what physical discomfort he had endured on her behalf—was still enduring. Not that she needed reminding—it was all she could think about. For every moment of that day following the incident in town, she thought of nothing else—repulsion at the thought of those terrible men and their intentions toward her—irritation at Cash Richardson's cowardice and having ever been mildly attracted to him. Still, it was the guilt mingled with delight she felt each time her mind reviewed Ryder's coming to her rescue, so powerfully and without pause, that confused her most. What an odd sensation it was —to feel completely guilty that the man she . . . that a man she was attracted to, and the others, would sacrifice their physical health for the sake of her honor and safety. Ryder had always been that way—Feller too. Her father as well, for that matter. But her father and Feller were more inclined to try talking first, as opposed to using intimidation and threats.

So as she went out to the chicken house to gather the eggs, she considered her feelings—the emotions so boiled together within her—and she thought about Ryder. She could still hear her mother—almost hear her mother's voice giving Ryder a talking-to about his quick temper and flying fists, where wrong and right were con-cerned.

"Ryder," Elly Hunter began, "you are gonna have to learn when to jump right in with fists a-flyin' and when not to!" Dusty noticed the way her mother shook her head as she held a cool cloth to Ryder's blackened eye. "Ya can't go a-punchin' everybody in the nose all the time. Ya gotta learn to try some other methods!"

Dusty and Becca sat on the kitchen floor, their legs folded, their chins resting snugly on their fists as they watched their mama clean up the cuts and bruises on Ryder's face. One of the drifters her daddy had hired to help bring in the field crops had said something disloyal about Dusty's family. After telling the man to "take it back" and being met with firm belligerence, Ryder had jumped on the man, both fists flying, and taken some hard hits himself before finally beating the man enough that Feller jumped in and pulled Ryder off him. Of course, Hank and Elly Hunter didn't allow fighting among their hands, but when Ryder told Hank what the man had said, the drifter was sent to drifting, and Ryder got off with only a firm reprimand from Dusty's father.

"I know it, Mrs. Hunter," Ryder mumbled as Dusty's mama dabbed at his bleeding lip with a wet cloth. "I tried talkin' to him. I did! But he just made me so darn mad that I—"

"I understand, Ryder," Elly said, smiling. "And, in reality, I should thank you for defendin' us the way ya did."

"What did he say, Mama?" Dusty asked. Her

curiosity burned so hot that she could hardly stand it.

"Nothin' that you're old enough to be hearin'," her mother told her.

She knew that would be the end of it.

It was obvious from Ryder's behavior in town he still battled a temper easily provoked when someone was treated badly. She smiled, recognizing something else about him that hadn't changed much in five years. Still, Ryder had taken her mother's advice and worked on other ways of defending truth and right.

As she left the chicken house, she headed toward the barn to put the eggs in the egg bin. She smiled, remembering the first time Ryder had tried something other than fighting and how well it had worked —that Fourth of July picnic when she'd been fourteen and worn the new dress her mother had made for her but never altered. Her mother hadn't had time to alter the one flaw in the blue calico dress—the dress Dusty Hunter would never forget!

The Fourth of July picnic almost five years ago—nope, Dusty would never forget that night! Yet as her mind began to travel back again, she stepped out of the barn hearing voices—voices that made her stop dead in her tracks. Stepping back into the barn, she hid in the darkness as Ryder, her father, and the other hands stood just outside talking.

"Miss Dusty looked 'bout like she wanted to shrivel up and die today in town," Ruff noted.

"She don't take to bein' noticed," her father told them. "And, boy, oh boy, did she get noticed today."

There was a low round of amused chuckles. Dusty was surprised when no indignant anger rose in her bosom as it usually did when she came across herself as the subject of conversation.

"You old boys got Miss Dusty all wrong," Ryder assured them. "She's as much a girl as any female. And she wasn't always wantin' to stay unnoticed. Fact is, I think Becca probably learned mosta what she knows from her older sister. Ain't that right, boss?"

"I'd say you 'bout pegged it there, Ryder," Hank chuckled.

"What about that there Fourth of July picnic dance some years back, Ryder?" Feller offered.

Dusty could not believe what she was over-hearing! It was uncanny! She wasn't sure at first that she'd heard correctly. Was Ryder actually about to tell the same story that had begun to bang around in her own mind? The picnic dance five years ago and the blue dress that hadn't fit right?

"There you go!" Ryder exclaimed.

"I hope Dusty ain't in earshot," Hank chuckled.

Dusty smiled at the irony.

"Dusty was, what . . . fourteen? Was she fourteen yet, Feller?" Ryder asked.

152

"More'n likely. I'd say she'd be that in order to be dancin' with the older people and . . . uh . . . wearin' a dress like that," Feller confirmed.

"Anyway," Ryder continued, "Dusty was fourteen, and her mama had made her this new dress. Sky blue . . . ya know, Dusty insisted that it be blue and all. So her Mama makes her this dress—ya know when a girl's fourteen and folks think they're old enough for a party dress with no collar and such. And somehow the top part . . . ya know right here . . ."

Dusty peeked around the corner to see Ryder indicate his chest, holding his hands out from his body where a woman's bosom would be. She was mortified.

"Somehow," he continued, "that dress didn't fit just right. It was a little . . . too big at the top here. And bein' as Mrs. Hunter didn't have time left to fix it, Dusty stuffed a couple a Mr. Hunter's old handkerchiefs in there . . . ya know . . . to fill the dress out and all."

Dusty began blushing when she heard the low, amused chuckles of the hands, including Feller and her daddy—even though she knew the men were completely unaware of her. Try as she might to stop it at the memory of the tale, she felt a smile spread slowly across her face—like the warm embrace of an old friend.

"I knew she'd done it when she come out to get in the wagon to leave that night. I knew she hadn't popped out overnight like that," Hank chuckled. "But what's a daddy to say?"

There was more chuckling from the group of men.

"So we all meet in town for the Fourth. And life's a-goin' merrily along and all. Ya never saw a fourteen-year-old girl get so much attention from hands and boys in town! And I mean even without them hankies!" Ryder told them, chuckling again, only louder.

"No doubt," Feller added. "Fact was, Miss Dusty got more attention anyhow. She was quite the fine piece a pie . . . even at fourteen."

"Mighty fine for fourteen!" Ryder affirmed. "All day them hankies stayed put. Don't ask me how . . . but they done it. All day . . . all through supper . . . and then the dance starts. Well, 'bout halfway through the dancin'," he continued, "I look over, and I see little Miss Britches a-dancin' with some cowboy . . . can't remember who."

Ryder paused, and Feller offered, "Brown Morrow. It were that boy who worked over on the Maxwell place. 'Member?"

"Oh, yeah, "Ryder agreed. "Dusty was a-waltzin' away with ol' Brown when I notice that he's a-lookin' down at her . . . at her . . . ya know . . . her . . ."

"Bosom," Hank finished.

"Thank you. He's a-lookin' straight down at her . . . bosom . . . and I see that one of them hankies she tucked in there is a-givin' her away . . . 'cause it's slippin' up out the top of her dress, you see."

All the men burst into laughter. Dusty stifled her own giggle. It all seemed so clear. She could see it all over again—Brown Morrow looking down at her bosom, her father's handkerchief slipping up and giving away the secret she'd tried to slide past everyone. The fact was, she'd stuffed the top of her dress in order to capture the attention of none other than Ryder Maddox. And capture it she had!

"That's terrible!" Ruff chuckled. "Poor thing. Havin' her bosoms . . . or the lack of 'em revealed to everybody there."

"Oh, don't worry. Good ol' Prince Charmin' here came to the rescue," Hank assured them, nodding toward Ryder as Feller slapped him on the back proudly.

"What'd you do, boy?" Guthrie asked.

"Well . . . I couldn't let Miss Britches lose her self-respect and good reputation there," Ryder explained. "Imagine what would've been goin' 'round town the rest of her entire life had Brown said something to her . . . or to anybody else."

"And so ya went at him, fists a-flyin' and . . ." Titch coaxed.

"Nope," Ryder corrected. "I grabbed little Alice Maxwell there . . . and we waltz on over near to Brown and Dusty. I fake a sneeze and say to Dusty, 'Hey there, Miss Hunter. You still got that hanky I gave ya to keep for me?' "

All the hands and Dusty's daddy burst into laughter.

When they'd finally settled themselves again, Ryder continued, "So bein' that Miss Britches is as smart as a whip . . . she reaches down the front of her dress and yanks me out a hanky or two. I let go another sneeze for good measure and blew my nose, then tucked the darn things in my pocket."

The hands hooted and hollered and laughed until they were complaining about their sides aching.

Ruff sighed. "I can't imagine it! Miss Dusty, a girl a fourteen and stuffin' her dress to go to a social!"

"Well, she don't need no extra stuffin' these days!" Titch said. "Ain't that right, Ryder?"

Ryder chuckled. "No, siree! She didn't need much stuffin' then neither."

"You hold on there. That's my daughter you all are talkin' about, boys," Hank reprimanded teasingly. Then, wiping the tears of mirth from his eyes, he added, "That Dusty was a character all right. The things she used to get into!"

Dusty didn't hear the rest of their conversation. Her mind was lingering back on that night so long ago. There had been a lot more to that night than Ryder had told the hands—a lot he probably wasn't even aware of. But she was. She remembered it all—how she'd panicked when she'd looked down to see why Brown Morrow was staring at her chest. What would she do? How could she possibly explain the handkerchiefs in her bodice without completely humiliating herself? Then Ryder had danced up with Alice and saved her life. She'd loved him all the more for being her hero that night. He was her hero all the time! She couldn't even remember or begin to count all the times he'd saved her. But she did remember that he'd danced with her after her dance with Brown Morrow that night. She remembered the feel of dancing with him—the strength of his arms about her—his mischievous grin as he pulled the infamous handkerchiefs from his pocket, sniffling into them and teasing her.

"You and me," he'd whispered to her during their waltz, "we're on far too intimate a terms now, ya know. Me a-usin' your . . . hankies on my nose and all."

Dusty glared at him gratefully for a moment before smiling and whispering, "You saved my life, Ryder Maddox."

"Oh, I did, did I?" he had chuckled.

Their dance had ended. Yet Dusty had waltzed with Ryder Maddox, and it had caused quite a stir among the other girls in town—the ones Dusty's own age and the ones older who'd all been trying to catch his attention all night. Alice could gloat too—for though his reasons for dancing with her may have been a bit desperate, no one else knew it! So Ryder had made Dusty and Alice the girls to be jealous of that Fourth of July—and Dusty had reveled in it. Even now, she felt the same silly schoolgirl pride welling up within her at the memory.

The men were settling their laughter now, and Hank sighed, "Well, let's get these chores finished up, boys. Daylight's gone, but it comes too early in the mornin'."

Dusty stayed in the barn for a while longer until she was certain everyone was gone and wouldn't see her coming out of the barn. It had been fun overhearing the conversation. It had taken her back in time to when things in life weren't so serious— when her heart was young and untainted and hopeful—when she'd still been that impetuous, wild girl always finding herself in a fix.

Finally, Dusty figured the hands and her daddy were busy enough not to notice her leaving the barn, and she started back toward the house. The sky was so clear that night. It seemed as if every star twinkled far more brightly than usual. Dusty paused and looked toward the north. The air was still warm, even though the sun had been down for a while, and Dusty inhaled deeply. Even for the cooler temperature of the evening, it was hot. A swim would be nice, she thought to herself. Yet she was weary from the trip into town and the events there. So, with a heavy sigh, she resolved to simply retire for the night. Turning back toward the house, she nearly ran headlong into Ryder, however. He had obviously been standing directly behind her. For how long, she could only wonder.

"Excuse me," she mumbled. Her heart had begun to pound furiously at the sight of him. She felt the need to escape at once. Had he seen her leave the barn? Had he figured she'd been there during the conversation he'd had with the other men?

"Hey there," he said, quickly reaching out and taking her arm. "Why don't you and me go for a little walk, Miss Dusty?"

Dusty clenched her teeth tightly together—conflicting emotions of elation at his invitation and trepidation as to the reason for it battling within her. She wanted to snap back at him a defensive, *Why?* and erect the wall of stone between her heart and the fabulous man—but she didn't. For some reason, she simply took a deep breath, turned, and began walking beside him—listening to the way the handle of the unlit lantern he carried squeaked rhythmically with his stride.

"Sorry if I seemed a little . . . grouchy today in town. Just let my temper get the better of me," he began in a mumbly sort of manner. "Never did ask ya if you were all right. Them fellas upset you too bad?"

Dusty could only shake her head, affirming the men hadn't done permanent damage to her. Why couldn't she talk? she wondered. It was as if her voice were lost to her. She could only walk beside him, as she'd done all those years ago—listening to his voice—hanging on his every word as if it were the very nectar of life.

They walked in silence for a while, until the light of the house was dim in the distance. Ryder stopped and drew a match from his pocket, running it quickly along his pant leg. The match ignited, and he lit the lantern. Setting it at their feet, he turned to face Dusty. Looking down at her—an expression of concern on his handsome face—he asked, "Do you have somethin' ya wanna say to me?"

Yes! Dusty's mind shouted. *Yes! Thank you for coming to my rescue today! Thank you for being born so beautiful and perfect! Thank you for coming back to my father's ranch so that I could have you near me again!* Yet the words actually escaping her lips surprised her.

"Why did you leave?" Dusty knew she didn't have to explain to him what she meant. He knew what she meant—rather, *when* she meant. Even though it was unspoken, he knew it.

Ryder paused for a moment, looking away from her, shrugging his shoulders. He didn't try to avoid an answer—didn't even seem surprised that particular question was the one she asked.

"I guess . . . guess 'cause I started thinkin' that maybe I was some sorta twisted . . . I started thinkin' somethin' was wrong with me," he stated finally.

"What?" Dusty exclaimed in a whisper. The

question, in her mind, had been simple enough to deserve a serious answer. Was he teasing her? "What kind of an answer is that?" she asked him.

"A truthful one," he told her. "I left because I started thinkin' somethin' was wrong with me. I thought I was turnin' into some sort of ol' letch," he explained. He seemed serious enough.

Dusty shook her head and sighed, rolling her eyes as she spoke. "The ranch was doin' really bad. That's the year we almost lost it. I remember that." Looking up to him suddenly—searchingly —for her heart and mind needed an answer, she added, "But . . . but Mama favored you, and you were the best hand we had next to Feller. Daddy would've kept you on through it all."

This intoxicatingly handsome man bent toward her then. Dusty noted how hot she felt being so near to him. It wasn't the warmth of the day left in the night. It was the excited warmth—the blissful warmth a woman feels when the man she cares for most in the world is near to her. It disturbed her that this sensation should still wash over her after all this time—after she'd worked so hard to deny it.

Lowering his voice, he said, "I was twenty years old, and I was attracted to a fourteen-year-old little girl I knew." He raised an eyebrow and tipped his head to one side, waiting for what he'd said to sink into her mind. When Dusty stood

161

still unbelieving, he added, "And she was the boss's little girl to boot. Do ya see what I'm sayin' here, Britches?" Moving his face even closer to hers, meeting her eye-to-eye, he stated, "I was afraid I was turnin' into some sort of pervert or somethin'!"

Dusty was infuriated that he would tease her so! Infuriated and very hurt. She couldn't believe how he was toying with her—making fun of her childhood crush on him. "It's a simple enough question, Ryder! Can't ya just give me a straight answer?" she pleaded.

He chuckled with frustration, retrieved the lantern from its place at his feet, and said, "Your daddy had to let us all go. That there was reason enough . . . but add to it the fact that in my spare time I was listin' off in my head how many girls I knew who went and got married when they was sixteen or seventeen . . . and then tellin' myself you'd be sixteen or seventeen soon enough!" He raised his eyebrows as the expression on Dusty's face must've revealed, at last, the beginning of belief. He told her, "I needed work, your daddy's ranch was flounderin', and I was turnin' into a pervert. So I left." He turned from her then— simply turned and walked away.

How Dusty loved to watch him walk! He had a rhythmic sort of saunter that defined him— caused him to stand apart from anyone else she knew. It was especially pleasant to be standing behind him and to watch him walk—even if he was a terrible, heartless tease.

The darkness swallowed him quickly—even for the light of his lantern. Dusty turned and started back toward the house. Yet her heart leaped for a moment. He had seemed sincere in the reasons he gave her for leaving. But she remembered herself at fourteen, remembered all the silly, stupid things she used to do—the ridiculous situations she used to stumble into. Stuffing her dress for the picnic was one of her milder antics. It was true: Ryder had always treated her kindly—more than kindly, actually. He'd always been chivalrous in saving her dignity anytime he was near, when she would plunge headlong into stupidity—like the handkerchiefs in her bodice at that long-ago Fourth of July picnic. He'd saved her today, hadn't he? In so many more ways than he would ever know! She could never admit to anyone the selfish, immature elation she'd felt when he'd knocked the stuffing out of Cash Richardson. It had been fabulous! He'd even saved her on that night he'd left so long ago. The night she'd confessed her young heart's obsession with him. On that night he'd . . .

"A pervert! Oh, please!" she mumbled, entering the house and not allowing herself to dwell on that incident five years ago.

"Who's a pervert?" Becca asked unexpectedly. She'd been standing at the sink cutting up berries when Dusty had entered.

"Uh . . . nobody, Beck," Dusty stammered, waving her hand in a gesture Becca should forget Dusty had ever said it.

"But you said, 'A pervert! Oh, please!' " Becca prodded, undaunted.

"Must be a man she's talkin' about," her father answered from his seat at the table. "Perverts. The whole lot of 'em. Ain't that right, Dusty?"

Dusty rolled her eyes, thinking her father was making fun of her. Yet when she looked at him to see his face completely serious, no sign of mirth whatsoever apparent there, she realized what he thought she must be thinking.

"I . . . I wasn't speakin' of . . ." she insisted.

Her daddy slid his chair back and stood up. Reaching up and retrieving his hat from the hat rack behind him, he told her, "Ain't all males of the species as low as them fellas in town, Dusty. As low as Cash Richardson, for that matter! It's way past time for you to be believin' that they are." Hank was always grouchy when he was tired, and tonight he must've been done in.

"But, Daddy, I wasn't . . ." she stammered again. Still, he left by way of the front door.

Becca stood looking at her sister with blatant disapproval. "It upsets Daddy when you dog all men. And it upsets him even more that ya let it ruin your life!"

"I wasn't talkin' about today, Rebecca," Dusty said, irritated. She sensed the hot sensation of anger and humiliation rising within her. Her face felt warm and red, and her hands began to perspire. Yet how else could she expect everyone to interpret her actions? She'd behaved this way for so long—what else did she deserve? "And it didn't ruin my life! He—"

Becca threw the knife she'd been using into the sink, exasperated. "It did so! You've been nothin' but prickles and burrs to every fella who comes anywhere near to ya ever since Cash done ya wrong. Won't smile at anybody . . . won't talk to anybody longer than absolutely necessary. You're even mean to me and Daddy half the time . . . sulkin' every minute of the dang day, sittin' around feelin' sorry for yourself! Workin' like a horse to keep yourself so tired and miserable that ya don't have time to remember you're a girl who likes to smell nice and look pretty! There's other people hurtin' in the world, Angelina. Hurtin' a whole lot deeper than you. And it's time you quit bein' so selfish and . . . and downright chicken . . . and started livin' life again! Heaven knows Daddy and I would be a lot better off!"

Had everyone in her family lost their ever-loving minds?

"What do you even know about how hurt I am, Rebecca? What do you even know about life and how it can burn you?" Dusty shouted, tears filling her eyes. For all her holding in her emotions and heartache, she'd held in everything else too. All her need to talk to someone, to be comforted, had been bound up.

"I know that for two years I've lived my life in the shadow of the great Dusty Hunter, who had her heart broken! I spend half the time with the new hands or with friends in town explainin' why someone as pretty as my sister is so miserable and cold. Dusty, Dusty, Dusty! That's all I hear! Heck, for the first year after you caught Cash with that saloon girl, I spent every Sunday doggin' him after church so's he wouldn't spend all afternoon beggin' me to win ya back for him!"

Dusty tried to ignore the tears escaping her eyes, streaming over her cheeks. She'd never considered how her own misfortune affected her family. She'd been so wrapped up in her own heartbreak, in her own grief, she'd been selfish and blind to what it had done to those around her.

"And I know a whole lot more about heartache than you think!" Becca continued, though she lowered her voice—though it cracked with emotion. Rebecca's compassion for her sister was spent that day as far as patience was concerned, and all the things she'd wanted to say to Dusty— all the things Dusty had needed to hear—burst out of her mouth. "You go on and cry, Angelina! It's time you felt somethin'!" Bursting into tears of her own, Becca ran out of the kitchen and into her bedroom, slamming the door behind her.

Chapter Six

Dusty stood for a moment, wiping the tears from her cheeks. When she couldn't stop more tears from escaping her eyes, she turned and grabbed a lantern from the front porch. Quickly lighting it, she fled the house. She ran and ran—tears raining over her face—until she'd reached the banks of the stream. This was where it fed the big pond by way of a serene waterfall. She leaned against a tree as she tried to catch her breath. Somehow the stars didn't look as bright or as beautiful overhead. She didn't care that the water was beginning to cool off. So what if she caught her death of cold! She loved an evening swim, and in that moment, it was the only thing in life that didn't cause her grief.

Crying, sobbing harder than she'd cried in so very long, she leaned back against the tree as the truth of what her sister had spoken sank in. Angrily, she unlaced her boots and removed them, stripping her stockings off as well. She unfastened her skirt, letting it fall to the ground around her ankles. Lifting her petticoat as she stepped out of her skirt, and holding the lantern high to light her way, she nimbly made her way along the boulders leading to the waterfall.

Setting the lantern on a nearby boulder, Dusty

stepped through the cold water and into the small alcove behind the waterfall. Hundreds of years of the waterfall eating away at the rock had created the alcove—the perfect place to hide—to be alone. Dusty cried bitterly for long moments, plunging her face into the water before her as it cascaded down from above. The cold water felt good on her face. It soothed the heat of her tears and calmed her. She wiped the excess water from her eyes, smoothed her wet hair, and leaned against the cool, wet slab of rock behind her.

Closing her eyes in trying to hold back more tears, she thought on what Becca had said. It had all been true. All of it! She couldn't fault her sister for having an insight to her pain and selfishness. The lantern light burned low and reassuring on the other side of the waterfall, but even its light did nothing to comfort her. Closing her eyes again, she tried to clear her mind. What Becca had said had all been true, except for one thing: it hadn't been Cash Richardson who had broken her heart. Cash had only driven the final nail into her coffin of heartbreak. It hadn't been Cash she'd cried over after she found him with the saloon girl. It had been Ryder. Dusty had cried years of tears—her heart breaking because there had been no handsome Ryder Maddox to rescue her from Cash. She'd merely gotten involved with Cash because Ryder was the only man for her and he was gone. She'd convinced herself she'd have to settle with whatever came along. It was Ryder who'd broken her—Ryder—not Cash.

"You all right?" Ryder asked, stepping into the alcove from one side of the waterfall. It wasn't necessary to walk right through the cascading sheets of water as Dusty had done. Dusty was startled by his sudden appearance. Immediately, she began wiping at the water trickling over her face from her wet hair. He set his own lantern down on the wet slab of stone beneath their feet.

"What are you doin'?" she asked him.

"I saw ya leave the house . . . and ya looked upset," he replied. He stood next to her, leaning back against the rock and looking out at the water rushing over them. "I came to apologize . . . figured I'm the one who upset ya." He wore an expression of both guilt and regret.

At that very moment, Dusty realized she wore only her shirtwaist, petticoat, and pantaloons. In an effort to convince him to leave—to leave her to her own thoughts and her humiliating lack of attire —she said, "I'm fine. It wasn't anything you said."

Still, he remained standing next to her. In fact, he removed his hat and plunged his own head forward into the water. He brushed the water from his face and smoothed his hair back. He looked at her for a long moment. Looking away, he said, "Ya know, Dusty . . . it's time ya got over that dog and went on with life."

Dusty couldn't believe she'd heard him correctly. "What?" she asked in a whisper.

"I've been watchin' you," he said. He looked at her—studied her—and the intimidation of being studied by a man so profoundly attractive caused her great discomfort. She looked away. "You've buried yourself. Ya got this old hard shell built around ya now . . . and nobody gets through it."

Someone gets through it, she thought.

She tried to settle the emotions running through her—overtaking her. Yet when she spoke, she knew the turmoil in her soul was evident in her raised voice. "Fine—go ahead. Tell me how awful I am—how selfish and uncaring I am. Go ahead!"

Ryder grinned. "Now that's more the hotheaded you I remember." Yet his smile faded quickly as he added, "I don't have to tell ya how you are now. You know it." She looked up to him as he continued, "And that's how ya want it. It's safer. It's safer to be a coward." He sighed. "It's safer."

Dusty looked away as the hot sting of tears seared her eyes again. Somehow hearing these things from this man hurt her more than hearing them from her sister or her father or Feller or anyone else. "Thank you. But I think I'm already feeling as bad about myself as I possibly can."

"And it's safer to stay angry," he added, seeming to ignore her plea for relief. "I don't know what all went on, Angelina," he added. Dusty winced at his calling her by her given name. It had always plucked at her heartstrings as some sort of delightful secret when Ryder called her Angelina. He shook his head and continued, "But there ain't one man on this earth worth ruinin' your life for." The hair on the back of Dusty's neck prickled slightly when he added, "One person can ruin your life for you . . . but you shouldn't ruin your own life over one person."

She wondered at the cliché implication of his choice of words. All this time she'd spent lamenting over what had happened to her since he'd left so long ago. Self-centered and selfishly caught up in self-pity, she hadn't even paused to wonder what life had dealt to Ryder Maddox. Besides, she thought, there *was* one man on earth worth ruining your life for. Suddenly, she consciously admitted again what she'd always known, all this time. The one person certainly wasn't Cash Richardson, though he'd hurt her deeply. Dusty's heartbreak had taken place long before she'd fallen almost in love with Cash.

"You and Becca sure pride yourselves on knowin' everything there is to know," she mumbled.

"I can't speak for Becca . . . but I do know every-thing, Miss Britches," Ryder stated, frowning down at her. "I've been watchin' you." He turned toward her, leaning one shoulder against the rock wall of the alcove. "Ya don't smile much. Ya laugh . . . once in a while, maybe. Ain't even a real laugh though. You pull your hair back all tight in a knot like some old widow . . . and your hands don't ever hang at your sides or lay in your lap all soft and relaxed. You got 'em clenched into fists anytime you ain't busy. And ya work almost harder than any man I know."

Dusty looked away quickly, realizing even as she stood next to him now, her small hands were indeed fisted. "And what does all that possibly matter to you, Ryder Maddox? Who are you to be worryin' about me?" She felt a betraying tear leave one eye and travel down her cheek.

"A boy you knew once a long time back. A boy who was a friend to you then . . . and who don't like to see how you've turned out," he answered plainly and not too kindly. As several more tears escaped her eyes at his almost cruel words, he added, "And I ain't talkin' about the wrappin' on the package, Dusty. When you were fourteen years old, it was obvious to the world that you'd grow up to be a sweet-lookin' peppermint stick. That ain't what I mean."

Dusty brushed angrily at her tears and wondered why she still stood next to him—listening— enduring his cruel words.

"It's what's inside you that you're hidin' from. And frankly, Dusty . . . I think ya know it's selfish. It makes your daddy unhappy, it makes Becca unhappy . . . and anybody else who tries to friendly up to ya."

172

"Then why are you standin' here?" she cried. "Why don't you walk your sweet little hind end back to wherever it was Daddy dug you up? Then ya won't have to be around someone like me who makes everybody miserable!" She plunged her head into the water, trying to cool the heat of her cheeks. She ran her fingers through her wet hair, keeping her eyes closed. It was too hard to look at him. It was painful to know Ryder stood so close to her—disappointed in her—unable to like her. Somehow, it actually hurt more now than it had so long ago.

"Thank you, but I already know my hind end is sweet," he said. She glared at him, and he grinned at her with sarcasm. "I like it here. That's why I brought myself back here . . . sweet little hind end and all!" His jaw was tightly clenched, betraying his anger. "I like it here better than any place I've ever been. I just don't like what's happened to you." Again Dusty buried her face in her hands, frustrated that she couldn't stop the tears. "You ain't only hurtin' yourself, Dusty," he mumbled. "You're hurtin' your daddy and Becca—"

"Yes! I know! You've told me and told me and told me!" Dusty interrupted. Somehow, she was instantly able to harden herself—able to stop her tears all at once. "Becca's adored you since she was eight years old, Ryder. You want to spend your time with someone sweet, untouched by disappointment and heartache? Then you spend your time with her! See how she turns out when you leave her!" She watched as he winced at the accusation. She reveled in the knowledge she'd made guilt bite at him.

"You blame me, more than you blame him?" he asked in a low mumble.

Could he truly still believe she'd actually loved Cash? She wanted to scream at him, *I loved you! I loved you, and you left me!* But instead she said, "I don't blame anybody. Just myself. I saw the world all rosy and pink—love, laughter, and sunny days! It's not your fault I was so innocent, is it?"

Ryder rubbed his eyes for a moment and then his whiskery chin. "Nope. It ain't my fault you were so innocent." He looked to her, the brown sugar of his eyes warm and mesmerizing as the light from the lantern flickered in them. "It's my fault you quit bein' innocent."

Dusty didn't argue with him. What was there to say? Call him a liar and prove to be a liar herself? He looked away from her—out at the thin wall of water before them.

"I had to leave, ya know. Your daddy was fallin' into hard times with the ranch, and that's what cowboys do—they go where there's work. I told ya that at the time. You'll never know how many times since then I've wished I wouldn'ta left. How different my life . . . but I had to go. I didn't want to cause a burden on your mama and daddy. And, anyway, I was startin' to . . ." He paused and turned back toward her. His eyes narrowed; his expression was completely sincere. "You were the most adorable thing . . . do you know that?" He grinned slightly. "Funny too. Always findin' yourself in some mess. Sweet as a sugar cookie on Sunday." He sighed heavily and looked away. "And you were fourteen years old." Looking back to her, he emphasized, "Fourteen!" He brushed at the water trickling down from his own wet hair onto his face and exclaimed, "For cryin' in the bucket, Dusty! You were fourteen!"

Dusty thought, *But I would've been fifteen. Then sixteen. I would've been seventeen if you'd waited.*

"I had to leave," he whispered. "Your daddy was havin' trouble a-scroungin' up money to feed his family. He couldn't afford hands. And you were fourteen."

He looked to her, and she knew by his expression he expected understanding—that he wanted her forgiveness somehow. He knew he'd hurt her. Probably he'd known it for the past five years—that he'd broken the heart of a young friend he'd cared for. And for the first time in five years, Dusty admitted to herself just how young fourteen had been. He'd been right to leave. He'd done the right thing—to the very end, the night before he'd left. He'd even tried, in their

175

last moments together, to fulfill her dreams as much as he could when he was already a man—and she was still a child.

"I know," she breathed, closing her eyes against the tears there and finally letting herself remember the night Ryder Maddox had said good-bye to the child that loved him.

Dusty had been crying off and on all day. Her mother was beside herself with concern and compassion for her daughter, and her father had explained several times why the ranch hands had to be let go. Becca cried too. She hated when Dusty was upset, and she knew why Dusty was so upset this time—even if she was only twelve.

Dusty Hunter was fourteen years old, and her world was shattering—or so it seemed to her. The droughts of the past two years had nearly ruined the Hunters' chances of keeping the ranch, and there was no way her father could pay the cowboys and ranch hands. He'd told them all that morning he couldn't keep them on; he could only afford to keep the top hand, Feller.

All day, Dusty had watched the cowboys ready themselves to leave. She'd watched Ryder Maddox—the best of them all, the handsomest of them all, the kindest, bravest, strongest, smartest of them all—watched him readying his saddle and bedroll to leave the next morning. Never again would she lie awake in the early, dark hours of the morning, listening to his low, soothing voice singing as he milked the cows, cleaned the stalls, and did other early-morning chores—other chores he'd volunteered to do because he liked to work in the early morning. Never again would she thrill when he flashed his dazzling smile at her or lifted her onto the fence to watch the men breaking horses or branding cattle. Never again would he cup her face in his rough hand and tell her not to worry about the other girls in town teasing her—tell her she was the prettiest girl in the country and they were just jealous.

That night Dusty sought him out. She'd been watching, waiting for him to leave the fire pit where all the hands were sitting—some lamenting their impending travels, some glad for the freedom. And when at last he did start toward the barn, she followed him—watched him from behind a tree as he entered the barn and some moments later came back out carrying his saddlebags. Then, mustering all the courage she could, she ran to him—scurrying along, trying to match his stride.

"Don't go, Ryder," she begged him in a whisper. "Daddy will keep you on! Mama's so fond of you . . . and Daddy too! You don't need to go!"

"It's time I moved on, Dusty," he'd told her—his voice not quite as deep as it would be someday, his shoulders not nearly as broad. "Gotta always be earnin' my keep."

"Ryder, please," Dusty begged him. Tears started down her face again. She reached out and took hold of his arm, and he stopped—turned to look at her. "Please, find a way to stay here, Ryder. I—I can't bear it if you go!"

The young man frowned and grinned at the same time. He reached out, cupping her face with one rough hand in his familiar manner, stroking her cheek with his thumb. "If you were a few years older, sugar . . . I'd move heaven and earth to find a way to stay 'round your daddy's ranch."

"I love you, Ryder," she confessed with the honesty and ignorance to consequence of a young heart. "Don't leave me."

He winced as if she'd physically struck him. "I have to, Dusty. I-I can't stay here. And anyway," he continued, dropping his hand from her face, "you only think you love me, sugar. Someday when some good-lookin' man comes along and steals your heart, you'll look back and think, 'That ol' Ryder Maddox! What'd I ever see in him?' "

"No," Dusty sobbed through her tears. "I'll never think that."

It was the first taste of the truth of life she remembered—that just because you confess your love for someone, it doesn't mean they confess it back. It doesn't mean they won't ever leave you. Turning from him, she ran as fast as she could. She heard him calling after her—knew he'd chase her. He always went after her when she was upset. Yet darkness was on her side, and she was fast. Darting here and there, she managed to lose him, eventually finding herself at the old well house west of the barn. There she threw herself into the nearby straw pile and sobbed bitterly. For a long time she cried, until she felt too tired to cry anymore and she was able to calm her sobbing.

"There you are, you little cuss," Ryder said, plopping down beside her—panting with the exertion of having hunted her down.

Dusty rolled to her other side in the straw pile, turning from him, too tired to run anymore—not wanting to face him with the shame she felt because of her confession and now her tears.

"I'm all right, Ryder. There's nothing more you need to say to me," she whimpered.

Ryder sat in silence for a few more moments. He took her shoulders and turned her to face him. "You're the prettiest little girl I've ever seen," he told her.

She winced at his words. It hurt her to be reminded of her youth. She'd never forget how handsome he'd been—lying there in the straw under the silver moonlight. Ryder's eyes were the softest, warmest, most enticing shade of brown. His smile was bewitching and somehow made her mouth water for his kiss—even though she'd never been blessed with the feel of it.

"Still, I'm a mite older than you, Dusty," he continued, "in case you hadn't noticed. And I have to leave. I have to leave . . . more because of you than because of your daddy havin' trouble with the ranch. Do ya understand?"

Dusty gazed into his eyes. She saw the sincerity obvious in their golden brown tone. "You're just bein' nice to me, Ryder. Ya don't have to do that." She was so deeply warmed by his concern for her.

"I ain't just bein' nice, Dusty," he said, propping his head up on one hand and letting his other travel from her shoulder down over her arm, finally taking her hand in his. "I love that little wag ya do with your fanny when ya look at me over your shoulder and walk away." Dusty's eyes widened in astonishment at his revelation. "The way ya smile at me and wave from your bed-room window every mornin'. But you're fourteen years old, sugar. Just a baby—and ya put my mind into thinkin' about you . . . and . . . and I shouldn't! Do ya understand what I'm tryin' to say?"

"I'm nearly fifteen, and I wish you wouldn't talk down to me!" she scolded him.

He looked away from her and shook his head. "That's my point, Dusty. If you were older . . .

you'd realize I ain't talkin' down to you. I'm tellin' ya the truth of it. You're a pretty baby. You make me laugh. You're smart, kind. And you're too young for me, Angelina."

Though she didn't say it—couldn't admit it to him—she did know it. He was a man. She was still a child. Though she would eventually grow up, he was much older, ready to live his life. It was wrong to make him feel guilty about anything concerning her. So moving toward him, she pulled her hand from his and wrapped her arms tightly around his neck, hugging him warmly, nestling against him there in the straw. She inhaled deeply the scent of him, swearing to herself she would never forget the way he smelled—the warmth of his body—how firm his muscles were beneath his shirt.

"You're right," she whispered, tears streaming down her face again. "And thank you for treatin' me so well . . . for puttin' up with me, and for . . ." But her words were lost as she felt his arms go around her, returning her embrace. She felt him place a firm kiss to the top of her head, and she thought she might melt in a broth of pure delirium.

"I don't suppose," he mumbled, "that it would hurt for me to give you one little good-bye kiss, now would it?"

As she looked up into his mischievous grin, Dusty's heart swelled with anticipation. She

181

loved his grin—the soft smile that meant Ryder Maddox was up to no good.

"No. It wouldn't hurt," Dusty assured him. She didn't understand—didn't know—the innocence of youth didn't warn her—warn her of how much it would indeed hurt her.

Taking her face between his strong hands, Ryder smiled at her and whispered, "You ever been kissed by a boy before, Miss Angelina?"

"Not yet," she answered, mesmerized by his expression. She realized that, if he did kiss her, she still never would've been kissed . . . by a boy.

Ryder's smile faded quickly as he caressed her lips softly with one thumb. He seemed to change his mind, for he bent toward her and placed a lingering kiss on her forehead. Disappointment washed over Dusty instantly. Yet a moment later, he mumbled something under his breath an instant before he pressed his lips to hers slowly, several times in succession—each time lingering just a little longer. The last time, his lips were slightly parted, and he seemed to be repressing something. Dusty fancied she might actually pass away from the intense delirium his kiss bathed her in. She'd never imagined—and she'd imagined a lot— never imagined that when he kissed her, it would be so perfect—so heavenly—so addicting! Dusty clutched Ryder's wrists as he kissed her once more. He held her face for a moment, gazing at her with obvious regret.

"I do love you, ya know. You are the most delicious thing on earth to me," he whispered, kissing her hard and quick—before yanking his wrists free of her grasp, rising to his feet, and walking away into the night.

Dusty buried her face in her hands and sobbed for a long time—sobbed until she heard her mother calling for her. She returned to the house to discover Ryder Maddox had ridden away into the night. He didn't wait until morning to leave like the other hands. Ryder Maddox was gone.

"I know," Dusty admitted again to the infinitely handsome man who stood beneath the waterfall with her. The expression of deep guilt was mingled with the brown sugar of his eyes. Ryder had done the only thing he could do—ridden away to look for work, letting the little girl who had touched his heart grow up for some other man to have.

Ryder breathed a heavy sigh. It was the breath of relief—the breath a soul exhales when someone they've wronged finally forgives them. He leaned back against the rock wall behind them.

"You know," he chuckled, "I used to wonder what you'd look like all grown up."

Dusty herself was feeling something besides

resentment finally, and though she still wanted to lose herself in bitter sobbing over the loss of such a wonderful dream so many years ago, she smiled back at him. "Am I what ya thought?"

"No," he answered. The familiar grin of mischief toyed at the corners of his mouth. Dusty felt the flutter in her heart at his familiar, beloved expression and fought wildly to suppress it.

"No?" she repeated. "What did you think I'd look like?"

"I don't know. I thought you'd look exactly the same . . . only in long skirts."

"And I don't?" she asked—for now she was curious. How did she appear to him?

"No." His grin broadened then. "But I'd be willin' to bet you don't need no handkerchiefs to fill out your dress now."

Dusty smiled for a moment—almost giggled. Yet melancholy triumphed again. "No. I don't use my daddy's hankies anymore." Then, in an attempt to lighten her own mood, she confessed, "I wondered what became of you. Did life treat ya well after ya left?" She didn't tell him she had wondered over him nearly every moment of her life.

Ryder's smile quickly faded, and she wished she hadn't asked—even though it seemed a natural enough question to ask in light of the conversation.

"Well enough. I worked hard and . . . got what I deserved, I suppose."

Dusty frowned. Had he been unhappy—as unhappy as she had been?

He tipped his head and studied her. "Now," he began, "how am I gonna get you to quit this fist thing ya always do?" Dusty looked down to see that indeed her hands were clenched tightly once again. "Though two more as tight as yours mighta helped me out today in town."

"Thank you for that, by the way," Dusty mumbled, ashamed. "I . . . I meant to say that before. I just . . ." She startled when he reached out and took her fists in his strong hands. She tried to pull away, but he held fast. "I . . . I can't help it. I didn't even know I . . ." she stammered.

The grin of naughtiness and the twinkle in his eyes alerted her to his mischief. "Ya know . . . I always wanted to come back . . . find ya all grown up . . . and kiss ya right," he confessed unexpectedly.

"Ryder . . . I don't have hard feelings toward you," she told him, thinking he still didn't feel forgiven somehow. "You don't have to try to heal me. I know it's me. It's not you or Cash or anyone else. Ya don't have to—"

"Oh, don't get me wrong, Miss Britches," he whispered. "I owned a lot of guilt where you're concerned . . . but I'm just talkin' lighthearted to ya now. I always did want to kiss you again when it was more . . . proper. What do ya say? For old times' sake? To close the book on all those years ago?"

Dusty stepped back from him, yet he held her fists tightly. Her heart hammered within her bosom. She couldn't! She couldn't kiss him. She'd die if she did—drop dead right there behind the waterfall, if not from a broken heart that never mended, then from pure ecstasy! "I don't think here . . . with me half-dressed and you . . ."

"Let me kiss you, Dusty," he mumbled. "For old times' sake. Just once . . . to close that ol' creakin' door and heal the wounds. All right?" His voice had a dreamy, low, provocative tone.

Dusty shook her head—felt the warm moisture welling in her eyes. She couldn't! She couldn't endure the pain of it, the longing, the hurt it would leave.

"We used to be friends, me and you. Old friends . . . that's what we are. Old friends that left scars on each other. Let me kiss you . . . and not good-bye this time. Just . . . I'm sorry, old friend."

He stroked her cheek softly with the back of his hand. He took her face between his hands, caressing her lip softly with his thumb. Immediately Dusty's heart ached with longing, loss, hurt, fear. Her hands went to his wrists as she tried to pull away. "Ryder, please," she begged him, a tear trickling down her face. "I can't let . . ."

"Let me close it, Dusty," he whispered. "We both need that."

But I don't want you to close it, she thought. She watched, completely unable to move as he moistened his lips with his tongue. He moved his body closer to hers. Her hands reached out, pushing gently at his chest to keep him at bay a moment longer. She could still taste his kiss—still smell the scent of him from all those years ago. After so long, she still could feel his arms around her, feel how badly it had hurt to lose him—to never have had him.

"Ryder," Dusty whispered. She would beg him next—beg him to stop. Yet with every fiber of her body and soul, she wanted him to kiss her—wanted to be held in his arms, kissed, even ravaged by him! She wanted that fourteen-year-old girl who had lost her heart so long ago to suddenly grow up into a woman and be able to win her cowboy.

"I'm sorry, Dusty," he whispered softly. "I never wanted to hurt you." His lips touched hers tentatively. She couldn't breathe! She thought she'd die for want of being able to embrace him—hold him—taste his kiss again. "I never, never, never wanted to hurt that little girl," he added.

"I know," she whispered.

His mouth was fully on her own—warm, moist, lingering, and much, much more firmly than it had been five years before. With each successive kiss, his mouth endeavored to coax her into joining him—into participating in the delirious physical dialogue. Dusty felt her hands relax and move down to his waist. He broke from her for a moment—a roguish twinkle in his eye as he whispered, "Maybe that little girl never did grow up."

It was a challenge, and it upset Dusty—caused her hands to fist once more. Only this time, they fisted at the waist of his blue jeans—clutching the fabric of his pants in her palms—and she reflexively tugged on his clothing, causing him to stumble and bump her back against the rock behind her.

"Did she?" he whispered, letting one hand leave her face and go to her waist, pulling her body flush with his own.

"Yes," she affirmed, and this time when his lips parted against her own, she tried to breathe calmly—let her mind float away in the dream.

Dusty endeavored to let Ryder kiss her, even attempted to return his kiss, though the trembling wracking her entire body made it difficult to do so. As his arms tightened around her, pulling her against him—as his kiss coaxed her and his mouth toyed with hers—she felt her body relax against his. Soon his proficient, demanding kiss rained the warmth of passion over her completely, beginning to rinse away so many years of hardness or heartlessness. It was as if she stood beneath the waterfall, its liquid elements having been changed to that of a warm, sweet drink. As the kisses between them intensified, his hands left her body, going to where hers still clutched the waist of his pants. Still intent on kissing her, he took her hands in his, pressing them against his chest until they relaxed. Placing his arms around her waist, he pulled her to him.

His kiss was entirely beguiling—powerful, irresistible, and fantastically passionate! The sure knowledge, *I was too young!* traveled quickly through Dusty's mind. Fourteen! Never would she have understood a man at that young age. Never could she have been a woman for a man while still a child.

Then, as if an evil entity had entered their hidden escape, she thought of how she had never allowed Cash to kiss her like this. Never had she wanted him to. And the moment was lost to her— for heartache, loss, and betrayal had reentered her thoughts. She pulled her face from Ryder's, putting a hand to her mouth to keep from returning to him.

"Please, don't," she whispered. "Ryder, please."

He frowned down at her—brushed a lock of hair from her cheek.

"You did grow up, didn't you?" he mumbled. "And you got all the weight of experience on your shoulders that goes along with it, don't you?" Sighing heavily, he took her fisted hands in his once more and forced them open. "Thank you, Dusty," he mumbled. "I needed to be forgiven." He took a step back from her and added, "And you need to forgive. You'll never get beyond it if ya don't." Raising her hands, he kissed each upturned palm. "You know . . . you were the sweetest thing on earth to me." Then he turned from her—and in a moment was gone.

Immediately, Dusty's hands went to her face in an effort to cool the blush born of passion blazing radiant on her cheeks. Her mind whirled, her heart beat frantically, and her arms and legs were so atingle they felt numb. What had she done? In forgiving him—in letting him kiss her—she had cursed her soul to endless, eternal heartache! His kiss had confirmed what she had already known: she would love him forever! She could never go on and lead a normal life now. Not ever! Not without him.

Hours later, Dusty returned to the house, wet, wrung out, and defeated. As she tried to slip into her room quietly, Becca stepped into the hallway.

"Are you all right?" her sweet, concerned sister asked in a whisper.

"I'm fine," Dusty lied.

"Do . . . do you need anything?" Becca ventured. "Do you need to talk?"

"No," Dusty told her, closing her bedroom door behind her. She didn't need to talk. She needed to love—to love and be loved. Yet that need would never be fulfilled—because the only man who could fulfill it wouldn't. She slept hard and awoke feeling more tired than she had before.

Chapter Seven

Dusty was quiet for days, hardly saying a word to anyone, even when spoken to. She answered questions in short, quiet responses. Yet the spirit of resentment and hardness about her had begun to dissipate somewhat. For that reason, Becca decided not to push her sister to talk. Becca sensed something about Dusty had changed—for the better. It was so hard not to ask what had happened with Ryder the night Dusty had come home so late—especially when Becca knew her sister had been with Ryder. She'd seen Ryder come home sometime before Dusty, completely drenched from the waist up. She had seen Dusty come home drenched from head to toe, and she knew Dusty's favorite private escape was the old waterfall. It didn't take a genius to put two and two together. Furthermore, there was the change in Dusty's countenance. Healing had begun— Becca was certain of it. While it delighted her to near elation, Becca's own affairs of the heart, or lack thereof, tainted her happiness in her sister's healing.

Becca stepped up onto the bottom rung of the hog fence and poured the contents of the slop bucket into the trough. She thought of her own heartache—her own very deep heartache. It seemed to Becca her own heartache was even more impossible to heal than Dusty's, though she was certain her big sister would disagree whole-heartedly.

Suddenly, the top rung of the fence against which Becca leaned began to give way, the crackling sound of splitting wood reaching Becca's ears the next moment. Dropping the bucket into the mess of mud and manure in the pen, Becca grabbed at the fencepost, hoping to stop herself from following the bucket into the mess. Yet her feet were so firmly rooted on the bottom fence rung—her knees locked against the next rung up—that she couldn't get a good grip. A split second before she would have gone toppling forward and into another round of bathing with the hogs, she felt someone pull on the back of her skirts. Falling backward, Becca Hunter found herself cradled in the arms of Feller Lance.

"You're just bound and determined to waller around with them hogs, ain't ya?" he grouched at her, though his smile revealed her predicament amused him. Becca was stunned at his rescuing her. He was holding her in just the same manner as he had many years before, when he'd carried her home at age twelve after she'd banged herself up falling out of an apple tree. Becca couldn't speak, rendered silent by surprise—and delight.

In a moment her wits were about her again,

however, and Becca explained, "You said to feed 'em over the fence! Last time I fell in, you laughed at me and asked why I never fed them over the fence. So I was feedin' them over the fence."

Feller chuckled and let Becca's feet fall to the ground. As she stood, blushing furiously and straightening her skirts, he told her, "I said feed 'em over the fence, girl. Not on the fence."

"Well, maybe you should just build a better fence next time," Becca scolded, still blushing. She hated the way she blushed so easily in front of Feller.

"Maybe I should," he surrendered with a handsome and alluring smile.

Becca straightened her back and walked away. *Oh, how wonderful Feller was! How fantastically perfect,* she thought as she walked back to the house. But her heart sank to the pit of her stomach in the next moment. How fantastically perfect—and how completely out of reach of a young, silly girl like herself.

Dusty shook her head and smiled as she watched Becca walking back toward the house. She'd seen Becca almost plunge headfirst into the hog pen again. If it hadn't been for Feller, she would've been covered in pig manure. Picking up the bowl of strawberry stems, Dusty left the house by way of the kitchen door and headed out toward the garden. She sloshed the stems out of the tub and into a pile her daddy or one of the hands would turn under for next year's garden spot and then turned and hurried back toward the house. There were still the supper dishes left in the sink. When she looked up to see Ryder striding toward her, she began to tremble.

Dusty's heart had begun to change that night under the waterfall. She'd done a lot of soul-searching once Ryder had left her with the taste of his kiss still burning on her lips. The things Becca and her father had said to her came to mind often, but it was Ryder who had given her more to think about. Silently, she could admit to feeling less hateful—more compassionate and concerned about others. It seemed to her the change had begun after her conversation with Ryder. Had the hard to hear yet kindhearted things said to her by Ryder and everyone else begun the change? Or had it simply been Ryder—his words, his admissions, his kiss—that had changed her? She wasn't certain. She *did* know that since meeting him behind the waterfall, she had not talked with him. With the exception of casual conversation with others present during meals, she had not spoken to him. Now he strode toward her intent, it seemed—intent on something.

"Berries, huh," Ryder stated as he looked at the empty tub.

"Pies for supper tomorrow," she told him. It was light, trivial conversation. Still, at least she hadn't snapped at him, scowling like she'd done before.

" 'Member how much time me and you used to spend talkin'?" he asked, reaching down and yanking a foxtail out of the ground. He put it between his teeth and began to chew on it a little. Dusty nodded but remained silent. "Near to every night after supper we'd sit out there by the pit with your mama and daddy and the other hands and talk about . . . whatever there was to talk about." Still she was quiet and looked away when he looked to her for response. "You ever spend much time talkin' anymore?" Without waiting for an answer, he added, "You used to talk the hind leg off a horse." He smiled. "Sometimes I wondered how ya didn't pass out cold . . . 'cause ya hardly ever stopped for a breath. Remember?"

"Yes," she admitted. "I rambled on for days at a time. I really did." She smiled and laughed a little. "How'd ya ever tolerate me?"

He chuckled. "But it was always so interestin' . . . whatever you were goin' on about."

"I'm sure it wasn't!" she argued. "You were just nicer than everybody else and tolerated me more."

He grinned down at her, still chewing on the foxtail stem. "Bet it was hard on your daddy when your mama died," he sighed. He turned and began walking toward the house.

Dusty fell into step behind him. She nodded.

"I really wondered if he'd make it without

followin' close behind her. I couldn't believe how lost he was. Mama was everything to him."

"Yep. I remember how he doted on her. Course, she couldn'ta been everything. He had you and Becca. That probably kept him goin', I'd imagine." Ryder looked up into the sky. He frowned and mumbled, "She was a wonderful woman."

Their conversation was light—nothing intimate about it. It was conversation he'd made with her because somehow he'd found himself talking to her. Still, she wasn't ready to leave him, and when they reached the back porch, she sat down instead of entering the house. She hoped he would join her—and he did. His voice was soothing, comforting. She remembered so many nights spent in conversation around the fire. They had been wonderful, some of her warmest, fondest memories.

"Did ya ever find your aunt?" Dusty asked him. She'd suddenly remembered his having an aunt somewhere—that he'd spoken of trying to find her. "The one ya lost track of?"

Ryder's parents had died of the fever when he was thirteen. That's how he'd started cowboying —out of necessity for survival. He didn't have any brothers or sisters, and the only family he had known was an aunt.

"My Aunt Milly?" he asked. "Oh, yeah! I tracked her down right after I left here. Found her over in Flagstaff, Arizona . . . if you can believe it. She died about a year back." He was pensive for a moment and mumbled, "She was a good ol' gal. I really miss her."

Dusty felt suddenly empty herself—sad for him and horribly lonely. How odd it must be not to have any family. How terrible! She felt rather depressed in the moment, wishing she were still that Dusty Hunter from years ago—the Dusty Hunter who would've hugged him with reassurance. Instead, she clutched her hands together in her lap and stared out at the horizon.

The silence hung too heavy in the air between them, and Ryder finally said, "Well, I guess you'll wanna be gettin' in to finish up."

Dusty craved his attention, and desperation drove her to keep their conversation going—by any means she could think of. She was nearly as surprised as Ryder looked when she blurted out, "What did that drifter say about the family that made you light into him?"

"What?" Ryder asked. His expression was of utter confusion—and well it should've been, for he had no way of knowing what memories she'd been dwelling on of late.

"That time ya beat the sauce out of—what was his name?—Larry. Larry Williams. Remember? You beat him up, and Daddy sent him packin'?"

"Oh, yeah!" he chuckled. "Where the heck did that come from?"

Dusty shrugged. "I don't know. I was just thinkin' about it the other day. Mama and Daddy never would tell us girls what it was all about. All I knew was it had to be bad for Daddy to let *you* stay after brawlin' and yet send him away."

"It was bad," Ryder mumbled. He covered his mouth as a yawn overtook him. "That boy was a snake in the grass, I'll tell ya that."

"What did he say?" Dusty sensed he was avoiding giving her an answer. He'd avoided giving difficult answers all the time when she was younger. He was always leery of telling her things he wasn't sure she should know. Yet when she was younger, she wouldn't let him squirm away without an answer—and she surely wouldn't now. "Tell me. You do remember?"

"Well, yeah," he confessed, shifting his broad shoulders. He seemed unsettled. "But I don't know if I should . . ."

"Oh, come on. Tell me."

Ryder looked at Dusty—seemed to study her for a long moment. It was obvious he didn't want to tell her—that whatever Larry Williams had said made him uncomfortable. Still, as he ever had in the past whenever Dusty pressed him, he relented. "He said . . . he told some of the other hands that . . . that . . ."

"That . . ." she prodded.

"That your mama was a-hankerin' after me . . . if you want the ugly truth of it."

Dusty's mouth gaped open in astonishment. "What?"

Ryder sighed and shifted, his discomfort obvious. "He was sayin' she treated me different than the other hands . . . that I was her favorite. And—and he was tellin' the other boys that she wanted to . . . to . . . that she had a hankerin' for me but that I wasn't interested in the mama for bein' hot after her little girl." He grimaced and nearly whined, "For Pete's sake, what does it matter now, Dusty?"

"You gotta be lyin' to me!" Dusty exclaimed. She was oddly delighted—as if some lewd secret had just been revealed to her. In truth, it had! Someone had noticed her mother's favoritism toward Ryder and his toward herself? "Why would he say somethin' like that?"

"Your mama sorta took me under her wing. I guess that ol' boy didn't like it. I'll tell you what," he continued, "if Feller hadn't been in town that day, I wouldn'ta been the only one to whup up on that idiot! And I know your daddy would just as soon a shot him than let him go. As far as the other goes . . ." He looked at her and lowered his voice. "If nothin' else . . . he was too right on where my feelin's about you were concerned for me to let it go. You know what I'm sayin'?"

Dusty looked away from him for a moment, embarrassed somehow. Yet the fact someone would accuse her mother of anything wrong tweaked her temper. "You *earned* your place as

Mama's favorite," Dusty told him. "You worked hard. And you were always the one who helped her out with things, regardless of the fact you were keeping me out of trouble all the time."

"That ol' boy was a weasel," he mumbled. "I woulda like to have beat on him a little longer, but your daddy came upon it and made me stop." He shook his head and chuckled. "Boy! Did I have a temper back then or what?"

"Yeah," Dusty giggled. "Mama used to worry you'd get your head beat in one day."

Dusty looked to Ryder when he didn't respond. He was staring out at the horizon. She could tell by the look on his face that something she'd said had bothered him profoundly. He seemed to shake it off after a few moments, however, and turned back to her.

"Your mama was a wise woman," he said with meaning—though Dusty couldn't quite understand what the meaning was. "She treated me like her own boy. She treated all of us hands like her own boys. Never worked for another rancher with a wife like that." He smiled at her as he stood. "Well, I'm anxious for them pies tomorrow. You make 'em as good as your mama ever did."

"Thank you," she said, standing and smiling at him.

He winked at her, delighting her completely. She watched him saunter away, rubbing one shoulder as he went. She wanted to run after him—beg him to stay with her—but no sooner had he disappeared around the side of the house than Becca appeared at Dusty's side.

"That was the most pitiful excuse for a conversation I ever heard, Dusty Hunter!" she scolded. "Couldn't you at least make him think you were interested in talkin' with him?"

"Eavesdroppin' is a sin, Becca!" Dusty spat at her. "Go find somethin' to do. It's late." She started to walk away.

"Be my sister again, Dusty," Becca pleaded in a whisper. "Please! I need you! I need someone to talk to! I . . . I'm so lonely all the time. I have so much I wanna say to somebody. I . . ."

A longing—a regret so intense she felt she might suddenly fly apart—washed over Dusty. Turning quickly to Becca, she took hold of her hands, pulling her down to sit next to her on the porch steps. "Help me, Becca! I don't know where I am. I don't know which way to turn or what to say! I don't know how to be a sister anymore."

Becca's eyes filled with tears. "I'm startin' to feel that way too . . . like I'm losing me, Dusty. I can't hardly hang on anymore."

"So," Dusty whispered, "where do we go from here?"

Becca smiled and brushed tears from her eyes. "Where we used to go when we knew ourselves and shared secrets we didn't speak to anybody else."

●●●

Sitting across from Becca, Dusty gazed at her beautiful little sister. What fun they'd had there as children! What secrets they'd shared! What days of make-believe and joy! Now, though Becca didn't know it, this place held even more magic for Dusty. This was the place where she and Ryder had begun making their peace with the past. As Dusty and Becca sat in the hidden alcove, the cool water cascaded over the falls, creating a tranquil peace as only Mother Nature could create in the evening.

"Pretend it all never happened, Dusty," Becca said. Her voice was soft and soothing. "Pretend you were never burned by Cash's low character . . . that you never even considered him. Pretend Ryder never left and that Mama is still alive."

"Pretend that I'm still the me I used to be, Becca," Dusty whispered.

It was a game they used to play as children. *Pretend I'm a princess and you are too. Pretend the alcove is our castle.* It had been different so long ago. Dusty knew Becca knew it had been different too. Still, Dusty also knew she needed to heal, and sometimes going back to the beginning helped a person to sort things out. Maybe it would help her find the Dusty who had been lost along the way. "Pretend you can tell me anything, and I can tell you anything, and everything in life is as beautiful and as sweet as Christmas."

Becca paused for a moment—bit her lip as if considering whether she could say any more. Then quietly she spoke, "Pretend that I'm in love, Dusty." Dusty felt her heart begin to ache for her sister—for something in her knew Becca was not pretending but spoke the truth. "Not in love like—like a crush . . . really in love. I've been in love for a long time . . . and I've had to hide it away."

"With who?" Dusty asked in a whisper.

"Pretend I'm not ready to tell ya who yet. But I *am* in love," Becca admitted, tears filling her eyes. "But pretend you're able to tell me anything. Do you love someone, Dusty?"

Dusty paused. She nearly began to build up the internal stone wall—the one preventing anyone from getting too close to her. Yet would she go forward instead, try to find herself again—the self she and everyone else had been happy to know? Or would she remain a selfish, hurt, emotional hermit heaping discomfort and pain on everyone around her? In an instant, she'd made her decision, the decision that had to be made—the right decision.

"Yes," Dusty cried in a whisper. Tears burst from her eyes, and she buried her face in her hands for a moment. Sniffling hard, she looked back to Becca, tears streaming down her face as well. Still, it was all she could confess.

"I have dreams, ya know," Becca offered. She

closed her eyes for a moment, tears trickling over her lovely cheeks like tiny rivulets of emotion. "Someday, he'll walk up to me, take me in his arms, and tell me that he loves me . . . that he can't live another day without me. He'll kiss me, and his kiss will be the most wonderful thing in the world! And then . . . then I'll be able to kiss him whenever I want to . . . to be held by him, talk with him, laugh with him, and—"

"You will," Dusty told her softly. "Does . . . does he love you yet?"

Becca sobbed for a moment, trying to do so quietly. She simply shook her head. "No. No, he . . . he doesn't even notice me."

"That can't be true, Becca," Dusty argued. "He has to notice you. Everyone notices you."

"He notices me, I'm sure . . . whenever I do something silly. But not—not like I notice him."

"But, Becca—" Dusty began.

"It's Ryder you love, Dusty," Becca interrupted. "It's always been Ryder."

Dusty knew Becca did not want to dwell on her own pain anymore. Here was the test. Could she confide in her sister the way she used to? Could she find the courage and the humility to do so?

"I do love him, Becca," she answered in a sobbing whisper. Still, when she saw the delight and hope in Becca's eyes, she hurried on. "But only wait. He . . . he doesn't like who I've become. He . . . I think he's lived a lot of life since he left here and . . . and . . ."

"Has he spoken to you about . . . about when he left before? Does he know how much it hurt you?" Becca interrupted.

Dusty nodded. "Oh, he knows. He feels, or at least felt, a heavy guilt about it. But . . . but I never stopped loving him, Becca!"

"I know," Becca said, tears still streaming down her face. "I never understood why you accepted Cash when you had never given up Ryder in your heart."

"What else could I have done? I knew Ryder could never come back . . . though I watched for him every day. Every time I watched a new cowboy ride in each fall or spring, I prayed it would be Ryder."

"Why did ya stop?" Becca cried out.

"I . . . I don't know exactly," Dusty admitted. "I used to dream he'd come riding in . . . arrive just as Cash and I were exchangin' vows and carry me off into the sunset. I don't think I ever stopped watchin' for him . . . prayin' he would come back someday, wishin' he would remember me as more than a little girl he once owned affection for a long time ago."

Becca smiled through her tears. Reaching out, she took Dusty's hands in her own. "But don't ya see, Dusty?" she whispered. "He did come back."

"But I gave up, Becca. The day I found Cash

with that girl," Dusty confessed, only just realizing it herself. "I gave up that day—on Ryder, on love, on dreams. That was my heartbreak . . . givin' up the dream of Ryder." She sighed, looking through the waterfall and into the sky. "I still caught myself lookin' to the horizon most days . . . more out of habit than anything else. And I realized . . . I didn't really care that I wasn't marryin' Cash. I had never really wanted to in the first place. I just kept thinkin' my dreams would actually come true."

"But he's back now," Becca reminded her. "He's back. He's still not married, and he's here!"

"And he's beautiful, and he's still a dream," Dusty told her. "He would never want what I've become."

"He wants you," Becca assured her. "He would never have come back here if he didn't. Think about it. You're still you, Dusty! The part of you that makes ya you is still there inside! This hard, ol', crusty shell will melt away easily enough if you let it. You can have him. I know ya can!"

Dusty glanced around the alcove—at the warm sun shining through the water and lighting the shadows for them. "He kissed me here, ya know," she whispered.

Becca gasped. "When?"

"The day of the fight in town. He said he was sorry for breakin' my heart all those years ago . . . and he kissed me. He said we needed to close that old book. He ended it. He doesn't want me, Becca. He needed to know he could be forgiven for somethin' he shouldn't even feel guilty about."

Becca was silent for a moment before commenting, "He closed that old book, Dusty. What about the new one? Do ya really think he'd be here now if there wasn't a first page to a new book?"

Dusty smiled. Reaching out, she cupped Becca's face lovingly in her hand. "Who's this man who's stolen your heart, Becca?"

Becca's eyes were filled with moisture again. "A wonderful man who deserves as much happiness as life can bring. A wonderful man who I've loved as long as I can remember . . . just like you." Dusty knew Becca didn't want to say his name—knew she was frightened that in saying the name of the man she loved, he might be lost to her forever somehow. "Remember who I've always loved, Dusty?"

There had to be no more than that. With a smile and a nod of encouragement, Dusty leaned back against the alcove wall. "Let's listen to the water, Becca," she whispered. "Can ya hear that . . . the locust in the trees . . . and the calves a-bawlin' in the corral?"

Becca closed her eyes and leaned back against the wall too. "I can."

In three weeks time, the fourth day of July dawned bright, hot, and filled with excitement. Becca had been buzzing around in a bee-frenzy for two days prior to its arrival. A glimmer of the excitement even spilled over onto Dusty—something akin to the way she used to feel in years so long gone by.

In the days since Ryder had made his peace with her, in the days since she'd opened the door to healing her relationship with her sister, Dusty had changed. Not completely, for she still battled fear. The ever-present fear of heartache and disappointment still wound itself around her heart. Yet she had begun to change. She found herself smiling during the course of any given day—found herself viewing Becca in a more understanding and sympathetic light. Dusty now saw Becca as an ally—someone who was frightened and hurt herself instead of the naive, innocent, perpetually blissful antagonist she'd come to think her to be.

As for Ryder—Dusty's heart hammered all the more whenever he was near. Her body tingled at the brush of his arm or the sight of his mischievous grin. Now she had something else to motivate her: hope. Becca's assurances the night at the waterfall had spurred her on—as did the memory of Ryder's kiss. Surely a man could not kiss a woman in such a manner if he did not feel something besides mere friendship toward her.

And there it began. In the days leading up to the picnic, the smallest, tiniest pearl of hope bloomed in Dusty Hunter's soul. Perhaps—just maybe—if she could find the self she lost so long ago, maybe Ryder would . . . it was only a maybe. Still, it was enough to give her cause to want to try. So she had. She had tried. In trying, she found that indeed it was easier to be kind than continually cross—that a smile did feel better on her face than a frown—that having Ryder there, whether his heart belonged to her or not, was better than when he had not been there. So it was Dusty found herself looking forward to the picnic instead of dreading it.

Becca was near to exploding with excitement. Sitting between Dusty and her father on the buckboard, she reached over and squeezed Dusty's arm. "I love the Fourth picnic!" she squealed. "All day long, from mornin' 'til midnight! I love it!"

Dusty, for all her trying to remain calm in appearance, couldn't help but smile. She'd been infected with a bit of Becca's contagious delirium. After all, she had always loved the Fourth of July picnic too. Everyone left their ranches and farms and shops in town, even all the hands and cowboys about. Everyone headed out to old man Leroy's enormous, ancient barn. Abandoned but in good repair, it stood in the middle of what was once a cornfield. Old man Leroy was too old to farm anymore. Both his sons had been killed in the war, and he'd sold off some of his land to another farmer. Yet the house, most of the pastures and fields, and the old barn were still his. Ancient trees extended quite a ways out from the north side of the barn, providing shade so desperately needed for the elderly folks and babies during the heat of the summer day.

Everyone in the county attended, bringing ham, chickens, turkey, beef, pies, cakes and cookies, butter and breads, potatoes, and greens—all manner of delicious food. There were tables and tables laden with good things to eat, stretching out the entire length of the barn. The barn itself was always decorated with pretty paper ribbons. Lanterns were hung here and there or set about in order to provide light for the dancing, which would begin in the early evening and continue until the fireworks were ignited in the field at about ten o'clock. It was indeed the most wonderful day spent outside all year long! Dusty felt the warm bubble of excitement well up in her bosom—threaten to burst from her and win over her indifference of the past few years.

She glanced over her shoulder. Feller and Ryder rode side by side, followed by the other ranch hands. Ryder winked at her and smiled. She turned away quickly, angry at the heated blush rising to her cheeks.

It had been during the Fourth of July picnic five years ago—the day Ryder had saved her reputation by asking for the hanky peeking out of the bodice of her dress. Still, she smiled at the memory—wondered if he too were thinking about that incident.

Becca glanced back at the riders for a moment as well. She leaned over to Dusty and whispered, "Doesn't Feller look just adorable today?"

Dusty couldn't help but smile. She quirked an eyebrow and asked, "Adorable?" She'd never imagined Feller Lance as being *adorable*. Still, it was true. Oftentimes—now that she contemplated it—Feller could indeed appear adorable.

"Adorable!" Becca repeated with excitement.

Dusty sighed, relieved to be leaving the ranch and responsibility behind for a day. Today she would try—truly make the grandest effort ever to enjoy herself—to fend off the feelings of annoyance and hatred that usually were her safeguard. Today she would try again to be the Dusty Hunter she was born to be.

Hank Hunter tied the team to a post under one of the big trees and helped Becca and Dusty down. The ranch hands chuckled and mumbled with rare excitement as they too secured their horses. Dusty realized just how thoroughly everyone needed a break from the arduous labor of the ranch.

"Come on, girls," Hank Hunter chuckled. He crooked both his arms, inviting his daughters to be escorted. "I can smell Miss Raynetta's rhubarb pie from here!"

They fell into step behind the ranch hands all

shined up in their best blue jeans and cleanest shirts. Dusty gasped quietly when she realized she was intently watching Ryder's saunter in front of her. Alice's words about his pants fitting nicely echoed through her mind, and she knew her cheeks were rosy. She heard Becca giggle and looked to see her sister bite her lip with understanding. She raised her eyebrows in delighted approval. Dusty shook her head to cool her blush, smiling as her attention was drawn to the eccentric woman walking toward them—her own familiar little wiggle and brilliant purple dress further endearing Miss Raynetta to anyone already admiring her.

"You look like somethin' that just walked out of a fairy tale, Miss Raynetta," Ryder greeted.

Miss Raynetta stopped, placing her hands on her hips. She tipped her head to one side, smiled, and offered him a flirtatious wink in return. "You'll go places with talk like that, Ryder," she said. Reaching out, she took hold of his shirt collar and pulled him toward her, placing her cheek to his for a moment in thanks for the compliment. In the next moment, her attention turned to Dusty. "I love it! I love it, I love it! I told ya it would become ya, didn't I now?" she chimed, taking Dusty's hands in her own and studying the dress she'd made—and the girl in it. "And you're wearin' your hair down these days," she commented. Leaning toward Dusty, she whispered in her ear, "Men like it when they can get to your hair and run their fingers through it."

"Miss Raynetta," Dusty scolded.

Turning her attention to Becca, Raynetta exclaimed, "And look at you! I never saw cream butter as soft as that yella!" She sighed, dramatically placing a hand to her bosom. "Only other woman that could wear that soft yella was your mama, child!" She looked to Hank, and Dusty was sure her voice broke with restrained emotion as she said, "Beautiful girls, Hank! Just beautiful!"

"Yes, ma'am," Hank agreed, releasing his girls and offering his arm to Miss Raynetta.

Dusty was pleased with the woman's reaction to her father's offer of escort. Miss Raynetta blushed. She put her hand to her own cheek with obvious delight a moment before placing one small hand in the crook of Hank's arm.

"I'm hopin' for that rhubarb pie of yours, Miss Raynetta," Hank chuckled.

"I only brung three this year, Hank . . . so ya better be quick about it," Miss Raynetta giggled.

"Becca! Dusty!"

Maudie Phillips was quickly approaching, and Dusty sighed. "Oh, help us all," she mumbled.

Jabbing an elbow at her rib cage, Becca whispered, "Hush, Dusty! She'll be gone soon enough. She just has to act like she's glad to see us so she can move on."

"You look like two angels a-standin' there,"

Maudie chirped as she approached. Dusty recognized the all too familiar syrupy tone in her voice—a tone that really meant, *I can't abide it when someone might look good enough to take any man's attention away from me!*

"And blue has always been your best color," Dusty said, forcing a smile. It was an honest compliment. Blue had always looked good on Maudie—dang it all!

"Well, with that Ryder Maddox back workin' for your daddy," Maudie began, dropping her voice, "I'm determined to catch his eye today!"

"Well, that blue should do it," Becca said. Smiling, she took hold of Dusty's hand, pulling her in the direction of the tables.

"Have fun, girls," Maudie called after them. Dusty frowned as she watched Maudie toss her golden locks as she turned.

"She makes me wanta smash her face in a cowpie!" Becca growled.

It was then Dusty remembered that, for the past several years, Maudie had been sweet on Feller Lance. Maudie followed him around mercilessly at every town social there was. Dusty figured Becca's irritation with Maudie was more in regard to Feller than to the fact she'd revealed she'd set her sights on Ryder.

As they approached the crowd gathered outside the barn and around the tables, old Leroy swaggered toward them.

"My, my, my," he mumbled through his gums—he only had six teeth left in his head. "If you Hunter girls ain't just about ripe for the pickin's!"

"Mr. Leroy," Dusty greeted. She was determined to overlook the rather inappropriate comment. It could be construed as lewd—if it hadn't been for the fact Mr. Leroy had been known as a man without tact for over fifty years. "Thank you for having us out."

"My pleasure, girls!" He winked at Becca and then hollered, "Hank!" Old Leroy offered his hand to Hank in greeting. "I was just tellin' your girls here . . ."

Becca and Dusty took the opportunity to escape the sweet old man's ramblings. With old Leroy involved in conversation with their father, they were quickly off in search of other entertainment.

"Lookie there, Dusty!" Becca exclaimed. She nodded toward a large oak tree nearby. A group of women were gathered beneath it. "They're quiltin' under the big tree. Who's it for? Have you heard?"

Dusty shook her head. She hadn't heard of anyone in town announcing a marriage. Usually a bee under the big oaks at the Fourth picnic was held to quilt for a young bride-to-be.

"Oh my heck!" Becca exclaimed, nodding in another direction. "Look at that! Maudie's all over Ryder . . . just like butter on bread! How can you stand there and let her go on, Dusty?"

"What can I do?" Dusty asked. What right did she have to be jealous? What could she do to acquire Ryder's attention—without looking as silly as Maudie did hovering over him like a fly to maple syrup?

"You can go over there and join in the conversation for one!" Becca told her, irritated at her sister's lack of fighting spirit. "He'll turn to you in a second! And probably be forever in your debt for savin' him from a fate worse than death . . . that being Miss Maudie Phillips!"

Dusty was silent. All she could do was watch Maudie flirting with Ryder—feel helpless, frightened, and angry enough to claw the girl's eyes out.

It was Cash who interrupted her thoughts.

"Excuse me . . . Dusty?" he asked.

Dusty turned to find Cash standing just behind her. He owned the same demeanor as a whipped dog. She sighed, recognizing his expression at once. It was the, *I'm so humble in asking your forgiveness* look in his eyes.

"Cash . . . go soak your head," Becca told him.

"Becca," Dusty scolded.

"I, um . . . I . . . uh . . . wanted to apologize for the other day . . . in town when those men were—" Cash began.

"Yeah, you'd better apologize, you skunk," Becca told him. "Be glad Ryder didn't mop up the whole town with your yeller hide!"

"Becca!" Dusty scolded again. Her sister owned no propriety where speaking to Cash Richardson was concerned. Becca had never been able to tolerate Cash, and she wasn't about to give him any way to hurt her big sister again. "Run on and talk to Maudie," Dusty told her with a smile. "Not a worry in the world right here." Becca looked to Dusty and sighed. She glared at Cash a moment before leaving them alone.

"You were sayin', Cash?" Dusty coaxed. Oddly, she found she was resisting the urge to burst into giggles. He looked ridiculous—all dressed up in his best black suit, his perfectly trimmed mustache combed neater than a dead man's. How had she ever gotten so lost as to find herself involved with Cash Richardson? It was ridiculous. Truly!

"The other day in town," he began again, "I . . . I'm sorry I wasn't more forceful in the beginning. I should've stood more firmly for my cause and—"

Dusty shook her head and interrupted him. "Cash, we both know you're not the type to get your hands dirty. And you're certainly not the type to get a new suit dirty."

Cash looked at her in astonishment. In fact, Dusty was astonished herself.

"Dusty, I-I," he stammered. "I can prove myself worthy. I swear! Just give me a chance to have you again."

It was the same old argument. No, it hadn't stopped over the past two years. It had lessened, yes. Yet Cash Richardson had never quit trying to win Dusty back. She felt sorry for him in those moments—sorry for him and guilty herself, for the grief she'd given him over his betraying her. Had he deserved it? Had he, when she knew deep within herself she would've eventually found another reason not to marry him anyway?

"Cash," she began, somewhat awash with guilt, "you never had me . . . never. Not even when ya thought ya did. I'm the one who's sorry."

"You're just saying these things because I hurt you, Dusty," Cash said. It was clear he didn't believe her—perhaps thought she was only trying to resist him somehow. "But I know I can win you back."

Dusty opened her mouth to offer further explanation. However, at that moment, she looked up to see Ryder angrily striding toward them. She glanced at Becca. She stood some distance away, talking with Maudie. Becca nodded, and Dusty knew her sister had sent Ryder to her rescue. As Ryder continued toward them, his eyes burned with annoyance, one hand already fisted. Cash took a step backward as Dusty stepped in front of Ryder, putting a hand to his chest to stay him.

"Ryder," she said, "here comes Alice and her family. Y-you need to meet her husband, Alex."

Ryder looked past her to Cash—furious. Yet, stepping back, he followed as she started toward Alice.

"I don't know why you even stomach him," Ryder growled.

"Because I'm realizing he wasn't the only one who was dishonest where he and I were concerned," Dusty explained.

Ryder stopped and scowled at her. "What do ya mean by that?"

"Dusty!" Makenna exclaimed. Dusty smiled as the little girl ran to her, wrapping her tiny arms around Dusty's legs.

"Hey there, sweetie," Dusty giggled. She quickly picked up the little girl—grateful for the distraction.

"You brung Ryder Magics?" Makenna asked, pointing a tiny index finger to the handsome cowboy.

"My horse brung me," Ryder answered. As the sweet little girl smiled at him, Dusty watched his anger and irritation fade. "You know I woulda broke Miss Dusty's back if I'da let her bring me to the picnic."

The clever little girl somehow understood Ryder's humor and erupted into giggles. Makenna stretched her arms toward Ryder, and he gathered her into his strong embrace. He chuckled as she kissed him soundly on one cheek.

"Dusty! Honey, you look wonderful!" Alice chimed, throwing her arms around Dusty's neck. The warm hug from her friend reminded Dusty that hugging had been all too absent in her life.

Alex Jones was carrying Jake on one hip as he reached them. "Hey there, Dusty," he greeted.

Alex was a handsome man—rather short with light hair and green eyes. His smile was his best feature, and Dusty nodded in greeting. He'd been a school chum of Alice's and Dusty's when they were girls. Dusty had been very happy for Alice when she'd married Alex; he was a good man.

"Ryder Maddox," Ryder introduced himself.

"Alex Jones," Alex said, taking Ryder's offered hand.

"Didn't you and your daddy run the grain chute in town years ago?" Ryder asked.

"Yes, sir," Alex confirmed, obviously pleased Ryder recognized him. "I heard ya were back as a hand over to Hank Hunter's ranch."

"Yep. Ain't no better place to hang your hat," Ryder told him.

"Hank's a good man. A good man." Alex bounced baby Jake a moment when the boy began to fuss and then continued, "I hear my daughter's expectin' a marriage proposal from ya when she grows up."

Ryder chuckled, and Makenna hugged him again. "Sweetheart, I'll look like ol' man Leroy by the time you're old enough to be gettin' married," he said to the girl. Makenna only smiled, pinching Ryder's cheeks.

"Well, Alice said Kenna took right to ya the other day." Again Jake whimpered, and Alex

220

paused a moment to quiet him. "Kenna, you run along and find the other children, darlin'. Let your mama talk with Miss Dusty." Kissing Ryder once more on the cheek, Makenna wriggled down from his arms and ran off in search of adventure.

"So," Alex began, winking at Alice, "I guess I have you to thank for givin' my Alice her first bird's-eye view of a bathin' man, huh?"

"Alex!" Alice gasped. "You shut your mouth!"

"You told him?" Dusty asked Alice in a horrified whisper. She couldn't believe Alice had told Alex about the two of them spying on Ryder way back.

"You know I tell Alex everything," Alice reminded her.

"Yes . . . but . . . Alice!" Dusty whispered.

Ryder and Alex both chuckled. "Yeah. Them two were always up to no good," Ryder assured Alex, "whether it was snitchin' cookies or a-sittin' up in a tree a-spyin' on me skinny-dippin'." Dusty and Alice gasped simultaneously. "What?" Ryder asked. "You two think I didn't know you were sittin' up in that tree?"

Alex broke into a roar of laughter at the look on his wife's face.

"We weren't spyin' on you," Dusty stated.

"You were," Ryder argued, grinning triumphantly.

"We were not!"

"Were too."

"Were not!"

"Ah, Dusty! Give it up," Alice giggled. "We were so!"

Dusty was completely flustered, her cheeks fiery red with an embarrassed blush. He'd known all the time?

As the two men stood chuckling, Alice simply linked arms with Dusty, straightened her posture, and said, "Fine. You two boys go on about your silly talk. Dusty and I are here to enjoy ourselves." Turning, she pulled Dusty with her and started toward the quilting.

"Just for that, Alex can get my turkey and candied yams out of the wagon *and* take care of Jakie," Alice giggled.

"I'm horrified, Alice!" Dusty said. "All this time he knew we were—"

"Ah, let it go. It's funny! And besides . . . Ryder never said anything 'til now. I think that's right sweet of him not to tease us about it." Alice giggled again. "Just imagine how horrified you woulda been if he'd taken to teasin' ya about it back then."

"Not to mention Mama woulda had my hide," Dusty added, smiling.

It was sweet to think Ryder had kept the knowledge to himself, especially considering what a tease he had been—what a tease he still was! It would've been perfect teasing ammunition. Dusty couldn't keep herself from glancing back over her shoulder to where Ryder and Alex stood talking. She couldn't stop a smile from spreading across her face when Ryder winked at her.

"Who's gettin' married?" Alice asked, and Dusty turned her attention to the quilt stretched out on a frame in the shade of the trees. "I haven't heard anyone announcin' anything. Have you?"

"No," Dusty answered.

"Well, let's find out." Alice tugged on Dusty, urging her to hurry her step.

Chapter Eight

The day was overflowing with amusement and lightheartedness. All the day long there were games for the children, quilting, eating, and endless visiting. The men competed in ax throwing, roping, riding, and team pulling. Ryder won several of the individual contests. After being awarded a blue ribbon in splitting wood, he sauntered toward her, and Dusty's stomach fluttered. A familiar grin of mischief spread across his handsome face as he approached.

"There you are," he chuckled. Holding out two of the many ribbons he'd won, he said, "I was wonderin' if you could look after these for me." His eyes quickly surveyed Dusty from head to toe. She squirmed uncomfortably under his gaze. Lowering his voice, he teased, "Beg yer pardon— I plum forgot. You're fillin' your dresses out in a mighty fine manner all on your own these days."

Dusty's mouth dropped open in astonishment. Chuckling to himself, Ryder winked, stuffed the ribbons in his pockets, and walked away. Dusty quickly glanced around. Had anyone heard him? Oddly, when she found no one was close enough to have been eavesdropping, she felt somewhat disappointed. Still, she silently gloated when Maudie Phillips arrived a few moments later to engage in trivial conversation.

While the men went about outdoing one another at being strongest and best at various events, the women visited endlessly. They quilted, wiped the runny noses and tears of playing children, and made certain the food table was always clean and heaped with good things to eat. Miss Raynetta flittered about like a little purple butterfly—here and there and back again—visiting and laughing and making sure everyone was having a good time.

Dusty found herself studying the eccentric little woman. She thought that though Miss Raynetta wore a perpetual smile, laughed, and seemed to be enjoying herself, there was something missing in her countenance. Dusty couldn't quite put her finger on what it was at first, but it bothered her—saddened her somehow.

Later in the day, as Dusty sat watching Miss Raynetta—trying to figure what it was about the sweet woman that seemed unsettled—the answer struck like a thunderbolt. Miss Raynetta was always alone! Even when she talked to the other women or to the children, it wasn't very long before someone else interrupted, and Miss Raynetta would flitter off to some other activity. As Dusty continued to observe her, it was obvious Miss Raynetta was intentionally trying to stay busy—every second busy. Several times throughout the day, Ryder approached and talked with her, and Dusty wondered if he too felt Miss Raynetta's masked discomfort.

Just after one of the team pulling contests, Dusty noticed Miss Raynetta locked in conversation with her father. Dusty smiled, noting her daddy's complete attention to the small woman as they talked. He chuckled several times, clearly amused by something she had said. Once during their conversation, Miss Raynetta reached up, straightening the collar of Hank's shirt as she babbled on. They talked for a long time. Though several people approached Hank briefly, Dusty was proud of his lending his attentions to Miss Raynetta for such an extended period of time.

"You gonna stand back and just watch your whole life?" Ryder asked as he sauntered over. He sighed and sat down next to Dusty on the old tree stump. "Scoot your fanny over," he mumbled, bumping and pushing her as he spoke.

"Are ya havin' fun?" Dusty asked, delighted he was sitting with her—especially when she saw Maudie Phillips looking at them from across the way.

"Yeah," he answered. "How 'bout you? You havin' fun just sittin' here watchin'?"

"Yep," she told him.

"What's so fun about it today?"

"I'm learnin' a lot." Dusty smiled. Ryder arched an eyebrow in doubt. "I am! For instance, I've learned that ol' man Leroy has a flask of whiskey hidden down the front of his pants." Ryder chuckled and nodded. "I've learned that Miss Raynetta isn't as happy as she always pretends to be . . . and I've learned that Ryder Maddox is still the most eligible bachelor in the county."

Ryder chuckled. "All right. What do you want?"

"What do ya mean?" Dusty was truly perplexed.

"What do you want? You ain't much into compliments . . . so I figure ya must want somethin'."

"I don't want anythin' from you," Dusty said. She sighed and tried to appear unaffected.

"Really?" he teased.

"Really." She was secretly delighted by their friendly banter. "What could you possibly have that I would ever want?"

"Well," he began, and she knew there was mischief in his mind, "ya did tell me awhile ago that I have a sweet hind end." Dusty gasped. "I figure maybe you want me to sit right down on my fine hind end and sit you right down on my lap . . . then spend some time sparkin' with ya."

"I can't believe you!" Dusty scolded, delighted at his flirting.

"And now that ya mention my sweet hind end . . ." he began.

"I did not mention it," she argued.

"It puts me to wonderin' . . . when did ya first think my hind end was sweet? Was it recent? Or was it after you and Alice sat up in that tree a-spyin' on me back when—"

Dusty shoved him hard, causing him to tumble off the stump. He chuckled, reached up, and took hold of her arm, pulling her off after him. She landed in a heap next to him and immediately looked about to see if anyone had noticed. The only people nearby were several young children playing in the grass, and she was thankful everyone else's attention was otherwise occupied.

"We closed our eyes, and you know it," she argued as she tried to stand up.

"Oh, bull," he chuckled, pulling her back down to sit next to him in the grass. He lay back in the grass, tucked his hands under his head, and sighed with contentment. "Now come down here, and let's get to kissin'!"

Again, Dusty's mouth fell agape. She shook her head in disbelief. "Let me get a whiff of your breath. I think you've been out with ol' man Leroy," she scolded.

He chuckled again. "All right. Come on down here and get a whiff of it then."

Dusty was completely flustered. She knew it was time—time to stop the teasing. She'd let her guard down too much, and her heart was beginning to ache. He was so handsome—so deliciously attractive lying there in the grass next to her—so friendly and witty and fun! And she knew she couldn't have him. Still, she wondered what he would do if she actually took him up on his teasing offer. Would he take her in his arms and kiss her so perfectly—the way he had under the waterfall? Or would he just laugh, having only been teasing all the while?

There was no more time to consider on it—for in the next moment a giggling, straw-headed little angel came bounding over from her play with the other children. With a quick leap, she landed herself squarely on Ryder's "lap." In truth, he had no lap —having been stretched out straight on the ground.

"Oof!" he choked in obvious pain. Makenna giggled and stretched over Ryder's stomach, reaching up to squeeze his cheeks lovingly. Dusty bit her lip, but she couldn't stop the giggle rising in her throat when he winced and choked, "Well, hello there . . . you little devil, you."

"We frowed up our ball, and it's stucked in the tree now, Ryder Magics. Please will you get it for us?" Makenna begged.

Ryder chuckled. Gently, he lifted the little girl off his body and struggled to sit up. Dusty smiled, biting her lip as Ryder sat silent for a moment. An expression of enduring discomfort and pain lingered on his face.

"Sure thing, sweetheart," he choked. "Just give me a minute, huh?"

Again Dusty giggled—simultaneously feeling sorry for him. He looked up and grinned through his pain-stricken frown.

"You go on and laugh, honey," he said, struggling to his feet. "But you'll be havin' a whole lot more sympathy when the day comes and you're wantin' to have my baby." He laughed heartily when Dusty gasped—when she nearly fell over flat from the shock of the remark.

"I can't believe you said that!" she exclaimed. She was mortified—yet oddly delighted at his inference that someday she might have his baby.

"Yes, ya can," he corrected her. "Now run off and involve yourself with these nice folks! Try havin' some fun for a change, Britches." He limped and limped to the tree under which Makenna stood pointing upward.

Dusty stood, leaving Ryder to help Makenna with her dilemma. There was nothing else to do. She was dazed by the things he'd said. For several minutes, she wasn't aware of where she was walking or who had stopped her along the way to chat. The sun seemed brighter, the food tastier, Becca's smile more radiant. Furthermore, try as she might to ignore the fact, Dusty's feet felt lighter as she walked along—lighter than they had in years.

However, late in the afternoon, when the sound

of fiddles announced the start of the barn dance, the old feelings of uncertainty and fear—the need to hide away and put up a defensive wall—began to overtake her again.

"Oh, come on, Dusty! It'll be so much fun!" Becca assured her, taking her hand and leading her into the barn. "You love to dance!"

I loved to dance, Dusty wanted to correct, but there was no reason to squelch Becca's enthusiasm.

"You havin' fun today, honey?" her daddy asked, putting a strong arm around her shoulders. The music started, and everyone began whooping and hollering with delight. Dusty nodded and forced a smile. "Good. Then ya won't mind a-beatin' the floor a bit with your daddy, now will ya?" Dusty smiled up at him. He was so considerate of her—so desperate she should have fun—that she should find herself again.

"You know I'd love it," she told him, linking her arm through his.

He led her to the floor, joining the others in the reel. Dusty thought, *I'd forgotten how much fun it could be.* As the dancers wove in and out, Dusty was delighted when Feller smiled at her and winked, obviously enjoying himself. Ryder too was there and winked as they passed. Miss Raynetta was his partner and was obviously delighted with his company.

The dancing continued for nearly two hours. Dusty found herself dancing with Cash, and not a harsh word or irritation rose within her. She danced with Feller and all the other hands including Ryder, though he never asked her to dance a waltz. It disappointed her that he never asked her during a slower, more intimate dance. He waltzed a great deal with Miss Raynetta and several of the elderly ladies in the county. Dusty watched, amazed when she realized this handsome bachelor—the man all the girls so obviously mooned after—saved his waltzes for those who needed the most attention. It was another testament to his good character.

"Are ya havin' fun, Dust?" Becca asked, smiling as she stood next to Dusty watching the others dance.

"Of course," Dusty assured her.

"No. I mean, really." Becca was uncertain of the truthfulness of Dusty's answer. And why shouldn't she be? For the past two Fourth of July picnics, Dusty had spent most of her time sitting in the wagon or working on the quilts outside—in no way involved with the socializing and dancing.

"I'm truly having fun, Beck," Dusty told her. There were hard moments she didn't mention to her sister. For example, every time Ryder led a woman other than herself to dance, whether young or old. Still, she wouldn't spoil her sister's good spirits.

All of a sudden, there arose a hollering and

whooping. Becca and Dusty whirled about to join the others in looking toward the dance floor.

"Oh, Dusty! Remember?" Becca squealed as she began clapping her hands in time to the music. Ryder and Feller began a stomp. They were astoundingly agile! Dusty too laughed as she remembered the two men entertaining her family long ago at the ranch with their stomp routines. Becca squealed with delight in unison with several other females as Ryder and Feller ignited the crowd's admiration by leaping into the air. Dropping smoothly to the floor to balance, stretched out, on their hands and toes, they pushed to their feet and continued with very impressive, fancy, masculinely awkward footwork.

Dusty was completely mesmerized by the smiles emblazoned on the men's faces. She was so intent on watching them, listening to the rhythmic stomping of a barn full of boots, that she didn't hear a fiddler shout, " 'Turkey in the Straw,' boys! Give us that one!"

Feller and Ryder stopped dancing as the familiar tune began. Bent over and resting their hands on their knees, they panted and shook their heads. Feller waved off the pleas of the fiddlers, but when the crowd roared with approval, moving aside to clear a path between Feller and Ryder, Becca and Dusty, Becca took Dusty's hand and pulled her toward them.

"Oh, no!" Dusty breathed.

"Oh, come on, Dusty!" Becca pleaded. "Remember what fun it was?"

"No, I can't!" Dusty breathed, horrified at what was happening—frightened into planting her feet firmly where she stopped. No sooner had Becca turned to her—her bright eyes pleading with desperation, filled with disappointment—than Feller and Ryder were upon them.

Becca squealed as Feller took her hand and pulled her to the center of the room where the crowd now cheered. Ryder reached out and took Dusty's hand.

"I can't—I can't remember," she stammered. She was lying, of course—looking for any reason to avoid being involved.

Ryder quirked a suspicious eyebrow and grinned down at her. "Come on now! It'll be fun!"

"Get that girl a-twirlin'!" the lead fiddler shouted.

Before Dusty knew his intent, Ryder pulled her arm over his head and hoisted her onto his shoulder. He carried her to where Feller and Becca waited, the crowd cheering them on all the while. He dropped her to her feet next to Feller and Becca. Dusty knew it was either perform or be eternally humiliated before every soul in the county.

"I'm not fourteen years old anymore, Ryder!" she scolded.

Still breathing hard from the jig, he smiled, taking her left hand in his right and saying, "And I ain't twenty!"

The lead fiddler drew his bow slowly over the strings twice. Speeding up the tempo with the following four singular notes, he and the other fiddlers burst into a rousing rendition of "Turkey in the Straw." Dusty hitched up her skirts and petticoats with her free hand. She felt as if something other than her own consciousness seemed to be telling her feet what to do. Indeed, she was matching Ryder step for step—just as she had as a young girl around the fire pit years ago. She glanced over to see Becca looking at her—delirious with exhilaration. Dusty couldn't help but smile. The crowd clapped out the beat of the tune, men hollered, and women squealed with encouragement as the two couples performed a series of quick turns and steps—just as they had years before on the same occasion.

I'll never remember it, Dusty thought as Ryder passed her to Feller, taking Becca in hand. "I can't keep this up!" Dusty panted as Feller took her waist and turned her around, pushing her out in front of him as the next series of quick clogging steps began.

His only response was a loud, "Ye-ha!" as she and Becca matched steps.

Ryder and Feller would change places behind them, she knew—and when she turned around it was Ryder who put his arm around her waist. Becca was now on her other side and Feller at the far end. They all four stomped out a beat on the barn floor while the music stopped for a moment to emphasize their steps. *Boom—boom—boom ba ba boom! Ba ba boom—boom—boom ba ba boom!* Dusty thought in her head as the sound echoed in her ears several times before the fiddlers joined in with the final chorus of the song. Ryder twirled Dusty under his arm, rotating himself as he did so, dropping to one knee, and pulling her to sit on his other knee as the music ended. The crowd erupted into shouts, whistles, and compliments. Dusty saw Ryder smiling at her as he brushed a bead of perspiration from his forehead.

"See?" he panted. "Ya didn't miss a step."

Dusty knew her cheeks too were glistening with extra moisture. Still, she returned the smile as he took her hand and helped her to stand. The feel of his hand gripping hers was so beloved—so familiar—it made her uncomfortable, and she needed to look away. Her gaze fell to Feller. She heard Becca squeal with delight and then throw her arms around his neck—as was her manner when someone pleased her. Dusty noted the way Feller's face paled—the way his hands did not linger a moment too long at her waist. Was it true? she wondered then. Could it be that Feller still saw Becca as no more than the boss's little daughter? Dusty's heart ached for Becca as she obviously sensed Feller's discomfort. Her arms fell away from him; a humiliated blush tinted her already rosy cheeks. Dusty and Becca had each hugged Feller enough times to know he was more than a bit uncomfortable in showing affection. Yet apparently having it flung on him in front of everyone in the county was nearly more than he could bear. Or was there some other reason? If there was, Dusty was unable to discern it just then.

Dusty felt Ryder drop her hand. He strode past her and directly to Becca, taking her in waltz position as the fiddlers began again. It was in that moment Dusty remembered why she'd decided to close herself off. What was the end result of fun and pleasure, the end result of falling in love? The heartache on her sister's face reminded her. Yet something again plucked a chord of gladness in her at Ryder's recognizing Becca's need to be rescued. He also leaned over and whispered something to Feller; both men's smiles faded. Still, when Ryder looked back to sweet Rebecca, a friendly grin spread across his face.

Dusty followed Feller toward the barn door leading outside. Before he could entirely flee, she caught hold of his sleeve. He turned to face her, his expression that of stone.

Yet she ventured, "I'd forgotten how fun that is."

"Yep," Feller mumbled. She saw his eyes glance up and toward the dance floor—to Ryder and Becca. "But I'm gettin' too old for this kind of horse sh—manure," he growled.

"That's a barrel of bull, Feller," Dusty reprimanded. "I've known you long enough to know when you're poutin', and I'm—"

"I ain't poutin', Dusty," he interrupted, irritated.

"You're poutin'!" Dusty stated. "And if you were me . . . you'd be tellin' me to buck up and quit feelin' sorry for myself."

Dusty could see Feller's jaw clenching and unclenching with frustration. Still, he nodded and simply walked a ways away. He leaned back against one wall, watching the waltzing couples gathered in the center of the room.

Dusty turned her attention to the waltzing couples too. She smiled at Ryder and Becca together. Yet the little imp of jealousy that resides in every female heart plucked at her brain.

"That was simply astoundin'!" Miss Raynetta sang as she floated toward Dusty, her brilliant purple dress glowing in the lamplight, a black ribbon with a cameo hanging about her throat. "I can't believe you children still remember them dances you all used to do together!"

"I wasn't sure I would," Dusty confessed. "It's been so long!"

"Hasn't been all that long in the way of things, sweetheart."

"Maybe not," Dusty admitted.

"And," Miss Raynetta dropped her voice to a whisper, "you know . . . I've always wanted a man to throw me over his shoulders like a sack of flour the way Ryder done you!" Dusty stared at the woman, her mouth again agape with astonishment. "Well, it's the truth of it, pumpkin!" Miss Raynetta affirmed.

They were silent for a moment, but only a moment, before Miss Raynetta led Dusty closer to the barn door—and privacy. There she continued with her predictable yet charming chatter.

"Mind a little advice from a voice of experience?" Miss Raynetta asked.

Dusty sighed. Still, she smiled at the woman. "I suppose you're gonna give it to me no matter what. Right, Miss Raynetta?"

"Don't waste your life. I seen your eyes light up when that Ryder Maddox walks through a door."

"What? That's the most ridiculous thing I ever—" Dusty began to argue.

"Now, don't give me that. I can see it. That don't mean everybody can. What I'm tryin' to say is don't let havin' your pride hurt and your heart broken strip ya of your life's happiness with a good, lovin' man, babies runnin' around, and all the joy they bring ya." Miss Raynetta smiled with an expression of incredible understanding. Dusty was astonished as she continued, "Believe me, honey . . . you're talkin' to somebody who knows what a waste it is."

Dusty stood silent—simply stared at the woman in wonder. She looked to the dance floor where Ryder and Becca had finished their waltz and now stood applauding the musicians.

"And wipe that thinkin' out of your mind. There ain't nothin' to be jealous of where your sister is concerned."

"I wasn't thinkin' that at all," Dusty began to argue. "I was—"

"Oh, yes, ya were. Any excuse to harden your heart against that cowboy. You're lookin' for any reason ya can to convince yourself ya don't want him," Miss Raynetta said.

"I don't want him! I . . ." Dusty insisted.

"Yes, ya do." Miss Raynetta's eyes misted. Her expression fought the natural frown accompanying tears as her chin quivered. "And don't give up. Once you're able to draw yourself outta that hole you've dug . . . don't let him go."

Dusty cast her gaze down for a moment, greatly unsettled by the normally jolly woman's obvious despair.

"I loved a cowboy once myself, Angelina," Miss Raynetta whispered. Dusty saw tears trickling down Miss Raynetta's lovely face—accompanied by a sad, sentimental smile. The sweet woman daintily brushed at the tears. "I was young . . . too young for him, I thought. I figured if I confessed to him how I felt, I'd just have to listen to him tell me what I already knew. But now . . . I've lived twenty years of my life wonderin' what would've happened if I'd have told him how I felt. He was a kind man. He wouldn't have made fun of me—I know it. Though I know it probably wouldn't have changed anything, because he really loved the girl he married, still . . . I shoulda tried."

Dusty felt tears escape her own eyes. She quickly brushed them from her cheeks as the woman continued, "So . . . I never married. I couldn't get that man outta my soul. Because, ya see, Dusty . . . whether or not he loved the girl he married . . . I never found anybody that I could love like I loved him." Miss Raynetta discreetly pulled a handkerchief from inside the bosom of her dress and wiped the tears from her cheeks. Sniffling and forcing a smile, she continued, "So you tell that boy how you feel. 'Cause ya ain't a little girl no more. You can love him legal and all you want. Don't drive him away and ruin your life." She paused and embraced Dusty warmly for a long moment. "You hang onto that man come hell or high water. You hear me?"

Dusty could only fight her tears. Her heart was pounding furiously. How could she? How could she overcome what even Miss Raynetta McCarthy hadn't been able to overcome? How could she confess her feelings to the man she so desperately loved?

"Now, I'm gonna go on over and freshen up that punch bowl," Miss Raynetta said, puffing up the sleeves of her royal-plum dress. "You run out and find that boy and give him a reason to hang around. You hear me?"

240

As Miss Raynetta turned to leave, Dusty asked, "Miss Raynetta?" The woman turned and looked at Dusty. "What . . . whatever happened to that cowboy you loved?"

Again heavy moisture filled the woman's eyes. Her forced smile faded, and she did not answer directly. She seemed to be deciding whether she should explain. Then she forced a smile somehow; another tear traveled down her cheek.

"He married the girl he loved, and she made him very happy. One horrible, sad day, she passed on without him. She was too young to die . . . far too young. But together they'd had a wonderful life." She paused, moved back to Dusty, and whispered in her ear, "And two beautiful little girls . . . named Angelina and Rebecca." Then she turned and hurried from the barn.

"Daddy?" Dusty spoke unconsciously in a whisper. Her own daddy was the cowboy Miss Raynetta had loved as a girl?

"You look like you've seen a ghost, Dusty," Feller said, stepping up from behind her.

Instantly Dusty turned to face him, accusing, "You never told me it was Daddy that Miss Raynetta . . ."

Feller looked shaken and angry. "Wasn't my place to tell you," he nearly snapped back. "I probably shouldn'ta told you nothin' at all about it!" He started to turn to leave. Dusty reached out, took hold of his arm, and stopped him—though his expression was of anger and secreted guilt.

"Please don't be angry with me, Feller," Dusty begged. "I had no right to scold you before. As far as Miss Raynetta is concerned . . . it was just such a surprise! I didn't know. I never even suspected!"

"People don't want everybody to know when they're hurtin', darlin'," he told her purposefully. "Ain't that right?"

Then something else occurred to Dusty. This man, her daddy's top hand—how often had she seen him courting a girl in recent years? She could remember several years ago when Feller had been quite the attraction to all the women in town. In fact, he'd been out nearly every Saturday night when she was younger. Yet about the time everything with Cash came crumbling down, he'd quit. She couldn't think of one solitary Saturday night in recent years when Feller had gone to town by himself. Always it was with the family to the town socials. He hadn't courted a girl in years. Dusty closed her eyes as tears threatened to stream down her face. How selfish she'd been—how completely wrapped up in self-pity! She hadn't sensed Miss Raynetta's pain or Feller's or Becca's or anyone else's for that matter. Had she been so blind as all that? Did Feller actually care for Becca deeply? Had he cared for her deeply for two long years? Perhaps waiting for her to grow up—to be old enough to have? Why then didn't he reach out and take what was standing so willing and ready before him? Was there more to Feller Lance's profound, insightful understanding of Dusty's broken heart? Was it wisdom born of experience? And was that what kept him from Becca?

"Have you ever been hurt, Feller?" she whispered.

"All the time. Got bucked off'n ol' Red just last week, and my tailbone is still achin'," he mumbled.

"No," Dusty interrupted, irritated. "You know what I mean."

Feller looked up to where folks were beginning to dance to another tune. "Like I said, people don't want folks knowin' 'bout their heartaches." He exhaled a heavy sigh and forced a smile. "You better swaller them tears, Dusty. Here comes your sister."

"Oh, Dusty!" Becca exclaimed, arriving on the arm of Ryder. "You've just gotta go dancin'! How can you and Feller just stand here, stiff as posts, when the music is goin'?" she asked.

"Well, Becca," Dusty began in her older-sister-who-knows-everything tone, "there's some things that . . ." But when Feller jabbed her in the rib cage, quite uncharacteristically, she stopped talking and looked to him, astonished.

"Some ol' cowboy has to ask you in order for you to go dancin'," Feller answered Becca. "Ain't that right, Ryder?"

Dusty looked to Ryder when he chuckled—the mischievous grin spreading across his face. "Dang right. Would you like to do me the honor, Miss Britches?" he asked Dusty.

Dusty felt sick and nervous inside—elated and enraptured at the same time. Why was this affecting her so? Hadn't she just danced with him several tunes before? Taking his arm, for she was determined to change—to find the Dusty that used to be—she allowed him to lead her to the floor.

"Grab that girl and come on, Feller," Ryder called over his shoulder.

It was a waltz. Of course it would be a waltz—considering Dusty was already thinking she might faint. Her nerves made breathing difficult. Her knees were trembling something fierce. When Ryder put a hand at her waist, lifted one of her hands to his shoulder, and took her other in his own, she noted how violently her hands were trembling.

"Come on there, girl," he told her. "It ain't like ya never danced with me before." He grinned down at her and, lowering his voice just as the music started, added, "Only this time the whole county won't be waitin' for me to stomp on your foot, and there ain't none of your daddy's hankies fillin' out your dress so nice."

Dusty gasped as he winked at her and began the waltz. "I can't believe you would say such a—"

"Yes, ya can," he chuckled.

As Dusty waltzed in his arms, her heart ached all the more. They'd closed the book. He'd told her they had the day under the waterfall. But she didn't want the book closed! The heat of his kiss that night was still warm on her lips, the feeling of being in his arms still too fresh. Moreover, his smile, his wit, his heroism, his way with conversation—all of it was something she'd dreamed of owning for as long as she could remember. Miss Raynetta's story flashed through her mind. She looked up to Ryder, and he smiled down at her. *The book was closed, wasn't it?* she wondered as her entire being warmed to his touch. And what about herself? Did she want to end up a crotchety old spinster, forever pining away after what she hadn't tried for? Even if she weren't grouchy—even if she ended up like Miss Raynetta, beautiful and cheery—her life would be forever empty, filled with nothing but regret, eternal heartache, and loneliness. But Ryder had said, *We need to close this book.* He'd said it. Looking up into the brown sugar of his eyes—to the fantastically good-looking man holding her —she doubted her ability to win him. Why would he want her anyway? He'd said himself he didn't like the way she'd turned out! How could she possibly attract him? Hold him?

Afraid tears were again brimming in her eyes, Dusty turned her head and looked away from him. What she saw caused an idea to begin forming in her mind—a way of perhaps mending her darkened soul. She needed to find Angelina "Dusty" Hunter. The Dusty Hunter who had loved people, cared about people, helped people—feared little and loved life! The Dusty Hunter who had cared more about serving others—making sure life was better for others, better even than her own. She needed to find the girl who was lost so long ago. Concentrating on others, making the lives of others whole and happy with someone to love—maybe that would unearth the Dusty Ryder could love. And what she saw at that moment she knew was her means of healing her own soul.

Hank Hunter was actually dancing! For the first time she could remember since her mama passed, her daddy was waltzing—and with none other than Raynetta McCarthy. Dusty noted Miss Raynetta wore an expression that certainly must've mirrored Dusty's in the moment Ryder had taken her in his arms. Nearby Feller was leading Becca in the waltz. Poor Feller—something had eaten his heart away too. Something had made him believe he wasn't capable of having a young, fresh beauty like Becca to love him. Four people primed for happiness—four people just needing someone to guide them along.

"Well, look at that," Ryder mumbled.

"What?" Dusty asked, her thoughts having been interrupted.

"Look at ol' Feller," he told her. "By dang if he

didn't find a gut or two left in his belly after all."

"What're you talkin' about?" she asked with irritation. She didn't want to admit that perhaps someone else had been as insightful as she where her sister and Feller were concerned.

Ryder's brow crinkled in puzzlement. "You ain't as blind as all that, are ya?" he asked.

"I have two perfectly good eyes in my head, thank you," she nearly snapped.

"Really?" he taunted.

"Yes!"

"Then why don't you see what I see?"

"What do you see?"

He was taunting her. She knew he was. But what if she were wrong? What if Ryder were referring to something else? She couldn't take the chance of breaking Becca's confidence where her feelings for Feller were concerned.

"What do you see?" he asked.

Sensing they were indeed thinking the same things, Dusty rolled her eyes and looked over to where Feller was leading her sister in a waltz. "I see Feller Lance dancin' with Becca." She paused and repeated her question. "What do you see?"

Ryder grinned with mischief, bent, and whispered in her ear, "Looooove."

Dusty couldn't help grinning with delight as goose bumps broke over the entire surface of her body. The sensation of his hot breath on her neck was divine! His speaking that particular word alone made her mouth suddenly begin to salivate. She had to consciously keep herself from turning and letting her mouth seek out the savor of his.

Desperate for escape, she glanced once again to Becca and Feller. She was warmed by the rather uncharacteristically flirtatious smile on Feller's face—by the way he held Becca a little more closely than was proper. She was suddenly more aware of her proximity to her own dance partner.

Dusty wanted to dance with Ryder forever. The stomp with Feller and Becca earlier was too fast, too demanding, and too much work for her to have had even a moment to linger on the thought of the fantasy come to life—the dream come true of dancing with Ryder then. But now—oh, heavenly now! In his arms again!

She wanted to have teasing conversations with Ryder—share in realizations about others with him. When she was a child he'd talked with her. All those years before he had to leave, they'd had times almost daily when they sat and talked. It's what she missed most about him. Talking—listening.

"You see Feller havin' feelin's for Becca?" she whispered.

"I didn't say that," he countered, no doubt afraid he'd said too much.

"Yes, you did!"

"Hm," he breathed as if he'd never said anything at all.

A sort of giggly joy rose in her chest at their friendly banter. "You're a pill!" she told him. "And I'm not blind," she whispered. "Nope. Not anymore."

"Hold on there a minute, brat," Ryder muttered as if he'd read her mind.

"What?" she asked, feigning innocence.

"You got that look in your eye. I know it well enough, and it's makin' me a mite nervous," he said.

"What look?" She was elated that something in her had seemed so familiar to him suddenly. "I just think it's very interesting that—"

"I remember that look. It always shows up a minute before you plunge headfirst into trouble," he chuckled. "Last time I seen that twinkle in your eyes, I ended up nearly gettin' hanged for lettin' you set the ol' cow shed on fire tryin' to light up a Christmas tree for ol' Flossy. Chee! You thought the danged old milk cow was lonely at Christmas 'cause her calf had died that spring and—"

"I'm not gonna set anything on fire," she told him. She'd forgotten about the Christmas tree for the ailing cow in the old shed. How she ever talked Ryder into that, she'd never been able to figure.

"Poor ol' Flossy," Ryder began, pitching his voice high and trying to imitate a fourteen-year-old girl he'd once known. " 'She's just beside herself ever since she lost that calf last spring. I just know a Christmas tree all her own would cheer her up! Pleeeeaaaase, Ryder! Help me put candles on a tree in the shed where Daddy's got her holed up. I promise I'll be careful!' " He finished his imitation of her and rolled his eyes.

Dusty giggled, that very strange, almost forgotten sensation she'd only recently begun to experience again. "I can't believe you let me do that!"

"Ah, you run me like an old dog back then," he mumbled, smiling down at her. The music stopped, and he caressed her cheek for a moment with the back of his hand. "Didn't you?"

She wanted to beg him at that moment, *Please love me. Give me another chance.* But she just forced a smile, hiding her heartache.

Chapter Nine

"Folks! Now settle down, folks! Settle down," the lead fiddler shouted. With regret at having to end their interlude, Dusty turned her attention from Ryder to the fiddler. "Now . . . this here's the Fourth of July!" Everyone clapped, hollering with good nature. When Dusty glanced up at Ryder, he winked, delighting her to the very core of her being. She watched him as he put his pinkies at the corners of his mouth and whistled in celebration. "And on the Fourth a July we always have us some fine fireworks at ten o'clock, now don't we?" Again there was shouting and whistling. "But 'fore we do . . . there's dancin', and there's gotta be fun and games! Ain't that right?" Everyone shouted in agreement. "So, all you young folk, single ones that is . . . you all get together here outside the barn. Time to pack 'em in!" The giggling of all the young unmarried girls in the county nearly outdid the sly chuckling of all the young unmarried men. "Everybody else—let's keep the dancin' goin'!"

"Come on then, Miss Britches," Ryder chuckled, taking Dusty's hand and pulling her toward the group of unmarried men and women gathering just outside the barn door.

"No, no, no," Dusty argued as Miss Raynetta, appearing from nearby, took hold of her free hand and began dragging her toward the others as well. "I . . . I . . . I don't want to . . ." Although her intentions to unearth her soul were sincere, the application of doing so was proving difficult, near to impossible at every turn.

"Of course you want to!" Ryder and Miss Raynetta exclaimed simultaneously. Before Dusty could argue further, she found herself pushed into the group.

"All right! All right! Now simmer down!" Maudie Phillips was saying. "Everybody know how to play?" There rose up a general noise of confirmation.

"Oh, no! I can't do this!" Dusty exclaimed under her breath. She turned around, needing escape.

"You done a jig with the whole county a-lookin' on, Dusty," Ryder stated as she ran smack into him as she tried to flee. "Believe me . . . you can pull this one off."

"Um," she paused. Suddenly her innards were trembling at being so close to him. "No, actually. Just spottin' Becca. Makin' sure she was—"

"Ah, come on. Be a sport, Miss Hunter," he dared. Dusty didn't like being dared. It ignited her temper, and she had a horrid habit of not backing down. "I mean," he continued, "what harm could it do? You might have a little fun . . . and that ain't gonna kill ya. No matter what ya think."

"Maudie, you're it!" Miss Raynetta hollered. "You got five minutes! No more. Get to hidin'!" Miss Raynetta leaned over to Dusty and whispered, "That oughta ruin her chances of latchin' onto any man!" Dusty's eyes widened in amazement at the woman's impish trickery. She watched as Maudie squealed with delight—not realizing she'd been had. Maudie took off running. Dusty knew the whole fun of the game was sneaking around in the dark, hoping to bump into whomever it was you were sweet on.

"Do you remember the object of this game, Ryder?" Dusty asked.

"I believe I do. But why don't ya tell me?" he chuckled.

As a younger girl, "pack 'em in" had been her favorite. It was the opposite of hide-and-seek. In pack 'em in, one person hid, and everybody went looking for the hider. The difference was when someone found the hiding person, the finder hid with the hider. This premise made for great fun—especially in the courting-age groups—because usually by the time the last seeker had found all the hiders, a fair amount of flirting, teasing, and sparking had transpired among them all.

"I'm not gonna tell ya what you already know," she told him.

"Then I'll see you . . . wherever I see you, Miss Dusty," he said, winking at her. He turned and joined several other ranch hands in their conversation.

"I'm so glad to see you joinin' in tonight, Dusty." Dusty rolled her eyes with irritation. Drawing in a breath of patience, she turned to face Brenda Rivers. "It's been so long since you were out like this," the girl said, adding insult to injury. Brenda was Maudie's best friend and as syrupy and fake as they came. She stood twisting a long strand of her ebony hair around one dainty finger.

Dusty smiled. "I just keep so busy helpin' Daddy with the ranch and all. But I do feel a bit more . . . tolerant tonight, I guess," Dusty told her pointedly.

"Hmm. Really?" Brenda sighed. "I thought maybe you was just keepin' an eye on Ryder Maddox."

"Why ever would ya say that, Brenda?" Dusty asked, feigning indifference.

" 'Cause if Ryder Maddox was my daddy's hand . . . I'd be keepin' more than my eye on him!" Brenda Rivers was the most shameless flirt Dusty had ever known.

"It's the nice weather that's got me feelin' refreshed tonight," Dusty sighed, ignoring her comment.

"I bet," Brenda said. "Good luck. Findin' Maudie, I mean."

"You too." Dusty forced a false smile in return.

As Brenda walked away, Miss Raynetta whispered in Dusty's ear from behind her, "There's one a them in every town. Two in this one! Just makes a woman wanna spit!"

Dusty chuckled and nodded. She'd always adored Miss Raynetta—now more than ever. She'd never look at her the same again—or her own daddy. Turning, she smiled at her. "You wanna join in the game, Miss Raynetta?" Dusty asked.

"Oh, my lands, no!" the woman giggled. "I'll just stay here and help out where help is needed." With a wink, a candle seemed to flame in Dusty's mind. Her daddy had always liked Miss Raynetta —spoken very highly of her. Maybe her sudden aspirations where they were concerned wouldn't be so difficult after all.

"Let's go!" someone shouted. Suddenly, young men and women were racing every which way.

Dusty paused, uncertain she really should get involved. Deep in her heart, she wanted to. But should she? Still, her eyes caught Ryder's daring stare and triumphant grin. Lifting her skirts, she spun around in the opposite direction, determined to find Maudie first—especially not last—and especially before Ryder found her. She wouldn't give Maudie a chance to even look at him too closely!

It was Feller Lance himself who handed everyone a lantern as they left the barn—along with instructions to blow it out once they'd found Maudie and were hiding with her.

"You're not joinin' in, Feller?" Dusty asked.

"I'm too old for this kind a thing, Dusty. You know that," the man answered with a chuckle.

"You're only as old as you feel, Feller. And you're not as old as you try to make everybody think ya are." With that, she left him frowning with puzzlement. No doubt over the past two years, her high spirits had become too unfamiliar to him, but that would change—somehow.

It was a fairly clear night. Not too many clouds threatened to darken the moon. Still, Dusty was grateful for the light of the lantern. She could see other lanterns dotting the night out in the fields, looking like fireflies hovering in a darkened meadow. Pausing, she looked around trying to decide where Maudie would hide. It really wasn't a very hard thing to figure out. The easy options were fairly obvious—lie low in the grassy field until someone stepped on her? No—Maudie was too pristine for that, though it would've been one of her least wise choices. The old oak clear down by the creek was a good one, but Maudie was too soft-skinned to climb it. Then Dusty saw a lantern flicker and go out near the old shed out behind the barn.

"Oh, surely you tried harder than that!" she mumbled to herself as she set out. She blew her lantern out immediately, knowing the way well enough to find it by moonlight and thereby not easily leading anyone else to it.

Carefully she stepped into the old shed, closing the door behind her. It was pitch dark, even with the moonlight streaming through the enormous crater in the shed's roof overhead. She heard muffled giggles coming from above.

"In the loft?" she whispered. "Maudie?" Dusty called. "You up in that loft?"

There was no answer. So draping her skirts over one arm and setting the lantern on the ground by the door, Dusty climbed the ladder to the loft of old man Leroy's shed. It was awkward at best, but when she reached the loft and peered about, it was to see at least five different smiling faces in addition to Maudie's—including Becca's.

Guthrie clamped his hand over Maudie's mouth and, motioning to Dusty, called out in a whisper,

"Come on, Dusty! Hurry! I can hear somebody else outside the barn!" Something about Guthrie calling her Dusty—just plain Dusty with no "Miss" attached—it suddenly warmed her heart so completely she thought she might burst into tears.

"Hurry up, Miss Britches! There's others nearby!" Startled at hearing his whisper just below her feet on the ladder, Dusty did as Ryder prodded and climbed up into the loft with the others.

"Just here," Becca whispered. Dusty followed suit with the others, lying down next to Titch. She hadn't even stretched out completely on her stomach before Ryder was beside her. He plopped himself down with a triumphant grin, obviously having ditched his lantern somewhere as well.

"Ssshhhhh!" someone whispered as Maudie and Becca both fought their delighted giggles. Dusty allowed a smile begging to spread to draw itself across her mouth, but she lost the battle to deter the giggles. It was Ryder's hand over her mouth that finally silenced her.

"Keep yourself quiet, girl," Ryder whispered with a low chuckle. "Or I'll find a way to do it for you."

"You cheater!" Dusty told him. She pushed his hand away, trying to squelch the immediate thrill traveling over her because of his threat to quiet her. "You followed me!"

"I figured you were still pretty good at this game," Ryder whispered in her ear. "So . . ." Goose bumps again broke over her entire body. She was bathed in delight as she lay there in the darkness waiting for her eyes to adjust to only the light of the stars and moon breaking through the tattered rooftop of the old shed.

"You're a cheater as well as a scoundrel," she told him, still smiling. He had followed her. How . . . how . . . how fabulous!

One of the girls erupted into giggles again; Dusty recognized it as Becca. "Ssshhh!" a man's voice scolded. "Stop that! Everyone'll know where we are!"

Minutes of silence passed before someone else entered the old building. Now Dusty waited anxiously—trying to restrain the giggling sensation overtaking her again at the excitement of watching whomever it was labor to find the hiding place.

"It's Cash Richardson," Ryder whispered in her ear.

Dusty looked at him irritated, only to find his expression utterly sincere. Cash? Why did it have to be Cash? So soon. After their altercation in town—even for their obvious ignoring of each other at the picnic thus far—Dusty feared Cash's presence might dampen Ryder's good mood.

They all listened as Cash ascended the ladder rungs and peeked up into the loft. Maudie and

Becca immediately burst into giggles. Smiling, Cash blew out his lantern and climbed up into the loft right next to Ryder.

Dusty felt sick. She certainly didn't want him in such proximity—and she didn't want him ruining Ryder's fun.

"Quiet down!" Cash chuckled. "Brenda Rivers was right behind me." His voice was pleasant and friendly, however, and Dusty relaxed a bit as she saw he and Ryder nod to each other in greeting. The game was too fun to be ruined. Maudie's and Becca's giggles were immediately muffled. Obviously some masculine hands were to thank. Closing her eyes, Dusty imagined how fun it must be to be in Maudie's place—when all flirting was romantic and there was no fear of heartbreak because it was, as yet, unknown to her.

Her thoughts were sent sailing into the night breeze, however, when she was suddenly pushed with great force, causing her to roll over onto her back.

"What are you do—" she began when she realized it was Ryder who had pushed her over. He put an index finger to his lips quickly, frowning at her in scolding at being so loud.

In that very moment, the few clouds that were in the sky drifted in front of the moon, blocking the faint light it let into the shed.

Dusty felt Ryder lean down, putting his mouth to her ear. She could feel the moisture of his breath as he whispered, "This situation just sorta demands I do somethin' inappropriate. Don't ya think?"

"What?" she exclaimed in a whisper, only to be met with a resounding "Ssshhhhh!" from the other occupants of the shed. She heard Ryder's amused chuckle, and her mind pictured the mischievous grin no doubt beginning to spread across his face.

"Don't worry about it bein' so dark," he whispered so quietly she could barely understand him. "I'll just . . . feel my way to makin' a devil of myself." She felt one of his hands at her waist; the other slid under her neck as he pulled her against him. The hand at her waist traveled slowly up her back and over her shoulder until it reached her chin, cupping it firmly. She could feel his breath on her cheek and in her hair. All she could hear was his breathing. Then suddenly a lantern light peeked over the ladder and into the loft.

"Ssshhh! Hurry up, Brenda!" Maudie giggled as Brenda lay down next to Cash and blew out her lantern. No one had noticed Ryder held Dusty. No doubt most had been too involved in their own little trysts to notice her and Ryder—except for Becca. Dusty knew that, although Becca giggled, her heart was back at old man Leroy's barn with Feller.

Dusty knew complete darkness and a sort of public privacy invoked by the game was what all these flirtatious young men waited for. She'd had a kiss or two stolen in the dark playing pack 'em in before.

As the cloud continued to completely block the moon's light from the shed, Ryder whispered, "Shoot, sugar . . . the whole point of this game is the sparkin' that goes on when everybody's packed nose-to-nose but can't see worth a darn. Ain't that right?"

His roughly shaven cheek brushed her own lightly. Dusty involuntarily clenched her hands into tight fists. Ryder's thumb caressed her cheek, slowly moving to her lips. He was indeed feeling his way in the dark to her mouth, and something buried deep inside her screamed silently, *Hurry! Oh, hurry before the cloud is gone and takes the moment from me!* Yet her trembling body reacted routinely—a small fist going to his chest, pushing gently against his body.

She whispered, "Ryder, stop it. I can't . . ." But in the next moment, she felt the warmth of his lips, softly toying with her own. A wave of heat, so intense she thought her body might burst into flames, broke over her so rapidly, she shuddered in the exhilaration of such awakening. He kissed her softly twice more before his tongue touched her upper lip teasingly, causing a small gasp to escape her lungs and providing him the means of deepening the kiss. For a moment, her mind fought surrender to him, but as his kiss wove a spell of enchantment over her senses, even her fist at his chest relaxed, her palm pressing gently against him now. His mouth was warm, moist—sweet with the nectared taste that was his kiss.

All too soon, the cloud left the moon, and with it went Ryder's kiss. He fairly tore his mouth from her, sighed heavily, and let his face drop into the straw on which they lay. The giggling that erupted from either side of Dusty told her she hadn't been the only young woman to be kissed in the dark. All she could do as other young people came into the shed and up to the loft was lie there in the blissful realization Ryder's kiss had been her own. Once in a while she'd glance over at Ryder, now lying on his back, hands tucked under his head as he gazed at the stars.

"Ol' beat-up pan Mama used to smack skunks with," he whispered. He smiled and winked at her as he gestured toward the sky and the Big Dipper so bright and visible in the starry night. Dusty sighed and smiled at him adoringly as he winked at her.

Moments later, and far too soon, the first round of the game ended simply because Maudie had picked such an obvious hiding spot and the last person had found it. Yet Dusty was glad, for as Ryder descended the ladder just before her, catching her around the waist as she stepped down from the ladder and onto the shed floor, she knew she could not again endure the euphoria mingled with heartache that his kissing her had caused in her.

All the young people walked back toward the barn together. Guthrie and Ryder talked about what all would have to be done the next day since the ranch had been abandoned for a whole day. Becca rattled on somewhat dejectedly. It was the lack of excitement in her voice that caught Dusty's attention.

"I'm tired," Becca had said. "I wish we could go home now." Dusty looked quickly to her sister. Becca did indeed look unhappy.

"What's the matter? You love the fireworks," Dusty reminded her.

Becca shrugged. Then, linking arms with Dusty and dropping to the back of the group, she confessed, "Truth is, Dusty . . . I don't really want to be here at all. Not like this."

Dusty frowned. "Why? You've always really looked forward to the picnic and all. Even today you—"

"I know. But . . . it's gettin' hard to pretend to myself. I want to be here . . . but not as one of the unmarried girls. I want . . ." Becca couldn't finish her thought; she didn't have to. Dusty knew how she felt. Becca wanted to be married—married to Feller—be his wife and come to the picnic on his arm—dance every dance with only him—make her own pies and cookies in a house they shared together.

"I know," Dusty admitted. Ryder's remark about her having his baby someday echoed through her own mind. When Makenna had jumped in his lap the way she had—every time she was near him, in fact—Dusty pushed away the desire to have it be her own little girl vying for his attentions—hers and his—theirs! Closeting her own thoughts in the back of her mind, she put her arm around Becca's shoulders. "We just gotta get Feller to realize he's worth havin' you."

Becca shook her head and wiped a lone tear from her cheek. "He sees me as a baby . . . still needin' him to keep me from fallin' headfirst into the hog pen," she mumbled.

"I don't think that's it at all! I—" Dusty began.

But Becca shook her head and begged, "Please. Let's not talk about it. All right?"

Dusty understood heartache and the need to try to bury it. So, smiling, she nodded, and they walked back to the barn in silence.

The fiddlers were still sawing away on their instruments, and people were still dancing and having a wonderful time. Dusty knew the fireworks would be soon, and then it would be time to go home. Only, unlike Becca, who longed for the night to end, Dusty did not. *How ironic,* she thought to herself. As much as she had dreaded it, she would be the one who had enjoyed it so thoroughly. As she thought about Ryder— the delight he'd caused her to feel in so many different ways that day—she glanced over to where he stood in a circle of young men sharing conversation. He smiled and winked at her and then raised his eyebrows as if he'd just remembered something. He reached into his pocket and pulled out the blue ribbons he'd offered to her as stuffing for her bodice earlier in the day. Silently he held them out toward her with an expression of, *Do you need these?* Then with a mischievous grin, his eyes traveled the length of her. He shook his head dramatically, winked at her, and stuffed the ribbons back into his pocket.

He was unbelievable! Dusty knew that had any other man in the world implied such things to her as he had that day, she would've been bound to slap him solidly across the face—and would've gladly done so! But there was something unspoken between them—a familiarity left over from somewhat growing up together that made certain allowances. *That was the reason,* she told herself. Nothing more—for she knew he was just teasing. Wasn't he?

The announcement was made that the fireworks would begin. Everyone began gathering outside near the big field to watch the amazing display of gunpowder turned into color light up the night sky.

Dusty hung back from the rest of the group. Perhaps she understood too well Becca's feelings of wanting to be with Feller, for she had no desire to join the others in the crowd and be painfully reminded that she was, for all romantic purposes, alone. So leaning back against one of the big trees, she smiled as she listened to the crowd "oohing and aahing" with each consecutive explosion toward the stars. She wondered where Ryder was and assumed he would be wherever poor Miss Raynetta found herself—offering friendly companionship. She still could not believe that particular revelation—her own daddy loved by someone and completely unaware of it? Not unlike Feller, maybe.

The hand suddenly covering her mouth from behind and the arm going around her waist startled her so that her heart seemed to skip a beat or two. But at once she recognized the chuckle from behind her and wiggled from his grasp. She turned, slapping Ryder on the arm in reprimand.

"Ryder, you scared the waddin' out of me!" she scolded.

Ryder chuckled at her but said nothing. The look in his eyes, however, was all too familiar. Dusty actually stepped back from him. "What are you up to?" she asked. He was up to no good; she knew from his expression.

"Unfinished business," he mumbled as he reached out, spun her around, clamped his hand over her mouth again, and, letting his arm go around her waist once more, lifted her off the ground. He pulled her behind the tree and into complete seclusion.

Dusty struggled, pulling at his hands, trying to loosen his grip. But he was much stronger, and she began to wonder whether she really wanted escape anyway. She ceased her struggling instantly when his arm left her waist, his hand now encircling her throat gently. Keeping his other hand over her mouth, he pulled her head to one side, and she nearly fainted from the euphoria of his kiss on her neck.

"Forgive me, Miss Hunter," he mumbled against her neck. Her flesh tingled from the delightful sensation. "But somethin's put the devil in me tonight, and that little frolic in the loft with you just wasn't long enough." As Ryder continued to kiss her neck playfully, Dusty tried again to push his hand from her mouth. At last, he yielded, releasing her body. Still, he took her face between his powerful hands, forcing her to look up at him.

"What're you doing to me?" she asked him breathlessly, stepping backward and leaning against the tree trunk.

"What're you doin' to me?" he sighed. He released her, rubbing his eyes with frustration. He reached up, taking hold of a tree limb as he leaned toward her.

"Nothin'," she squeaked out, not understanding his accusing manner.

"Let me ask you somethin'," he mumbled. His

eyes were narrowed with deep intensity as he looked at her—almost hatefully somehow. "All that time you was hooked up with Richardson . . . how much time did you spend lettin' him kiss you?"

"What?" Dusty breathed.

"I want to know," he growled. "How often did he kiss you? And how did he kiss you? Tell me."

He was angry—suddenly and unexpectedly angry. It sounded as if he were battling jealousy, but Dusty knew it couldn't be. So what did he want her to say?

"I don't think I have to tell you anything about it," she told him. His chest rose and fell with angered breathing. "And why would it matter to you? I'm sure you've had your share of women since you left me . . . left here."

"I've kissed my share of women, yeah," he admitted bluntly. Dusty tightly closed her eyes against any vision that might try to imprint itself on her mind. Yet when she felt him take hold of her chin, she opened them again to find him glaring down at her. "But there's kissin'," he mumbled, leaning down and kissing her multiple times in lingering succession. She was angry at herself for letting him do it—for returning his kiss even when they were in the midst of arguing. His arms went around her. He pulled her against his body, and the warm brown sugar of his eyes narrowed as he gazed at her and said, "And there's kissin'."

Immediately, his kiss was different—far more intimate and demanding. He paused, taking her face in his hand and caressing the outline of her lips with his thumbs. When he pressed his body against hers, pinning her back against the tree, she gasped slightly, and he took immediate action in capturing the vulnerability of her parted lips with his own. Dusty let the tears of heartbroken bliss escape her closed eyes as she clutched at his shirt with a frightening desperation. His whiskery face was chafing the delicate flesh around her mouth, chin, and cheeks. Yet the scratchy feel of it was invigorating—the strength of his body against hers overpowering in its dominant security—the moisture of his mouth, as ever, warm and sweet.

"Which was it?" he asked, pausing the exchange. "How did you let him kiss you?" Dusty turned her head from him, embarrassed because of her tears and clutching at his clothing less possessively. "Tell me!" he demanded. "How did he kiss you? The first way or the second?"

"He—he never kissed me the way you . . ." she stammered.

"Because he never tried . . . or because you never let him?"

"B-because I never wanted him to," came her quiet answer.

"Because you never wanted him to?" he asked. His embrace of her loosened as his attention was arrested by her confession. "You were gonna marry him!"

"I didn't want him!" she cried out suddenly, searching his face for understanding. She found only confusion. "You don't understand at all, do you? Not really."

"I—I think that I . . . maybe I don't want to understand," he admitted.

And she thought, *Because you aren't in love with me.* "Why are you here . . . with me . . . right now, Ryder?" she asked him.

"Because my mouth has been waterin' after you all day long," he angrily confessed.

She wanted to ask him why, but she feared the answer too much. Feared his answer would be far less than she dreamed of it being. She could not endure the disappointment then—or ever. Better to live in ignorant bliss than have him tell her what she could not bear to hear—that she was only someone to have fun sparking with, not someone he loved. He leaned forward, taking one more deep, impassioned, succulent kiss from her mouth before starting to leave her.

But when he tried to step back, Dusty felt the tug on the front of her dress, reached out, and pulled him closer to her again and begged, "Wait!"

He looked down curiously, following her pleading glance. Somehow during their interlude, the latch of his belt buckle had gotten caught in the lace at the waist of her dress. They were so entangled that Dusty knew his pulling away from her would tear the lace and ruin the dress.

"What now?" she asked him in frustration.

He grinned and wiped the tear from her cheek with the back of his hand. "I guess we'll just have to keep—"

"Hey there, young folks! What're you all up to?" It was old man Leroy. He was drunker than a skunk and watching the goings-on between Ryder and Dusty with an amused grin.

"Oh . . . um . . . I just had somethin' in my eye, Mr. Leroy. Ryder was helpin' me . . ." Dusty replied.

"You take me for a fool, girl?" the old man chuckled.

Ryder smiled down at Dusty and then looked over to the kindhearted man. "Actually, Leroy," he began, "I was out here makin' love to this gal, and looks like the lace of her dress is all a-tangled up with my belt buckle."

Dusty held her breath and closed her eyes in humiliation.

Old Leroy chuckled. "Well . . . you two folks keep a-fiddlin' at it. It'll all work out in the end." With a wink, he rather staggered off toward the field.

"Wise man," Ryder said, smiling down at Dusty. She felt his hands slip between their bodies at their waists, and she looked away as he kept grinning all the time he struggled with their clothing. In a moment, he had freed the lace of her dress, and she smoothed it down, unable to look at him again for feeling shy at sharing such intimate moments with him.

But Ryder would not have her feeling ashamed or shy. He put a hand under her chin, forcing her to look up at him. "It's been quite a picnic, hasn't it?"

She nodded. It had been. For as tired as she felt, it had been a welcome day—a welcome memory. He leaned toward her, to kiss her again, but she turned her head, unable to endure kissing him again—knowing that it was only in fun. He grinned understandingly.

"You work on your sister, Britches. I'll work on Feller," he told her. "Surely we can stay out of trouble doin' that . . . and somebody in this world deserves somethin' good. Don't they?" He walked away. Dusty watched as he caught up to old Leroy, throwing an arm around the man's shoulders and smiling down at him.

Dusty watched him go, her mind and spirit in complete turmoil. The night . . . the day . . . the entire day and night had been so wonderful—so hurtful. Her mind was tired. As she watched the last few colorful explosions light up the night sky, she was tired. It had been a day filled with too many things—too many confusing emotions for her mind and body to handle. Suddenly, all she wanted was what Becca had wanted—to go home.

Chapter Ten

There was a mountain of work to be done on the ranch to prepare for the coming autumn and winter. The days turned quickly into weeks. Even as summer was still heating the earth, July was filled with haying, canning, field crops, branding, and more.

Hank had the hands in the fields from before sunup to way beyond sundown every day. Dusty and Becca found the three weeks following the Fourth of July picnic in town to be a lonely time. On occasion, Miss Raynetta visited, and there was a stormy day when rain beat down so heavily the hands were forced in from the fields. Yet most of the time the men were so beaten and tired after the day's work, they dropped down in whatever pasture they found themselves, sleeping out under the stars. Feller cooked their meals over an open fire, and Dusty and Becca were left at the ranch house to their own tasks—gardening, preserving food, milking the milk cow, making butter, tending the chickens, and more. Their hearts' desires were nowhere near. All this meant long, hot days with little diversion.

Dusty spent days upon days mulling over in her mind every moment spent and every conversation she'd had with Ryder since his return. At times, she felt hope rise within her. If she were able to soften herself—to find her real self again—maybe, just maybe, he would be interested in knowing her again. And yet self-doubt and the lack of his flirtatious presence caused a gray cloud to hang over her wishes and dreams.

They'd never spoken of it again—his outrageous conduct at the picnic, her all too accepting behavior. They'd both let it remain an unspoken, uncertain past. Yet Dusty wanted desperately to ask him why—why had he treated her so adoringly? Why had he felt such a need to kiss her so recurrently and with such extreme emotion? But they'd arrived home so late from town that evening—and immediately after her father had the men out to tent under the stars, mend fences and windbreaks, count and tend the herd—there hadn't been a moment to talk with him, even if she'd had the courage.

Dusty could also see her sister's misery. It was obvious Becca was truly and thoroughly in love with Feller. She was miserable without him and even more miserable for lack of her love being returned. And there was Miss Raynetta. Dusty was convinced Miss Raynetta was as in love with her father as ever she had been twenty years ago! Her own heart ached for Miss Raynetta's. After all, she knew how agonizing it was to have the man you loved standing right in front of you and not be able to call him your own, draw from him your strength, sleep in the comfort of his arms, and bask in the bathing ecstasy of his kisses. All these thoughts Dusty pondered for days upon days upon days, until her mind was so tired she thought she could not rise another day.

August did arrive, and with it the mending of windbreaks and fences was finished. Hank Hunter and the rest of the men came home. They slept long and late the first day back in their bunks. Dusty left muffins, butter, and ham out for them when she left the house one late morning to enjoy the summer day while it still tarried. It was, in fact, almost noon when she decided to refresh herself with a wade in the pond. The waterfall looked cool and refreshing as she approached, and she quickly unlaced her boots. Tossing them under the big willow, she gasped with horror as they almost conked Ryder squarely on the head. He was stretched out beneath the tree—obviously sleeping quite soundly, for Dusty's boots landing nearby did not startle him in the least.

Quietly, Dusty moved toward him. Standing over him, she simply stared down, studying him at her leisure. He lay stretched out on his stomach, wearing only his trousers. She detected a slight snore. As a young girl, she had simply adored coming upon Ryder asleep in the barn or the field and staring at him—marveling at his attractive face and well-formed body.

Suddenly, as her eyes traveled from his feet

toward his head, she noticed for the first time the deep and painful-looking scars he bore on his back across his shoulders. Never before had she seen them! She was certain they had not been there before he'd left the ranch years before. She studied the scars intently, for they were strange. There was one very long horizontal scar, perhaps eight inches in length, lying just above and parallel to his left shoulder blade. Two more converged on either side of this scar and traveled vertically downward perhaps four inches. Multiple smaller scars were here and there surrounding the longer wounds. Dusty assumed these were from stitches having held together the once-maimed flesh. The scars looked unendurably painful! They were thick—very thick, raised, and still very purple. Still, Dusty could not begin to guess what had caused them. They did not look like anything she had seen before. One was perfectly straight, as if it had been made by a knife. The others looked more as if the flesh had been . . . torn. They were deep, and what else could have made such deep scars but a thick blade?

These scars on Ryder's back had definitely been acquired since he'd left five years ago. Dusty was certain she would have remembered seeing such awful wounds before. After all, many had been the times she'd stood just as she did now, studying him in secret as he slept. As she stepped toward him to investigate the wounds further, her foot snapped a twig. Ryder did not awaken slowly as she would have expected. Rather, his eyes popped open instantly. He flipped like a hotcake from his stomach to his back, seeming very relieved to see her standing there—almost as if he had expected something much worse.

"You scared the waddin' outta me, girl!" Ryder grumbled as he sat up and buttoned up his britches.

"I'm sorry," Dusty apologized. "I didn't mean to . . . I just . . . I just . . ." she stammered. It was startling to catch him so unguarded. He seemed nervous—as if her surprising him were far more unsettling that it should've been.

"I know, I know," he apologized. "It's your favorite spot, and now I've trodden on holy ground, so to speak." He remained sitting on the grass, bootless, sockless, and shirtless. It was obvious he'd been sleeping deeply, for he wore a frown and groggy expression.

"No, it's not that. I . . . everyone can come swimmin' here. I—I . . ." Her eyes fell to the scars.

Instantly, his expression was that of anger—yet also disgrace. He rubbed at his shoulder and quickly retrieved his shirt, putting it on and leaving it unbuttoned and hanging open. "Pretty gruesome, huh?" he mumbled as he rolled up his sleeves.

"No," she answered honestly. "Just . . . I don't remember . . ."

"That's 'cause they weren't there before," he growled. "You want a closer look?" he asked angrily. He pulled the shirt down over one shoulder and turned his back to her. "Come on now, Dusty. Why don't ya take a good, long look? Wouldn't want ya to miss anything."

It was obvious he was very self-conscious about the scars—that they provoked a deep anger in him. Yet she knew it wasn't vanity stirring his anger. He'd run around plenty without his shirt since he'd come back. It was something much deeper.

"Look here," he said, looking over his shoulder at her. He motioned to his back, just above his left shoulder blade. "You tell me, Miss Dusty . . . what do you think made them scars? What do you think happened to me to put scars like that on my back?"

"I—don't know. I . . ." She couldn't fathom how she'd come from simply walking to the pond intent on a refreshing swim to having infuriated Ryder so completely.

"Come on now! Make a guess!" he demanded.

"Ryder . . . it isn't any of my business. It's not important if—"

"It ain't important to you?" he almost shouted, jumping to his feet. "What do ya mean by that?"

"I mean . . . it can't be a good memory . . . the way you were injured. So if ya want to keep to yourself about it . . ." She shook her head, irritated she was in the situation at all. "I just came down here to relax! I didn't mean to disturb you. You need to lie back down, go back to sleep, and wake up on the right side of the bed this time!" she told him angrily. She turned and began to walk away.

"Ain't ya ever wondered what happened to me over them five years?" Ryder asked. His question was completely unexpected. "Or are ya still so wrapped up in what happened to you that it really never entered your mind to ask?"

She turned around and met his angry, hurt glare. *I wondered what happened to you every day of my life for five years! That's how I spent my time,* she thought. "Of course it entered my mind. But I figured you would've told people if you'd wanted them to know."

Ryder nodded. "A few men caught up with me a year or so ago. And 'cause you're right—I do keep my business to myself most times—here's the short of it. These men had a bone to pick with me . . . and they intended to pick—literally. Now, I make a perty good accountin' of myself in a fight—even a fight that ain't fair like this one was." He didn't have to tell her. She already knew it from firsthand experience. "But there were four of these hombres, and I didn't have it in me that day to get 'em down . . . bein' that I was still sick with somethin' rattlin' in my chest. Well, these fellers put my arms 'round a tree and tied my hands on the other side of the trunk . . . tied my feet too. And then you know what they did there, Miss Hunter?" He glared down at her. "One of them took a big ol' knife out of his boot and made that first big, long cut 'cross my back. Then he leans forward like this . . ." Ryder leaned forward and put his mouth right next to Dusty's ear, sending a wave of goose bumps erupting over her. "And he said, 'We're gonna skin you, boy! We're gonna skin you clean one strip at a time!' He stuck the blade of his dirty old knife—the kind a man uses to skin an animal—he stuck that blade real deep into that cut he made and started tearin' my skin away from my body. He yanked on it first, tearing the skin down some. I thought I was gonna pass out it hurt so bad. I never imagined anything like that in my life! Any kinda pain like that! Then, very slowly, so that it hurt all the more, he tore the skin down and down and down. Oh, I know them other scars are only a few inches down, but believe me, sugar . . . when someone's skinnin' you slow as they can . . . it hurts like hell!

"Someone had seen them come upon me and had run in town for the sheriff. If they hadn't, I'd be dead now . . . if not from bein' without my skin and bleedin' to death, for the sake of the pain. The doctor sewed me up as best he could, and thank goodness he cleaned me out good first . . . which was painful too, I might mention. I still have nightmares about them devils and what they did and intended to do to me. The physical pain on its own was more than I can tell you . . . but emotionally it messed me up a while too. So, like those close to you have been tellin' you for some time now, you need to be riddin' yourself completely of that attitude of yours and look around to see who else might have their own scars to bear!" With that, he simply glared down at her.

By now the tears were flowing freely down Dusty's cheeks. She could see in Ryder's eyes that the memory of the abuse he endured had somehow hardened his soul against her for that moment in time. His eyes were cold and angry as he looked at her. She could only stand in shock—unable to comprehend such horrors. To endure something the like! To live through it! What kind of a man . . . how much strength he must have had! And she was angry—angry anyone would hurt him so—that anyone would dare to touch him—to maim his perfect body—to cause him such pain!

"Why?" she asked in a whisper. "Why would anyone want to do that to you?"

He sighed and looked away for a moment and then back to her. "You've been angry at me before? Ain't the thought ever crossed your mind?"

She suddenly realized something then—actually consciously realized how very unselfish he was. All the time he'd been back, all he'd ever done was try to encourage her—try to draw her out.

281

And all this time she'd never thought he might have pain of his own. She had never comforted him. It was an aspect of who she'd been that she'd lost along with everything else. She felt it come back to her in that very instant! She felt the desire to be compassionate and helpful strengthen within her—even beyond what it had in emerging little by little before. It was at that moment she realized she now felt it. Now she wasn't just doing what she knew she had to do to give comfort and happiness. She felt it. Her bosom felt warm and hopeful inside. He'd done it again. Even now, again Ryder healed a part of her without even trying. She also realized he didn't want to tell her any more. For whatever reasons—and her curiosity would nearly kill her, she knew—he did not want to tell her any more.

"No," Dusty stated kindly. "I've considered slappin' you a time or two, kickin' you hard in the seat of the pants, but I've never considered skinnin' you alive." She smiled warmly at him, and he sighed with relief.

Ryder grinned, rubbed at his eyes, and mumbled, "I'm testy sometimes when I wake up."

"I figured that out," Dusty told him, wishing in her most secret of wishes she could be the one to wake him up every day forever.

He grinned and asked, "You goin' swimmin'?"

Dusty shrugged. "I was thinkin' about it."

"Well," he said, stretching, "if you're plannin'

on a bit a skinny-dippin' . . . I might hang around. Otherwise . . . I got some things to do."

Dusty's eyes widened, and she smiled, unable to completely hide her delight at his flirting with her. He grinned, obviously pleased with having made her smile. Dusty wondered why she fought so hard to conceal her delight with him. Why didn't she just throw her arms around his neck, confess to him everything she still felt—everything—and be done with it, consequences be hanged? But she couldn't—not yet. Find the Dusty he could love first. Dig her out, and then offer that woman to him. It was the only chance she would have.

"Well," she said, unfastening her skirt and letting it drop to her feet. After all, he'd seen her many a time in just her petticoats. Besides, it was the only weapon against his shocking, flirtatious remarks she had. "You go on and do what ya gotta do. I always swim in my clothes."

"Oh, I know it," he said in a low, alluring voice, feigning disappointment. He sighed, retrieving his hat from the ground. He put it on his head and picked up his boots in the other hand. "But . . . it's a good thing you came along after my swim . . . 'cause you know I don't!" With a nod and a wink, he turned and sauntered away.

The water felt good, cool, and revitalizing. As Dusty waded and swam, she thought of Ryder. Something had changed. Even for his being gone for near to three weeks with the other men, only popping in during storms and on other rare occasions, she'd somehow managed to keep the doors she'd opened where people, especially Ryder, were concerned. He hadn't acted strangely toward her because of their moments together on the Fourth. Rather, he had confided in her—a deep and painful secret. The water was soothing, as was the long nap Dusty took under the willow. She intentionally lay down just where Ryder had lain. It gave her a sense of being close to him.

She was refreshed when she awoke—strangely alive and refreshed as she walked back to the house.

ಎಚ

Dusty was astonished when she entered the parlor to find Ryder sitting in the rocking chair with Makenna on one knee, Jakie on the other. He was reading a book to them as they both lay with their heads resting contentedly against his chest. As always, Jakie had his two middle fingers in his mouth, and Makenna nuzzled Ryder's chin with the top of her head.

"What's goin' on?" Dusty asked, perplexed. "Is Alice here?"

"Dusty! There is mercy in the world! I thought you'd never get back!" Ryder exclaimed. An expression of profound relief spread over his face. Standing up, he set both of the children down snugly in the rocking chair. Handing

Makenna the book, he told her, "Now, you show Jakie the drawin's, ya hear?" The little girl nodded and smiled as he bent and kissed her affectionately on the forehead.

"What's goin' on?" Dusty asked again, suddenly very unsettled.

Frowning, Ryder put an index finger to his lips, silently shushing her. He took hold of her arm and led her out onto the back porch. "Danged if I even know! I was out saddlin' up that new stallion 'cause your daddy wanted me to start breakin' him in . . . and all of sudden, here comes Alice a-cryin' like anything. She hands me the two babies and says, 'Watch my children for me, Ryder! Where's Mr. Hunter?' I started to ask her what was wrong, but she goes off a-screamin' at me askin' where your daddy is. I told her he was in the house to rest a spell, and next thing I know, your daddy, Becca, and Feller are in the wagon with Miss Alice headin' off somewhere! Your daddy's a-hollerin' at Ruff and Guthrie to run in town and get the sheriff and the doctor, Titch is a-headin' on out to fetch Miss Raynetta . . . and here I am with two squallin' children and a saddled-up stallion in the barn!"

"What in the world?" Dusty exclaimed. "Well, what happened?"

"I don't know," Ryder assured her, shrugging his shoulders. "They didn't give me the time a day . . . just headed off like hell was nippin' at their heels!"

"Well, did ya try askin' Kenna?"

"Heck no! She was a-bawlin' like she'd had her leg cut off when I got her! I wasn't gonna upset her again. Took me danged near half an hour to settle 'em both down."

"Well, somethin's goin' on! They might need you over at Alice and Alex's. We've got to ask Kenna."

Going back inside, Ryder at her heels, Dusty smiled warmly and reassuringly at Makenna when the little girl looked up from her book. "Hey, sweetheart," Dusty cooed, crouching down beside the rocking chair and smoothing Makenna's hair from her forehead. "Did your mama decide you needed a good long visit with Ryder today? Or is somebody sick at your house?"

Immediately Makenna's lower lip pursed and began to quiver as big tears filled her eyes.

"Now, there you go, Dusty. Gettin' her all upset," Ryder grumbled from behind her—though he made no move to interfere.

"Daddy was . . . bringin' in the cattles. Some men came. There was shootin', and them cattles started runnin', and Daddy falled off his horse, and they runned over him, and he got hurted, and the bad men left," Makenna told them through her sobs.

Dusty turned to look up at Ryder and was even further frightened when she saw how pale his face was—how utterly horrified his expression.

"Where'd them cows kick him, Kenna honey?" Ryder asked.

Makenna shook her head, crying again, and Jakie followed suit. Dusty gathered them both in her arms as she crouched before the rocking chair. "Rustlers," she whispered to Ryder.

He nodded in agreement. "I'm more worried about where that boy got kicked," Ryder mumbled.

"Let's get these babies settled down, Ryder," Dusty said. She watched as he bent down, picking up Makenna and heading toward the back of the house. "Then maybe you oughta get over to Alex's and see—"

"No," he stated. "It ain't safe to leave you here alone."

He was right. Dusty knew her daddy's ranch was the closest to the Joneses'. If there were rustlers in the county, they might come there next. Still, she could see that Ryder was itching to leave, unsettled and uncharacteristically nervous.

"You all right, Kenna honey?" he asked as he pushed Dusty's bedroom door open and carried her inside.

Makenna nodded. "Mama said them men was after the cattles." Ryder nodded, seemingly unconvinced, and something in Dusty was frightened. His expression was oddly worried—too intensely worried for Ryder Maddox.

"Let's lay you and little Jake down here. This

is my bed, Kenna," Dusty said in a soothing, maternal voice. "Don't ya think it's soft?"

Makenna sniffled and nodded.

Ryder glanced nervously at the bedroom window. Dusty tried to keep the panic welling in her bosom from escaping its tight restraints. Jakie would not let go of Dusty, and she finally had to lie next to him to calm him down.

"Do ya want me to tell ya a story, Kenna?" she asked. Ryder stood looking around the room as if he didn't know what to do next.

Then Makenna begged, "I want Ryder Magics to sing me a song." Ryder started to shake his head, but when his eyes met Dusty's concerned ones and then the pleading blue pools belonging to Makenna, a slight smile and a heavy sigh escaped his lips, and he nodded.

"Sit here with me," Makenna told him, motioning to the bed next to her. Instead, he knelt down beside the bed, took one of her small hands in his own, and brushed a lock of hair from her forehead.

"What do you want me to sing to ya, honey?" he asked. Dusty could only watch him— mesmerized at the little girl's power over the man.

"The one about pretendin', Mr. Magics," came her answer.

He chuckled. "Why is it little girls like that song so much?" he asked the child. He was looking at Dusty, however.

Dusty couldn't help but smile. She remembered too being so sick with the fever when she was eleven and Ryder coming in through her window one night. He'd sung the same song to her—kneeling by her bed just as he did now and holding her hand while he smoothed the fever from her brow with his callused fingers.

" 'Cause it's pretty," Makenna answered. "It makes me dream."

Ryder bent, kissing her tenderly on the forehead, and began:

Are you pretendin' tonight, little darlin',
   Pretendin' I'm your Prince Charmin',
   Though I'm nothin' but a cowboy . . .
      a-ridin' for the brand?
Are you pretendin' I'm a gentleman . . .
      a-askin' for your hand?
Well, I'll kiss you tonight, little darlin'.
And I'll hold you real tight, in my arms.
And if you're thinkin' that my kisses . . .
      aren't really who I am,
   I'm not pretendin', little girl,
   A dream unendin', little girl,
   No more pretendin', little girl . . .
      I'm your man.

"Again," the girl demanded sleepily when he'd finished.

Ryder looked to Dusty and smiled. Jakie was

already asleep, middle slobber-drenched fingers relaxed at his side.

"All right then," he agreed. "But do ya promise to go to sleep when I'm done?"

Makenna nodded and smiled. Her little heart-shaped mouth placed a kiss in her chubby little hand and held it out to Ryder. He smiled and kissed her palm before starting his song again.

This time, by the time Ryder finished the final chorus, Makenna slept soundly. He stood and stretched as Dusty maneuvered her way off the bed.

Shutting the door behind them as they left the sleeping children, Dusty asked, "Now what?"

"Hurry up and wait, I guess," he answered.

"What's goin' on here, Ryder?" Dusty asked. He still seemed unusually unsettled.

"Couldn't tell ya," he answered. "I can say it's a whole heck of a lot harder sittin' here with the women and children than it is a-goin' along to help."

"Now ya know how the women and children always feel," Dusty teased. He nodded. "Come into the kitchen," Dusty said. "You can help me get some supper on in case anyone ever comes home."

Dusty was beginning to feel as if she were caught up in some dream come true, even for all the drama and worrying about Alex, Alice, and the sleeping children. She and Ryder alone on the ranch, children asleep in the other room, and supper needing doing—it was like a dream. The sun was setting fast. She knew when it was dark they'd both feel all the more agitated. It was best to keep a fretting, impatient man busy.

Still, Ryder wasn't much help. He kept glancing out the windows and pacing the floor anxiously. He was more company than anything else—and that was best anyway. They talked about nothing substantial, just biding their time. The sun set, the children slept, and no one came home. It was nearly eight o'clock and still nothing.

"You sleep in there with them babies tonight," Ryder said. Standing, he took his hat from the rack behind the door.

"Where are you goin'?" Dusty asked, fairly leaping to her feet.

"Well, sweet thing," he began, "as much as I would like to stay in here and sleep with you too . . . I'm not sure how your daddy would feel—"

His words and her smile were stifled instantly by the sudden bawling of calves and the sounds of restless horses out in the corral.

"Shhh!" Ryder told her. "Blow out the lamp!"

Dusty didn't pause—simply blew down the chimney of the lamp sitting in the middle of the table. She peered through the darkness as Ryder went to the door. Taking down the rifle her father kept above it, he cocked it in readiness.

"You get down on the floor," he whispered.

Dusty was terrified. "Ryder?" she whispered.

He put an index finger to his lips. Carefully, he peered out the window and into the night.

"Somethin's spookin' the horses in the corral," he said. "Someone's out there."

"Maybe it's Daddy," Dusty offered in a whisper. "Or Ruff or Guthrie come back."

"The horses wouldn't be spooked . . ." His voice trailed off. Suddenly he flung the door open and shouted. "Who's there?"

The answer came quickly in the shrill repeat of gunfire. Dusty saw a woodchip fly off the doorframe where a bullet hit. She watched Ryder aim his rifle and fire several rounds in return before slamming the door. "That wasn't very bright," he grumbled. Bullets immediately riddled the kitchen window, sending glass crashing into the sink and over the floor. Dusty screamed and covered her ears.

"Get the babies and bring them closer to us!" Reaching over and pulling a piece of glass out of his arm, he shouted, "Now!" The blood soaking the sleeve of his shirt caused Dusty to pause, horrified at what was happening. "Go on, girl! And stay down low!"

Quickly Dusty began crawling toward the bedroom, trying to keep her wits about her. Even though the gunfire had stopped for the moment, the fear in her was almost paralyzing. She could hear the children crying and reached the bedroom just as Makenna came running out, carrying her brother as best she could.

"Dusty!" the child cried.

Dusty took both children in her arms and hugged them quickly before carrying them back toward the kitchen. She stood to carry them, crouching over all the same. As she entered the kitchen, Ryder lifted the enormous kitchen table, turning it on its side, and motioned to Dusty and the children to get behind it. Then, going to one of the broken windows, he knelt below it, carefully peeking outside and then aiming his rifle.

He was patient and did not fire. He would make certain he was sure of his shot. It seemed to Dusty it would be impossible for him to hit anything in the dark. When he did fire three times in succession, Dusty heard a shout from outside and knew he'd been successful. Almost immediately, however, whoever was left outside returned fire. Ryder scrambled behind the table. The children were frightened into silence, though tears profusely streamed down their faces. Dusty comforted them as best she could—holding them tightly to her.

"Who are they?" she asked him in a whisper when the gunfire died down again.

Ryder shook his head. "We'll stay back here. It gives me a good shot if they try to—"

More gunfire interrupted him. This time, however, the shots were not hitting the house. Dusty heard her father shouting above the noise.

"They're back!" Ryder breathed. Jumping to

his feet, he bolted for the back door before she could stop him.

He started to open the door, no doubt to join the fight now that the threat seemed to be distracted from the house. Looking and seeing Dusty and the children huddled in fear, he paused, his attention arrested by something else. Slowly he turned toward the parlor and peered into the darkness. A shot split through the room. Dusty saw Ryder reel back a moment before firing his rifle into the darkened room beyond. Blood immediately stained his shirt at the shoulder as he fired several more shots. As he headed toward the parlor, Dusty reached out and caught hold of his leg.

"Wait," she begged.

"It's all right," he muttered without looking at her. Carefully he disappeared into the parlor.

"He's down," he called. She heard him growling angrily at someone and could hear scuffling, and in the next moment, her father burst through the front door.

Dusty screamed, startled at her father's abrupt entrance. "Ryder's been hurt! Where's Becca? What's going on?" she babbled anxiously as she pointed her father toward the parlor.

Ryder entered the kitchen, nodding a greeting at Hank and saying, "Got one tied down in there. Son of a—gun got into the dang house!"

Hank reached out and tugged at Ryder's torn shirt to inspect the wounds in his shoulder and arm. "There's four more out in the yard there. Two were already down when we got here. The others . . ." He trailed off and looked to Dusty. "Rustlers. Went after Alex Jones's steers. Guess they weren't satisfied with 'em and decided to come here 'fore makin' for the hills."

"Is Alex well?" Dusty asked. "Kenna said he was injured and . . ."

Hank glanced to Kenna, her large blue eyes filled with fear and sadness. "Alex's fine. Couple a broken ribs, I think." Then he nodded to Ryder and added, "Looks like this boy's more banged up than Alex. You better get to it, Dusty. Clean him up." Reaching out, he smiled, hefting Kenna up onto one hip and Jakie onto the other. "We'll let Feller and the other boys help the sheriff, and I'll take care of these little bits." With a chuckle, he trotted down the hall with the children, rattling off something about having peppermint sticks hidden under his bed.

Dusty stood, mouth gaping as she stared after him. That was it? Her father waltzes in after a confrontation the likes of rustlers and just gallops the children back to the bedroom? And where was Becca? Certainly she wasn't out in the yard cleaning up dead rustlers with Feller and the sheriff.

She turned quickly as she heard Ryder's boots heavy on the kitchen floor headed for the door. "Hold on there," she scolded, reaching out and taking hold of his pants by the waist. "You're not goin' anywhere!"

"It's just a scratch or two, Dusty. I don't need—" he began to argue.

"Sit!" she commanded, pointing to a chair.

With a heavy sigh, Ryder turned the chair around and, straddling it and sitting down hard, stripped off his shirt. She knew he was near to crazy with wanting to be outside where the excitement was. Yet she also knew how fast infection could set into a serious wound. So with great trepidation, she mustered her courage, inhaled, and bent down to investigate his injuries.

"It's a pretty bad graze at your shoulder," she mumbled more to herself than anyone, "but this one on your arm . . ." It was a deep wound the glass had made. Undoubtedly, Ryder Maddox would have another nasty scar to add to his collection.

Dusty bustled around boiling water and retrieving ointments and bandages. All the while, Ryder sat patiently watching her scurry about. At last, she set the kettle of hot water on the floor and began sponging his wounds clean. She glanced up to see him smiling down on her. A frown immediately puckered her brow.

"What?" she asked.

"Nothin'," he chuckled, wincing as she cleaned the wound on his arm.

"What?" she demanded indignantly. What could he possibly find amusing about their situation?

"Just you . . . so frownin' and serious."

His answer seemed absolutely ludicrous. Of course she was serious! Alex and Alice had been attacked! Ryder had been injured! Becca was who knew where, and there were dead men lying in the yard! Then she remembered something else. There was one in the parlor as well!

"There's a man in the parlor!" Dusty exclaimed, leaping to her feet.

"Oh, he's out cold," Ryder assured her. "I made sure of it. The sheriff can get him when he's done out there."

Dusty looked at him and shook her head. Men! Was everything always so trivial in their eyes? Again Ryder chuckled, and Dusty scowled at him.

"I'll have to stitch this one shut, you know."

"I know."

"Then what are you still grinnin' about?" She had lost any amount of patience she might have possessed.

"You," came his answer. "A-scurryin' around like a little mother mouse."

"Would you prefer I left ya here to get infected and die, writhin' in pain and the stench of gangrene stinkin' up my kitchen? Maggots eatin' out your eyes?" She sighed with irritation as he laughed wholeheartedly.

She flung the cloth she'd been using to tend to his wounds at him and turned to leave. But he reached out and caught hold of her skirts. She turned to face him indignantly.

"Now don't go hissin' your tail up," he said, smiling and standing up from the chair. He put his hands at her waist and pulled her toward him. The syrup of his eyes sent her heart to pounding a different beat than when she'd been scared such a short time before. "I was just thinkin' . . . I like playin' house with you now a whole lot more than I did when you were little." As Dusty's eyes widened at his flirtatious manner, he added, "Well . . . let's just say . . . it's a mite different these days."

Quickly, she swallowed the impulse to throw herself against him, wrap her arms around his neck, and draw blissful rapture from his mouth. Instead she calmly stated, "I imagine that it is . . . bein' that you're standin' here bleedin' your life out all over me."

"I ain't bleedin' to death, and you know it," he mumbled, brushing a strand of hair from the corner of her mouth.

Almost instantly, the realization she'd been trying to ignore for the past while hit her fully in the midsection. Tears sprang to her eyes and tumbled over her cheeks.

"But you could've been!" He could easily have been killed in the shooting—walking into the parlor as he had done—even by the glass flying everywhere when the windows shattered.

"Naw," he breathed. "Not me. It would take a lot more'n rustlers to take me down." His reassurances comforted her—no matter how unrealistic they were. She smiled, brushing the tears from her cheeks. He endeavored to pull her closer to him, but she pressed her hands against him with resistance.

"I'm upset," she whispered. "I . . . I don't want ya to tease me just now."

"I'm not teasin' you, kitten," he mumbled, kissing the top of her head. Then he did what she wanted him to do. He gathered her into his powerful embrace as he said, "I'm holdin' you close to my heart so you'll hear it beatin' and know this whole mess is over . . . and I'm just fine."

Dusty laid her cheek against the warmth of his mighty chest and indeed drew greater comfort than she had imagined possible from the soft rhythm originating within him. The beat of his heart was so soothing—so strong. She knew why babies liked to lie against their mothers' breasts to go to sleep—understood why she had often seen her mother with her head lying against her father's chest as they lay stretched out under the big oak watching their girls wade in the creek. It was an embrace of security—an assurance that the person you loved indeed lived.

"Now, finish playin' house with me and bandage me up so I can get out there and find out what needs doin'. All right?" Dusty unwillingly pushed herself out of Ryder's embrace and nodded. She directed him to the chair, and she continued patching him up.

"Them babies will probably have nightmares for a year after all this," he mumbled, wincing as she worked on him.

Dusty nodded, guiltily distracted by the smooth contours of his arms and shoulders as she tended him. Ryder was exactly what her rather outrageous Aunt Gertie would've called "a mean piece of work." *How could any woman not throw herself at his feet and beg him to love her?* she wondered briefly.

"They're tucked in snugger'n bugs in a rug," Hank said, stretching and yawning as he came down the hall. "That yeller dog still out in the parlor?"

"Ain't heard a peep from him," Ryder answered.

"Well, I left Miss Raynetta and Becca over at Joneses' . . . figured they needed 'em more'n we did. But lookin' at the likes a you makes me wonder, boy," Hank said, leaning over Dusty to inspect Ryder's injuries again.

"Oh, I been way more cut up than this, boss," Ryder assured him with a meaningful wink at Dusty. "I think I'll fare fine."

"Well, when Dusty's got you sewed shut . . . come on in here and help me drag this filth outta my house." With that, Hank disappeared into the parlor.

Dusty's hands trembled as she secured several stitches of blue thread through the wound on Ryder's arm. How she'd hated having to be the one to sew up the hands since her mother passed away. But working on Ryder had been almost unendurable! Still, she managed not to faint as she stitched and bandaged. Then she could only sit in the chair where he'd sat and watch Ryder and her father awkwardly drag the unconscious man from their parlor and out into the yard.

"If you don't let that arm rest, it'll bleed all night!" she called after them. But she knew it was useless. Ryder would work himself into the grave before he'd admit to being licked. All she could do was hope her stitches had been secure and her bandages tight enough.

Laying her head on the table, she meant only to rest her weary eyes for a moment. When she felt something warm brush her cheek, her eyes fluttered open, and she realized she'd fallen asleep.

"Come on, Britches," Ryder mumbled quietly. "Let's haul your fanny to bed so you can get some rest." She realized, as he put his fingers to her face once more, it had been the back of his hand caressing her cheek that had awakened her.

"I'm not tired," she said as she closed her dry, tired eyes once more. The quick vision of the way Ryder used to so often carry her from the creek, the haystack, or the porch swing when she was a child—the way he'd carry her into the house and to bed—the memories flittered through her half-conscious mind. As a child, she'd often worn herself into a sleep before reaching the house. Ryder would come lugging her in, and her mother would scold him for pampering her daughter so.

"You always do this," he grumbled as he pulled her to her feet and began to gather her in his arms. "Won't just walk the ten feet to your bed. Gotta sit down somewhere first and . . ."

Dusty pulled herself to full consciousness when she realized he intended to lift her and carry her to bed. Had his arm and shoulder been well, she would not have thought twice about letting him do so—merely because she was so very tired and her defenses were down. But he was not well, and the strain of lifting her could only serve to hurt him.

She squirmed out of his arms. "Fine, fine, fine," she grumbled. "I'm going." She staggered down the hallway into her bedroom, delighted by the dreamy warmth of his chuckle.

Chapter Eleven

There it was—the feeling someone was watching. This time, Dusty opened her eyes to see Kenna staring at her with an expression of profound impatience.

Dusty smiled, rubbed at her still dry and tired eyes, and said, "Good morning, sweet pea."

Immediately, Kenna burst into excited chatter. "We has been awake, Dusty. I'm hungry, and Jakie's drawers were soakin' wet! He wet clean through onto Mr. Hunter's bed, and Feller didn't have nothin' to diaper him in but one of your aprons, and he's so fussy!"

Dusty smiled at the thought of Feller Lance having to give a go at changing a baby's diaper—especially with nothing at hand to use for one.

"Who's fussy?" she asked Kenna. "Feller or Jakie?"

Kenna rolled her eyes impatiently. "Jakie!"

"So I guess it's time I was gettin' up," Dusty said.

Kenna nodded and smiled, her tangled curls of hair bouncing along like a happy tune.

Dusty dressed quickly and entered the kitchen to find Feller shoveling breakfast into Jakie's mouth. She clamped her hand over her own mouth to stifle the giggle wanting to leap out at the sight. There sat Jakie in one of the big kitchen chairs, an apron at his waist—the ties wrapped around him and the back of the chair and knotted securely to hold him steady. He kicked his feet with delight as Feller awkwardly fed him applesauce straight from a quart jar with one of the biggest spoons owned by the Hunter family.

"Now ain't that good, boy?" Feller chuckled.

"Yeah . . . you eat your applesauce good, and it'll put hair on your chest!"

Dusty wondered if Becca had ever seen Feller in such a light. Knowing Becca would be delighted at the sight, she felt sad her sister had been the one to be away for the night helping Alice.

"Good mornin', Feller," she greeted with an amused grin.

"Mornin', Miss Dusty," Feller grumbled, clearing his throat. He seemed humiliated at having been caught with his perpetual guarded manner absent. "Just sloppin' the piglets . . . though that Miss Kenna's finickier than all get out."

"I'm not surprised," Dusty sighed, going to the cupboard and removing a loaf of bread and a jar of jelly. Experience had taught Dusty that, indeed, Kenna wouldn't eat well when away from home.

"Quite a ruckus last night 'round here, wasn't it?" Feller sighed, lifting the apron at Jakie's lap and clumsily wiping his face.

"I was wrung out! I didn't even stay awake long enough to find out what happened after Daddy went out to talk to the sheriff," Dusty admitted, a little ashamed. All she'd cared about was making sure Ryder had been tended to.

"Your daddy sent Ryder over this mornin' to fetch Becca—Miss Becca and Guthrie home. Your daddy's gone into town to round up a couple a hands to help Alex out 'til he's up to snuff, and Ruff and Titch are long gone to the pastures a-countin' head." It was amazing how much information Feller could give a person in two sentences.

"Well, it looks like you've got things well in hand in here, Feller," Dusty teased. "I guess I'll just be about my business cleanin' up the mess in here and the parlor. I'm glad you swept the glass up though."

"Couldn't have them young-uns a-runnin' around with it like that," Feller mumbled.

"You'll make a mighty fine daddy to somebody one day," Dusty told him. He simply rolled his eyes and shook his head the way he did when he was embarrassed.

The parlor was destroyed! The lamp in one corner had been shattered, no doubt by the gunfire the night before. Whoever the wounded man was, he had bled all over the carpet her mother had ordered all the way from Chicago. It was lost, and it made Dusty profoundly sad to have to roll it up and pitch it outside to wait to be cremated. Feller helped her right the table and ran around after Kenna and Jakie like he hadn't ever been so amused in his life.

Before lunch, Ryder and Guthrie returned, Becca riding behind Ryder, arms tightly around his waist. Dusty felt a small shiver of jealousy run through her and scolded herself in silence. She knew where Becca's heart belonged, and her poor sister looked completely done in as she slid off Ryder's mount.

"You look whipped," Dusty said, hugging her tightly.

"I am," she exclaimed with a fatigued sigh. "I've never been so tired. Alex was so miserable all night, and Miss Raynetta and I sat up with Alice, and . . . oh, I've got to sit down a spell."

Dusty looked up to where Ryder had dismounted and was walking his horse to the corral. He nodded and tipped his hat with a smile. She turned and led Becca to the porch swing.

"How banged up is he?" Dusty inquired as she sat down next to Becca. Pushing with her toes at the porch floor, she started them rocking back and forth.

"Pretty bad. Both eyes black . . . one's completely swole shut. I'm certain he's got half his ribs, at least, crunchin' up in there . . . probably a broken arm. Doc's out from town again this mornin'. Ol' Alex looks like somethin' the dog upchucked." Dusty smiled at her sister's use of one of Ryder's terms.

Feller and the children came out of the house. Becca stared at Feller, an expression of wonderment in her eyes at the sight of him with the children. Kenna jumped up in Becca's lap, and Becca gave the child her attention, smiling lovingly at her as Jakie sat completely content on

Feller's hip. Dusty giggled as she watched Jakie inquisitively staring up at Feller's unshaven face and ever sucking his two middle fingers.

"Did you see my daddy, Becca?" Kenna asked.

"I did! He's gonna be just fine. A few bruises and all, but otherwise he's ready for you to come home and give him some sugar!" Becca said, kissing Kenna's forehead and smoothing her hair. "Miss Raynetta's gonna come get you in a while and take you home to see your mama and daddy. I bet you're ready to sleep in your own bed." Kenna nodded.

Feller slapped at some insect on his arm. "Flies are bitin'. Hope Miss Raynetta don't waste too much time a-gettin' here." Dusty knew flies nipping at something other than the stock was a sure sign of a storm.

"Maybe I oughta take these babies home now," Ryder offered, stepping up onto the porch. "That litter of puppies out behind the barn are chewin' the grass down to nothin'."

"Storm. Bad one. Bad lightnin' for sure," Feller agreed.

"I'm goin' in. I am so tired," Becca mumbled. She stood and stumbled toward the house.

Dusty watched her exhausted sister go into the house and then looked at the two tired cowboys.

"How long 'til the storm gets here?" she asked.

Feller looked up at the clouds starting to gather in the west. "Don't know. But I figure we better get these kids home now if they wanna be sleepin' with their mama tonight."

Ryder looked so tired. Dark circles shaded his eyes, and the dried blood on his sleeve told her the wound on his arm had been bleeding again. "I should check your arm, Ryder," she said.

"Naw. I just bumped it in the barn this mornin'. It'll be fine. Let's get them kids home." He yawned, and Feller, ever chivalrous and realizing Ryder's need to recover, took Kenna by the hand and descended the porch stairs.

"You let Dusty tend that arm, boy," he grumbled. "I'll take the kiddies home."

"But I'm saddled up and . . ." Ryder began. Feller turned and raised his eyebrows. Ryder nodded in agreement. "All right then."

"Bye-bye, Dusty!" Kenna called. "We're goin' home now!"

Dusty smiled and waved at the little chubby-cheeked angel. "You give your mama my love now! Tell her I'll be over as soon as I can." Kenna waved her assurance and skipped along contentedly beside Feller. Dusty paused to note how natural Feller looked walking alongside the girl, hauling Jakie on his hip. Yep. She'd like to see Feller Lance be the daddy to her nieces and nephews someday.

"Now," she said, turning to Ryder, "as for you . . . strip that shirt off, and let me see your bandages."

A low chuckle rumbled in his throat as he stripped off his shirt in one swift move. "I understand you wantin' to see me with my shirt off . . . but my arm's gettin' sore now, and I don't know if I want you pokin' at it."

Dusty felt the blush on her cheeks—though she tried to act unaffected. "You hush up," she said. She examined his arm and determined the bandages needed to be changed. Taking his hand, she led him into the kitchen and directed him to a chair.

"Bossy little thing today, ain't ya?" Ryder asked, smiling as if he had some secret amusement. His persistent, teasing smile unnerved her as she worked to change the bandage. There was mischief in his tired eyes. Although her heart began to hammer furiously, the door of fear within her soul, struggling to protect her, began to bolt itself against him.

"There," she sighed as she finished tying the bandage. "All done."

She smiled down at him, expecting him to stand up and leave. Instead, he reached out, taking hold of her forearm with both his strong, roughened hands. Turning her palm up, he kissed her wrist softly, trailing his thumb along the vein showing itself beneath her smooth skin. Pulling her closer to him so her knees were now pressed firmly against his thigh, he kissed the bend in her arm.

"What . . . what are you doin'?" Dusty breathed, trying to pull her arm free of his control.

Instantly and unexpectedly, Ryder was on his feet, defensive and determined. "Now . . . I've kept my hands offa you for a long while," he stated. He spoke as if reminding her—as if she were able or even wanted to forget the bliss of being in his arms and the moist power of his kiss.

"As—as well you should," she stammered.

"Why?" His eyebrows puckered into a sincere frown.

"Because . . . because it's not proper for you to," she told him.

"Proper? I used to ride you around on my back half the darn time when you was fourteen, and that wasn't proper! But it never seemed to bother you then!" She didn't understand his sudden agitation. "Your mama got all over me for that . . . but . . ."

"I don't understand this, Ryder," Dusty finally said as he let go of her arm.

"Do you know why I came back here?" he interrupted.

"Because you like it here," she snapped, quoting the reason he'd given her that blissful night under the waterfall.

"I came back here to kiss you!"

"Yeah. You told me that before too, and—"

"I meant it. I came back here," Ryder lowered his voice to nearly a whisper as he leaned toward her, his eyes narrowed, his mouth tight with frustration, "I came back here to kiss you, Dusty. To get a good, long, tasty drink of your mouth and satisfy the desire I couldn't satisfy five years ago. I came back here to do that, sugar. And if you think I'm gonna stand around while you go on a-teasin' me night and day—"

"Teasin' you?" Dusty exclaimed in her own defense.

"Teasin' me!" he nearly shouted in a whisper. "Just like ya always done right before I left. I don't even think ya always knew you were a-doin' it . . . but sometimes ya did. And sometimes ya do. I know you too awful well."

She ignored his preaching about her teasing him. She had a more important question. "If that's why you came back then . . . then why didn't you just do it when you first got here? Why did ya—"

"You were so stuffed up in your own misery . . . you wouldn't even look me in the eye when I first came back! I can just imagine what ya woulda done to me if I had thrown you on the ground and had my way with you right then and there!" He was nearly shouting now, and Dusty suddenly remembered Becca had gone into the house earlier to rest.

"Sshhh!" she hushed him. "You'll wake Becca."

"I don't care if I wake Becca! I don't care if the whole world hears me 'cause you and me, we're gonna have it out right now!" With that, he

311

swooped her up in his arms and headed for the door. "I'm sick a this cat-and-mouse bullsh— manure!"

"Your arm!" she exclaimed, not wanting to struggle for fear of hurting him.

"Dang the arm, Dusty! You better get to worryin' about your own safety!" he growled as he lumbered out onto the porch and down the stairs. All she could do was put her arms around his neck and listen to him mumbling under his breath as he walked toward the barn. "Swishin' your little fanny around like nobody's business! Smilin' all sweet and sugary! Runnin' your hand over my arm like that." He paused in his grumbling and looked to her as he stood still for a moment. "Grass or straw?" he asked.

"What?" she breathed. "What're ya doin'? And what in tarnation are ya talkin' about?" He was mad! She was certain he'd lost his mind.

"Grass or straw? Where do you prefer I do this? Grass or straw?" he repeated.

"D-do what?" she stammered. The excitement that had begun to burn in her chest now spread throughout all her limbs. He meant to . . .

"Fine. Grass. It don't itch!" he answered for her, turning on his heels and heading toward the creek bank.

Thick clouds had gathered overhead, ushering in the beginnings of the storm. There was an ominous excitement in the air. As Ryder reached the grassy bank of the creek, Dusty couldn't understand how they'd gone from dressing his wounds to arguing over his assaulting her. He rather roughly set her down on the ground and stood, muscles tensed and jaw clenched, staring down at her.

"Ryder," she began.

"Hush your mouth, girl!" he ordered.

She watched every muscle in his torso flex as he clenched and unclenched his fists. She was quiet for a moment until she noticed the blood seeping through the bandage on his arm again.

Leaping to her feet, she reached out and took hold of his arm. "You're gonna tear those stitches out if you don't . . ." But her words were lost as she felt his hand caress her cheek.

"You're never gonna forgive me for breakin' your heart back then, are ya?" he asked her. His face was no longer angry, his shoulders slumped with defeat.

"I have nothin' to forgive ya for," she whispered as his thumb traveled over her lips. Then a courage she thought she'd lost forever surfaced in her soul for a brief moment. "You know, don't you?" He frowned and looked at her uncertainly. "You . . . you know that . . . just now for a second . . . for an instant I wanted . . . I wanted you to . . ."

"And ya don't want me to now?" he asked. She was astonished by the intonation of hurt in his voice. Or did she imagine it? "Now, you don't want me to—"

She put her fingers to his lips to silence him—afraid of what he might speak. "What did ya plan to do?" she asked him.

"Kiss you," he mumbled. "Just kiss ya, sugar. That's all. You know that."

"No, I mean . . ." She paused. Yet it was something that had been eating at her very soul ever since he'd spoken of it at the picnic in July. She'd forced it to the back of her mind, not wanting to endure the visions it evoked—not wanting to be conscious of it. "You told me that . . . there were other women these past years . . . other women you . . ." She interrupted herself in an effort to control the wave of jealousy, hurt, and anger washing over her.

"And I told you that I never kissed them the way I—"

"You never hauled them out of the kitchen and down to the creek bank?" she asked. Ryder smiled sympathetically and shook his head, no. "Promise?"

"I never hauled nobody down to the creek bank . . . especially with the intentions I had today," he answered. "You ever touch Cash Richardson's bare naked stomach?" he asked, and she immediately drew her hands away from his waist where she'd been slightly caressing him—unconsciously.

He chuckled as she shook her head and placed her hands on her crimson cheeks. She took a step back from him, but he took hold of her wrists and held them at her back—pulling her body flush with his own.

"Did you? Did you ever touch him like you do me?" Dusty could only shake her head, mesmerized by the intensity of his gaze. "Don't you ever be afraid to touch me, Dusty."

He paused and placed a long, heated kiss on her neck. Releasing her wrist he'd been holding behind her, he put his hand at the small of her back, running it up her spine. Even through her corset she could feel the power and warmth of it there. He'd done it again. As her body melted helplessly against his, she realized that once again he'd vanquished her will to resist him—broken the lock on the door keeping her safe from heartbreak.

"I'm gonna have my way with you yet," he chuckled in her ear.

Dusty locked the first two fingers of each hand into the belt loops at either side of his hips as his hands held her face, drawing her mouth to his own. His kiss was so familiar, so perfect. *Please,* she thought to herself. *Please, Dusty . . . don't be afraid to touch him.*

But even as his kiss breathed passion, led her into a kissing she'd known with only him, only cared to know with him, she could not return his embrace. The times in the past when he'd kissed her, she'd never been able to embrace him—to let her hands slide up and over his chest to his shoulders—caress him as she wished in her innermost soul to do. Her mouth surrendered to him more than willingly enough, every thread of her lost in delirium. Still, she could not completely let go of her fear. She wanted to run her fingers through his hair, feel his jaw under her palm working to weave his spell of ecstasy. But she couldn't. And, after long moments, she sensed the frustration—the defeat in him. Though he smiled at her wistfully, stroked her lips with his thumb, she knew she'd disappointed him. The passionate kiss he'd meant to give to her from the moment he returned—it would never be fulfilled if she couldn't be completely lost in it with him.

Ryder tweaked her nose playfully, actually slapped Dusty on the bottom as if she were still a child, and said, "Run along now. You've wasted enough of your time tendin' me today."

"Ryder," she began. She wanted to beg him to give her another chance—plead with him to be patient with her—tell him she would die if he left her again.

"Run along, sugar. Ain't no more to say . . . today." And he began walking toward the barn.

She watched him go, drowning in agony. *Why?* she wondered. Why couldn't she reach out and try to win his heart? He'd kissed her so intimately! Surely he would be willing to fill her heart if she could just reach out and take hold of him for once.

කර

The bright flash of lightning followed almost instantly by a crash of thunder startled Dusty from her sleep. The exhausting night before coupled with the emotional twisting she'd endured at Ryder's hand during the day had drained her, and she'd fallen asleep fast and deep. Now the rain was pouring down harder than it had all summer, and Dusty couldn't believe she'd slept through the beginning of the storm. Almost at once there was another flash of lightning and simultaneously a crack of thunder overhead—so loud that Dusty let out a startled scream. In the next moment, her bedroom door flew open to reveal a completely rattled Becca.

"Dusty! This storm—the lightning is so close!" Becca exclaimed. Dusty immediately rose from her bed and went to look out the window. "For Pete's sake, Dusty, don't stand so close to the window! Are you crazy?"

The next bolt was almost blinding as it shot across the sky, but it wasn't until Dusty covered her ears before the attending crack of thunder that she noticed the next bolt hit the ground near the center of the corral.

"Is Daddy up, Becca?" she asked. "It's gonna hit the house!"

The words were no sooner out of her mouth than a streak of blinding light struck the chimney of the bunkhouse as Dusty looked on. As the accompanying thunder cracked, deafening in its volume, the fire sparked on the bunkhouse roof caught like dry grass in a prairie field.

"Daddy!" Dusty screamed. Turning, she fled from the room without a word to Becca. "Daddy! The bunkhouse is on fire!"

Hank Hunter burst out of his room wearing only his long underwear and boots. Not even pausing to answer her, he was through the kitchen and out the back door.

"Daddy!" Dusty called after him. The lightning was still striking too close for comfort, and she knew the fire from the bunkhouse might also attract it. Yet even as Becca rushed into the kitchen, Dusty shouted, "Come on! Somebody might be hurt!"

Oh, how she prayed silently and in mumbled words for Ryder's safety—for the safety of all the hands! Becca's face was void of color, and Dusty knew she was saying her own silent prayers.

The rain was torrential! Dusty wondered as she stepped off the back porch and into the sheets of water how it was the bunkhouse continued to burn with such drenching moisture—but it did. As Becca and Dusty raced toward it, they saw the men stumbling from the bunkhouse, dazed and coughing from the smoke.

"Anybody hurt?" Hank shouted. Even though the lightning and thunder were moving away, the downpour was still deafening.

Dusty listened and watched—wiping the water from her eyes.

Ruff coughed, and Titch answered, "Guthrie got conked on the head by a beam that fell! I couldn't get to him, and Ryder and Feller are still in there!"

With unspoken understanding, Dusty looked to Becca, who looked to Dusty—fear of an unrealized nightmare blazoned across both their faces.

"Lord, help us!" Dusty heard her daddy pray as he started toward the bunkhouse.

"No! Boss! It's blazin' in there!" Ruff shouted, taking hold of Hank's arm.

"Those are my men in there, boy!" Hank shouted, angrily yanking his arm free.

As he ran toward the burning building, Ryder and Feller exited, dragging Guthrie by the feet and arms. For a moment, a vision flashed in Dusty's mind of another fire—long ago. Another fire and another rescue by Ryder, but the danger at hand left no time to reminisce.

After depositing the injured man at the feet of Dusty and Becca, Feller turned to Hank. "You want us to bucket line it from the well, Hank?"

Dusty only wanted to tend to Ryder, who stood before her, coughing and covered in black soot. His right hand went to the stitched wound at his arm and pressed against it for a moment as he winced. Still, he seemed to be breathing all right, with no new visible injuries. Guthrie, though still breathing, was unconscious. A large laceration across his forehead bled profusely.

"Let it burn. There's no savin' it now," Hank mumbled as he stood watching the fire. "Least everyone's out."

Dusty and Becca knelt and studied Guthrie's wound.

"Let's get him to the house," Dusty ordered. As she stood and looked at all the ranch hands standing about, some dressed in nothing but trousers, some in their underwear and boots, she added, "Let's get everyone into the house."

"Titch and Ruff, you boys get Guthrie on in!" Hank ordered. "Feller, you, me, and Ryder are gonna get the stock out of the barn . . . just in case the wind changes and whips that fire over thata way." He pointed to Dusty and added, "Get that boy tended to, girls. Then get them boys dried off and warmed up. Get a fire goin' in the kitchen, Becca."

Dusty watched as, without a pause, Ryder, barefoot and wearing only trousers, started toward the barn. It was obvious his arm was giving him pain, but he ran off behind her father anyway. Feller, who had managed somehow to be wearing his boots and trousers, followed close behind.

"Just lay him out on the table in the kitchen,"

Dusty instructed Ruff as he and Titch worked to carry Guthrie inside.

Becca was close at Dusty's heels. Almost immediately after entering the house, Dusty and Becca both began to shiver with cold. Realizing only then that both she and her sister stood there before the men in only their soaking wet night-dresses, she said quietly to Becca, "Run get a shawl for each of us, Becca." Becca blushed and obeyed as Dusty began dabbing at Guthrie's wound with a dishcloth.

"Put a kettle on for me, Titch," Dusty instructed. "Put somethin' under his feet, Ruff. He's as pale as a ghost."

It was a long while that Dusty and Becca tended to Guthrie, cleaning his wound and then making him comfortable. He was just beginning to gain consciousness when her father, Feller, and Ryder entered, dripping wet and looking like they were dead on their feet.

"It didn't catch the barn," Hank announced. "Bunkhouse is nothin' but smolderin' ashes now. How's Guthrie?"

"He's comin' around, Daddy. He's got a big ol' goose egg on the back of his head . . . but it's swellin' out, so he oughta be fine except for a headache," Dusty answered.

"Good," Hank breathed with relief. "Then let's get these boys laid out somewhere."

Dusty and Becca scrounged what extra blankets

they could to help the men settle in on the floor of the parlor. Most of their own belongings, including clothing, had burned. After her father built a fire in the parlor hearth, and she and Becca had seen the men all bedded down as comfortably as possible, Dusty retired to her own bed and attempted to sleep.

The events of the past twenty-four hours—the fire, the rustlers, and mostly the moments spent in intimate exchange with Ryder—however, kept her mind too alive for sleep. So it was that in the early hours of morning, even too early for her father or the ranch hands to be up, Dusty carefully made her way among the sleeping men. She checked each one to ensure they were as warm and as comfortable as possible. Here and there she'd pull up a blanket, and as she did, she wondered how long they'd all have to run around in their bare feet and underwear. She'd always worried about the men who hired on at the ranch, even when she was little. In the winter or during big storms, she would beg her mama to let them all sleep on the floor in the house, completely convinced they wouldn't be warm and safe enough in the bunkhouse. As she grew older, she still worried. Guthrie and Titch coughed in their sleep, and Dusty winced, knowing the smoke in their lungs, coupled with the fact they'd all been drenched to the bone, would surely cause someone to take on a cold.

Feller slept soundly on his stomach, his head resting on his hands, and she almost tripped over one of his elbows bent at the side of his head. Reaching down, she pulled his blanket up over his back. Then she looked to where Ryder lay nearby.

Ryder slept on his back, hands folded beneath his head, bare feet crossed as if he were awake and simply staring at the ceiling. As she silently approached him and stood gazing down at him, she scolded herself. She had the sudden urge to lie down next to him and snuggle close—sleep there in such a blissful state. His blanket too had slipped away, and Dusty stood in silent awe at the perfect form of him. Even as he slept, the muscles in his arms and chest were so well-defined they were indeed far beyond merely admirable. Uncon-sciously, she exhaled a heavy sigh of admiration and longing. She wanted him for her own so much more than she'd ever wanted anything in her entire life. Almost half of her life she'd wanted him. He was so wonderful— so witty, strong, and extraordinary!

Her mind drifted to the conversation they'd had the day before. *Don't you ever be afraid to touch me,* he'd said. She wanted to! Just to brush the hair from his forehead, hold his hand. He'd never know how much she wanted to hug him, throw herself into his arms as she once did, caress the smooth surface of his skin when he kissed her, feel her fingers tangled in his hair.

But Dusty could only stand gazing down at him. Only now were the moments quiet enough, with everyone safe in the house—only now was peace restored so she could let her mind wander back. It seemed so long ago, as it always did, and yet like yesterday in many ways.

The hayloft of the old barn had always been Dusty's secret, quiet-thinking, and daydreaming space. Her grandpa had built the barn, and somehow Dusty always felt as if he were up in the loft with her—watching her think as she'd been told he'd watched her daddy so many times when Henry "Hank" Hunter was a little boy. Sometimes she let Becca come up with her, and they'd talk about their dreams or just about nothing. But that crisp, autumn evening, Dusty's mind and heart were in turmoil. Soon she would be fourteen, and with each passing day she felt her heart binding itself tighter and tighter to the young cowboy who had been hired on by her daddy over three years before. It was some- thing she didn't know how to manage. Ryder was ever so much older than she. She was still a child in the eyes of the world—and in his. Yet she loved him—more dearly than anything! She knew the drought was bad for the ranch. She'd heard her daddy telling her mama that very afternoon that, if the weather didn't change come spring, they might actually lose the ranch.

So on that cool autumn evening, Dusty Hunter sat in the hayloft trying to understand the guilt she felt for wishing the weather would change so her daddy wouldn't lose his ranch—and for the mere fact that she didn't want to lose the ranch hands along with it. The guilt she felt was horrible! For, admittedly, she cared more for the fact that Ryder might have to leave than she did about whether her daddy would lose every-thing he'd worked so hard to maintain.

Sighing heavily, with tears on her cheeks, she had lain back in the soft straw and fallen asleep for some time. What woke her was the thick scent of smoke—the sharp crackle of fire. No one knew for sure what started the blaze—though Feller always suspected Bill West had been smoking in one of the empty stalls. Dusty's mama didn't allow the hands to smoke—at least in her presence or where she could see them. Bill had been notorious for hiding away and rolling a smoke now and again. Whatever the reason for the blaze, as soon as Dusty realized the barn was afire, she quickly dashed to the ladder leading down from the loft. Yet when she reached it, the fire below was so terrifying she couldn't force herself to climb down! All she could see below were flames—everywhere! Even when she saw Feller leading two horses out of their stalls, holding a cloth to his face and cough-ing as the smoke burned his eyes and lungs, she could not call to him—paralyzed by fear.

She ran to one of the loft windows and pushed at the shutters. But it was the window her father never opened, and the latch was so rusty she couldn't budge it. Quickly, she ran to the opposite side of the barn and pushed at the large doors there. The doors had been bolted against the autumn winds after the loft was filled with straw for the winter. If it had been summer, they would've been open all the time so straw could be pitched out through the doors and down to the ground below. But they'd been bolted, and it wasn't until Dusty began struggling with the bolts, realizing she would indeed be burned alive if she didn't find a way out, that she began to scream for help.

"Help me! I'm in here! I'm in here!" she screamed. She could actually hear the blaze increasing below and knew it would only be a matter of minutes before the fire engulfed the loft as well. At last, the bolt gave way, and the loft doors swung outward. Looking out and coughing as the smoke now increased, devouring fresh air, Dusty could see the commotion on the ground below. It seemed like a dream—so unreal! All the hands were running this way and that. They'd begun a bucket line, but she knew it was doing very little good. She saw her daddy and screamed, "Daddy!"

Instantly, Hank looked up to see his daughter

at the mouth of the loft doors, the smoke from the fire billowing out past her.

"Dusty!" he shouted.

Dusty saw her mother gasp and burst into tears as she too looked up and saw her. Without pause, her father ran to stand just below the loft.

"Jump, Dusty! You have to jump!" he shouted.

"I—I—I can't!" she cried. Her body was stiff and motionless with fear. No matter how she willed herself to even fall out the opening, she could not.

"You've got to!" her daddy shouted.

Her mother dashed toward the burning barn, intent on entering to try to save her daughter. Dusty saw Ryder dash past her mother as Feller grabbed Elly Hunter around the waist to stop her from going in. Somehow Ryder managed to fling a wet blanket over his head. Dusty turned when she heard the crack of his whip to find he had snapped it at one of the large beams of the loft until it was secured there. He climbed it like a rope to reach her since the ladder to the loft was ablaze with flames. She could only stand and stare at him, terrified with panic as the blanket fell from his shoulders when he awkwardly climbed into the loft.

The open loft doors worked like a magnet to the fire. Ryder slapped at the seat of his pants, which were smoking when he reached Dusty.

She could only stare at him as he came at

her in a dead run, shouting, "Dang it all, girl! Jump!" The next thing she knew, he'd wrapped his arms tightly around her. Spinning them around so his body left the opening first, he flung them out the door and into midair!

The blanket the other hands had quickly stretched above the ground beneath the loft did little to buffer their fall. When Ryder hit the ground solidly, still holding tightly to Dusty, she knew something in his body had broken; she heard the crack of bone and the moan a man makes when grievous pain is dealt him suddenly. It had been near to six weeks before Ryder's broken ribs healed sufficiently for him to be able to move comfortably.

Dusty brushed the tears from her cheeks as she now stood looking down at the man who'd saved her life years before. Reaching down, she began straightening his blanket. She gasped, startled, as he opened his eyes and took hold of her wrist.

Putting an index finger to his lips he mouthed, *Ssshhh.*

Dusty looked around her to make certain none of the other men were awake. She tried to pull her wrist from his grasp, but before she could move to escape him, he was pulling her down onto the floor next to him.

Sshhhh! he mouthed again, frowning at her and then grinning mischievously.

In one swift move, Dusty found herself lying on her back on the floor, one of Ryder's powerful legs across her own. He threw his blanket over their bodies as he leaned over her, gazing down into her face.

"What're you doin'?" she scolded in a whisper.

"Shh! You'll wake 'em all up!" he whispered.

"Get off me!" she ordered quietly. "Let me go!"

Ryder grinned. "No," he told her. The expression on his face comprised pure mischief.

"Let me go, Ryder!" she ordered in a whisper.

Kiss me, he mouthed.

Her eyes widened with astonishment at his demand. *No!* she mouthed back to him.

"Why not?" he teased.

Dusty rolled her eyes and shook her head in disapproval. She was thankful for the loud snoring of several of the sleeping men so her voice wasn't the only sound in the room. Had their flirtatious banter been the only sound, it surely would've awakened the others. She whispered, "Everyone will hear!"

Ryder raised his eyebrows and smiled. "Really?" he whispered. "It's gonna be that good, huh?"

"Ryder!" Dusty whispered between clenched teeth. "Let me go."

She was completely delighted! His playful manner was beginning to penetrate her guarded shell more and more each time he used it. Still, she must be proper. To lie on the floor smooching with him among the other men littered hither and yon—it was unthinkable!

With a shake of his head, Ryder suddenly rose to his feet, pulling Dusty to hers. Wincing only slightly from the pain caused by his injuries, he lifted her quickly, cradling her in his still-able arms, and made his way to the front parlor. With each step he took, very adeptly walking over the sleeping cowboys, Dusty's heart began to pound more furiously. What if someone was awake? What if someone was watching Ryder carry Dusty, him only in his trousers and her in her nightdress, to another part of the house? What would they think? Then she looked at Ryder, his face so close to hers, his body warm as he carried her, the mischief apparent on his face—a promise of a dream about to be fulfilled. It had to stop, she thought to herself, these secretive flirtations with Ryder. Yet it could stop tomorrow—couldn't it?

When they reached the kitchen, Ryder let her feet drop to the floor yet still held her tightly against him. She let her hands rest against the strength of his chest, trying to push him away, but not trying as hard as she should have.

"What is wrong with you?" she whispered as his eyes narrowed.

He studied her face intently. "Got a bit of devil in me tonight, I suppose," he answered.

"Apparently," she confirmed. "Now . . . let me go."

"Hm? Let me think," he hummed, frowning as if he were contemplating a large decision. Then, smiling, he shook his head. Dusty held her breath and struggled to resist him as he bent and placed a lingering, moist kiss on her neck.

"Why do you do this?" she asked in a whisper. Her desire to let herself be comfortable in loving fought with her fear in letting her heart surrender to him.

" 'Cause I like to," he told her. "And 'cause you want me to." The tone in his voice was low, affecting her like an intoxicating liquid.

"I don't," she lied in a whisper as a thrill traveled through her body when he kissed her neck again.

"Don't lie to me like that, sugar," he chuckled. He took her face between his hands and whispered, "Don't lie to me . . . and don't lie to yourself anymore."

"Stop," she demanded then, taking his face in her hands.

"Why?" he asked.

"Because I want to say something to you," she whispered.

"Really?" he teased. "You say things to me all the time."

"Be serious," she told him.

"I was. But you said, 'Stop. I want to say something to you,' so I—" he teased again.

"I know why my mama favored you so," she whispered to him. Desperate to distract him, she said the first thing that had come into her mind.

Indeed he was silent for a moment, having been surprised by what she'd said. "What do you mean?"

"You were savin' my bacon every time she turned around, weren't you?" she asked him. "Every time I got myself in a fix, there ya were to bail me out." Dusty swallowed the emotion rising in her throat. Ryder was apparently uncomfortable enough with her remarks that he was hushed into silence. "I heard her call you my guardian angel once. Do ya remember that?"

Ryder cleared his throat and looked away for a moment. "Yeah," he mumbled. "You got in more fixes than a kitten in a string factory." He smiled at her for a moment.

"I did. I did," Dusty agreed, smiling back. "She talked about you the day she died, ya know," she told him softly. She saw the emotion wash over his face and his jaw clench, signaling his discomfort.

"What'd she say?" he asked, and the moisture in his eyes betrayed the deep feelings he'd had for Elly Hunter.

Dusty knew she could never tell him everything her mother had said pertaining to Ryder Maddox the day she died. She could never tell him she'd sat next to her mother's bed, holding her hand as her mother told her to never, never marry some-one unless his character was as magnificent as Ryder Maddox's had been. That her mother told her, in fact, she wouldn't be surprised if Ryder returned one day when Dusty was older to pick up where he'd left off protecting her and caring for her. She couldn't tell him all of it—but she would tell him the rest.

"She said," Dusty began in a whisper, "that Ryder Maddox was as fine a young man as was ever born on earth." Dusty's heart ached for his in that moment. The tears in his eyes told her the fine young man of so long ago had carried her mother in a special place in his heart as well. "She said she missed you and would've liked to have had you with her before she went." Ryder looked away for a moment, brushing angrily at a tear that escaped and traveled to his chin. "And I know that she'd be disappointed in me if I didn't thank you for not letting me burn alive the night Grandpa's barn burned."

He released a nervous chuckle and looked back to her, whispering, "You already thanked me. That night—remember?"

"Yes, but . . . I want to thank you now. For every time you pulled me out of a tight spot," she told him.

He smiled. "I drug you in here to pull you into a tight spot . . . and look where it got me. All mushed up like some—"

"Then go ahead," Dusty interrupted him.

Her heart began to pound wildly. What was she

doing? What was she saying? Resisting him would be her only survival! Had she suddenly become completely bent on self-destruction?

"Go ahead and what?" he asked, frowning his familiar puzzled frown.

"Pull me into a tight spot," she mumbled, casting her gaze down suddenly—humiliated at her brazen flirting.

He quirked an eyebrow. "You tellin' me you're gonna let—"

"Not if you're gonna keep talkin' about it," she grumbled, as her grip on a thread of courage and hope began to slip away.

"Then let's stop talkin', sugar."

The familiar grin of mischief spread across his lips. As he cupped her chin tenderly in his capable hand, Dusty held her breath. Oh, how she loved the way he held her face for a moment as he began kissing her! The way he'd take her face between his hands and caress her cheek or cup her chin the way he was doing now, always, always letting his hand travel down over her throat as he deepened the kiss before taking her in his arms. As his kiss intensified, his arms encircling her body and pulling her close, Dusty could not keep an audible sigh of delight from escaping her lungs—let her own tentative pair of hands rest on his stomach. He broke their kiss for a moment, and she felt his smile against her mouth.

"I like that," he whispered, "when ya touch me."

An instant before Dusty's resolve to resist him could take control of her again, Dusty leaned forward and captured his mouth, kissing him almost fully—almost the way she'd always dreamed of having the courage to kiss him. His response was immediate. He embraced her even more tightly and rather fell back against the wall behind him as the passion detonating between them rose to a fury—a fury that almost scared Dusty. Her skin tingled at his touch, for she'd never been lost in his embrace while wearing such thin clothing. The absence of her corset allowed her to feel more definitely the warmth and strength of his arms and hands as he held her. She could not pull herself from him! Why should she? It was where she wanted to be—locked in his arms, melting in the heat radiated by his powerful body—delirious from his impeccable kiss! Then she grimaced, gasped slightly, and pulled away from him as the vision of being fourteen and seeing him for the last time—the pain of that moment—stabbed at her heart again, intruding like a violent and rapidly spreading disease.

Ryder knew her well. It was all too evident by the way he closed his eyes, clenched his jaw tightly shut for a moment, and then sighed with disappointment. "Don't," he breathed.

She squirmed out of his arms, but he did not force her to stay—simply kept hold of one of her hands.

"It's late," she mumbled, looking about nervously.

"Don't do this, Dusty," he whispered.

"I've got to get to bed. I'm done in," she told him, smiling and pulling her hand from his. "This can't happen again," she told him. Turning, she hurried down the hallway toward her room.

Escape! It was her only hope! She'd gone too far—let herself feel too much—let her guard against him down. Now she wondered if it weren't, indeed, too late to save herself. As she crawled into her bed, her body still tingling with having been in his arms, her lips still moist with their kisses, she tried desperately to cling to her broken heart. Yet it was leaving her. In a moment of panic, she realized it was leaving her. She must hang onto it! She must! It was the only way to save it from happening again!

Ryder inhaled and let out a long, frustrated breath to try to calm his varying emotions. Turning, he walked back into the room where the floor was lined with his snoring, worn-out fellow cowboys. He held his breath for a moment and then sighed and smiled with relief as he saw it was Feller who stood leaning against the wall on one shoulder— a knowing grin on his face as he stood there in nothing but his soot-covered trousers.

"What ya been up to, boy?" Feller asked quietly.

"No good, as usual," Ryder chuckled, running his fingers through his smoke-scented hair.

"Oh, I think you're doin' fine," Feller grinned.

Ryder raised an eyebrow and grinned proudly. "Think so?"

"Oh, yeah!" Then Feller chuckled. "But you're a mighty brave boy to be corruptin' the boss's daughter under his own roof!"

"You oughta try it sometime, Feller," Ryder whispered. "You'd be surprised how much more their kisses confess to you in such circumstances." Ryder winked at his friend, though Feller's smile faded instantly. He walked back to his place on the floor and settled in for the short time of rest remaining.

Dusty stood at the sink peeling apples for breakfast. The sun was just coming over the eastern horizon, spilling saffron warmth over the fields. Dusty loved mornings! She decided that the morning following a night part of which was spent in Ryder's arms was the loveliest of all. Still, her hands began to tremble nervously at the thought of her own unguarded behavior with Ryder the night before. She'd spent most of the remaining hours before dawn rebuilding her resolve to resist him—reminding herself he would be leaving at some point, that she could not endure her heart breaking for him again. Yet even for the hours spent in trying to dredge up resentment and fortitude, her heart fluttered at the thought of his holding her—at the memory of their sweet, tender conversation beforehand and at the lingering feel of his kiss. She was dangerously close to the brink of losing her self-control, of opening up the most tender and vulnerable part of her heart—dangerously close.

She was startled from her thoughts as two arms slid around her waist. A warm kiss savored her neck from behind. Trembling, she dropped the apple and knife. She knew Ryder's touch—the feel of his breath on her neck. Struggling in his arms, she turned to face him.

"What are you doing?" she scolded in a whisper.

Ryder released her, smiling down at her with amusement as he reached behind her and retrieved the apple. "Good mornin' to you too," he chuckled, taking a bite out of the apple. Dusty couldn't help but smile. She bit her lip and placed her hand over her mouth as she studied his tousled hair.

"I've always wanted to do that, you know," he said, leaning forward. He placed a hand on either side of her, meeting her nose-to-nose as he chewed the bite of apple in his mouth.

"Do what?" she asked, still smiling at his boyish appearance—boyish, that was, except for the fully matured, muscular nature of his bare chest and arms.

"That," he repeated. "What I just did." With a mischievous grin and another bite of the apple, he turned and went out the kitchen door and onto the porch. He paused, standing next to Hank as he surveyed the damage from the fire.

It must be the kitchen, Dusty thought. Why did she so often find herself at his whim in the kitchen? Yet as she watched him talking with her father—as she dreamed of how wonderful it would be to see them talking like that forever—the blackness in her heart began to spread again. She tried to fight it off—to tell herself and her will she didn't want it there anymore. She tried to force her mind to let go of the hurt of heartache and loss, of resentment. Still—it triumphed. After nurturing it for so long, intentionally seeking it out in her soul, the darkness and the fear won out, and Dusty felt the door slam shut on her heart. Ryder would hurt her again. He would. Even if he didn't intend to, fate would lead him to do it. And if it happened—when it happened—she would die. This time her heart would stop, shatter into pieces. And so there, at the kitchen window, watching him walk away with her father and toward the smoldering pile that was once the bunkhouse, Dusty ended her dream. After trying so hard and so long to live it, she decided it must end—before it killed her.

పోఖ

Dusty waited until after breakfast, when the other hands were about their work and she had seen Ryder go into the barn to saddle up. Quickly, she rushed out of the house and over to the barn. As she entered and saw him, still wearing his soot-covered pants, having borrowed a shirt from her father, her heart fluttered, and she almost changed her mind. Yet when he turned around and looked at her, the dazzle of his smile and the twinkle in his eyes threatening to seduce her from her intent, she plunged forward.

"Don't do this to me anymore, Ryder," she said, turning away from him. If she looked at him, she would be in his arms in the next minute. She knew she would. She wanted to be there now, and it was why it was so necessary for her to tell him what she must.

"Don't do what? I'm puttin' on a bridle," he told her, obviously puzzled.

"Don't tease me. D-don't make me think that . . . don't try to . . ."

"What?" he asked. He seemed completely naive. As she turned and looked back to him, she saw understanding dawning on his face. "You tryin' to tell me not to . . ." he began.

"Yes!" she stated emphatically. If she even heard him utter the word *kiss* again, her resolve would be lost! If he said anything clever to her at that moment, she would be undone.

He didn't say anything at first. Then he spoke, and the sound of his voice was like glimpsing heaven—yet his words were a slice of hell. "All right. If that's what you think you want."

Then she turned to face him. "It has to be that way."

"Why?"

His question was so simple, but the answer was so complicated! "Because . . . because . . ." she stammered.

"Why?" he repeated angrily, frowning as he studied her.

"Because . . . because . . ."

"Because you don't trust me. And ya don't think you can take heartbreak again. Am I right?" he demanded.

She couldn't answer him—only stood drenched in heartache, longing, regret, and fear.

Suddenly, he was furious. "You're not the only one who's had a long road of it, Dusty! But I'm here! And I'm here for my own reasons. So you either get on with me . . . or get over me, sugar!"

Dusty knew he was right, but to admit it would be to fail completely.

"Who do you think you are?" she nearly shouted at him. "I am over you! I've been over you since—"

"Don't lie to me either!" he growled, his frown deepening. Reaching out, Ryder took hold of her chin firmly. "Now, I won't play with you anymore . . . since you think that's what I'm doin'. I won't play if that's what you're wantin'. But it's up to you to burn the book this time . . . or open it. It's up to you." He paused and then added, "And we'll leave it at that . . . for the time bein'." He released her face, turned, and checked the cinch on his saddle before mounting. Straddling his horse's back, he looked down at her angrily, shook an index finger, and said, "Anytime you're ready. Use me, abuse me, or whatever you want. You walk right up to me, give me the word, and I'll kiss you in a way you never dreamed of! And that goes for anything else." He took the reins in hand and growled, "That offer stands . . . for now. But it's up to you, girl!"

He left the barn at a full gallop, and she watched him go. What had she done? Her heart screamed for her to call after him, but she didn't. She clenched her teeth tightly and watched him go. He'd be going again and again and again— perpetually riding away from her. And one day . . . one day, he wouldn't come back for supper.

Turning back toward the house, willing her eyes to stay dry, she was mortified to see Feller step out from behind the barn, his arms folded disapprovingly across his chest.

"What do you think you're doin', girl?" he growled at her.

"Protecting myself," she spat at him.

Feller shook his head, his jaw tight with withheld anger. "You know . . . I almost thought you'd given up that selfish way you found a few years back. I was startin' to hope in ya. But now . . . now you've gone and let the devil win, Dusty. It ain't God a-tellin' you to turn that man away!"

Dusty couldn't stop the tears, and they streamed freely down her face. Still, she remained strong —strong, indignant, and hateful. "And who's tellin' you, Feller? Who's tellin' you to bury your heart from Becca?"

She saw the fire leap to his eyes. For all the hard feelings she was trying to brandish, she felt guilty and disgusted with herself for hurting him. Still, he only shook his head and said, "You worry about yourself, little girl . . . 'fore you start gettin' so big for your britches as to be tellin' me what to do!" Turning from her, he strode away.

After watching him go, Dusty glanced up to see Becca looking at her from the kitchen window. Who did they all think they were? She'd tried to dig out of the grave of heartbreak she'd buried herself in. She had! She thought she could! But to dig out only to be murdered again? And yet her inner voice broke through the door to her heart and screamed at her, *You selfish coward! You've lost your mind as well as your heart!* Dusty knew then she deserved heartache. She deserved loneliness. She wasn't like Miss Raynetta, who'd remained a good person having lost her only love—for Miss Raynetta had no choice, but Dusty had. And she'd pushed it away. Looking in the direction Ryder had ridden, she secretly wished, *Please let him leave before I have to see him with someone else.* Having to watch Ryder rain his affections on another woman—that truly would take her life.

Chapter Twelve

Days passed. The tension between Dusty and Ryder grew for a time, yet it was Ryder who seemed to settle down first. His smile returned, and Dusty fancied he hadn't cared for her so much after all. He seemed to be faring far better than her tear-saturated pillow was!

One morning nearly a week later, Dusty dried her hands on her apron, left the kitchen, and stepped out onto the porch. As she did, she saw Miss Raynetta riding up astride her black mare, wearing a fiery red dress.

"I picked up your family's post while I was in town," she said, reining in next to the porch. The pleasant woman handed a large handful of letters and small parcels to Dusty. "Looks like Ryder Maddox even has somethin' today."

"Really?" Dusty said as she glanced through the post.

"I gotta get on home, hon," Miss Raynetta apologized as she turned the mare. "Wish I could stay and visit. Come out to my place soon! We need a long talk."

"All right," Dusty said, waving. "Thank you for bringing the post."

Miss Raynetta returned Dusty's wave, and Dusty watched her ride away. Returning her attention to the post, she thought it odd—odd that someone would send Ryder a rolled-up newspaper tied with twine and nothing else. Tucking a loose strand of hair behind her ear and without thinking, she untied the twine and unfolded the paper.

"*Abilene Times*," she read aloud. "So . . . have you been in Abilene all this time, Ryder?" she mumbled to herself. Then she began reading the titles of the articles, "Cattle Prices Soar . . . Mayor's Daughter to Wed." She opened the paper, and her eyes fell to a small article on the right-hand bottom corner of the paper. Someone had circled the article in black. "Miss Lillian Montgomery Dies." A frown puckered Dusty's brow as she read the article aloud to herself. "*Lillian Montgomery, daughter of Kirk and Emily Montgomery, who own the Montgomery Cattle Ranch south of Abilene, died yesterday. Miss Montgomery would've been nineteen next month. The community joins the Montgomery family in their sorrow at the loss of their beloved daughter after such a long ordeal. The* Abilene Times *says, 'May she finally rest in peace, safe in the warmth and beauty of heaven.' "*

The tiny hairs on Dusty's arms prickled; the

hair on the back of her neck stood so on end she had to reach back and rub at it. Carefully, she folded the paper, returning it to its original shape and tying it with the twine once more.

Her mind was simply swimming in thoughts, ideas, and possibilities for explanation. The girl who died must've been someone Ryder knew. After all, it said in the article her father was a rancher. It made sense Ryder would've ended up in Abilene at some point, working cattle for a rancher there. But the girl—she was nineteen, Dusty's own age, a ripe age to have captured Ryder's attentions. Shaking her head, she tried to dispel the thoughts of Ryder even knowing another woman. It was simply informative— simply someone letting Ryder know a member of the family of a man for whom he'd run cattle had died. But what if there were more? And if there were, Dusty had no right to know, especially now.

For days, she'd been trying to find a way out of the mess she'd gotten herself in. Almost instantly after sending an angry Ryder off, her heart had softened—broken the darkness within once more. But now, now she'd pushed him too far. She knew it. He would go on. After all, he'd done what he'd come to do—several times!

"After such a long ordeal," she repeated out loud. "Serves me right for reading other people's post," she grumbled, heading into the house. She simply tossed the handful of assortments

onto the table—paper for Ryder Maddox and all.

Still, try as she might, Dusty couldn't quiet her curiosity about the paper. It ate at her for the rest of the day. Something told her it wasn't as simple as it appeared. Had Ryder been close to the girl? Had this Lillian been the woman he'd kissed differently than he kissed Dusty? Had he even been in love with her? The thought caused Dusty's bosom to ache with insufferable pain. It caused her throat to constrict; she had trouble drawing breath on occasion. She found it nearly impossible not to cry. Yet she swallowed it—all of it—as his words echoed through her mind again. *Anytime you're ready. Use me, abuse me, or whatever you want. You walk right up to me, give me the word, and I'll kiss you in a way you never dreamed of! And that goes for anything else. That offer stands . . . for now. But it's up to you, girl!*

He'd said it—but had he truly meant it? Had he truly understood, as he always seemed to, that Dusty would leave that black moment, regret it, and need a window left open to reach for him through? He'd been patient, hadn't he? Understanding? Surely he would give her another chance. Was there hope? Or had she put the final nail in the coffin of her true and only love?

After supper, when the hands were sitting around the fire outside, Dusty approached Ryder. Each step she took toward him felt as if she were pacing toward the hanging tree.

"Mighty fine supper, Miss Dusty," Ruff offered as she approached.

"Thank you, Ruff," she accepted, pausing to study the worn-out men. "You all look positively wrung out!"

They all only nodded, their fatigue too great to offer a spoken answer. A few rather grunted in confirmation. She walked up to Ryder, his smile broadening mischievously as she approached. She was encouraged. It seemed the anger was gone from him. Had he forgiven her?

"Miss Raynetta went to town today," she told him.

"Did she?" he asked, grinning up at her from where he sat on one of the old logs.

"She picked up our post for us and . . ." Her words were lost in her throat as instantly his smile faded. The color drained from his handsome face, and he looked as if she'd just told him someone in his family had died. And now she wondered—had she?

Without another word, he held his hand out to her. Slowly, she placed the paper in his strong hand. Somehow she wanted to snatch it back from him, wishing she'd never told him that Miss Raynetta had gotten the post. She saw his jaw tighten as he looked at the paper's title—his eyes closing for a moment as if something he'd only experienced in nightmares was about to come true. Without looking at her again, he opened the paper, and just as Dusty's had been, his attention was drawn to the circled article. She watched him as his eyes traveled left to right, left to right, and left to right again as he read. When he finished, he sighed heavily, dropping his head and closing his eyes tightly as if trying to dispel a terrible vision in his mind. He seemed completely overwhelmed, burying his face in one hand for a moment as if struggling to control his emotions. All at once, he fairly leapt to his feet, threw the paper into the fire with the force of a man possessed of grief and anger, and, without looking at anyone, stormed away into the darkness of the night.

"For Pete's sake, Dusty," Feller exclaimed. "What did ya do now?" It was the first thing Feller had said to her for days—since she'd hurt him too.

"I-I just gave him some post that came for him today," she stammered.

"Well," Feller said, standing beside her and staring out into the darkness after Ryder, "you'd best go apologize then."

Dusty frowned and looked at Feller. *Apologize for giving him his post?* she thought. Feller winked at her, and she understood. Now was the time—the time to give back to Ryder in some small amount what he'd given to her. Without hesitation, she followed him into the darkness—this time to perhaps be forgiven.

"Ryder?" she called after him. "Ryder?" She found him in the barn, his hands pressing against one wall, his head hanging forward as he violently kicked an old leather horse collar with one foot. "Ryder?" she ventured.

"You don't wanna go down this road with me, Dusty," he growled, and she did not miss the crack of emotion in his voice. She wanted to shout, *I'd go down any road with you.* But she just stood quietly for a moment when he again repeated, "You don't wanna go down it."

"Who is she?" she asked, stepping onto the path.

He looked at her, frowning and angry. "You read my post?" he growled.

"I . . . I thought it would be . . ." she stammered, searching for a good excuse—knowing there was none.

He shook his head and repeated, "Who was she?"

"Yes. You're obviously very upset and—"

"She's a girl. She was a girl," he answered bluntly.

"Did you love her?" she asked quietly. Already the tears were heavy in her eyes as she anticipated the dreadful answer.

He chuckled with a sort of grief-stricken hysteria. "Did I love her?" he repeated. "I don't know if that's really any of your business, now is it?" His manner was so uncharacteristically cruel that it seemed to answer the question itself. It was a manner provoked of great pain. He added with defeat, "No, I didn't love her."

Momentary relief washed over Dusty so strongly she thought she might faint. "Well then, why—" she began.

"You want me to trust you, is that it?" he asked, turning to her—fury evident on his handsome face. "You want to know why I'm so upset by that paper?" His voice cracked with emotion. "You can't even find the smallest reason to trust me. Why do ya think I should trust you?"

"Ryder, I . . ." She reached out, taking hold of his arm in a gesture of support, but he yanked his arm free of her grasp.

"Don't touch me right now." His usually warm eyes were ablaze with anger. "I'm mad at you."

Dusty felt as if someone had shoved her heart into a cider press and was grinding. "Me? Because I read the paper? I'm sorry, Ryder. I know I shouldn't have! I just—"

"No," he countered, wrinkling his nose and shaking his head. "I don't care that you read the dang paper. I'm mad because . . . I need to tell you about this, and I can't."

"You can tell me anything! We've always talked about everything. Just because I said somethin' stupid . . . because I was afraid and I . . . just because I won't let myself . . . does that mean you'll never be my . . . my . . ." she stammered.

"Your what, Dusty?" he growled. "Your what?"

"M-m-m-my . . . my . . ." she struggled for the word that wouldn't betray what she really wanted him to be to her. All she could utter was, "My friend."

"Ah, but you're wrong on both counts, sugar," Ryder countered, shaking his head. "I am your . . . friend." He said the word as if it left a bad taste in his mouth to do so. "And we don't tell each other everything. Now do we?"

He was right. As she stood, face drenched in tears before him, trembling in the presence of his pain and anger, she knew he was right. She hadn't told him everything. She hadn't told him how much she dreamed of him, longed for his kiss, desired to be the cause of his smiles and happiness. She hadn't told him everything. She hadn't told him she loved him so desperately in spite of her efforts not to. And what hadn't he told her? That there had been a woman in his life since he left so long ago? That she'd scarred him, maybe far worse than the scars he now wore on his back?

"No," she admitted in a whisper, "we don't." Then a panic gripped her, prompting her next unexpected question. "Will this . . . be what makes you leave?"

"No," he confirmed in a low, much calmer, and somehow humbled voice. He looked to her, his eyes seeming so far beyond sad and discouraged that her tears increased. "The only thing that would make me leave . . ." He paused, and Dusty thought her heart might beat free of her chest so viciously did it pound as she waited for him to continue. "If it happened . . . it wouldn't matter to you if I left or not."

Dusty buried her face in her hands and sobbed, "How can you say that? How can you, when ya know . . ." When she raised her eyes to him again, there slowly crossed his face an expression of horrified enlightenment.

"You're thinkin' I'm gonna leave again. Is that it?" he asked. "All this time . . . you've been buildin' up this wall against me because . . ."

"Did you love that girl, Ryder?" Dusty finally cried out as the pain of jealousy and heartache silently but vigorously insisted on another confirmation. She had to know! She had to know his kisses had been sincere—that he did mean to kiss her, wanted to hold her in his arms—that he hadn't been pretending it was a girl in Abilene he couldn't have anymore for whatever reason.

"Why, Dusty? Why does it matter to you? Tell me!" he demanded. "Tell me everything!"

Dusty cupped her hand over her mouth for fear she might indeed confess to him her life had become whatever and whoever and wherever he was.

He seemed to take pity on her and sighed. "No. I told you I didn't love that poor girl. And she died." It seemed an odd way to put it—but it did calm her somehow.

Dusty instinctively leaned toward him, but he held up a hand. "I'm not mad at you," he whispered, "for readin' the paper." A heavy sigh escaped his lungs. "I'm just . . . worn out. I'm turnin' in. Good night." It was so plain and final.

All she could say in response was, "Good night."

All night she worried about him—wondered if he had lain in his bunk for long hours in turmoil —if he would even be in his bunk come morning—if his horse and his bedroll would be anywhere to be found. But when the rooster crowed and she heard him clanging around in the barn, grumpily cussing at the milk stool, she cried her last fearful tear and drifted to sleep. It was almost an hour later when Becca, having already finished feeding the men, came in to check on her sister, finally waking her up.

"What in tarnation is the matter with Ryder?" Becca asked when Dusty entered the kitchen after having hurried to dress.

"What do you mean?" Dusty asked. She knew, of course, about the newspaper he'd received. But Ryder was usually so adept at pasting on a happy face that she was curious about Becca's experience.

"He stormed in here and ate his breakfast like he'd knock you flat if you even talked to him!" Becca shook her head. "Somethin's eatin' at him."

Dusty paused. Should she confide in her sister? She wanted to—desperately! But should she? "He got some post yesterday. Someone died. That's all I know. It upset him so badly that I—"

"Who?" Becca interrupted. "Who died?"

Dusty swallowed hard and continued. "A girl. A girl in Abilene."

"A—a girl? A little girl, like nine or ten? Or a big girl, like—"

"A big girl, like nineteen."

Becca sighed heavily and then began her own explanation. "Dusty . . . I'm sure she was just an acquaintance. I'm sure she didn't mean anything to him and that—"

"If she didn't mean anything to him, Becca . . . then why is he so upset?" Dusty burst into tears. She burst into a quick confession of what she'd told Ryder days before in the barn.

"Dusty!" Becca scolded, horrified. "You didn't!"

"I did! I swear I've never been so stupid!" Dusty cried.

"Well, you got that right," Becca agreed. Dusty wiped angrily at her eyes. "But," Becca continued, "even if this girl was something to him, she's dead now and—"

Dusty shook her head. "That's not the point! He should've loved me, Becca! He should never have left. And even then . . . he should've come back for me!" Dusty sank into a chair and sobbed into her hands.

"Dusty," Becca began, kneeling before her, "he—"

"You should've seen him yesterday, Becca!" Dusty screamed in a whisper. "I've never seen him like that! He was . . . that girl was somebody to him!"

"Maybe like Cash was somebody to you," her sister offered softly.

"No! No, it was different," Dusty insisted. "H-he . . . oh my heck, Becca," Dusty sobbed. "When I think of him with her . . . I—"

"Stop it!" Becca stood up and covered her ears for a moment in frustration. "You have to take control of yourself, Dusty! Look at you! One minute you're tellin' him never to touch you again, and the next you're ready to tear his eyes out because he might have—"

"Don't say it! I don't want to hear that!" Dusty cried.

Becca bent and took Dusty by the shoulders, shaking her to rationality. "Listen to me! Just let it go, once and for all! Just let go of everything that's holding you back. This isn't you! Back and forth, back and forth! Angelina Hunter is a strong, persistent, confident woman. You love Ryder. Quit pushin' him away! If you keep doin' it—keep kissin' him one minute and slappin' him the next—if you keep doin' that to him . . . then, Dusty . . . he will leave you again."

"I-I know that." Dusty sniffled, closing her eyes

356

to calm herself as she inhaled deeply. "B-but I can't . . . I can't get beyond this . . . this . . . this . . ."

"Fear."

Dusty knew Becca was right. Fear—more than past heartache, more than pride, more than anything—was what kept her from surrendering herself to loving Ryder completely. It kept her dreams at bay, kept her arms from returning his embrace, kept her hope and faith from fulfilling her greatest desire.

"Yes. I'm too afraid." Dusty looked to her sister.

Becca nodded, and there was true—desperately true—true understanding in her eyes. Becca was afraid too. Dusty understood more fully than ever before how truly akin their heartaches were.

"I should just walk up to him and . . . and say . . ." Dusty began.

"And say, 'I love you, Feller. Can you love me back? Imperfections and all?' That's what I should say," Becca whispered.

Dusty nodded. "But it's not that easy . . . facing rejection and heartache head on."

"It's like standin' still when a mad bull is chargin' ya." Becca reached out and hugged Dusty. "But you've had so much offered to you from Ryder! He ain't the kind to be insincere."

"I know."

It seemed that day dragged on forever! And even longer was the night Dusty spent worrying over

Ryder's despair and fighting her own. Time and again Dusty would sit up in her bed, determined to march out into the parlor and wake him up—to tell him she loved him, that she was sorry for his pain, and would he give her a chance to heal it as he had endeavored to heal hers. Time and again she lay back down, afraid. Once she even made it to standing in the parlor door staring down at him as he slept. But courage was not hers that day. Maybe the next it would be her companion —tomorrow—when daylight gave her strength. And so she fought to find comfort of any kind— through another long, lonely, anxious night.

Miss Raynetta arrived early in the morning to help prepare the food for the bunkhouse raising planned for the next day. All morning long she chattered away like a cute little squirrel—busily preparing pies and trying to lift the glum moods of both Dusty and Becca. Finally, just before lunch, Miss Raynetta dried her hands on her apron and, turning to the Hunter girls, fairly snapped, "What in all get out is wrong with you girls?"

Becca shrugged her shoulders innocently, and Dusty mumbled, "Nothin'."

"Well, that's a lie if I ever in my life heard one!" Miss Raynetta argued. "All mornin' you two been mopin' around like whipped dogs! Let's get out of this kitchen and soak up some sun!" Tossing her head, she untied her apron and rather dramatically dropped it to the floor. Then, linking arms with both girls, she led them out onto the porch.

Dusty couldn't help but smile. Becca exchanged an amused glance with her as well. It was almost impossible to maintain a blackened mood when Miss Raynetta was anywhere near. Again, Dusty's thoughts turned to the woman's loneliness—her secret longing for one man, hidden for more than twenty years. She thought of her father—still lost without her mother at times, but so young to be living out his life alone. She thought of her sister—Becca's tender heart breaking from longing for the love of such a seemingly unobtainable bachelor. It had all gone on long enough. Today, she told herself—today it would begin to change. Today she would begin to beat down her fear! Truly this time.

"Do you remember Feller ridin' through town when he was little . . . ." Dusty began.

"Naked as the day he was born!" Miss Raynetta finished, erupting into twinkling giggles of merriment. "Hang my garters in the window, but that was a sight to behold!" Miss Raynetta tried to say more, but her laughter was uncontrollable. It only took a few moments for Dusty and Becca both to begin giggling, having caught the contagious delirium. "Lookin' at him now," Miss Raynetta sighed, "can you ever believe it? Can you even imagine that sour-pussed ol' goat a-doin' somethin' the like?" Again she burst into giggles.

"Of course, he ain't all garlic and vinegar like he pretends," she said when she could talk again. Wiping tears of mirth from her eyes, she added, "Ain't that right, Becca, honey?"

Dusty's heart swelled with delight. Miss Raynetta had taken the bait and swum off with it. Furthermore, it seemed she wasn't as blind as Dusty had been for so long. Still, Becca's smile faded immediately.

"I don't know what ya mean, Miss Raynetta," Becca mumbled, blushing wildly.

"Oh, honey," the maternal woman comforted. Miss Raynetta wore a copper-colored dress; it made her look warm and approachable. "We women who have tendencies toward hired hands know each other's hearts better than we care to admit. No need to go tryin' to fool me. I been there before!"

"He thinks I'm a baby," Becca confessed, dabbing at the tears springing to her eyes.

Miss Raynetta put an arm around Becca's shoulders and smoothed more tears from her cheeks. Dusty stood in awe, realizing Becca had suffered greater from the loss of their mother than even she had, for Dusty was older when their mother passed on. Furthermore, instead of stepping in as nurturing, teaching, caring big sister in her mother's absence, she'd selfishly withdrawn. It was both a hurtful and a fantastic thing to watch Miss Raynetta mothering her sister now.

"Oh, honey, he knows you ain't a baby!" Miss Raynetta told her, smiling slyly. "I had to slap his face the other day 'cause he was so near to droolin' all down the front of his shirt at watchin' your fanny wag as you were walkin' away from him!"

"You don't have to try to make me feel better, Miss Raynetta," Becca sniffled. "I've known Feller a mighty long time and—"

"I would never lie to you, honey! Now you keep that in mind." Miss Raynetta smiled again. "Test me out." The woman glanced over to where Feller was at that very moment, working on the corral fence. "You go on over, and you have yourself some silly little conversation with Feller. Then, when you walk away, you take five steps, and you turn around as fast as you can . . . and you'll catch him at it! If I'm wrong, I'll eat crow for a month! But I ain't ever wrong." Becca's eyes began to glisten with the thought of the tantalizing dare. "Go on now. Go on."

Becca looked to Dusty for either encouragement or discouragement, and when Dusty nodded emphatically, Becca turned and took out toward the corral.

Dusty followed Miss Raynetta's gaze as she watched Becca approach Feller. "I ain't wrong about this. Take my word for it. He won't disappoint her," the petite matchmaker whispered. Still, Dusty sensed Miss Raynetta was as anxious as she was when the woman nervously linked arms with her again.

Come on, Feller, Dusty thought. *For once, be your same old, predictable self.*

Becca approached Feller, and he did indeed cease his labor. Dusty noted Becca's state of agitation was obvious by the way she stood swishing her skirt back and forth as she talked to him. Becca nodded, and Dusty was aware of the simultaneous breath-holding she and Miss Raynetta were enduring as her sister turned from Feller and began to walk away.

"Keep watching her! Keep watching her!" Miss Raynetta whispered. Then she began to giggle with delight. "See the way his eyes drop from the back of her head to . . ." Dusty's merciless, sudden clutch on Miss Raynetta's dress sleeve interrupted her, and both women fairly squealed with delight as Becca then, having taken far more than five steps, turned to catch Feller watching her. He immediately twitched a shoulder and waved to her when she waved at him. In her excitement, Becca nearly skipped back toward the henhouse.

"She's a wise girl not to draw his attention back this way," Miss Raynetta whispered as she and Dusty instantly bent over and studied the ground —trying to appear as if they'd missed the whole scene, in the event a humiliated Feller Lance should glance their way. They giggled together so uncontrollably that finally Miss Raynetta took hold of Dusty's arm and led her to the far side of the house, where they clamped their hands over their mouths and continued in their merriment.

Finally, with heavy sighs, they were both able to gain control of themselves. Miss Raynetta straightened her posture and proudly announced, "Was I right? Or was I right?"

"You were very right!" Dusty lovingly smiled at her, and Miss Raynetta seemed suddenly uncomfortable under her gaze.

Looking away, she sighed, "That was a hard thing for her to do . . . have the faith to overcome her fear and test him."

"I know," Dusty agreed.

Miss Raynetta looked back to Dusty, her smile fading completely. "And what if a man has already passed that test? What if a man has already proven trustworthy and loyal and a woman still pushes him away?"

The questions were very pointed. But Dusty wasn't ready to hop from Becca's affairs of the heart to her own. As further proof the old Dusty Hunter was beginning to win over, Dusty was not surprised to hear herself blurt out her own pointed question.

"You still love my daddy, don't you?" she asked Miss Raynetta without pause.

"Oh, honey!" Miss Raynetta tossed her head and forced an indifferent expression. "That was a long time ago." But Dusty didn't miss the familiar pain in her eyes—familiar not only because she'd seen it there before but because she'd felt it herself.

"But you still love him, don't you?" Dusty repeated.

Miss Raynetta brushed at her cheeks, which were already the bright pink of blush. She stared at the sky, at nothing for a long moment, and then shook her head and seemed to swallow her tears. "I suppose that we never get over that first love of our life. Some people are lucky enough to have it forever." Then, looking to Dusty meaningfully, she added, "If they have the courage to hang on to it."

"Daddy's still a handsome man, Miss Raynetta. And you're still a beautiful woman. He's very fond of you and very attracted to you," Dusty said in a whisper. "I've been noticing lately how often he talks about you and thinks about you with that big grin spread smack across his face."

"Your daddy wasn't meant to be mine, honey. He was meant for your mama, and she deserved him. You know," she said as tears filled her eyes, "it broke my heart when she died." She looked to Dusty and put a dainty hand to her breast and continued, "I never once thought bad of her or resented her marryin' Hank. I want you to know that! She was a wonderful woman, and she was far good enough for him in my eyes. They were so happy together, and I could never try to fill his heart now like she did."

"Not like she did. Of course not," Dusty told her. "But Daddy's got more love left to give than most men can give in a whole lifetime. You and Daddy are so young, Miss Raynetta! You can fill his heart . . . the way you will."

"Sweet thing," Miss Raynetta sighed as she wiped at her sentimental tears, "I'm goin' on thirty-six!"

"But that's so young!" Dusty interrupted. "My granny didn't have Mama until she was forty-three!" She lowered her voice again, "Don't you long for a baby of your own, Miss Raynetta? I've always wanted a little brother."

Miss Raynetta smiled and shook her head. "You sure have changed your tune about things of the heart lately, Miss Angelina Hunter. And you're a mighty big hypocrite to boot." She was quiet for a moment. She looked to Dusty again. "I'll tell you what. I'll make you a proposition. You show me you're a-lettin' Ryder snuggle in close to you once in a while . . . and I'll . . . I'll . . ."

"You'll start lettin' it show to my daddy that you care for him!" Dusty finished for her.

"It's a deal," Miss Raynetta giggled.

"Do ya give me your word?"

"Shake on it!" Miss Raynetta offered her hand, and Dusty grasped it, shaking it firmly. Could it be there was another woman, other than Dusty and Becca Hunter, who was trying to find a way to fight her fear of offering her love to the one man she wanted to have it?

Almost as if angels themselves had stepped in, Ryder sauntered out of the barn and tossed some trappings to the ground. Hunkering down, he began to fiddle with them.

"Hm?" Miss Raynetta hummed. "Fancy that. Ask and ye shall receive?"

Dusty swallowed hard. Miss Raynetta was innocent in exactly how much harder it was for Dusty to walk up to Ryder at that point than it had been even for Becca. The angel of mercy had no idea Dusty had demanded Ryder not touch her—that he'd been given such grievous news the day before, after she'd dropped off the post.

Anytime you're ready, he'd said. His words—the vision of his face that day in the barn—both flashed through Dusty's mind. *I'll kiss you in a way you never dreamed of!* he had promised.

Slowly Dusty turned toward the barn. She took several steps toward him, but he stood up and disappeared into the barn again. Letting out the breath she'd been holding, Dusty turned to Miss Raynetta.

"I can't. He's gone now and . . ."

Miss Raynetta quirked an eyebrow and nodded toward the barn. Ryder had just returned, carrying an ax. He began splitting wood. Taking Dusty's shoulders, Miss Raynetta guided her in his direction a few steps before letting go and stepping back.

Dusty walked to where he worked, pausing just a few feet from him. His back was to her. He hadn't seen her yet. She could still escape, but then fear would have won, and her father would never know of the secret love waiting for him. She took one more step toward him. Ryder worked at splitting wood, his skin bronzed from work in the sun, and as usual, his shirt, still tucked into his trousers, hung down around his legs. Dusty smiled and took another step toward him. *How funny,* she thought. How funny that he would take the time to completely unbutton his shirt when it hampered him but leave it hanging down about his lower body instead of taking the slight effort required to toss it aside.

She watched his muscles work as he swung the ax, and she could feel Miss Raynetta's increasingly astonished expression burning into her back. Before she could think twice, she reached out and placed her hand on his shoulder as he set the ax aside and bent to gather the wood. He startled and turned his head. Dusty was encouraged to be greeted by the handsome smile spreading across his face.

"Whatcha need?" he asked innocently.

Dusty opened her mouth and drew in a quick breath, but no sound came out. What would she say? Could she simply say, *I need you to make love to me here . . . now . . . out in the open so Miss Raynetta will see?* Something inside her told her that were she truly to answer Ryder's question so boldly, it would not make a difference. He would react however he would react whether she spoke or not. For an instant, she closed her eyes, biting her lower lip for courage, and drew in a deep breath. When she opened her eyes once more, Ryder had turned around and stood facing her.

"What?" he asked, obviously perplexed.

Without meeting his gaze, Dusty focused her attention on the body before her, placing her hands against the smooth, solid contours of his broad chest.

Don't you ever be afraid to touch me! His words echoed through her mind. Afraid! Fear! It had been her destroyer. It would lose Ryder for her! Her hands betrayed her inner battle with a trembling that could not be seen by Miss Raynetta from her distance but could be neither missed nor ignored by Ryder. She forced her soft caress upwards toward his shoulders. Their words in the barn several days before had been so harsh, and unfinished somehow. Then the newspaper had come, bringing more discomfort between them. She wondered—if he did find the patience to deal with her, would he remember what he'd promised her about his kiss?

Her hands traveled the breadth of his broad shoulders, up over his neck, finally resting on his face. When she finally found the courage to glance up at him, it was to find that his eyes had narrowed, his expression that of completely pleased anticipation. It gave her hope and courage—that playful, mischievous smile she loved so much. Quickly, she focused her attention to his mouth and moved slightly to kiss him. Yet panic and fear stalled her, and she winced at the pain in her frightened soul. What if he refused her? What if he refused her there with Miss Raynetta looking on? How would Miss Raynetta ever find the courage to approach her father? But when she looked up at him, he smiled warmly, the sweet brown sugar of his eyes reassuring her he would not fail her. Again she looked at his mouth. *Simply kiss him,* she thought. It was simple enough, wasn't it? She'd kissed him before, hadn't she? But this was different. There was no reason for it! Nothing had led them to it.

Watching Ryder's mouth until it was so close she had to close her eyes, Dusty moved toward him until she felt the softness of his lips against her own. He was still. Yes, he let her kiss him, even returned the kiss, as much as he could— considering how softly and how quickly she kissed him. Casting her gaze down for a moment before facing his, she drew in a deep breath. When she looked up at him again, he quirked one side of his mouth in a smile of satisfaction. His expression was nothing less than entirely inviting, and with every shred of courage she had left, she moved closer to him, letting her body press lightly against his. Still, his arms did not go around her; his strong hands were not at her waist. And she wondered—had it taken such profound courage as this for him each time he'd kissed her when she had not responded with a reassuring touch? No inviting caress?

She ran the fingers of one small hand across his lips before raising herself to kiss him again. This time, she did not pull away so quickly but let herself breathe of the scent of his face. Her kisses, however self-propelled, were met with perfect acceptance and delight. He did not deny her. In fact, a moment later, she went limp against him as his hands caressed her waist for long moments before he finally locked her in the power of his arms. Instantly, Dusty surrendered to his dominant power and confidence. His will was paradise! Everything else was driven from her mind, including the existence of Raynetta McCarthy looking on. His mouth suddenly left hers and traveled to her neck. She pressed her hand against the back of his head, enraptured by the feel of his kiss on her skin. His chin nuzzled her collar, forcing it down so he could kiss her throat briefly before his hands cupped her face, his obsessively craved kiss finding her mouth once more. A matter of a week had been far too long to deny herself the attentions of Ryder. A day would've been too long, she thought. An hour—a minute!

In the next moment, when he broke from her

and swept her into his arms, carrying her hurriedly toward the barn, she faltered in her confidence and whispered, "I'll explain later."

"You don't have to explain," he mumbled.

"I-I do," she told him.

By now, he had reached the barn and let her feet drop to the ground.

"You don't have to . . ." she began, wanting to release him from any obligation he felt to kiss her further because of what he'd said to her.

"You know I want to. And besides," he whispered, putting his mouth to her ear and causing her knees to buckle, "I haven't kept my promise."

Taking advantage of her weakened state, he pressed her body back against the barn wall with his own. He took her face in his hands for a moment as he began to fulfill the promise of a kiss she'd never dreamed possible. There in the shadows and privacy of the barn, Ryder Maddox proceeded to weave a spell of passion about Dusty breathing of magic. With his simple caressing of her throat, arms, face, and hair, he somewhat hypnotized her—kissing her tenderly, teasingly, furiously, and demandingly—thereby sending her sense of reality to some sort of obliteration for a time. But was it, she wondered, because he kissed her any differently? No. It was because she had sought him out and in doing so had surrendered the resistive part of her present between them each time before. His kiss wasn't any different, only more delicious and thirst-quenching because she received it differently. He'd known it would happen! He'd known that once she came to him without being coaxed or trapped or teased, it would indeed seem all the more dream-fulfilling to share in it with him.

She had never fathomed how incredible it would feel to run her fingers through his hair—to caress the broad expanse of his shoulders—to find that she could kiss him! Often his mouth would leave hers to scatter tender kisses along her nose, forehead, and neck, teasing mercilessly. Each time she would whisper some quiet hint to him she preferred his kiss on her mouth, he obeyed her without hesitation. She delighted, somewhat impishly, at her ability to control him so completely with a simple whisper or a hand pressed to his stomach.

"I've got chores to do," he mumbled between kisses once.

"I know," she answered breathlessly.

He released her then, stepping back and running his fingers through his already tousled hair. They looked away from each other shyly for one moment before he grinned at her with mutual understanding.

"There's wood to chop now." He pointed an index finger at her, winked, and chuckled, "But anytime you want me for somethin' like that again, you just let me know."

Dusty knew her cheeks were burning with the blush seeming to cover her whole being. What had she been thinking? She watched him leave the barn and shake his head in apparent wonderment before retrieving his ax and going about his labors.

Still trembling with delight, Dusty straightened her skirt and smoothed back her hair before leaving the barn. She blushed deeper still when Ryder looked over, winking at her again. She returned to where Miss Raynetta had retired to the porch swing.

As Dusty approached, Miss Raynetta frowned rather nervously and began fanning herself with her hand. "I guess I better be careful what kind a wagers I make in the future," the now terribly agitated woman sighed.

"Don't lose your nerve, Miss Raynetta," Dusty warned, sitting next to her. "You'll never know how much courage that took for me!"

"But the . . . the rewards were bountiful in your favor, sweet thing. I'm an old woman!"

Dusty smiled. She understood all too well Miss Raynetta's worries, her fear. Again, heaven seemed to intervene, and Dusty looked up to see her father striding toward them, a contented smile on his handsome face.

"Oh, my dear, no!" Miss Raynetta sighed as Dusty glanced at her with daring.

"Daddy!" Dusty greeted dramatically as Hank

stepped up onto the porch in one smooth stride.

"Hey there, punkin!" he greeted. "Miss Raynetta . . . I can't tell you how it warms my heart to see you and my girls gettin' on so well." Dusty was encouraged, and she couldn't help but elbow Miss Raynetta in the ribs. The woman immediately scolded her silently with a poke in her own. Yet she felt the woman's heart aching as her father added, "It's like having three purty little girls to my name rather'n only two." Yet Dusty didn't interpret the comment the same way as Miss Raynetta, no doubt, did. She sensed more hidden meaning than her father would care for her to have. Miss Raynetta's anxieties fairly oozed from her every pore, and as Miss Raynetta began to wring the fabric of her skirt, Dusty determined she needed a little shove.

"Well, I've got too much left to do in gettin' ready for tomorrow, Daddy." Leaping up from the swing suddenly, she offered, "Why don't you sit down here and take the weight off your feet for a minute? I'm sure Miss Raynetta is plum sick of my chatter."

"Don't mind if I do," Hank Hunter sighed, sitting down promptly, stretching his feet out before him. He propped one heavy boot over the other and sighed again, stretching his arms out on either side of him along the back of the swing.

Dusty almost giggled and yet felt profoundly sympathetic for Miss Raynetta, who squirmed uncomfortably as Hank's arm brushed her shoulders. Odd to realize she knew exactly how Miss Raynetta felt. No doubt the woman's heart was beating so hard inside her bosom she feared Hank could hear it. No doubt his arm brushing her shoulders had sent her body bubbling up in goose bumps.

In that brief moment, Dusty looked at her father differently than she ever had before. Hank Hunter was a profoundly handsome man—not just because he was her daddy but because it was factual! His shoulders were broad. He was tall and his body still muscular and strongly defined—a very youthful build. It amazed Dusty all at once to realize that her own father was someone who could easily send women of all ages swooning.

"Well," Dusty sighed, "I'm off. You two have fun now."

Dusty felt a little nip of guilt pinch her stomach at Miss Raynetta's widened eyes and mortified expression. Still, it was just a little nip. Calmly going into the house, she immediately motioned to Becca, who was sitting at the table shelling peas. The two sisters quietly dashed into their mother's old sewing room with a window looking out onto the porch.

Shhhh, Dusty mouthed. She and Becca crawled on their hands and knees to finally sit beneath the open window. Becca's eyes sparkled with excitement, and Dusty was certain that at least part of their radiance was the lingering knowledge Miss Raynetta had been right about Feller.

"Well, now, Miss Raynetta McCarthy." Hank's voice was clearly audible in the sewing room. "What have you and my girls been up to all mornin'?"

"Um . . . um . . . just bakin' and all for tomorrow," the sweet woman stammered in nervous response.

Hank chuckled. "You're an angel to come out here and spend your time with us a-helpin' out." There was silence for a moment, and then he continued, "Been a mite longer than I'd like to admit since I sat out here on any porch swing a-jabberin' on to a girl." Becca and Dusty both looked at each other delighted by their father's calling Miss Raynetta a girl.

"Been a mite longer than I'd like to admit since I was a girl, Hank Hunter," Miss Raynetta sighed.

"Ah, now go on! You look as fresh and sweet as the day I left your daddy's ranch."

"Hm. Good thing you're good with cattle, Hank . . . 'cause you sure are a rotten liar!"

Dusty motioned for Becca to follow her back out of the room, satisfied the conversation between her father and Miss Raynetta was going to continue.

Once they were both back in the kitchen, Becca whispered, "Do ya think we can get them two married, Dust?"

Dusty shrugged but smiled hopefully. Suddenly, everything seemed brighter—filled with possibility. Perhaps her father and Miss Raynetta would find happiness. Perhaps Feller would somehow find whatever he needed to make Becca's life perfect. And maybe she and Ryder—no. She wouldn't push her luck. She'd overcome a great deal of her fear, of her emotional trauma that day. She wouldn't jinx it all by hoping for something that, though more possibly tangible than it had been before, was still a dream too good to be true.

Chapter Thirteen

Everyone arrived on time for the bunkhouse frame-raising the next morning. Dusty and Becca and Miss Raynetta too kept busy carrying water to the men and making sure lunch was ready—and then supper. The frame was up, as well as some of the side boards, by the time the sun began to set. Hank Hunter had asked several of the men who fiddled to bring their instruments and invited the wives and children of the men who had helped out to the ranch for pie and dancing.

It had been a long, hot day filled with hard work. Dusty hardly had a chance to say more than a few words to anyone in passing—especially Ryder. Still, she and Becca had enjoyed a nice chat or two with Miss Raynetta. Dusty was even more determined that no more time should be wasted where her father and the woman who loved him were concerned.

The setting sun left the fire in the pit, the moonlight, and lanterns to warm the dark of the night for the gathering of county folk. Even though the men were tired, everyone was enjoying the get-together. Summer would be gone too soon, and the warm nights were to be savored.

Ryder had gone out behind the house to the rain barrel to scrub his face and arms and change his shirt. Dusty watched him go. Though her heart pounded in anxious desire for him to return so she could capture his attention somehow, her own attention was drawn to the corral fence. Her father stood leaning against a post, smiling contentedly as he watched the gathering.

"You tired, Daddy?" Dusty asked him, giving him a warm hug and then joining him in observing their friends and acquaintances.

"Done in, honey! Just about done in," he admitted with a wink and a tired sigh.

"The men got a whole lot more done than I thought they would," she commented. Without giving him even a chance to respond, she barreled ahead. "Daddy . . . you ever think about gettin' married again?"

"Good grief, girl!" he grumbled. "What kind of a question is that?"

"What about Miss Raynetta? You seem very fond of her. She's a good lady and—"

"Stop it. Stop it, right now, Dusty," he growled. His cheerful manner instantly disappeared. He seemed angry. Dusty followed the direction of his gaze and found his eyes did indeed follow Miss Raynetta as she walked from her seat toward the pie table. "I loved your mother so much. You know I still love her. I'll always love her."

"I know that, Daddy," Dusty said softly. "And I know you'll never stop. But . . . but there's room in your heart for—"

"I couldn't go through that again," he mumbled. "I couldn't love somebody and lose 'em. I couldn't stand it."

"But wouldn't it be better to love her all up close and right there . . . than from far away, wishin' you could have her close to you?" she ventured. "Wouldn't you rather have somebody in your arms and lose 'em one day . . . than to have watched her for so long and lose her somehow . . . never havin'—"

"What're you gettin' at?" he asked suddenly. "You tryin' to hitch me up with Raynetta McCarthy? What an idea, Dusty. Really!" But his eyes had an odd twinkle to them—though guilt was written there as well.

"Daddy," she said softly, taking his hand, "Mama would want you to be with somebody. You're still so young with so much to give someone. She wouldn't want ya to be alone and sad and wastin' what ya have to give. And Miss Raynetta is so completely different from Mama that nothin' would be the same! It wouldn't make ya feel guilty to love her, Daddy. If you'd just—"

"You're talkin' hogwash, Dusty." He shook his head. "Look at her . . . happy as a puppy in a mud puddle. All fresh and pretty. Don't look a day older than she did as a girl. And look at me . . . a forty-two year old man . . . an old man . . . with two grown daughters and—"

"And no sons," Dusty interrupted.

Hank chuckled, looking back toward Raynetta. "What would Raynetta McCarthy ever see worth havin' in me?"

Dusty swallowed hard and wondered if she were about to do the right thing. "Miss Raynetta loved someone once. Did ya know that, Daddy?"

"I heard the gossip in town. Folks say it was some hand of her daddy's. But I was there up until she was fourteen or fifteen. I don't remember her bein' sweet on nobody. I figure . . . nobody ever had the guts to go after her. She's quite the pistol . . . and a beauty at that."

"It's true, the gossip. It was a cowboy she loved," Dusty blurted.

"Really? And how is it that you know so much?" he asked.

"She told me," Dusty answered plainly.

"Is that so?" Hank chuckled and returned his

attention to Raynetta. "Well, he musta been a horse's hind end not to snatch her up without a second thought."

"He was a very, very wonderful young man, Daddy. You see . . . he didn't know she loved him. She never told him."

"Why the heck not? She ain't the type not to tell somebody what she's a-thinkin' about 'em."

"Well," Dusty ventured, "he . . . he was a mite older than her. Not too, too much older . . . but she was young." Dusty had her father's undivided attention now. No doubt he sensed the similarity between the story she was telling of Miss Raynetta and her own. "And he loved someone else . . . truly loved someone else. Someone Miss Raynetta thought the world of. Someone she thought deserved such a fine man."

"Hm," he mused, "musta been quite the woman he loved to keep his attention from Miss Raynetta McCarthy."

"Oh, she was. A marvelous woman." Dusty stroked the back of her father's hand and said softly, "Daddy, who do you think that cowboy was who didn't notice Miss Raynetta when she was fifteen and he was workin' for her daddy?"

"I can't imagine." His eyes widened as he asked, "You mean you know? You mean to tell me that she told ya?" He shook his head again. "I was there when she was about that age, sure enough. Did I know him, do ya think?"

Dusty smiled lovingly at her father. He was truly naive as to who the cowboy was who had unwittingly broken Raynetta McCarthy's tender heart. "I think ya did, Daddy," was all she said.

She wondered if she should've told him—for an expression of understanding captured his face, and with it came disbelief, guilt, regret.

"No, sir," he argued, his voice breaking with emotion. "I woulda known that. I never woulda been blind to somethin' like that," he assured himself, looking away. He looked sickened, pale—so much so that Dusty was sincerely concerned.

"Daddy?" she asked. "You all right? I'm sorry. I shouldn't have told ya. I . . . I just thought it might help ya to . . . to . . ."

"To what, Dusty?" he asked. He was very emotional. She hadn't realized fully how much he already cared for Miss Raynetta. The knowledge he'd hurt her in the past might now indeed serve to drive him further away from her rather than toward her. "To what?"

"I don't know, Daddy," Dusty cried suddenly. "Don't keep yourself from happiness outta guilt about Mama! I can see you have feelin's for Miss Raynetta, Daddy! Don't—"

"You tryin' to tell me that it's my fault she never married anybody else? You sayin' that?" he asked. Since her mother's death, Dusty had never seen her father so disturbed and weakened.

"No, Daddy. I'm not sayin' that." She swallowed hard. She'd come this far; she might as well tie her own noose completely. "But sometimes, Daddy . . . sometimes ya love someone so much . . . so real . . . that it doesn't matter who comes along. Even if ya try your hardest to love someone else . . . it doesn't matter. Sometimes . . . you can't love somebody else." How well she knew the truth of her own words.

"Little Raynetta," Hank whispered suddenly. Dusty felt tears streaming down her face at the sight of tears welling in her father's eyes. He scratched his whiskery chin for a moment. "I remember that day . . . the day I left her daddy's farm 'cause me and your mama were gettin' married." All the time he talked, his eyes were on Raynetta McCarthy—on Raynetta McCarthy and full of tears. "She . . . she come out to the barn to say good-bye . . ."

During his pause, Dusty closed her eyes against the pain in her heart. She knew all too perfectly what the young girl must've been feeling, what she'd wanted to say. Only hadn't.

"She cried when she said good-bye," Hank continued. "Told me she was cryin' because she was so happy for Elly and me. She gave me a . . . a scarf she'd been knittin'. Told me to congratulate Elly and said good-bye." Her father coughed, choking back tears. Then he said, "I loved your mother so much, Dusty."

"I know, Daddy," Dusty whispered through her own tears.

"It's only been this past year or so that I've been findin' myself in mind of Miss Raynetta. I tell myself it wouldn't be right . . . that it would be disrespectful to your mama and unfair to Miss Raynetta. I been tellin' myself that there ain't nothin' left in an old goat like me to offer somethin' as young and full of life as her. And yet sometimes . . . when she's around . . . I feel twenty again! All those silly notions that go through your mind when you're younger start up and . . ."

They were both silent for a moment as they fought to control their emotions. In fact, they had both been shedding tears and looking down at their feet, so when Raynetta McCarthy spoke, it was the first they realized she'd approached them.

"Well, you two seem awful sour tonight!" Miss Raynetta announced. Guiltily, both Dusty and her father looked up, revealing the obviously serious nature of their conversation. "Oh, pardon me. I-I'll leave you two alone. I'm sorry I interrupted," she apologized, turning to leave.

"Raynetta," Hank called out. Dusty noticed the way Miss Raynetta paused before turning around. Her father always called her "Miss Raynetta," and in being so familiar he'd revealed something that had unsettled the darling woman. Slowly she turned around and looked first to Dusty and then to Hank.

"Yes?" she asked. Her almost perpetual smile was gone; her eyes were wide and frightened.

"I . . . I . . . uh," Hank stammered. "Could you and I have us a little chat?"

Immediately, Miss Raynetta's hands began to wring, and she looked to Dusty desperately. "Dusty?" she asked. "Dusty, what have you been talkin' to your daddy about?" Dusty could see the panic and tears rising in the woman's eyes.

"Raynetta," her father began. Lifting her skirts, Miss Raynetta turned and lit out toward the barn. "Raynetta!" Hank called. He didn't waste a moment in pursuing her. Dusty knew Miss Raynetta would never be able to outrun her father. He was still one of the fastest runners in the county. No matter how spry Miss Raynetta was, and she fairly darted away like a spooked fairy, her father would track her down.

Tears fairly gushed from Raynetta's eyes as she ran—so many tears that her vision was blurred, and she had trouble seeing where she was going. How could she? How could Dusty tell Hank her secret? He knew now! He knew! She'd seen it in his eyes as he turned and looked from his daughter to her. She stumbled and fell, picked herself up quickly, and ran on toward the barn.

"Raynetta!" she heard him call after her.

How she wanted to stop and face him—to tell him what she had never had the courage to tell him so many years ago—had never been brave enough to tell him since his sweet wife had passed. But she couldn't. She couldn't face him. She could never face him again!

"Stop it!" he growled, and Raynetta felt a strong arm catch her around the waist—hold her still against a strong body. There would be no escaping him. As good to face the executioner as run from him, she squirmed about in his one arm, which soon became two until he released her.

Facing him, she cried, "How could she tell you? How could she?"

"She shouldn't have had to," Hank mumbled. "I should've—"

"I trusted her! I watched her go through a heartbreak . . . the kind that feels like it will kill you! I bled inside for her! I trusted her!" Burying her face in her hands, she sank to her knees in the straw covering the barn floor.

"Did ya ever tell her not to tell me?" Hank asked bluntly.

Raynetta looked up to him in pain and disbelief. "No! You shouldn't have to tell people not to tell some things!"

"Don't be mad at my girl, Raynetta, please," he said, in a soothing voice she'd come to know all too well. "She was only tryin' to help me."

"I loved Elly, Hank. I swear to you! No one was happier for her than me. I—I never resented her! I never . . ." she sobbed, desperate to defend herself against any betrayal he might suspect her of.

386

"I know," he said, reaching down to put a hand on her shoulder.

She moved away from him. Standing and turning from him, she hugged herself and whispered, "Just leave me be, Hank. Please."

For the first time in her entire life, Raynetta McCarthy felt ridiculous wearing a red dress. She wished it were brown or straw-colored so she could sink away into the corners of the barn and not be noticed.

"Raynetta," Hank began.

"I thought she was the prettiest girl I had ever seen. And when she had your babies . . . I thought, 'He's lucky to have her. No one else could've had babies that pretty for him. I could never have had babies that pretty for him.' " She didn't see Hank wince as he stood behind her. She felt cold—as if she were living in a nightmare—and she just kept talking. "I wished so much that I coulda had babies for you. I wished that those little girls coulda belonged to me. I tried not to think that way. I tried to love so many men who offered me marriage, but—"

"Raynetta," Hank interrupted, "I never, never woulda hurt you on purpose. Forgive me."

She turned to him suddenly. "Forgive you? For what? That's like Ryder Maddox a-beggin' forgiveness from Dusty when there weren't nothin' he coulda done different than to leave all those years ago. You did nothin' wrong. Nothin'.

And neither did I." Turning from him, she added, "And let's leave it at that now, all right?"

"I don't want you bein' angry with Dusty, Raynetta," commanded Hank. "She's lickin' her own wounds finally, and I know she had my best interest at heart. She knows I . . . she's seen me a-hankerin' after you and . . . and not reachin' out and takin'. She wanted to give me a shove forward, I suspect."

Raynetta watched as Hank turned and closed the barn doors, shutting them in alone. Someone had left a lantern burning on one of the rafters, and Raynetta marveled at how wildly alive Hank's eyes seemed in the lowered light—how possessive of what he was looking at—of her!

He turned to her and said, "I'm scared, Raynetta . . . more scared than I've been in a long, long time. And in a manner I ain't never been scared before." He took several steps toward her, causing her to stumble backward—so intent was he in his sudden appraisal of her. "I been watchin' these youngsters . . . the way they tiptoe 'round all proper and slow-like in courtin' each other. I figure . . . it ain't for me. Not anymore. I don't have the time for it."

"Hank," Raynetta began. Even as her heart swelled with hope and elation, she suddenly had a vision of Ryder picking Dusty up in his arms the day before—disappearing into the very same barn. Still, she feared to dream, and she tried to deter him. "It's in the past. I don't want your guilt toward me makin' ya think ya have to . . ." But her words were lost as he reached out and brushed a tear from her cheek with the back of his hand.

He was still so handsome—even more so in many ways than he'd been all those years ago. His hair, once so perfectly black, was salt-and-pepper now, his temples almost completely white. Yet his eyes, still as black as the night, were the same and made more appealing somehow by the wrinkles at the corners—testaments of years of happy living. His chin was firm and square and just as commanding as it always had been. As he stepped closer to her, taking her face in his hands, Raynetta McCarthy's heart began to beat so brutally within her chest she gasped several times—her breathing labored in trying to withhold sobbing.

"I'm tellin' ya this . . . and I mean it. It's the truth," Hank mumbled as he gazed down into her eyes.

"What?" she managed to whisper.

"Raynetta McCarthy . . . you're the most beautiful woman I ever kissed," Hank told her.

Raynetta smiled at him as a tear trickled down her lovely cheek. "You never kissed me, Hank Hunter."

"And I'm a fool for it," he chuckled, bending toward her.

Yet heartache still ebbed in her bosom—next to

hope. She put her hands softly on his chest to stall him. "I'm not Elly," she told him through more tears.

"I know that, Raynetta," Hank whispered and moved again to kiss her. But she turned her face from him.

"I . . . I won't be the same. I won't be her," she whispered.

"I know, Raynetta," Hank repeated. Then, taking her face in his hands again, he forced her to face him. "I want to have you, Raynetta. I'm not lookin' for a ghost." His eyes were moist with tears, but she knew they were tears for her sake—not tears over what he'd already loved and lost. "The past ain't standin' here next to us. All I'm seein' . . . all I'm wantin' is you."

He bent to kiss her again, but she took his face in her own hands. "I'm not very good at this, I don't think."

"Raynetta," Hank chuckled, trying to silence her.

"I mean . . . it ain't like I never kissed anybody before." Not liking the way that had sounded, she rattled on. "Not that I've kissed a lot or anything! I mean . . . I haven't. I mean, I have enough to know how and all . . . just not a lot. So, I might not—"

"Hush up, Raynetta," Hank chuckled in a low, alluring voice.

"All right," she agreed, dropping her hands from

his face. "All right." Hank kissed her lightly on one cheek, and she breathed, "Oh, my goodness."

As Hank Hunter kissed her tenderly, letting his lips linger on her lips for a moment, Raynetta thought she might indeed swoon away. She'd given up on her dream of belonging to him—long, long ago. Yet she dared to hope for it once more as his powerful arms wrapped her warmly in his possessive embrace—further proving his impatience with proper courting as his mouth seized hers in a blazing exercise in passion. Her timidity was vanquished almost immediately, and she let her own arms go around him.

Hank Hunter is kissing me, she thought. And his kiss was more perfect, more deserving of praise in its blissful perfection, than even she had ever dreamed. She kissed him in return, unbridled and unashamed of having loved him for so long. His hands caressed her face, her neck, his arms holding her possessively then again. And for all her joy, for all her rapture in living a dream in his arms, she could not stop the tears—tears of joy mingled with disbelief and fear of ending the dream. He eased the intensity of their affectionate exchange and, without releasing her from his embrace, broke their kiss, studying her face as he brushed away her tears.

"I'm not gonna bolt and run, if that's what you're thinkin', Raynetta," he assured her.

She looked away shyly. It was so unearthly to be

in such a situation with him. She began to doubt she was awake.

"Dusty, for all her tryin' to harden herself up, could see it in my eyes. Can't you?" Still she didn't look at him. She turned her face toward his. "Can't ya see yourself in my eyes? I do love you," he whispered without any pause or stammering. And she looked to him. He grinned at her and brushed a lock of hair from her forehead. "You think you can love a worn-out ol' cowhand like me, Raynetta McCarthy?"

She breathed a giggle—a sigh of believing what he was telling her. "I've loved you my whole entire life."

"Good," Hank mumbled. "Then ya think someday soon you'd marry me and we could get busy on that little brother Dusty's always wanted?"

Raynetta burst into tears—buried her face in her hands for a moment before looking up into his handsome, sincere, and loving face and crying, "Yes! Yes, yes, yes, yes, yes!" She threw her arms around his neck and hugged him, never wanting to let him go.

Dusty stood outside the barn, perched on an old rain barrel. She brushed the tears from her cheeks as she peered in through the barn window. Miss Raynetta would make her daddy happy! There was no doubting it. Hank Hunter would love Miss

Raynetta just as she'd always dreamed—perhaps even more.

"Shame on you, Miss Britches! Spyin' on Miss Raynetta and her beau!"

Ryder's voice from behind her startled Dusty, and she lost her footing on the barrel. Her arms flailed wildly, trying to find something to hold on to, but in the end she lost the balance battle and tumbled off the barrel—knocking Ryder to the ground. He chuckled, and she quickly scrambled up from her place on top of him, smoothing her hair and skirt and trying to find some semblance of dignity. He simply lay on the ground smiling up at her for a moment before extending his hand in a gesture indicating she should help him to his feet.

"Oh, like you need help gettin' up," she said. Still, she reached down and took his hand anyway, yanking hard. He yanked harder, however, and before she could regain her balance, Dusty was lying on the ground next to him. "You're a pill!" Dusty exclaimed, sitting up and kneeling beside him.

"And you've turned into quite the little matchmaker, haven't ya now?" Ryder grinned and put his hands behind his head. It appeared as if he meant to lie in the grass for some time.

"I'm not gonna talk to you if you're gonna be a stinker," she told him.

He seemed to ignore her and simply said,

"You're gonna have a harder row to hoe with Feller and Becca though." He raised himself and leaned on one elbow. "I'd be willin' to help ya with that one."

"Don't pretend ya didn't do nothin' to help that one in there," she giggled, motioning to the barn.

He chuckled. "Now . . . what do ya want to talk about?" he asked.

"What?" she breathed, completely puzzled and yet amused at his lighthearted manner.

"Me and you. Let's talk. What do ya want to talk about?"

Dusty paused. She didn't want to ruin his good mood, but the question had been banging around in her head for days. "Well, if you wanna talk . . ." He nodded encouragingly. "Let's talk about exactly why that paper ya got in the post the other day seemed to upset ya so much."

Immediately, his manner changed; so did his expression. His playful grin turned to a severe frown. Yet he didn't leave or reprimand her. He simply said, "Someone died. And . . . and that's sad most of the time, ain't it?"

He'd answered her question. She had no desire to upset him, so she simply nodded—even though her curiosity and the jealousy in her heart, burning over what she assumed were the reasons the paper had upset him, still ate at her soul.

"So," he said then, "why did you ever hook up

with a frog like Cash Richardson in the first place?"

Though his question upset and rather vexed her, it was fair enough—considering hers. There was nothing to do but answer him.

"Do ya really want to know? Do ya want to know what really happened?" Dusty asked him. "I know you've heard it all already. So why hear it again?"

"I want to hear it from you."

"Fine. I'll tell ya." Dusty inhaled deeply and crossed her legs beneath her skirt. Unconsciously she began picking blades of grass from the ground one at a time. "I've known Cash for a long time. To be honest . . . I never gave him a second thought until I was about sixteen." She realized her story would sound blunt and lacking emotion. Still, it was the truth—and the only way she knew how to tell it. "He started courting me then. He was nice . . . thoughtful . . . handsome." Ryder sniffed and coughed in obvious disagreement. Dusty couldn't help but smile. "He is fairly handsome, Ryder."

"For a frog, I guess he is."

Dusty smiled and shook her head. "He treated me very, very well . . . like I was special . . . like I meant everything to him. Nobody had treated me like that since . . ." She glanced at him, and he smiled guiltily. "For a long time," she finished. "And he wasn't a cowboy, so I knew . . ." She stopped herself but not soon enough.

"You knew he wouldn't leave ya," he finished for her.

"Yes," she admitted, looking down at the grass she was picking. "Every other man around seemed so . . . so . . ."

"They were all cowboys. Like someone else ya knew once," he finished again.

"Yes," she admitted. "Cash seemed . . . I really thought I could be sort of happy with him."

"That's the dumbest thing I ever heard!" Ryder growled suddenly. "You thought you could be sort of happy with him?"

"You asked me about it. I'm telling you the truth," Dusty reminded. It had been hard for her to start the tale—humiliating. And she was suddenly beginning to feel silly for confiding in him. "He was the only choice I had, Ryder."

"Please!" Ryder grumbled, sitting up completely and scowling at her. "You were seventeen when he asked you, weren't ya? Dusty! It ain't like you were an old, shriveled-up prune."

"I'm sorry I even told you," she spat, jumping to her feet and stomping away.

"Come on now. I'm sorry." Ryder was at her heels instantly, and she stopped as he took hold of her arm. "He just gets my dander up, that's all." He turned her to face him. "Don't stomp off mad again. Finish it. I really want to know what happened from you."

Dusty looked up into his magnificently

handsome face. The all too familiar pang of heartbreak stabbed at her heart. She felt the need to escape him now, as she always did when she knew she was weakening toward him—when she dared to think her dream might become reality. Even after their tender, intimate moments yesterday in the barn, she battled fear. She'd won so many battles with the emotion, but the war raged on.

"Yes, seventeen." She paused, reflecting on how mature she'd thought she'd been then. "We were engaged to be married, and about a month before the wedding, I went over to the Richardsons' to see Cash . . . to surprise him one evening. I'd just made him a cake for his danged birthday. When I think of all the effort I wasted on him . . ." she mumbled out of context. "Well, as I was walking toward the house, I heard somethin' comin' from the Richardsons' barn. I went over and looked in, and there was Cash and one of the saloon girls from town." Ryder let out a breath of exasperation, and then she continued. "They weren't doin' any more than kissin'—at least then—but . . ."

"And what did ya do?" Ryder interrupted.

"What do you think I did? I smashed the cake in his face and went home," she answered.

"I thought he was such a gentleman. So high and mighty . . . so much better than us lowly cowboys," Ryder grumbled.

"He was a gentleman! To me," she continued. "That was the ridiculous part of his story. He had too much respect for me, you see. But he had all this . . . this penned-up desire for me. And he couldn't endure it any longer. Have ya ever heard such a cockamamie excuse?" she asked him.

Ryder raised his eyebrows for a moment and mumbled, "A real gentleman would just ride off one night . . . don't ya think?"

Dusty didn't really think on what he said at first. She simply went on dramatically venting her old frustration. "He told me that to expect any man to resist . . . well, molesting me . . . was just too much to ask! How could he be expected not to falter and place his affections on someone else until he could have me . . . completely?"

"Oh, hand me a bucket 'fore I throw up!" Ryder exclaimed disgustedly. He sat down in the grass again. His anger and his disgust with Cash's actions were obvious. "Can't expect a man to keep control of hisself, huh? That's a real good excuse for bein' that kind of a jackass!" He shook his head in irritation.

Dusty shrugged. "He tried to make excuses, tried to explain, said he loved me . . . couldn't lose me . . . that he'd die if I walked away from him. So . . . I walked away."

"Hopin' he'd die?" Ryder chuckled.

Dusty couldn't stop the smile from breaking across her face. "Probably . . . now that I think back on it."

"But he didn't have the gumption to up and die, so . . ." he prodded her.

"So," Dusty sighed heavily, "he destroyed my pride, and I realized I wasn't hurt enough to have really been in love with him. And I hated myself for that. I realized what a shallow person I'd let myself become . . . settlin' for less than I lived my life to deserve and—"

"Interestin' that you should put your pride before your heart," he mumbled. "It's also very interestin' that it's your pride that keeps you from completely warmin' up to people now."

"I'm plenty warmed up to people!" Dusty defended herself, knowing full well he was right.

"Oh, yeah!" he chuckled with sarcasm. "A right hot apple pie!"

He winked at her teasingly. Still, she felt the heat of being provoked rising in her ears. It quickly died, however, the moment she looked down at him sitting in the grass—his legs stretched out long in front of him, his hat tipped back on his head as he leaned back on his arms looking at her. She was instantly calmed and delighted by the fact he sat so relaxed and attentive to her—that she had somehow found herself confiding in him. She wanted to be like an apple pie to him—wanted to warm him, share sweet, delicious kisses with him—wanted to satisfy him through good conversation and companionship.

"I . . ." Dusty began. She was about to tell him she was finding her way up from the darkness of hurt, letting go of pride and hardheartedness, when Makenna bounded up, plopping herself directly in Ryder's lap.

Ryder let out an, "Oof!" and a slight moan as he helped Makenna situate herself farther down on his legs. "There now, darlin'," he groaned as he smiled at her. "What can I do for my Kenna?"

Makenna giggled and took Ryder's face in her hands. "Mama said we could come over to Mr. Hunter's ranch even though Daddy is still sore. He's sittin', and Mama's talkin' wiff the ladies, and now there's dancin'!" she exclaimed excitedly. "You have to dance wiff me, Ryder Magics!"

"Is that so?" he asked, grinning delightedly at her.

Dusty smiled, filled with pure joy and amusement. How she loved to watch Makenna tag along after Ryder. How she loved to watch Ryder respond to her—completely enchanted by the little girl, a slave to her every whim.

"Um-hum!" Makenna nodded. "Come on, Ryder Magics! The musics is startin' again!"

"Pardon me, Miss Dusty," Ryder chuckled, rising awkwardly to his feet and taking Makenna by the hand. "I'm goin' waltzin' with the prettiest little angel in town!"

They began to walk toward the others, Makenna tugging mercilessly on Ryder's hand to hurry him along. "Hold on there, angel!" he groaned. "I got me a hitch in my get-along here."

Dusty giggled. But as Ryder limped away, her heart began to feel cold and lonely. Dusty nodded and winked, however, at Makenna, who threw her arms around Ryder's neck. He bent down and waved at Dusty happily as he lifted Makenna into his arms, carrying her the rest of the way.

Little girls would always love Ryder, she thought. She certainly hadn't been the last! She was sure of that. She wondered again what the girl who had died meant to him. Slowly, she walked over to where everyone was dancing next to the corral. The music was so pleasant, that oh-so-familiar tune. She watched Ryder's lips move, singing the words of the tune to Makenna as he danced with her, her tiny feet swinging this way and that in the breeze. Dusty smiled and bit her lip as Makenna giggled with delight in Ryder's arms.

"Well, I'll kiss you tonight, little darlin'. . . and I'll hold you so tight, in my arms," Ryder mouthed, kissing the toddler tenderly on the forehead. Makenna laid her head on Ryder's shoulder, delirious with joy as Ryder continued to sing to her.

Dusty stood humming and watching everyone dance until she felt someone tap her on the shoulder. She turned to see Feller standing next to her.

He smiled, nodded, and said, "You enjoyin' the evenin', Dusty?"

"Now and then," she answered teasingly. "You?"

"Now and then," he mimicked with a friendly smile. "You been up to no good where your daddy and Miss Raynetta is concerned." He winked approvingly at her.

"I've been up to very good where they're concerned," she told him.

The song ended, and the fiddler called out. "Grab your partners, folks! It's hot out tonight, and it's a flea-swappin' dance!" Everyone clapped and hooted and hollered, and Dusty, glancing to where Titch was leading Becca out to dance, saw an opportunity.

"Aren't you gonna be a gentleman, Feller, and ask me to dance?" she coaxed.

"It's a flea-swap, Dusty. I hate them kind," Feller grumbled.

"Oh, come on. Toughen up!" she told him, linking an arm with his and dragging him over to the dancing.

A flea-swap dance was something she'd always disliked too—especially if she were dancing with someone she wanted to be with. During a flea-swap, every once in a while the fiddler would shout, "Old dogs a-scratch 'em!" and everyone had to change partners.

Ryder had set Makenna down and was striding toward them. Catching his sleeve quickly and coaxing him to bend near, Dusty whispered, "Would ya watch and tell them fiddlers when to start and stop the swappin'?" He raised his eyebrows in admiration as he glanced at Feller and nodded.

"Oh, I can't believe I let you drag me on out here," Feller grumbled as the music started and they began to waltz.

"It'll be fun," Dusty told him. "I promise."

As they danced, Dusty noticed the way Feller's eyes kept glancing to where Titch and Becca were dancing nearby. "Oh, look," she whispered. "There's Becca. She doesn't seem to be havin' much fun."

"Hadn't noticed," Feller grumbled. Dusty was delighted by the blush rising to his cheeks.

"Really? The way you don't notice that little wiggle she's perfected when she walks?"

Feller's eyes widened with indignation just as the fiddler shouted, "Old dogs a-scratch 'em!"

Ryder stepped up and caught Dusty as Feller more than willingly released her and took Alice in his arms.

"Oh, he's mad now!" Ryder chuckled as he saw the glare Feller shot to Dusty across the way.

"He'll get over it," Dusty assured him—though a mild case of guilt did travel through her. It vanished quickly, however.

"They're gettin' closer . . ." Dusty whispered, not even realizing she and Ryder were hardly dancing at all—more holding each other, both staring expectantly at Feller. Ryder raised his hand and nodded to the fiddler again.

"Old dogs a-scratch 'em!" the man shouted, and Dusty and Ryder each exhaled with disappointment as Feller turned the opposite direction from Becca and ended up with someone else again.

"You in or out, Ryder?" Titch asked as he approached Dusty.

To Dusty's great surprise, Ryder took hold of her hand and fairly yanked her out of the circle of dancing couples. "We're out for now," he told his friend, who happily took someone else as a partner.

"That was nearly rude," Dusty scolded him.

Ryder shrugged his shoulders. "I don't feel like sharin' anymore," he mumbled as he intently watched Feller.

A smile escaped across Dusty's face; an odd fluttering in her stomach delighted her. How possessive of him! How fantastically possessive!

Dusty followed Ryder's gaze, and sure enough, Feller and his current partner were dancing directly next to Becca and hers. If Feller avoided Becca now, it would be too brutally obvious. Dusty knew he wouldn't take the chance at hurting her so terribly. Ryder raised his arm, nodded to the fiddler again, and this time—success! Feller turned to Becca, inhaled deeply, and took her in his arms. Dusty couldn't help giggling with delight and wrapping her arms around one of Ryder's large, powerful ones. He chuckled too, grinning down at her.

"Ryder!" Makenna squealed as Dusty turned in time to see the curly-topped child run headlong at Ryder. Throwing her arms around his thighs, her head, which had been bent toward him, hit his body hard, causing him great distress in his lower extremities.

"Oof!" he breathed again, doubling over this time and tugging patiently at the child's arms until she released her vise grip on him. Dusty bit her lip, once more trying to stifle the amusement she knew she shouldn't be experiencing. *Poor man,* she thought.

"There now, sweet thing," Ryder breathed to Makenna as he hunkered down awkwardly to face her. "You need to be more careful with ol' Ryder, or I ain't gonna ever be able to have my own babies to spoil."

Dusty secretly thrilled as she remembered the last time Ryder made such an implication at the Fourth of July picnic. A giggle escaped her throat next as Makenna actually seemed to understand Ryder's plea.

"I'm sorry, Ryder Magics," the child cooed, taking his whiskery face in her hands. "My daddy keeps tellin' me we won't have no more babies at our house either if I don't watch better where I sit."

"Wise man, your daddy," Ryder chuckled. He kissed her tenderly on one chubby cheek. "Now, you run along and find some younger boys to dance with for now. Okeydokey?" Makenna nodded and, contentedly humming to herself, turned and skipped away.

"You all right?" Dusty asked, biting her lip as she watched the way he straightened to a nearly upright stance.

"Yeah," he breathed. "Just gotta stand here a minute if you don't mind." He shifted his weight onto his other foot with a groan, and Dusty couldn't stop another giggle. "What're you laughin' at?" he asked. "I thought you'd be on my side where my ability to father children is concerned."

Instantly, Dusty's laughter ceased; her smile disappeared. The fluttering beginning in her stomach fairly erupted into chaos now. "What . . . what do you mean by that?" she questioned.

Ryder smiled and shook his head. "Sugar . . . if you haven't figured it out by now . . . I ain't gonna be the one to tell you!"

"I can't believe you!" she exclaimed. She was simultaneously aghast and elated. It was an odd sensation, to say the least. But he only chuckled at the blush on her cheeks, took her hand, and nodded toward the dance.

"Come on," he mumbled. "I'm well enough to join this next one." But she did not follow his lead.

Her feet were planted firmly where she stood, still trying to overcome the shocking delight of his inference. "You don't wanna dance with me?" he asked. But Dusty still could not respond—still struggled to absorb the previous remarks he had made. "Fine. Let's go for a walk. Me and you." He turned away from the dance and toward the barn. "Oops," he grinned. "Our barn is already occupied, ain't it?"

"Ryder!" she scolded. "That's my daddy in there!"

He raised his eyebrows, a broad smile spreading across his face. "I know it! Good ol' boy, your daddy." With a wink he turned in the direction of the creek and whispered, "Come on. I know a place we can be alone to . . . talk. A half-naked girl showed it to me once."

Dusty's mouth again gaped open in astonishment. Still, her feet betrayed her, for they willingly propelled her forward to follow him as he pulled her along. He glanced back at her several times, obviously amused by the uncertain expression on her face. Chuckling, he pulled her closer to him, putting a strong arm around her shoulders.

"Come on now, girl. Nothin' to fear." Then, leaning over and whispering in her ear, he added, "I ain't in no shape to threaten your good name . . . not after havin' Kenna Jones 'round here tonight."

"Ryder! You stop it!" she scolded in a whisper as he threw his head back and laughed.

Then quickening his step, he told her, "Come on! There's a full moon. It'll be right nice out there tonight." Smiling blissfully, Dusty won another battle with fear and cowardice, letting him lead her to the pond, across the rock path, and behind the waterfall.

It was indeed a beautiful summer night. The moon shone brightly through the cascade of water illuminating the alcove, giving it a magical quality—like a fairyland, hidden in secret from the rest of the world. Ryder reached out and let the water run over his hand for a moment. Dusty simply sat down on the inner edge of the alcove and watched him.

"Well, I'll tell you this," he began. "I sure am glad the bunkhouse is gettin' done. The parlor floor's givin' me cause to wake up with a backache every dang mornin'." He shook the water from his hand and dried his fingers on his pant leg. Turning to Dusty, he added, "Yep! Sure will be nice to sleep in a bed for a change. Of course . . ." Dusty knew mischief was about by the sparkle in his eyes and the grin on his face. "Been plenty of moments this last week . . . that I was tempted to slip into your bed a time or two."

"Ryder! You stop that!" she scolded, jumping to her feet. She could admit to herself inwardly she wasn't scolding him because his remarks of late were improper. She was scolding him because of the way they made her heart race even faster than it already did when she had him to herself.

"Boy! I found your switch, didn't I?" he whispered, going to her and taking her face in his hands. Without further warning or pause, he kissed her hard, intimately, and with an air of possessiveness that thrilled her. After the one, driven kiss, he pulled back from her, still holding her face and caressing her lips with his thumb as he mumbled, "Won't be long and you and I will be havin' to share all our hideouts with Becca and Feller—your daddy and Miss Raynetta too, for that matter!" He smiled at her, the warm magic of his eyes soothing her, relaxing her. Suddenly, she found her hands at his waist, tugging on the waistband of his pants—silently begging him for another kiss. "Yep! Me and you make a good little pair of matchmakers, now don't we?"

"I suppose so," she admitted, completely mesmerized by his mouth as he talked.

"You think you and me will ever get around to . . ." His words were lost as his attention seemed to be completely arrested by her own mouth. He swallowed hard, and she tugged at his waist again, "Angelina," he whispered, "you make my mouth water . . . and make me thirsty all at the same time."

Dusty inhaled triumphantly as he fairly attacked

her. It seemed as if he were frustrated with not being able to pull her body close enough to his. His kisses were demanding, surging with a passion he seemed unable to quench. He whispered her name over and over between worshipping her neck with moist kisses and commanding the responses of her mouth to his.

I love you! she wanted to confess to him. *I love you so much deeper than I even thought I did!* But she was silent—except for whispering his name once when he had ceased in ravaging her momentarily, his face poised above her own as if waiting for the next invitation. She wanted to hear him tell her he loved her among the things he was whispering now and again.

"Stop me," he begged her once. But she shook her head, and he fairly winced as his mouth took hers again. "There's something I need to tell . . ." Ryder began during another pause to allow her to catch her breath. Yet Dusty shook her head again and embraced him frantically as they continued to kiss. Finally, the cheers from the revelers back at the ranch house signaled them both that the dance had ended and everyone would be leaving.

"They'll miss us now," she whispered as he held her head against his chest. The mad hammering of his heart and his heavy breathing caused her to reach up and stroke his face soothingly. He kissed the palm of her hand and held her away from him.

"You don't think they already have?" he asked her. His expression was that of extreme mischief mingled with desire. "And look at you." He brushed a strand of hair from her cheek. "You look like . . ." His fingers caressed her lips, which were somewhat sore from the length and passion of their interlude.

"Like what?" she asked, standing back from him, straightening her skirt and blouse and running her fingers through her tangled hair.

"Like your daddy will string me up if he sees you just now," he chuckled.

"He won't be in the frame of mind to be noticin' it." Dusty grinned at Ryder.

"Not after the way Miss Raynetta must look by now, you mean?"

He winked at her and took her hand, leading her out of the alcove. She smiled, warmed by his arm about her shoulders. Still, as they approached the party of departing people, he dropped his arm to his side again.

Is this all there will ever be? she thought. Kissing and passion under the waterfall—only to return to the world as if nothing had happened? The look of panic and, yes, fear must've been far too evident on her face. Ryder immediately took her by the shoulders and glared down at her.

"Oh, no, you don't!" he whispered. "No, sir! Don't you give me that look!"

"What look?" she managed.

"That look that says, 'Will you be here in the mornin', Ryder?' " He shook his head. "I hate that look! It lets me know you still don't trust me. And believe me, Dusty . . . if that next step with me and you is ever to come . . . it won't be until that look is gone!"

"What next step?" she asked. Surely he would say it now—give her hope—hope of him.

"Ryder!" her father shouted. Ryder's attention was immediately turned to Hank, and he guiltily dropped his hands from Dusty. "Come on over here and help load up some of these supplies for Alex and Alice, would you, boy?"

Ryder let out a relieved sigh, winked at Dusty, and confessed, "I thought I was on my way to the hangin' tree!" He reached out and tweaked her nose before hurrying toward the Joneses' wagon.

"We'll pick up all the rest of what you need tomorrow when the boys are in town," Dusty heard her father tell Alex.

Alice waved to Dusty and gave her a knowing wink. Dusty smiled and waved back before noting how her father held Miss Raynetta's hand tightly as he walked her to her own wagon. He helped her up onto the wagon seat after tying a saddle horse to the back of the wagon. Never again would any of the other hands see Miss Raynetta home— Dusty knew that for certain. Going into the house then, Dusty found Becca sitting at the table, her head propped up on one hand as she stared rather dismally out through the window to the starry sky.

"What's wrong?" Dusty asked, though she already suspected what it was. Actually, she knew. Becca looked up at Dusty, and her eyes made a quick appraisal of her from head to toe.

"What's wrong is . . . I never come back from a walk with Feller lookin' the way you do after a walk with Ryder!" Becca told her simply.

"What are you talkin' about?" Dusty turned away shyly for a moment.

"He's gonna marry you, Dusty. Ryder's gonna marry you and give you babies and make you happy, and he's gonna spend the rest of his life kissin' you out in the barn or under the waterfall."

Immediately the fear and doubt began to chill Dusty. "Don't Becca. Don't say that! You'll—"

"My sayin' it ain't gonna make it not happen, Dusty. I caught him, you know."

"What? Caught him what?"

"I caught Ryder the other night . . . standin' in the doorway of your bedroom watchin' you sleep. Just standin' there with that deep ol' frown on his face, just watchin' you sleep." Dusty shook her head, unable to believe it. "I've seen you too. Standin' in the parlor, watchin' him. Truth be told, there were moments that I thought the bunkhouse fire may end up causin' a shotgun weddin' between you and Ryder."

"For cryin' out loud, Becca! How you do go on!" Dusty scolded, although her heart was beating frantically at the thought of Ryder so close to her when she was unaware. Hadn't he only just told her, that very night—hadn't he just told her there had been moments when he'd thought of her bed? "Anyhow . . . I saw ya dancin' with Feller tonight. You—"

"The flea-swap, ya mean?" Becca shook her head. "Well, that was the beginnin' and the end of me havin' his attention tonight!"

"You mean he didn't even . . ."

"Know why I caught you and Ryder a-starin' off at each other in the dark?" Dusty shook her head. "Because after the two of you would finally settle down every night . . . it was my turn to dream over a sleepin' man." Becca rose and, with tears in her eyes, went to her room.

"Feller Lance, you coward!" Dusty whispered angrily. Immediately, however, she repented. Who was the biggest coward of all on the Hunter ranch? It wasn't Feller Lance or Becca or even her father. It was Dusty—it was still her.

Chapter Fourteen

The next morning, after feeding the chickens, Dusty sought out Feller. She found him saddling up his horse. She knew he, Ryder, and Ruff were going into town to pick up supplies, and she'd made up her mind to talk to him before they left.

"Feller," Dusty began.

"Mmm hmm," Feller mumbled as he worked.

"Do ya . . . do ya fancy Becca?"

Feller seemed to nearly choke—dropped the horse's hoof, causing the animal to step directly on his own foot. "Dang!" he exclaimed, slapping the animal's flank. The horse lifted its foot, and Feller stepped back. He looked up to Dusty, his expression revealing his sudden anxiety.

Dusty secretly delighted in the way the color completely drained from his face. He deserved to feel uncomfortable after not having asked Becca to dance again the night before.

"Well, do ya?" she prodded.

"Do I what?" he asked with irritation, feigning ignorance.

"Do ya fancy my sister? Are ya sweet on her? Do ya like her, Feller?" Dusty was amused, watching him angrily grab a currycomb and begin roughly brushing the horse's neck.

"You beat all. What kind of a question is that? I got things to do," Feller mumbled.

Dusty had known Feller almost all her life. She knew him well enough to know that the only time he tried to get someone to leave him alone by saying he had things to do was when he was uncomfortable.

"Well? Do ya?" she asked again.

"Of course I fancy her! I've known her since she was in diapers almost. She's a fine girl. I fancy you too. What's all this about?"

"But . . . do ya like her, Feller? Do ya more than like her?"

Feller quit brushing the animal for a minute. He looked to Dusty. "She's seventeen, Dusty. She's got her whole life ahead of her. She's young."

"When I was seventeen, I was engaged to be married, Feller," Dusty reminded him.

"And Cash was twenty-one, Dusty. Not thirty." He went back to brushing. "Besides . . . weren't that almost the biggest mistake of your life?"

"Yes. Because if I had married him, it would've been dishonest . . . to him and myself. Because . . . I think ya already know, Feller . . . I never loved him like I should've," she confessed.

Feller only continued to brush the horse.

"Why don't ya let Becca know how ya feel?" she asked.

"There ain't nothin' to let her know."

"Don't do it, Feller. Don't waste your life for fear of rejection."

"You're the one to be tellin' me that, huh?" he growled at her. He turned to her. Dusty could see the pain in his eyes. It was unnerving—for never had she remembered seeing such hurt in Feller Lance's eyes before. "What about you? Huh? Who are you to be tellin' me what to be afraid of?" He threw the curry brush to the ground, took his gloves from their place in his back pocket, and angrily began pulling them on. "She's a girl, Dusty. Seventeen! I'm thirty years old.

Heck, I'm only twelve years behind your daddy!"

"You go on like you're a hundred, Feller!" Dusty felt the tears leave her eyes and travel down her cheeks. "Don't let happen to her what happened to me. Please!"

"You said it yourself. Cash woulda been the biggest mistake—"

"I wasn't talking about Cash, and you know it." Tears flooded her cheeks then. "Nothin' on this earth coulda kept me from tryin' my best to win Ryder if I'd been seventeen when he was here instead of fourteen. Nothin'!" Her voice cracked with emotion, and she brushed the tears from her face. "Don't break Becca's heart any longer, Feller. I swear I'll hate you forever if you keep doin' it!"

He was silent for a moment, his jaw clenching and unclenching with anger and frustration. "What do ya want me to do, Dusty? Huh? Waltz up to her and—"

"Yes," Dusty answered without letting him finish. "Walk up to her, and tell her how ya feel. Kiss her mouth raw! Kidnap a preacher, and marry her. I don't care! Just quit lettin' her think ya don't care." Dusty smiled for a moment through her tears—shook her head at the irony. "To think of all the times . . . all the sermons you've given me over the past years. I never knew what a hypocrite you really are."

Feller tightened the saddle cinch and pressed his forehead against the saddle for a moment. "I ain't even fit to touch her . . . let alone kiss her mouth raw, as you put it."

"Why not?" Dusty whispered, afraid for a moment that maybe there was really some reason Feller wasn't worthy of her sister. Maybe some secret criminal act or . . .

"Because she's perfect and I'm a scroungy ol' cowboy." Mounting quickly, he rode out at a mad pace—as if hell itself were nipping at his heels.

Dusty's heart ached for Becca. All day while the men were gone to town or out working in the pastures, Dusty's heart ached for someone other than herself. Becca was becoming quiet, withdrawn, unfriendly—not so unlike Dusty had been. It couldn't happen to her Becca. It couldn't! Not heartache, fear, and hate!

ॐ

It was almost suppertime when the hands rode in from their various endeavors. Ruff drove the wagon and team, and Dusty watched from the kitchen window as Ryder and Feller unloaded the rest of the supplies. Twice Ryder's eyes were drawn to the house. She could've sworn that he saw her, but he looked away—almost guiltily. And then, very unexpectedly, he didn't even come in for supper. Dusty's fears began to grow, her imagination running toward wild venues. He'd changed his mind about her—felt ridiculous for saying the things he had said to her the night before!

When the dishes were done, the evening talk

quieted, and the men bunked down in the parlor, Ryder still had not come in. Perhaps it wasn't that he'd changed his mind. He seemed to be in the same defeated mood he'd been in after receiving that danged newspaper! *Perhaps something happened in town,* she mused. Fortunately, Feller wandered into the kitchen in search of a cup of water.

"Feller, I'm sorry for earlier today! I just . . . I just . . ." Dusty stammered.

Feller nodded and held up a hand for her to stop her apology. "There was a woman in town today, Dusty."

Immediately, Dusty began to feel sick. A woman? Ryder's black mood? She nodded and listened as Feller continued in a hushed voice.

"I ain't never seen her before. I didn't hear what she said to him, or him to her for that matter . . . but she's stayin' at the Richins' boardin' house, and when she and Ryder met up . . . well, she was a-bawlin' like anythin' when they finished arguin', and Ryder's been madder'n a hornet ever since."

Dusty began wringing the fabric of her dress, tears brimming in her eyes.

"I ain't tellin' you this to upset ya, girl. Somethin's wrong, and you need to help him through it. He ain't told me what . . . but I've been in mind of somethin' since the day he rode in here. Five years is a long time and—"

"Maybe she's his wife! Maybe he got married

while he was gone and . . ." Dusty sobbed in a whisper.

"No, no, no, sweet pea!" Feller reassured her, taking hold of her shoulders. "It ain't nothin' like that, I'm sure. But . . . but I think he's carryin' around some deep scars and—"

"I've seen them," Dusty blurted out. "On his back! He—"

"I've seen 'em too, Dusty. But that ain't what I mean. If everythin' is ever gonna be right between you two, ya need to help him now." Then he turned away—simply retired to the parlor.

Dusty was in a state of panic. A woman! Her worst fear! Yes, it had always been her worst fear—to find out maybe some other woman had been held in Ryder's arms, caressed, and kissed behind a waterfall or in a barn.

Still, Ryder was nowhere to be found. When she looked in the barn, at the creek, even at the waterfall, he was nowhere. Had he abandoned her again? Had he ridden off, breaking her—destroying her completely?

Even as Dusty lay in bed listening for every sound that might signal his return, his very presence, she cried. He was lost to her! Ryder would never be hers! The dreams had been only that—dreams.

❧

She awoke slowly, comforted a bit by the night breeze breathing through the windows, softly billowing the curtains into the room as it whispered with the fragrance of honeysuckle and ripening apples from the orchard. The quiet midnight lowing of the cattle in the fields brought her mind out of sleep and into consciousness. Her body was tired—ached from the strenuous emotions still lacing through her. As her head lay on the comfortable, down-filled pillow, she wondered if merely the single hour of rest would give her back the strength she had lost.

Closing her eyes, Dusty listened again for some sound that would tell her Ryder was there—that he hadn't left but had merely gone for a late, late, very long walk to ease his mind about whatever the woman in town had said to him—or meant to him. The air was still warm from the lingering heat of the late summer day, and the crickets still chirped their lullabies of the night.

Her senses were suddenly alerted by a noise. She opened her eyes again, looking toward the open window. It took her anguished mind a moment to realize that something besides a summer breeze was entering her room by way of it. She startled, all at once fully awake when she realized Ryder was climbing into her room through the window.

"What on earth are you doin'?" Dusty asked, gloriously relieved to see him there—hopeful! Still, propriety demanded she act appalled. Didn't it? "What on earth . . ." she began again, sitting upright in her bed.

"Ssshhh," Ryder shushed her firmly, a deep scowl puckering his brow as he stepped into the room and began striding toward her.

"Don't you dare to shush me," she scolded. Obediently, however, she'd lowered her voice to a whisper.

He looked angry. He'd looked angry and determined even before he had completely entered the room. Before Dusty could act in any manner, let alone decide what manner to act in—for she was in rather a state of shock—Ryder Maddox had stripped off his boots, quietly gone and closed the door leading from her room to the house, and now sauntered toward her bed.

"What are you doin' in here?" she asked him. Her senses were completely alive!

In the very next moment and fully clothed, he slipped beneath the covers of Dusty's bed. Stretching out next to her, he propped his head on his hand, his elbow planted firmly on the mattress, as he stared at her—almost furiously.

"Excuse me? Are you listenin' to me? What are you doin'?" she asked, looking down at him—silently giving up prayers of thanks for his very presence.

Ryder gave no explanation. He simply reached out, took her chin firmly in his strong, callused hand, and forced her head back down to her pillow. She now lay looking directly up at him. Dusty was dumbfounded—completely mute with shock—delirious with delight! She could say nothing. She couldn't move. All she could do was lie there—in bed, for pity's sake—staring at the man who had her completely under his control!

"Is this my place?" he asked through clenched teeth. His jaw was so tightened Dusty could hear his teeth grinding with agitation. She knew he was angry—but at what? She knew it wasn't directed at her. What then? The woman in town?

"Is it?" he demanded in a booming whisper.

"Wh-what?" she stammered, still unable to comprehend the entire situation—let alone his reasons for placing her in it and the meaning of his question.

"Here!" he stated, releasing her chin and literally pounding his index finger on the mattress on which they lay. "In bed . . . next to you . . . every night! Is this my place?"

"Ryder . . . I—I don't . . ." What did he mean to ask? Where had the question suddenly come from? It was madness!

Again he took her chin in his hand and leaned over her, his face so close she could feel the warmth and moisture of his breath on her lips as he spoke. "I should leave," he said. "Now! Tonight! If I had any brains a-rattlin' around in my fool head . . . I'd leave! And I will . . . if this ain't gonna be where I find myself one day soon."

Dusty still didn't understand what he was trying to convey to her, but she had heard him say that he should leave. He couldn't leave! She would die if he left! Where had this come from? Why was he wanting to leave so soon?

"What do you mean, you're leaving? You can't leave me—I mean . . . you can't leave!" she exclaimed. "There's too much to be done, and . . . you said ya weren't gonna—"

"Shut up, Dusty!" he commanded through clenched teeth. "Shut your delicious little mouth and listen to me!"

Oh, how she wanted him to hold her—wanted to hold him! To kiss him! He was so close. His beloved face, unshaven and handsome as it was —the smell of straw and lye soap and leather about him—his body pressed warmly against her own. And yet his words were causing panic to overtake her.

"I should leave, Dusty. I know ya don't understand why. I can't tell ya why. Not now. Not yet. But I . . . if ya tell me that someday you're gonna come outta this . . . if you can tell me now, tonight, that if I stay, someday you're gonna let me take you into my bed . . . our bed . . . that somehow you're gonna give up your fool pride and give yourself to me completely . . . then I'll stay. If not . . ." He looked away for a moment. "If not . . ."

"You're telling me that either I—I . . . let you . . . sacrifice my virtue for you . . . or you'll . . ." she stammered. How could she do it? Yet the thought of losing him was intolerable, unthinkable, murdering to her soul!

"For Pete's sake, Dusty!" He closed his eyes tightly for a moment and drew in a deep, calming breath before looking down at her again.

Dusty allowed her mind to ponder on what she felt her heart knew he was saying. He wasn't asking her to sacrifice her virtue. He was asking—could it be that he was asking if someday she'd marry him?

"Stay or go, Dusty?" he asked. "Understand this. If I stay, it could be the last decision I ever make. If I go . . ."

"If you go . . . I'll die, Ryder!" It was that simple.

Dusty sniffled as tears began running from the corners of her eyes down her temples. She had read his spirit. He was asking if she loved him still—enough to marry him. Could it be possible he was truly unaware that she did? She'd answered him truthfully—as truthfully as she could. In that moment, she'd risked everything: her heart, her pride, her sanity—her life! He had to know it. He had to! He couldn't press her further, not yet, or she would crumble. He exhaled heavily, proving he'd received the answer to his question.

"So it's down to which one of us dies first, huh?" he whispered, grinning somewhat regretfully at her. "That's an easy enough choice for me then."

Cupping her face in his hands, he searched her eyes, his lips hovering only a breath from hers. "Say it to me," he mumbled. "Why can't ya just say it to me?"

Dusty opened her mouth to speak. She told her throat to utter the words, but the sharp pain in her chest, the fear of rejection even though he was lying in her bed, telling her he would stay for her no matter what—fear kept her from confessing to him. He hadn't spoken the words to her. How could he expect her to admit something he himself had not said?

He sighed, a hint of disappointment in his expression as he half-grinned at her. "Don't hurt yourself with talkin' if it's that hard, sugar. Just show me."

Her lips were still parted, trying to force the words from her throat. His open mouth, hot and demanding, seized hers in one of his passionate, rapturous kisses. There was no pause in her reflex. Her arms went around his powerful body, endeavoring to hold him closer to her. His hands left her face as the fierce, impassioned exchange between them continued, his arms striving to embrace her—caress her—hold her. His kiss was nearly suffocating in its euphoric power! He kissed her fiercely, as if it were impossible to kiss her long enough—deeply enough! As if he . . . as if they both were unable to satisfy an infinite craving and, yet at the same time, as if their kiss were the only thing on earth to give them happiness, security, and fulfillment. Finally, with one last powerfully driven kiss bruising Dusty's tender lips, he broke from her, caressing her face with his hand as he gazed into her eyes.

"You see how much warmer you'd be in the winter with me in here 'stead of out in the parlor or the bunkhouse?" he teased.

She couldn't help but smile at him. "Don't leave me, Ryder," she whispered as he bent, kissing her neck just below her ear once more. "I . . . I can't lose you again."

Ryder chuckled warmly. Then, tossing back the covers and quickly climbing out of the bed, he strode to the window. "If I don't leave ya now, your daddy'll have my hide!"

"No," she explained quietly. "Don't abandon me. I promise that . . ." But she was unable to speak what her heart wanted to tell him.

Smiling with understanding, he raised an index finger to her as his eyebrows arched with warning. "Don't abandon me, Angelina," he said.

He picked up his boots and climbed out through the window—into the soft summer night. She heard his footsteps on the porch and then in the kitchen as he made his way to the parlor—heard a deep voice raised in question and Ryder's answer.

Dusty lay in her bed in stunned euphoria for a moment. He loved her? After all this time, he loved her! He hadn't said it, granted. But to imply that he wanted her to be his wife—surely he had to love her. There entered into the blissful knowledge a tiny seed of fear. Why had he thought of leaving? Why had his question about whether she wanted him to stay been so mysterious? Did it have to do with the woman in town, the woman Feller had spoken of earlier? Who was she to him? Why a sudden urgency about whether he would stay or go? But Dusty pushed the jealous, frightened thoughts aside and dwelt only on the feel of being in his arms. She was warm with relief and hope at having, in part, admitted her love for him—her incredible desire for him never to leave her.

There came a breeze through the window—a whiff of honeysuckle nectar and warm, ripening fruit. Ryder wouldn't leave her again! He'd said as much, and she knew it was true. He would never leave her again. The sure knowledge was the last piece of the puzzle she needed—the last piece to fit into place in order to make her whole. Her heart was light; her body and mind were warmed. She felt momentarily void of fear. She was completely excited by life—by the prospect of belonging to Ryder Maddox—by the feel in the night air signaling the imminent ending of summer. The thought came to her that she would have a mother. Somehow she would have Feller Lance for a brother-in-law. And someday— someday, somehow, she would be the one to wake up Ryder Maddox each morning—send him from their bed out to whistle a tune in the barn.

In the morning she would say it to him—tell him what she knew he needed to hear her say. She was whole again! Here was the Dusty that had been! And in the morning she would tell him.

ಬಬ

Dusty listened to Ryder whistling—singing as he clanged around in the barn early in the morning. She caught his eye several times during breakfast and gifted him with her own mischievous smile —caused his eyebrows to rise inquisitively. Her father had sent the hands to ride the range that morning and get an idea where the cattle had wandered during the summer. It would be lunch before she would have the chance to talk to Ryder—maybe supper. But she would! She would tell him, and things would be different. Dusty had it all planned out. She would lure him to the waterfall. Yes! That's where she must tell him—in her own magical place, with no one else around.

The hands had been out most of the morning. Becca and Dusty worked together making apple pies for supper that evening.

"Do ya think . . ." Becca began, pausing in crimping the edge of a freshly rolled piecrust.

"Do I think what?" Dusty prodded.

"Oh, nothing," Becca sighed. She continued to shape the edges of the crust along the edge of the tin pie pan.

"Yes. I think he does." Dusty giggled, having read her sister's thoughts.

"What do you mean by that?" Becca asked, blushing.

"Yes, I think Feller loves you! I've told you that a million times, Becca," Dusty reminded her. "He's . . . he's uncertain . . . lacks confidence. But he'll find his way to tellin' ya sooner or later."

"I can't wait any longer for later, Dusty! I mean . . . I think he . . ." Becca sighed heavily again. "Nevermind. And anyway . . ." She glanced out the kitchen window. "Here comes somebody from town. Can't quite make out who it is yet."

Dusty followed her sister's gaze through the window to where a buggy with one passenger, a woman, approached. Dusty's neck prickled as she watched the woman stop the buggy near the back porch. She watched the graceful stranger step down from the buggy and look about. She appeared to be disoriented.

"Well?" Becca asked. "Are we gonna stand here a-gawkin' at her?" She dried her hands on her apron and walked out onto the porch.

"Hello!" Dusty heard Becca greet the woman as she slowly followed her sister. "What can we do for ya?"

Dusty stepped out onto the porch next to Becca. The young woman's eyes locked with Dusty's an instant. She studied Dusty from head to toe.

"Uh, yes," the young woman answered Becca, still looking at Dusty. "I'm . . . uh . . . is this the Hunter ranch?" she asked.

"Well, yes it is," Becca answered when Dusty didn't.

Dusty's stomach churned with fear. This must be the woman Feller had seen Ryder talking to in town the day before. And now she'd come here! Who was she to Ryder? Even with no true knowledge of her beyond the fact Feller had seen her talking to Ryder in town, Dusty knew this woman was no friend to her.

"Are you . . . are you Dusty?" the woman asked, still staring at Dusty.

"Yes," Dusty answered shortly. "And you are?"

"Rose Montgomery," the woman answered. Dusty stood speechless.

The name was unknown to her and yet somehow familiar. Then, like a horrible glimpse into a suffocating nightmare, Dusty remembered the newspaper. She remembered with perfectly terrible clarity the name of the girl in Abilene who had died—the name of the family in the newspaper article Ryder had received in the mail. Lillian Montgomery had been the name of the girl who had passed away—the name of the girl whose death had so unsettled Ryder.

"From Abilene?" Dusty asked.

The young woman frowned, obviously astonished Dusty knew of her. "Yes."

Becca frowned and looked from the woman to Dusty and back.

"Ryder isn't here. He's out in the pastures," Dusty curtly informed Rose Montgomery.

This girl was beautiful—long auburn hair pinned up to perfection. This was a young woman who would never be caught dead wearing her daddy's old shirts—as Becca and Dusty did at that very moment. Her eyes were as green as emeralds, her skin as fair as porcelain. She was rosy-cheeked.

"I-I came to talk to you," Rose Montgomery said then.

"Dusty?" Becca asked in a whisper. From the pale look on her face, it was apparent Becca too felt impending doom.

"Run on in and work on the apples, Becca," Dusty ordered. "It'll be all right."

It would be. It had to be! The night before Dusty had put the pieces of her soul in order. Nothing would take Ryder Maddox from her now—nothing and no one! She would have him. No one else!

Without another word, Becca went back in the house. Dusty descended the porch steps—soon stood face-to-face with the woman.

"Ryder has told you about Lilly then?" Rose asked forthrightly.

"No." Dusty's answer was impolitely blunt. "I know she was a young woman who died in Abilene recently. That's all."

Dusty could see the sudden excess moisture in the young woman's eyes, but she seemed to blink back the tears—inhaled a deep breath.

She studied Dusty for a long moment and then, smiling kindly, said, "I knew you'd be beautiful."

Dusty frowned, completely confused and taken back by the woman's remark. She shook her head.

The woman continued, "He told us stories about you . . . all the time. He described you perfectly—from the way your eyes flash with emotion to the perfect shape of you."

"What are you talkin' about?" Dusty asked. She felt frightened. This woman was there to destroy her happiness, and she knew it. So why didn't she just get on with it?

"Ryder," the woman answered. "It's why he came back here. He couldn't keep away. I knew he'd end up back here one day . . . for you."

"I'm sorry for my lack of . . . of . . . for being rude, Miss Montgomery," Dusty told her, anger and fear apparent in her voice. "I know your comin' here upset Ryder . . . and I can't really believe that you bring good news with ya. Just say what you came to say to me, and let's get it over with."

Rose dropped her gaze to the ground for a moment. Looking up to Dusty with pure defiance, she demanded, "You can't have him! He can't

433

stay here. If he stays here with you, he'll die!"

Dusty hadn't expected threats. A jealous woman maybe—a woman grieving of a broken heart even. But not threats against Ryder's life!

"Who do you think you are comin' in here and threatenin' my sister like that?" Becca growled as she once again came out of the house and onto the porch.

"I'm not threatening," Rose stated calmly. "It's the truth. There are men . . . dangerous men looking for Ryder. They mean to kill him. And they are close to finding out that he's here. I only came to warn him." She stepped toward Dusty, and Dusty could see the pleading in her eyes. "They will find him here. They've found him before and . . ."

A vision flashed before Dusty's eyes—the painful vision of Ryder's scarred back—the story he had told her of the way he'd sustained them. The torture he'd endured!

"Why are they lookin' for him? Who are you that you would know?" Dusty cried out, stepping forward and taking the woman's shoulders in her hands. "What did he do to cause them to come after him?"

Tears streamed over Rose's cheeks as she sobbed, "They blame him for Lillian's death. At least one of them does."

"Why?" Dusty forced her. "Why do they blame him? Was it his fault?" She shook the young woman slightly to try to bring her back to attention. "Tell me! You come ridin' up here and tell me that I can't have the only thing I've ever wanted in my entire life! I want to know why! Why are these men after him?"

Dusty felt Becca's arms at her own shoulders, and she drew in a calming breath. "No one will take him from me. Do you understand?" Dusty mumbled. Dusty Hunter was healed. She was back. And no one would take her happiness, her very soul away from her!

"There . . . there was an accident. About two and a half years ago. A stampede. Lilly was caught in the midst of it . . . and . . . and Ryder rode in to try to help her. B-but she was thrown from her horse. He reached down and took her hand . . . but she slipped and fell. She pulled him off his own horse. He was able to remount, but by the time he got to her, she'd . . . she'd been kicked in the head, and . . . and she . . . she woke up a week later. Her mind was gone. She just . . . she could eat and stare out into . . . into nothing. But she was gone. Her mind was gone." Dusty listened as Rose continued, "For two and a half years, our family tended to her like that. Then she died . . . this summer." Rose pulled a handkerchief from the sleeve of her dress and dabbed at her tears.

"That wasn't his fault. No one could possibly fault him for that," Dusty mumbled.

"I know. I know," Rose agreed. "But Wesley blamed him. He was so heartbroken. He accused Ryder of . . . of not trying hard enough to save her."

"Who's Wesley?" Becca asked.

"Wesley was Lilly's fiancé."

"Is Wesley the man huntin' Ryder?" Dusty asked bluntly.

Rose nodded. "He rides with two other men . . . men I don't know. I don't know where he met them or how. And he hired a criminal . . . an Indian man . . . a one-time warrior who had broken the laws of his tribe and been cast out. He's a butcher! He's hired him to kill Ryder!" Dusty closed her eyes for a moment, trying again to block the vision of the scars on Ryder's back from her mind. "He'll kill him! And they're close." Rose dropped her voice as if she expected them to hear somehow. "I know they're close. Wesley wrote to me from Santa Fe. I know they're closer than that by now."

"How do you know?" Dusty asked. "How could you possibly know where they are? And why does he write to you? Are you in it with him?"

"No! No! I would never hurt anyone—especially Ryder! I loved him as much as anybody! I don't want him hurt. But Wesley writes to me. I . . . I don't even know why! I do know that he's close. Wesley has Ryder's dog Dusty with him. Ryder had to leave her behind when he left our place. Wesley's usin' the dog to help him find Ryder."

Dusty felt as if she might faint of the sickened, anxious state of her mind and body. *I named me a dog Dusty once,* Ryder's voice echoed through her mind.

"His dog's name is Dusty?" Becca asked in a whisper.

Rose nodded. "The dog is very unusual. It looks like a wolf and has one blue eye and one brown eye. It's easy to identify, and when I was in Alamosa, the storekeeper there said she saw four men, one of them an Indian, and a dog like that. She heard one of the men call the dog Dusty." Rose reached out, taking Dusty's hand. "Ryder told me in town yesterday that he won't leave you, Miss Hunter." Rose's tears were streaming down her cheeks as she pleaded with Dusty. "I begged him! I told him they're on their way. But he's blinded by loving you! He told me he wouldn't leave you. He said he'd rather die facing the past than lose you now. But you have to let him go! You have to make him go!"

It's down to which one of us dies first, he'd said to her. As he'd lain next to her in bed last night, he'd said it. Tears streamed down Dusty's face, mirroring those Rose cried.

She shook her head and mumbled, "I won't let him go! And I won't let him be hurt!"

Rose attempted to calm herself slightly. "He

used to tell us about you. Tell us stories of things you did as a little girl. Tell us that he knew you'd grown up to be beautiful. He told us this was the best place on earth to him . . . for so many reasons . . . but truly because of you. But you can't let him be butchered like a penned-up pig! He'll be hurt . . . he'll be killed if you don't let him go!" Rose cried.

"They'll have to kill me to get to him and—" Dusty began.

"They will!" Rose cried. "Wesley doesn't care who gets in his way! Nobody . . . nobody matters to him anymore!" Rose squeezed Dusty's hand pleadingly. "He has to leave here! They will come for him!"

"You leave!" Becca shouted. "You leave now! You've warned us. Now get out!"

"Listen to me!" Rose pleaded. "Just—"

"You heard my sister," Dusty growled. "Leave now."

Rose Montgomery's beautiful, sad, emerald eyes implored Dusty still. But she was met with only cold denial. And she left.

"Dusty . . . Ryder will tell you the truth. Don't despair until he gets in from the pastures. He—" Becca told her.

"I won't wait for him to come in from the pastures!" Throwing her apron to the ground, she set out toward the barn. "Becca . . . where's Daddy?" she asked.

"Over at Miss Raynetta's."

"Go bring him home please."

Becca nodded and threw her own apron to the ground.

෴

Becca arrived at Miss Raynetta's to find their father and Miss Raynetta were off picnicking somewhere. She returned home to discover Dusty had been unable to find Ryder or the other hands. So after hours of searching and waiting, all there was left to do was to wait. And wait. And wait.

Becca was near to wringing her hands raw as she sat on the porch with Dusty—waiting. Her sister's nerves only served to further strain her own, so Dusty suggested Becca finish the pies they'd started that morning—the pies they'd started before Rose had appeared like the angel of death to ruin Dusty's dreams. Dusty knew Rose felt for her—that somehow Rose understood and ached for Dusty and her love of Ryder. Had it been Rose who had loved Ryder? Did she still love him? She'd admitted as much—said that she loved him. But was there more? Was she *in* love with Ryder?

Back and forth, back and forth—the porch swing rocked for an hour as Dusty struggled to hang onto a shred of sanity as she waited and waited. She heard a horse approaching then. Standing up, she shaded her eyes from the sun and looked toward the rider in the distance. It was Feller. Her heart sank, and yet there was hope. He might know where Ryder was.

Dusty had spent hours in contemplation. Her decision was made. Though she was disgusted to admit it, Rose Montgomery was right. She couldn't keep Ryder in danger. He had to leave. And she couldn't go with him. She'd be a hindrance—slow him down, distract him, and trip him up. She may already have! So as she approached Feller, as he unsaddled his mount, her determination changed. Her happiness and her dreams had been dashed to death. But she was whole now—the Dusty she had been born to be, the Dusty who had been lost for some time. And not everyone had to live in eternal misery. Not everyone—certainly not her family. Dusty's pain was so excruciating, yet her tears had ceased. There was no question. She would have to give Ryder up to save him. And she would save him—and there were others to save along the way.

Feller came out of the barn and tossed his saddle onto the fence, as was his habit when he meant to clean it. He didn't seem to see Dusty at first, but when he glanced over and saw the look of despair, of utter surrender to despair, on her face, he stopped. Dusty walked over to him—stood before him in silence for a moment.

"Dusty? You all right?" he asked.

"Stop it, Feller," she stated. "Just stop it."

Dusty watched as Feller's brow wrinkled with a

deep, perplexed frown. "Stop what? I ain't doin' nothin' but cleanin' my saddle."

"Exactly," Dusty confirmed. "You ain't doin' nothin'."

"Now, hang on there, girl," Feller began defensively.

"You haven't said anything to her, have ya?"

"What are you goin' on about, Dusty? I—"

"Have you, Feller? You haven't said anything to Becca. Not one thing. You haven't given her any kind of hope that ya care for her . . . haven't—"

"I ain't goin' down this road with you again, Dusty," Feller growled. "It's plain as day some-thin's stuck in your craw, but don't you go tellin' me—"

"Don't do it, Feller," Dusty interrupted. "Don't fritter away one single moment longer you could be with her. Don't take the chance somethin' will come along and take her from you . . . or you from her . . . leavin' ya with nothin' but a life of loneliness and regret."

"What's the matter, Dusty?" he began. It was obvious he now sensed the seriousness of her mood. "Come on now. You gotta tell me."

"She's in the kitchen right now. I think she's upset about some things. She needs you. She's miserable without you." Dusty swallowed hard and looked away for a moment. Then, looking back to him, she continued, "You've known, haven't ya? All these years you've known it was because of Ryder that I . . . became what I did. All this time you knew, didn't ya, Feller?" He didn't say anything, and his silence was all the confession she needed. "Well, then I suspect ya know how completely you're breaking Becca's heart by bein' such a coward and not—"

"That's enough, girl!" Feller nearly shouted. "Don't you be talkin' back to me like that! I—"

"You should be my brother-in-law by now! Don't you talk to me like I'm still ten years old! And crawl outta your hidey-hole, and quit tellin' yourself Becca's still ten—because she's not! You're breaking her heart! If you fiddle around any longer, somebody's gonna show up on the front porch one day and tear your world apart!" He seemed stunned by Dusty's outburst.

Suddenly panic set in; Dusty experienced pure panic. This man had to confess his feelings to her sister. He had to! "Please, Feller," she begged him then, not in anger but in deepest sincerity. "Please. Go in the house . . . right now. Don't waste another minute. Please."

His expression turned from anger to something like having been beaten. "Dusty . . . I'm thirty years old. I—"

"You're only five years older than Ryder, and you don't think he's too old to do it. Do ya? You don't think my own daddy's too old!" He was silent. "I know you, Feller. You've been tellin' my daddy to reach out and take Miss Raynetta, and you've been tellin' Ryder ever since he got here that he shouldn't waste his time in waitin' for me to come around. I know you. Well, practice what you preach for once, Reverend Feller Lance!"

Feller let his head droop for a moment. When he looked back to Dusty, he whispered, "She's so . . . so perfect! But, Dusty . . . I used to take her swimmin' in her bloomers, for pity's sake! I taught her how to ride a horse. I showed her how to play marbles!"

"And now you're gonna show her how wonderful it is to have the man you've loved for so many years finally belong to you." Dusty paused. She could see the fear in him. She could see his struggle with his feelings. "She's no little girl anymore, Feller. And you're not just some new cowboy with a fancy for the boss's daughter." Dusty looked away. "I'm . . . I'm goin' for a walk." She looked back at him. "And when I get back, I don't want to find Becca in the kitchen cryin' over you again." She turned around and walked away from him.

Whatever it was, it was bad. Feller knew that for sure. Dusty looked like she'd met death face-to-face and lost. His mind's first inclination was to go after her, take hold of her arm, and force her to tell him what had happened. Yet his heart caused him to look toward the house. Whatever had happened to upset Dusty had no doubt upset

Becca as well. And after all, Dusty was right. How many people had he watched waste their lives away because of pride or fear? Inhaling deeply and summoning all the courage in him, Feller ran to the house. He didn't even knock—just leapt onto the porch in one clean move, burst through the back door and into the kitchen.

"Becca?" he hollered. He didn't see her at first. Then he heard a whimper. He looked down to see her sitting on the floor, leaning against the wall— tears streaming down her face as she dabbed at them furiously with her apron. "What is it, honey?" he asked, going to her immediately, pulling her to her feet and gathering her into his arms.

"It's fallin' apart, Feller," Becca sobbed, wrapping her arms tightly around him. "Everything I dreamed for her! It's gonna die and . . ."

"No," Feller mumbled into the softness of her hair. He inhaled deeply, filling his lungs with the purely feminine scent of it.

"He has to leave," Becca cried, looking up into his face.

"He won't leave her," Feller told her.

"He has to! He's in trouble! If he doesn't leave . . . a woman came to the ranch and told us . . . and Dusty'll let him go. She doesn't have a choice!"

Feller took Becca's sweet, beautiful face between his rough, strong hands. He brushed the tears from her cheeks with his thumbs. "It's not her choice to make, Becca. And Ryder won't leave. I know it," he assured her lovingly.

He watched as the fear apparent on her face deepened. "You'll never leave, will you, Feller?"

"I may leave your daddy's ranch someday," he whispered, "but not without you." There, he'd said it. He'd set his foot firmly on the path, and he'd follow it now—wherever it led. "If ever I leave here . . . I'll be takin' you with me."

He watched as Becca struggled to believe she'd heard him say what he had. Her tears slowed, and her pain-filled eyes searched his for confirmation somehow. "Wh-what do you mean?" she managed.

"I mean exactly what you're standin' here hopin' I mean." Feller smiled down into her beautiful face.

"Wh-what do you think I'm hopin' you mean?" She was so adorable. He couldn't help but chuckle.

"I think you're hopin' that I'm gettin' ready to say somethin' to you I shoulda said long before now." He could see the excitement light up her eyes like the fireworks all those weeks ago had lit up the night skies out at old man Leroy's.

"All right," she whispered. "What is it I'm hopin' you'll say to me?"

"I love you," Feller said without pause. He watched as her tears began again—in profusion. "I'm sorry it took me so long to tell ya."

Becca collapsed against him, her head resting on the power, strength, and security of his chest as she cried. He returned her tight embrace for a moment before taking her face in his hands again.

"Really?" she asked him. "Do you really?"

He chuckled as he let his thumb brush her tender lips. "Yes."

"As much as I love you?" she asked. A moment of fear passed over her expression.

"More," he confirmed.

"You couldn't possibly," she told him, smiling through her tears.

"Do ya trust me?" he asked her then.

Her brow puckered in a puzzled scowl. "I've never trusted anyone like I've trusted you," she told him.

"Then trust me now. Ryder won't leave Dusty. I promise you. He won't leave her again. And he won't die either."

Becca nodded, trying to believe him. "Okay," she whimpered.

"And now that you know he won't, that it'll be all right . . . somehow . . . let me just warn ya that I ain't too awful good at courtin' and all. I've gotten kinda rusty in waitin' around for you to grow up."

"Don't lie," she said, smiling. "I remember the girls in town. I know how they still—"

"There's girls in town?" he teased. "I hadn't

446

noticed for 'bout . . . oh, least two years now."

"Really?" Becca sighed delightedly.

Feller chuckled. He adored the way she melted against him, the way her eyes twinkled as he teased her. She was an angel, his Becca—a beautiful, wonderful, fully grown-up angel he held in his arms. "Yes, really."

"I love you. You'll never know how much or how long I've been lovin' you," she whispered.

"How long?" he mumbled as he looked at her lips again. He couldn't keep his eyes off her tiny, soft, pink mouth.

"As long as I can remember. And I can prove it."

"Can ya now?" he chuckled, his head descending toward hers.

"Yes," she breathed as his lips touched hers for the first time.

Feller Lance realized how important restraint was. He wanted to fairly attack his Becca with a demanding passion—a passion he'd spent so long secreting. Still, he taught her how to kiss him—taught her very carefully, very tenderly. This wasn't marbles, after all. Yet when she let her arms go around his neck, pressing her body firmly against his, he could resist her no longer and gave into his love for her—his desire to hold her and own her. She tasted like heaven! Felt like heaven! Becca Hunter was heaven! And he knew by her kiss, by the sigh of blissful relief escaping her, Dusty had been right: all along Becca had belonged to him.

ꙮ

Shortly after their confessions of love to one another, Becca told Feller of Rose Montgomery's visit to the ranch—of the devastating news she bore. If Ryder's life were in danger, Feller would not let his Becca find cause to grieve over her sister's world falling apart. It wouldn't. He wouldn't let it happen to Dusty. He wouldn't let it happen to Ryder. And he certainly wouldn't let it happen to Becca!

Feller hated to leave Becca—for more reasons than he had time to list off in his head. Yet he'd set out immediately to fetch Hank home. He'd ride to Miss Raynetta's and somehow find Hank—tell him what was happening. But first, he pulled his horse to a halt beneath the big old willow growing on the creek bed—the one he'd watched Becca and Dusty play tea party under in their bloomers so many times so long ago. Dismounting, he looked around on the ground until he did indeed spy a rock looking like a "pile of dried-up cow manure," as Becca had described it. He chuckled at the fact two little girls so many years ago should dub the stone "the cow pie rock."

Hunkering down, he dug the dirt out from around its base until he was able to pry one edge up. Lifting the rock, he brushed dirt and potato bugs from the top of a rusty and ancient-looking old candy tin and pulled it from its hiding place. Quickly he removed the lid and looked inside.

The contents he found were exactly as Becca had described—an old bootstrap she'd torn from his boot when she was ten. He remembered then waking up one morning a long time ago to find the strap on the inside of his right boot was missing. He reached in and withdrew a rusty old straight razor and chuckled. Hadn't it been the same morning, as he was bellyaching around about his missing bootstrap, that a young Ryder Maddox had misplaced his razor?

Then, reaching in the tin again, he pulled out two small strips of paper. Both were curled up tightly and tied with pink ribbon. He carefully unrolled the first.

"When I grow up," he read aloud, *"I'm going to make Feller Lance fall in love with me. He'll marry me and we'll have 5 children and be happy forever. Signed this day that I turned 10, Rebecca Hunter."*

He squeezed his eyes tightly shut and tried to keep the moisture there from escaping as his heart ached with joy—beat with severe melancholy for a moment. Although it poured more joy into his body than he thought he could consciously endure, there was a twinge of heartache for the little girl who had to wait so long to grow up. Carefully, he unrolled the other small paper.

"All I want in my whole life," he read, though his voice still broke from the emotion the first revelation had caused, *"is Ryder Maddox. Someday he'll love me and we'll get married and have the sweetest babies and most beautiful life that anyone could ever dream of. Signed this day that Becca turned 10 and I am still 12, Angelina Hunter."*

Wiping at a tear on his cheek with the back of his glove, Feller awkwardly retied the ribbons and returned the tin and its contents to their secret hiding place. There was another man who would want to be sent to find it. Another man, in trouble now—a man Feller Lance was determined would live to find the buried treasure of the Hunter girls!

With pure tenacity to make happy the family and heart of the woman he loved, Feller rode off to find Hank Hunter—to tell him—to tell him of the devastating threat to his family.

Chapter Fifteen

The cascading water of the falls helped cool the hot sting of her tears. Dusty plunged her head forward into it again. *How can I go on without him?* she thought. Over and over she thought it. How could she wake up each morning knowing he wouldn't be in her day? How could she go to sleep at night not being held in his arms? How would she make herself do what she had to do to survive, knowing he was gone?

"I can't bear this," she sobbed.

How could she truly enjoy watching other children grow up—especially those of Feller and Becca? Even of her father and Raynetta? How could she love life without the one thing making life worth loving? She'd tried it before—and failed. What would she do? She'd thought of everything. *I'll go with him,* she thought again. They'd be together then! Until she slowed him down somehow, she reminded herself—caused his guard to unwind—thereby leading him into tragedy. She'd kill the other men first! Certainly they wouldn't expect a young woman to be an assassin out for vengeance. Yet that wasn't realistic either. First of all, she knew they'd kill her long before she had a chance to even react— and finding her body bloody and skinned somewhere out in the pastures would do nothing to improve Ryder's life.

It had been nearly an hour since she'd left the house, and still her mind fought to accept losing him. It was impossible!

"Fancy findin' you here."

Ryder's voice startled her. She wiped the water from her face and eyes quickly. When she turned to find him stepping through the waterfall, wearing only his pants, she felt as if someone had plunged a knife into the center of her heart. He was so wonderful—so perfect for her soul! His smile was so handsome—so unknowing. Still, it didn't take him long to realize she'd been crying.

"What's the matter?" he asked, a frown owning his brow.

There was no lying to him. He wouldn't believe her if she said nothing. She may as well face him now as later.

"I planned to tell you somethin' today," she told him quietly.

"Yeah?" he prodded. Obviously, he hadn't been back to the house or seen anyone else before coming to the waterfall. He was purely innocent to Dusty's recently acquired knowledge.

"Last night," she began. Unable to look at him, she stared at his feet instead. "After you left . . . I found me." He was quiet, probably not wanting to interrupt—knowing how much she needed to say it. "I found the me I started losin' when you left years ago." She looked up at him. She fancied her heart began to tear in two—for the pain in it was unbearable. The look of residual guilt on his face did not deter her. "The me I wanted to give . . . to you," she confessed. "I found her last night."

"So give her to me," he mumbled in the low, provocative tone that melted her bones. Though she knew he was flirting, the expression on his face revealed he was waiting for the slap she was about to deliver—for the stinging pain accompanying it.

"I did . . . forever ago . . . and since you've come back," she whispered. "She's always been yours. But . . . but you can't have her, can you?"

"What are ya talkin' about, Dusty?" he growled.

"It's why you haven't given yourself to me completely. Isn't it?"

"What?" he questioned. Yet by the look on his face, she knew he knew what.

"Rose Montgomery came to the ranch house today," she stated flatly.

He swallowed hard and shook his head. "I'm not leavin' you again, Dusty . . . if that's what you're worried about. No matter what you would've answered me last night in bed . . . I'm not leavin' you." Her skin erupted into a field of goose bumps at the memory of his lying next to her in her bed.

"Did ya love that girl, Ryder? Even though she was engaged? Did ya love her?" Dusty couldn't help but ask. She had to know the depth of what had brought Ryder to a life of running. "Or—or did ya love Rose?"

"No. Neither one. Not one bit," he answered flatly. "In fact, I couldn't stand Lilly. That makes the guilt I feel all the worse." He was furious then—furious. In a rage! "I told Rose to let it lie! I told her that I wouldn't leave. Yes, Dusty! I met with a woman in town yesterday!" he shouted. "I know ya heard about it from one source or another. Yes, it was Rose. She came here to tell me

Wesley and his hounds are closin' in on me again. Yes . . . again! But I ain't runnin' no more. I'm finally back where I want to be after all these years. It's worth too much to lose!"

"But ya have to go!" Dusty cried. "There's no other choice! I won't have them find you!"

Ryder leaned back against the rock wall—sank to a sitting position. "When I left here five years ago, I cowboyed around for two and a half long years . . . waitin' . . . bidin' my time. Do ya know why?" Dusty shook her head and wiped the tears from her cheeks. "I was waitin' . . . just skimmin' through life until you were older." She could only stare at him in expectant disbelief.

"Do you think I left here feelin' like I did with no plans of ever comin' back and seein' what would happen between us when you'd grown up some? You can't really think that little of me." He shook his head and continued, "I did a winter in Montana, then Wyomin'. When you woulda been turnin' about sixteen, I started home . . . back here. But there was a bad storm 'tween here and there, and I stopped over down in Texas. Had me a bad case in my lungs, and it was warmer there. I figured I'd just winter it out. Stopped over and hired on to a man named Montgomery. So . . . I was impatient . . . but I wintered it out, figurin' you'd be almost seventeen by the time I got here and still young enough that maybe no slimy banker's son had snatched ya up yet." He

454

looked up at her for a moment. She looked away.

"So, come spring, Mr. Montgomery brings in some new cattle. We get through the calving . . . and I make ready to leave. I'm packin' my saddlebags. Dusty, my dog, is as happy as any hound ever was at my side . . . and I hear it start. I could hear the ruckus and the girls screamin'. I run out to see Lilly caught in the path of the herd hellbent on tramplin' anythin' in their way. I jumped on my horse, bareback . . . only a bit on . . . and rode out there." He swallowed hard and looked down at his hand as he made a fist. "I had her . . . right there. I had her, and she slipped. I don't know how she slipped, but she pulled me off my horse too, bein' that it wasn't saddled proper . . . and by the time I scooped her up again, some mad steer had kicked her in the head. Though she woke up after a week, it was obvious she never would be in her right mind again, and Wesley . . . well, he was needin' somethin' to throw his anger at . . . so he blamed me.

"Wesley and me had a go-'round. But I was tryin' to understand what he was goin' through. When he threatened to track me down and kill me . . . course I thought it was just pain eatin' at him. But I figured I'd play it safe awhile and not drag you and your family into the mess. So I cowboyed around for a few months until I felt it was behind me. Went down to Arizona. And just as I was feelin' I could start out for here again,

Wesley and his boys showed up. They did me in pretty good that time. I was beat near to death before they tried to . . ." He paused and shrugged his scarred shoulder. " 'Cause, ya see . . . they don't come at me head on. They sneak up in the night or like when I'm not payin' as much attention. If it hadn't been for the townfolks a-knowin' and lovin' me . . . that meetin' in Arizona probably would've been the end of me. I realized I couldn't come back here."

He looked up at her. "But when I seen your daddy with that herd goin' through Tucumcari . . ." He stood up, went to her, and took her by the shoulders. "I won't leave, Dusty. I'm tired of runnin' from somethin' that wasn't my fault. Heaven knows I'm lucky Cash Richardson is a big enough idiot to show his true colors, or I mighta come back to find I was too late after all."

"Don't touch me," Dusty breathed, stepping back and out of his grasp. "Don't touch me again. Get on your horse and leave before they find you here."

"I know what you're tryin' to do, and it won't work," he growled.

"You can't stay, I can't go with you, and—" she sobbed.

"I'm stayin'. I will not leave you. Do you understand that?" he growled.

"But . . ."

He walked forward and took her face firmly

between his powerful hands. "Give her to me, Dusty!" he demanded. The moisture in his eyes was profuse—threatened to spill over as he spoke. "Give me that girl you found . . . that girl or the other one that was here when I came back. I don't care which. But I want you now. I'm tired of waitin', and I've wasted enough time. I won't leave you. I love you. Girl, I've loved you since you were a brat of a thing with dirt all over the sweet little fanny of your britches. And I love you more every minute that goes by. You're in my dreams . . . day and night. In my mind . . . in my soul . . . in my blood!"

She could not resist him—would not lose him! Dusty fell into his embrace, wrapping her arms tightly around him. She'd never let him go! No matter what was to come, she would keep him. She had to! She inhaled deeply the scents that were about him. She let her lips rest on his neck for a moment, and then she drew back and took his handsome face in her own small hands.

Ryder nodded. "And you need to stay away from me like this." His eyes flashed with desire. "One of these days . . . once it's all legal on paper and in front of the preacher . . . I'm gonna take ya out to this waterfall, strip ya down, and—"

Dusty clamped her hand over his mouth. "Ryder," she began to scold. "There are things you still shouldn't say to me." She kissed him on the cheek and whispered, "Yet."

She dashed out from under the waterfall intent on finding help and protection for Ryder. She ran along the rocks looking back at him as he pursued her. She needed to get him back to the house where there were more people—where they'd be safe.

The strong arms wrapping around her body like steel bands caused her to gasp. Looking up, she screamed as she saw the frightening, intimidating war paint of a renegade warrior.

"Dusty!" Ryder shouted as two men appeared from behind the large willow. They took hold of him and immediately ceased his struggle when the renegade holding Dusty put a knife to her throat. "Don't hurt her," Ryder pleaded angrily through clenched teeth.

"Ah," another man's voice sighed, thick with sarcasm. Dusty glanced over to see another man, a young man perhaps Ryder's age, holding a sobbing Rose Montgomery by the back of the neck. He held to a short length of rope—a rope tied around the neck of a dog. The dog began barking and straining on the rope, trying to get to Ryder. The man was tall, blond, blue-eyed, and powerful-looking. His eyes lewdly traveled the length of Dusty as he said, "Is this the famous Dusty?"

"Don't you touch her, Wesley," Ryder growled.

The man named Wesley only chuckled. "What's that, Maddox? You don't want me to throw her in front of a stampeding herd of cattle?"

The dog finally succeeded in pulling the rope from Wesley's grasp and ran to Ryder, barking and excitedly panting at his feet. The wolf-like animal with different colored eyes growled menacingly when one of the men holding Ryder kicked at her.

"Sit, Dusty," Ryder commanded. The dog immediately sat on its haunches, panting with delighted expectance.

"Amazing, Maddox," Wesley chuckled. "How do you keep such a hold on dogs, women, and children?" Again Wesley made a full and quite intimate visual appraisal of Dusty. "Of course . . . I guess that little girl you were always pining away after grew up in the end, didn't she?"

"Let her go, Wesley," Ryder ordered. "You don't have anything to blame on her!"

Wesley's triumphant smile disappeared. "An eye for an eye perhaps?"

Ryder began to struggle violently, shouting, "No!"

Dusty shrieked as Wesley snapped his fingers and the two men holding Ryder began dragging him toward one of the smaller trees nearby.

"You see, my dear," Wesley whispered, bending toward Dusty's ear, "he could get away easily enough . . . but he knows I've got you!"

"It wasn't his fault, you filthy coward!" Dusty shouted at him.

She was met with the stinging force of the back of his hand. It was too much for Ryder. Breaking free from his captors, he lunged toward Wesley.

"Stop," Wesley reminded Ryder, pointing to the knife at Dusty's throat. Ryder stopped his aggression. When the two men began pulling him back toward the trees, he simply glared at the villain.

"You don't understand it all, Wes!" Rose pleaded suddenly, struggling in the madman's grasp. "There's more to it than you know!"

"Shut up, Rose!" Wesley shouted. "Bind him up for it, boys!" Wesley threw Rose to the ground, growling at her, "Stay." Then he took hold of Dusty. "Carve him up," he told the renegade. "Slowly."

Dusty screamed, sobbing hysterically—clawing at Wesley. Yet again the knife was at her throat, and she froze as she watched the men loop one end of a rope around Ryder's wrist and tie the other to a large branch of the tree. She could already see what they meant to do. They had him between two trees, a rope looped at each ankle and wrist. They would draw him up between the trees to torture him! The knife at her throat didn't matter anymore, and she struggled to get away from Wesley's grip. She almost succeeded in freeing herself, but he took hold of the back of her blouse and slammed her to the ground.

"Wait! This girl just gave me an idea!" Wesley laughed.

Dusty gasped as she felt him tear the back of her blouse open—cut the strings to her corset. He tore at the fabric of her camisole, and she felt the cool breeze of the willow's shade on her flesh.

"Should I, Maddox?" Wesley growled. "Should I make you watch your precious boss's daughter . . . watch her bleed as Crazy Bear skins her before he does you?"

"You put a mark on her, and I will kill you!" Ryder threatened. His eyes were blazing with anger and fear.

Wesley laughed. "Really? Kill me? While you're being skinned yourself?"

Ryder began to struggle with the one arm stretched out toward the tree by a rope. But the cold blade of the knife held against Dusty's back stopped him, and he stood still—frantically looking about for an answer to save her.

"Stop it, Wes!" Rose cried out again. "You don't know it all! You don't! You wouldn't be doin' this if—"

"If what, Rose?" the man shouted. "You've said that to me before, and yet you never have anything to say, now do you?"

"It was all Lilly's fault!" Rose screamed. "Sh-she started the stampede that day, Wesley!"

"What?" he asked.

Dusty felt the pressure of the knife on her flesh lessen. She looked up to see Ryder, although frowning, nod at her encouragingly as he began to test the strength of the rope keeping him too far away to help her.

"Lilly started the cattle running, Wes! On purpose . . . so that Ryder would have to come to her rescue!" Rose sobbed into her hands for a moment.

"That's absurd, Rose! Why would she do that?" Wesley asked.

Dusty knew he didn't completely disbelieve Rose—else he wouldn't have paused to listen. Ryder twisted his hand around the rope holding his wrist and began to pull. The other men were distracted by Rose's story and didn't notice Ryder's efforts. Dusty could only watch him—hope for his strength to be even greater than she knew it to be.

"She was in love with Ryder," Rose suddenly sobbed. Dusty looked to Ryder, who, startled by what the girl had said, momentarily ceased in his efforts of escape.

"What?" Ryder himself asked.

"Lilly was certain she loved Ryder, Wesley. She was afraid to tell you. She wasn't going to tell you until she was sure Ryder cared for her! I-I knew that he didn't . . . b-but . . . I loved you so much, Wes! I thought that if she left you for Ryder . . . maybe—"

"Why would she cause the stampede?" Wesley shouted, leaping to his feet. "Why?" Dusty immediately rolled over onto her back and sat up.

"She wanted Ryder's attention! She had tried

for so long . . . gotten so tired of the stories about the little girl he'd known so long ago. She told me to stand on the fence and wait, and when the cattle were coming, she would ride out in front of them. Then I was to call for Ryder. He was in the barn, and she knew it. But she didn't know his horse wasn't saddled yet. We thought his horse was saddled. She paid Ben Dorian to spook the cattle and—"

"You're lying, Rose," Wesley growled. "You're lying to save his skin!"

At once, Wesley was on Dusty again. He pushed her down into the grass and straddled her waist with his legs sitting heavily on her abdomen. He tugged at the front of her blouse. Since it was cut away at the back, her neck and shoulders were now exposed.

"Does she taste good, Maddox?" Wesley asked, stroking Dusty's cheeks with his knife.

"I'll kill you if you touch her! I'll kill you!" Ryder shouted. He was enraged and began pulling harder on the rope holding him. His hand was turning purple from the lack of blood flow caused as the rope tightened on his wrist.

"Oh, I will touch her . . . and then I'll kill you!" Wesley shouted. "Stop fighting it, Maddox."

"Wesley!" Rose pleaded. "Listen to what I'm saying! It was Lillian's fault! Mine and hers! I loved you, Wesley! I was as blind crazy in love with you as she was with Ryder. I thought that if

Ryder could get Lilly to leave you then . . . then . . ."

Dusty saw an expression of realization, of guilt, of regret in Wesley's eyes for a moment—but only for a moment. Then it was gone, and his knife was at her throat again. Ryder stopped his struggles and tried to control his breathing.

"Cut him, Crazy Bear," Wesley ordered as his fingers caressed Dusty's shoulders for a moment.

"Wes, don't do this thing!" Rose pleaded, sobbing hysterically.

Sobbing, Dusty looked at Ryder. She watched the long-haired, face-painted butcher cut Ryder deeply on his arm just above his armpit. Ryder winced, and blood ran profusely from the wound.

"You can carve me up all you want, Wesley . . . but leave Dusty out of it. She didn't do anything to you," Ryder growled.

"I'll carve you and her, Maddox. No matter what," the man assured him.

"That's what I figured!" Ryder whistled sharply. "Dusty!" he shouted. Immediately, the dog leapt to its feet—burying its teeth into Wesley's arm. Dusty squirmed from beneath Wesley's body as he shouted and fought with the dog. The man called Crazy Bear lunged at Ryder, but Ryder ducked, kicking the man squarely in the midsection and sending him crumpling to the ground.

"Help me, you idiots!" Wesley shouted. The two men restraining Ryder ran to Wesley's assistance, kicking at the dog and trying to get hold of the rope hanging from its neck.

"Run, Angelina!" Ryder shouted. With both hands, he pulled on the rope binding him to the tree.

Dusty was momentarily awed as his muscles strained, blood flowing from his new wound. The sound of splitting bark crackled a moment before the large tree limb gave way to the strength of the man, and he was free. Crazy Bear had recovered and was wielding his knife as Ryder picked up the tree limb and swung it at him.

Another man kicked the dog hard enough that its grip on Wesley was broken. The animal fell to the ground dazed and wounded. Ryder still wrestled with Crazy Bear, the rope on his wrist still tied to the tree limb. Dusty and Rose simultaneously screamed as they saw the large silver blade of the Indian's knife plunge toward Ryder's chest. Quickly, Ryder lifted the tree limb, and Crazy Bear's blade was buried in it instead of Ryder's body. Twisting the limb, Ryder caused the renegade to lose his grip on the weapon. Dropping the limb to the ground and in one smooth motion pulling the knife from the wood, Ryder cut the rope binding him. Turning, he ducked as Crazy Bear lunged at him.

Suddenly, Wesley took hold of Dusty's arm. He paused and winced because of his own injuries. Weakened from the attack of the dog, Wesley stumbled, and Dusty broke away. Again, Dusty screamed as Crazy Bear lunged at Ryder. This time the two men struggled to the ground, wrestling—brutally locked in mortal battle.

"Cowards!" she heard Wesley shout as the other two men ran off. "Get back here, and do the job I paid you for!" One of the men paused, shook his head, and then continued to retreat.

Dusty looked to Ryder—watched the struggle —held her breath as the body of Crazy Bear went limp. Ryder rolled the dying man over and pulled the knife from his chest. He turned his furious glare on Wesley.

"It's not my fault," Ryder growled as his chest rose and fell with labored breathing. "None of it . . . none of this!"

"Ryder," Dusty sobbed. He held his hand up, signaling it would be dangerous for them both for her to distract him now.

"Let it go, boy," Ryder urged. "Walk away. Alive."

"No," Wesley growled as he strode to meet Ryder.

It was then the true coward in him reared its ugly head. He must've realized he was in no physical condition, because of the dog bite or otherwise, to face one such as Ryder Maddox. Instead, he turned toward Dusty, raised his knife, and lunged at her.

"No!" Dusty heard Ryder shout. She turned to

see Wesley with the knife high above his head, plunging it toward her. It was a nightmare! Time seemed to slow as Ryder miraculously reached her first. Catching Wesley's arm as he plunged the knife toward Dusty, Ryder twisted his hand—burying the blade deep into Wesley's stomach. Wesley's breath stopped; his face contorted in pain. He dropped to his knees, looking in horrified realization at his own blood on his hands. Closing his eyes, he moaned and slumped at Dusty's feet.

"No!" Rose sobbed as she rushed to him. She turned him over, crying and stroking his pain-stricken face.

"Rose?" he whispered. His eyes closed—his last breath exhaled.

Dusty looked from the dead man on the ground and the woman sobbing over him to the pale, regretful face of Ryder before her. The dog began to bark as it struggled to its feet. Though Dusty looked in the direction of the dog's barking to see her father, Feller, Becca, the sheriff, and others approaching on horseback—though she heard their questioning and angry shouts—she cared for nothing but the fact Ryder was safe—that he was free—that she was free!

Dusty and Ryder stood for several moments looking at each other—so much said with their eyes. Yet Dusty was all too aware of the blood streaming down Ryder's arm. Tears unashamedly escaping her eyes—for the thought of him in pain caused pain in her own soul—she reached down, lifted her skirt, and proceeded to tear a strip of cloth from her petticoat. Working quickly, she bound his wound. Even as his hand caressed the tears from her cheeks, she labored to ensure not one more drop of his precious blood would be lost.

"Dusty," he breathed.

Gathering her into his arms, he led her away from the dead men on the ground, and they collapsed to their knees in a desperate embrace.

"Dusty!" her father called. "Are you all right?" But she did not answer him. She was locked in Ryder's arms. His mouth was sweeping her neck and shoulders with relieved, loving kisses.

"Ryder," she whispered, drawing his kiss to her mouth. Though their passion was unrestrained, their bodies were weak. Ryder gently pushed her down in the grass—continuing to ravish her with caresses and kisses.

"What went on here?" the sheriff asked.

"I can explain," Rose said. She released the dead man's face, brushing the tears from her cheeks. She stood and walked toward him.

"Ryder!" Hank demanded. Still Ryder and Dusty continued to ignore anyone's presence but their own. "Ryder!" Hank reached down and pulled hard at the waist of Ryder's pants, tugging at him to get off of his daughter and tell him what had happened.

With a heavy sigh, Ryder released Dusty and struggled to his feet. He pulled Dusty to her feet as well, and Hank grimaced at the amount of blood covering them both.

"Boy, you do beat all," Hank mumbled as he studied the wound on Ryder's arm. "And the way you're eatin' up Dusty here . . . you got anythin' to talk to me about?" Hank frowned and then smiled at the young man. Ryder shook his head and smiled, still out of breath from the fight—or the passion. Hank didn't seem sure which. "All this aside, that is," he added, looking around at the dead men and blood.

"Well, sir," Ryder said, "I have to marry your daughter."

Hank quirked an eyebrow. "You have to marry my daughter?"

Ryder smiled and shook his head. "You know what I mean. I want to marry her. I don't have to marry her . . . yet."

Dusty gasped, and Hank burst into laughter at the look of astonishment on his daughter's face. "You have at it, boy! It's been too long a-comin'! A long, long time!" As Hank turned and looked to his own adorable wife-to-be, perched up on her bay mare and dressed in vermillion, his attention was drawn to Feller, helping Becca down from her horse. "Feller!" he called.

"Yes, boss," Feller nodded.

"You got somethin' to say here?"

Feller cleared his throat nervously. "I don't have to marry your daughter yet either. But . . ."

Hank laughed. He looked back to where Ruff and Titch were helping Guthrie and the sheriff tie up the two men they'd caught running off as they approached.

"Good thing I only got two daughters, Raynetta! My hands are droppin' like flies!" He pulled Raynetta from her saddle and gathered her in his arms, quenching his own thirst for the kiss of the woman he loved.

"Boss . . . your family is somethin' else," Guthrie sighed, pausing as he looked at the scene around him—dead men, blood, and people of all ages—in love.

Epilogue

"You be careful gettin' that turkey out of the oven, honey!" Raynetta Hunter mothered her daughter Becca.

"Oh, Mama! You worry too much," Becca said. She smiled as she carefully took the turkey from the oven to baste it.

Angelina Maddox stood in the doorway of the parlor watching Becca and her mother work on the turkey. Angelina had brought the pies, rolls, and potatoes for Thanksgiving dinner. She was glad her dinner preparations were finished, for now she could stand back and watch the two women she loved most in the world bustling around in the kitchen—listen to the low, masculine voices of the men she loved most as they sat talking in the parlor.

"What you boys thinkin' you'll have to pay to start your herd come spring?" she heard her father ask.

"Too much!" Ryder chuckled.

"Dang right," Feller agreed. "I ain't leavin' though. 'Til Becca's had the baby, I ain't goin' for cattle."

"Me neither. I worry about Raynetta. She's so small," Hank mumbled. "All of a sudden I'm rememberin' how downright scary havin' babies is. Raynetta's hopin' for a boy. But I hope she's carryin' another girl. I like 'em."

Dusty turned and smiled at her father. He winked at her. Ryder saw her attention was not on the kitchen at that moment. He rose from his chair and sauntered seductively to where she stood in the doorway dividing the two rooms. Putting his hands caressively at her waist, he gazed down upon her with a mischievous grin—silently telling her only the present company was keeping him from ravishing her.

"Well, I guess I can hire on enough hands to drive home Feller's cattle and mine come spring.

Ol' Leroy's ranch cost a bit . . . but it can be done," Ryder told the men, though his eyes saw only his wife.

"Sorry 'bout that, Ryder . . . but I can't leave Becca," Feller apologized.

Ryder bent down and whispered in Dusty's ear, "I love you." He kissed her neck several times, causing her to flinch from the delicious tickle.

"Ryder can't go for the cattle," Dusty announced. "We'll all have to depend on Guthrie, Titch, or Ruff to go."

Ryder smiled and kissed her again. "Dusty gets cold at night," he explained with a wink to Feller.

The men chuckled, and their merriment caught the attention of Becca and Raynetta.

"What's goin' on in here?" Raynetta asked, drying her hands on her apron. Dusty noted how green Becca looked and wondered if she'd be able to even enjoy her Thanksgiving dinner. She wondered if either of them would be able to eat and keep it down. The way they'd both been lately, she doubted it. And even though her own stomach was upset, she smiled.

"Dusty don't want to let Ryder go for cattle come spring," Hank answered.

"Well, of course not!" Raynetta exclaimed. She squeezed Ryder's arm lovingly. "She's gonna have a new brother or sister and a niece or nephew to help look after. She'll be plum worn out if Ryder's gone!"

"It's really not so much that, Mama," Dusty corrected, hardly able to contain her smile. "I just want to make sure Ryder's here when his own baby's born." She squirmed with delight—blissful in her husband's arms. Ryder's smile faded; he even paled a little as he understood what Dusty was saying.

"My own baby?" he whispered. She nodded.

Hank whooped and hollered, and Feller chuckled as Becca and Raynetta linked hands and began skipping around the kitchen. Dusty giggled with gladness as Ryder's hands left her waist and rested on her tummy. When he looked up at her, she was astonished by the tears in his eyes. She thought maybe she should've chosen a more private moment to reveal her secret to him.

"Ryder?" she whispered as the others began to talk excitedly about how wonderful it would be to have three new babies in the family all at once.

"Aw, he's all right, Dusty," Hank chuckled. "He's just been afraid Kenna Jones plopped down too hard in his lap one time too many!"

With that, Ryder's smile returned. Dusty saw the glow of wonder in his eyes as he looked at her. Still, he seemed quite melancholy.

"What's the matter, Ryder?" she asked.

"I just . . ." he stammered. He looked about at the relatives Dusty knew he adored. The next moment, he swept her up in his arms and carried

473

her down the hall toward her old bedroom. "You all go about your business, you hear?" he called over his shoulder. Becca and Raynetta giggled; Feller and Hank chuckled.

Once he'd carried her into the bedroom and kicked the door closed behind them, he laid her gently on the bed, covering her body with his own.

"What is it?" she asked him again as moisture filled his beautiful eyes.

"Just for a moment . . . I was thinkin' how adorable you were that first day I ever saw you a-draggin' that little old table over them tree roots. And I was thinkin' of how hard it must've been for your daddy to be givin' you over to me. And now . . ."

"And now I'm havin' your baby?" she softly asked him.

"Yeah," he breathed, his smile that of perfect joy. "What if you'd married Cash? What if I hadn't seen your daddy on that drive? And what if Wesley . . ."

"And what if somebody comes in here?" she teased. Dusty reached up, smoothing the worry from his brow, trailing her fingertips lovingly over his lips.

"Naw," he chuckled. "They know better." He brushed the hair from her face, and Dusty felt the tears leaving her eyes to travel over her temples.

"What, sugar? Now you're all soppy too." His smile was beautiful—the most beloved sight in all the world to her.

"I love you, Ryder," she whispered as he brushed her cheek affectionately with his own.

As Ryder's wonderfully capable hands lovingly caressed her tummy where their baby grew, he kissed her—the kiss that would forever send her heart racing—the kiss assuring her of his boundless, eternal love for her.

"I love you," he breathed. Moments later, his mouth wandered down her cheek to tarry at her neck. The tears cascaded from Angelina's eyes as she realized again the absolutely benevolent magnitude of her dreams forever coming true—when he whispered, "My little Dusty Britches."

Author's Note

I can't quite put my finger on why *Dusty Britches* seems to be such a favorite—not only to me but to my friends as well. Perhaps it's simply the final realization and triumph of vanquishing unrequited love—of it being quite fully requited at long last! (When unrequited love is no longer unrequited, is it called "requited love"? Hmm . . . I may have to research.) Or perhaps it's the fact two other love stories intertwine with Dusty and Ryder's—Feller and Becca's and Hank and Raynetta's.

Secretly, I imagine Hank and Raynetta to be my good friends Joel and Rhonda—although they've been married for 17,511 years and have six children. Joel is a cutie, and Rhonda has big brown eyes and loves to wear red. Becca and Feller live only in my mind, yet to me they are as real as anyone else—and I adore them!

Then again, it might be the fact so many little details of *Dusty Britches* are mirrored moments from my own life . . .

Incident #1: The Singing Ranch Hand. I was seven years old—our handsome hired hand, Dale, milking the cows at three and four in the morning, singing "Make Believe" from *Showboat*, his gorgeous Howard Keel–type voice wafting from

476

the milk barn, over the clear morning air, and in through my bedroom window. How romantic!

Incident #2: Old Man Leroy/Lace in Belt. Leroy, my friend's dad—a very intimidating man—once came upon my older dream-boy mercilessly flirting with me, my older dream-boy's metal belt loops having gotten caught with my belt buckle whilst he'd gathered me into a romantic embrace and proceeded to verbally seduce me in the hallway at church. Maybe I could write a short essay on this titled, *"How Your Most Romantic Moment at Age Fourteen Can Best Be Ruined by Humiliating Circumstances."*

Incident #3: Pack 'Em In. Based on the age-old game "Sardines," which I played as a teenager and always enjoyed—especially the time one of my long-lasting crushes captured me out in the tall grasses in the field behind his house and, of course, stole a kiss! Initials of Romantic Culprit Boy: W.M.—City of Incident: Albuquerque— Age of Delighted Victim: Twelve—Weather Conditions When Tête-à-Tête Was Perpetrated: Warm Summer's Eve.

Incident #4: Dusty Stuffing Hankies in Her Bosom. Based on the antics a cherished friend of mine (who will, *of course,* remain nameless) when we were twelve. She once told me the "hankie-stuffing incident" worked out much better in *Dusty Britches* than it had in real life! Implements Used Instead of Hankies: Kleenex Tissues—In Profusion.

. . . to list a few.

Still, in truth, I think Ryder and Dusty endear the story to me. (I mean, Ryder *is* a good kisser, and that *does* count for a lot. I mean, let's just be honest with ourselves, shall we?) Yet it's the journey—Dusty battling to overcome her fear and heartache, Ryder risking his life to be with her—maybe that's why the story speaks to me so deeply.

In any regard, it's important to me that you know *Dusty Britches* is real! Fiction, yes—but in my mind all the characters are there! I see their faces, hear their voices. The story plays out in my head as vividly as any of the aforementioned incidents of my real life—sometimes even more vividly!

So whatever my reasons are for the story of *Dusty Britches* meaning so much to me (important or not), I hope it brings *you* joy—smiles, goose bumps, giggles, sighs, tears, and hope! My wish is when you read or reread this book, you find yourself transported into the story—that your heart is lightened and your optimism fortified when you close it—that you can hear Ryder singing in the barn in the early morning hours and feel Dusty's joy when she realizes her "unrequited love" was always entirely "requited."

Marcia Lynn McClure

About the Author

Marcia Lynn McClure's intoxicating succession of novels, novellas, and e-books—including *The Visions of Ransom Lake*, *A Crimson Frost*, *Shackles of Honor*, and *The Whispered Kiss*—has established her as one of the most favored and engaging authors of true romance. Her unprecedented forte in weaving captivating stories of western, medieval, regency, and contemporary amour void of brusque intimacy has earned her the title "The Queen of Kissing."

Marcia, who was born in Albuquerque, New Mexico, has spent her life intrigued with people, history, love, and romance. A wife, mother, grandmother, family historian, poet, and author, Marcia Lynn McClure spins her tales of splendor for the sake of offering respite through the beauty, mirth, and delight of a worthwhile and wonderful story.

Center Point Large Print
600 Brooks Road / PO Box 1
Thorndike, ME 04986-0001 USA

(207) 568-3717

US & Canada:
1 800 929-9108
www.centerpointlargeprint.com